JULIE MYERSON

Julie Myerson is the author of nine novels, including the bestselling *Something Might Happen*, which was longlisted for the Booker Prize, and three works of non-fiction, including *Home: The Story of Everyone Who Ever Lived in Our House* and *The Lost Child*. In the words of the *Observer*, she 'has a talent for making the unthinkable readable. The results are riveting.'

'This is a book that you will turn through the night to reach its conclusion — Myerson has you dying for the end and even surer that you will do just that when you get there'
The Times

'It's the sort of book you cannot put down, partly because it is so addictive and partly because if you do put it down, you know you will spend the next few hours startling at every creaking door . . .'
Observer

'A brilliantly unsettling read. Myerson's elegant prose creates a suffocating feeling of dread as the psychological consequences of loss and violence are mercilessly revealed'
Mail on Sunday

ALSO BY JULIE MYERSON

Fiction

Sleepwalking
The Touch
Me and the Fat Man
Laura Blundy
Something Might Happen
The Story of You
Out of Breath
Then
The Quickening

Non-Fiction

Home
Not a Games Person
The Lost Child

JULIE MYERSON

The Stopped Heart

A Novel

VINTAGE

1 3 5 7 9 10 8 6 4 2

Vintage
20 Vauxhall Bridge Road,
London SW1V 2SA

Vintage is part of the Penguin Random House
group of companies whose addresses can be found at
global.penguinrandomhouse.com

Penguin
Random House
UK

First published in Vintage in 2017

First published in Great Britain in hardback by
Jonathan Cape in 2016

penguin.co.uk/vintage

A CIP catalogue record for this book is available
from the British Library

ISBN 9781784701314

Printed and bound in Great Britain by Clays Ltd, St Ives plc

Penguin Random House is committed to a sustainable future
for our business, our readers and our planet. This book is made
from Forest Stewardship Council® certified paper.

for Gill Coleridge

I

It was a sunny day. The sky was thick and high and blue. Addie Sands was standing in the lane and she was screaming. There was blood everywhere. On her skirts, her wrists, her face. A dark hole where her mouth should be. There were no words. Nothing but the black taste of her screaming.

Nobody knew what to do. We all stared. We dared not go to her. I think some of us stepped away. At last my mother went over, grabbing her by the shoulders, seeing the blood, the mess of her hair hanging down, tears and cries and wet on her face.

For the love of God, Addie, what is it? What's happened?

Addie moaned. She tried to twist her head away. She would not let herself look at my mother's face.

Just tell me, my mother said.

Addie kept on weeping. She could hardly breathe for weeping. My mother had her by the shoulders. She kept a hold of her.

Are the kiddies all right? Has something happened? Is it the school?

The kiddies. A quick, burnt feeling went through me.

Addie moaned and dropped to her knees. Right there in the lane with the sun high up above and dandelions and dust and horse dung all around.

I didn't know, she said. How could I know?

My mother kept very still.

Know what? she said.

Addie could not look at her.

I thought he'd come to fetch the kiddies home.

Now my mother got it. Her face turned white. When at last Addie lifted her chin, her eyes did not go anywhere. They went straight through.

I thought he'd come to fetch them. I didn't know what he was going to do. He had this great big happy smile on his face—

Addie gazed at my mother.

He was smiling all the time he did it, she said.

Mary Coles stands in the lane. Sky still dark, but already birds are singing. The cottage too. Dark and unsteady, turned in on itself. She keeps her eyes on it, unsure at first what she's looking for, wondering if she's even got the right one. The second cottage you come to after the humpback bridge, Graham said. Is it this one? Does she want it to be? Brick and flint. Run-down. One smashed windowpane under the eaves. Paint flaking off the door. The little gate – yes, the gate – so rotten it's coming right off its hinges, he said.

She pushes the gate. The hinge gives, but the part that ought to move doesn't. Some kind of plant or vine stopping it. She hesitates, not wanting to force it. It didn't want me to go in, she hears herself telling him, it seemed to want to keep me out.

In the rented bungalow, in the middle of the night, she woke him up and told him her plan.

'What?' he said. 'Drive there right now? On your own? Why on earth would you want to do that?'

She did not reply.

'Come here,' he said. 'Come on. Come back to bed.'

But she was already up. Pulling on her jeans, sticking feet into boots, looking around for her keys.

'I need to see it. In the dark. I want to see what it's like.'

He stared at her, pushing hair and sleep from his eyes.

'But you'll see it tomorrow—'

'I want to do it now.'

'What, in the bloody middle of the night?'

'It'll be light in an hour.'

He gazed at her. His face unreadable, a man used to absorbing the blows. He threw back the covers.

'All right, at least let me come with you.'

She lowered her eyes.

'Please. I don't want you to. Don't make me explain it. I just want to go there on my own.'

Now she shivers, fingers closing around the car keys in her pocket. She knows it's empty. Empty for at least a year, he said, maybe more. More than a year? She lets go of the gate and stands for a moment, breathing in the earthy dawn smell of light and damp and things warming up. She thinks she hears an owl.

She had meant to go right up to it, look through the windows, see if she could get an idea of the inside. That's what she told him. And she knows she could do it if she wanted to. But she doesn't. She doesn't even try.

Instead she stands there motionless for perhaps thirty or forty more seconds and then, as if someone had walked up and shoved her out of the way, she turns and hurries back to the car.

She hopes he'll be asleep when she gets back, but no. Eyes open, iPod in one ear. Curtains half-drawn to let the light in. The open suitcases still spread on the floor. A sweater. Her unzipped, kicked-off boots. He turns his head.

'That was quick.'

'You're supposed to be asleep,' she says.

He smiles and puts an arm out from under the duvet, reaching for her. She stands there looking at it, the hand.

'Well?' he says.

'Well, what?'

She sits down on the edge of the bed, a little more heavily then she meant to. Feels him shifting his legs. She lets him hold her hand, warming her.

'You found it?'

She nods.

'And? Tell me?'

She hesitates.

'It's nice.'

'Nice?'

'All I did was stand in the lane. I heard an owl. I think it was an owl. And then I came back.'

She feels him thinking about this. His eyes on her. His hand moving to her bare knee.

'You're freezing.'

She says nothing. He takes hold of her hand again.

3

'All right but what do you think? Is it what you imagined? Do you like it?'

'I don't know what I imagined,' she says. 'But yes.'

'Yes, what?'

'I like it. I do.'

He sits up, encouraged, grabbing another pillow to push under his head.

'It needs a few repairs, I know that – the roof and so on. And I'm sure there's a bit of damp. But the basic structure is fine. Did you go round the back? Did you see any of the garden?'

She shakes her head.

'You'll be amazed. It's enormous. Seriously, I think there was once an orchard. It goes on forever.'

She looks at her hand lying there in his.

'That's nice,' she says.

He smiles.

'Just imagine. You'll be able to garden again.'

She sighs. Feels him squeeze her hand. A moment of silence. Both of them thinking the same thing.

'So you can see us living there, then?' he asks, his voice suddenly shaky.

She swallows. Remembering the gate that would not budge. The heavy darkness of the glass-eyed windows, sucking up the light. She tells him that she can.

The night he came, a storm. Just like him, it seemed to come from nowhere. A freezing wind. We woke before dawn to the crack of thunder. Greasy light. Rain coming down. The dog pestering at the door.

My father was already up to do the cows. My mother, feeding the baby, dark-eyed and vacant and fidgety from no sleep. I think he told her to get back to bed but she wouldn't, just kept her eyes on him while he made a cigarette.

They'd been angry with each other for a long time and not just because of Isaac Roper. And then when the kid came along, he wasn't expected to live and all in all my father said that would be the best outcome. But he was two months now, lusty and alive, and sometimes I thought he would suck the life out of her.

4

We sat in the kitchen while the storm raged. It was a big one. It lit up the walls, the floor, the table, the hearth. We heard the rain pelting on the roof of the privy. The dog grew so afraid she stopped crying and turned her face to the wall.

With the next crack of thunder, my mother pulled the baby against her and went over and opened the door. A cold gust of rain and blackness blowing in.

Sally, what the hell? my father said.

She shut it again, shushing and joggling the baby. He lit his cigarette. Lightning ripping across the sky.

I didn't want to count, but I couldn't help it. One, two – three and the sky cracked open. Upstairs the little ones started to scream.

Over us now, my father said, putting the cigarette in his mouth.

My mother's eyes were on the ceiling.

Eliza, she said.

What?

Up you go.

I sighed.

They'll calm down in a minute.

Keeping his eyes on the table, my father folded his tobacco pouch. Another clap and upstairs you could hear Lottie and Honey wailing. Maybe the twins as well. My father looked at me.

Just do it, he said.

I began to go, but even as I did, there was another bright flash and then a sound like the whole world tearing itself into pieces. The ground shuddered and the air outside the window turned black. My mother screamed. I ran to the door.

No! she cried, but I'd already pulled it open.

For a moment we didn't understand what it was, the thing that we were seeing. Then we did. Suffocating the house and blocking out the light, the great big tangle of its roots standing stiff against the flashing sky.

My mother screamed again. My father swore. The old elm tree that used to stand beside our cottage was standing no longer. It was down on the ground and under it was a man.

The sale goes through very quickly. Ten days later, they've exchanged and are told they'll have the keys by the end of the week. Mary is glad. She is beginning to realise how much she needs to get out of the rented place with its shiny brown furniture and smells of frying and Febreze.

It's a bright, warm day. Blue sky. Late spring. They know they can't get inside yet, but they drive over anyway. To look at the garden, he says. Now that we know it's ours. To stand there and think about the possibilities.

Possibilities. She knows that all he means is to encourage her, to scoop her up and carry her along.

'I love you,' she says, understanding exactly how much his optimism costs him.

'What?'

Biting her lip. On the edge of her vision, bright fields of something — corn, is it, or barley? — speeding past.

'I just do. I love you.'

He glances at her.

'Well, that's good.'

'It is?'

He smiles, his eyes back on the road, fingers brushing her knee.

'Yeah. It is.'

He slows down when they get to the village.

'Look,' he says, 'a post office — that's rare enough these days. And a Co-op. Useful.'

Her eyes are on the neat, clipped green with its swings and slide and hanging rubber tyre. Grateful for a reason to look away, she takes in the Co-op with its metal racks of newspapers and black buckets of bright roses and foil trays for barbecues.

'But I think there's also a Farm Shop up that road beyond the church,' he says. 'Local produce—'

'What about it?' she says.

'Well, it's what we want, isn't it?'

She looks at him and he laughs and for a few quick seconds, the laugh could almost be his old laugh — warm and permanent and real.

The cottage looks smaller than last time. Smaller and darker. They stand there together in the lane, shocked all over again that it's theirs.

When he brought her here a week ago, the morning after her night-time visit, they had to walk around with the stupidly young

6

estate agent following them. At one point, moving across the upstairs landing in an attempt to get away from him, Mary had cried out so loudly and abruptly she'd made them all jump.

'Christ almighty!' Graham had grabbed her shoulder, turning her towards him. 'What is it, darling? What's the matter?'

She glanced down the long passage that led to the second bedroom, her heart still thudding.

'There was – I don't know – I heard something.'

'What do you mean? Heard what?'

She took a breath.

'Someone said my name.'

Graham tried to laugh and so did the boy estate agent.

'Your name?'

She nodded.

'Mary Coles. They said Mary Coles.'

'And where exactly was this person?'

She stared at Graham.

'Just there.'

'Where?'

'Behind me. It felt like they were right behind me.'

The boy made a face.

'Whoa! You're freaking me out now.' He pulled his phone out of his pocket, glancing at it as he rubbed at his hair. 'Well, I'm one hundred per cent certain there's nobody here,' he said.

Mary felt embarrassed.

'I know that. I don't know what it was. I imagined it, obviously. I'm sorry.'

The phone buzzed. The boy threw them a look of apology and walked over to the window where a pile of dead bluebottles lay on the sill.

'These old houses,' he said as he dialled a number. 'I don't know what it is with them. All sorts of strange noises, I guess.'

'That's right,' she said.

'Could it have been the pipes?' said Graham.

She looked at him.

'No,' she said. 'Not pipes.'

The boy walked back towards them, texting now.

'It's been empty for a while. I guess that can feel a bit creepy.'

She watched his white, bitten fingers moving over the phone.

'It's not,' she said.

'You what?'

'It's not creepy.'

He blinked at her, put the phone back in his pocket.

'Well, of course, it's full of potential.'

She couldn't help it, she smiled. I'm going mad, she thought with a casualness that took her breath away. Don't expect too much of yourself, the counsellor had said. There will be good days and bad days, ups and downs. The trouble was she had become so used to not expecting too much of herself that these days she seemed to expect almost nothing.

Graham touched her shoulder again.

'Are you OK? Do you want to go and sit in the car?'

She laughed and told him of course she didn't want to do that. They finished the tour.

As they walked out into the bright, leafy garden, the boy asked Graham if they'd seen the movie Scream. He said they hadn't. He told him they should see it. The first one, anyway, which was by far the best. 'But don't worry,' he said, 'it was only your wife that made me think of it. I'm sure there are no slasher maniacs here.'

Now she walks up the path with its fringe of greying forget-me-nots and, shielding her eyes, peers in through the dark kitchen window. There it is again – the steep, narrow staircase with its flimsy wooden door, the range, the rough old scrubbed-pine table which the estate agent said came with the house.

She feels him behind her.

'What are you looking at?'

'Nothing. Just everything. The kitchen.'

'That room needs a bloody good lick of paint.'

'Yes.'

He takes her hand.

'Come on. Come with me. I have a plan.'

He takes her round the back. Across the surprisingly big yard – once a real farmyard, she supposes – with its old stone trough and water pump. 'Nice old original feature, nice that they kept that,' he says. And then on into the overgrown garden where they find a white wrought-iron bench under an apple tree. He brushes fallen blossom and a crust of bird shit off it and they sit down.

Insects are hovering all around them, alighting on the tired, half-dead cones of lilac and buddleia. They watch a bee crawl over a bloom before falling backwards into the air and then lifting off and away.

At the bottom of the garden, just beyond where they sit, an enormous tree – or the vast, rotten trunk of one, anyway – lies in the long grass.

Graham is looking around him, interest and delight and expectation on his face.

'All it needs is a bit of TLC,' he says.

'Yes.'

She tilts her head back to look at the sky.

'It's huge,' he says. 'The garden. Do you realise that? The other day, with that silly boy, we only saw about half of it. I don't think he had a clue. It goes back even further than you can see.'

'You can show me,' she says. 'In a minute.'

He smiles.

'I think that's a walnut tree over there. And see the apple trees? Loads of them. I told you – I'm sure this used to be an orchard once upon a time.'

Once upon a time. She turns to look at him and as she does, he opens his old corduroy jacket and shows her: a bottle and two paper cups. He smiles.

'I told you I had a plan.'

They thought he was dead but he wasn't dead. He was the luckiest man on earth. He was alive. The tree had missed him by about an inch.

I waited for them to find this out. I watched as my father went out in the solid sheeting rain and bent his head and said something to him. And I saw the man lift up his own head and say something back.

My mother gasped.

He's alive. Bloody hell. Thank God.

I said nothing. My heart jumping now.

My mother shouted at Frank to run and wake Isaac Roper. I watched as my father touched the man on the shoulder and said

9

something else. Maybe he told him he was going to be all right or one of the other things people say when they think someone's going to die.

I wonder if he'll lose his legs, my mother said.

I stared at her.

The legs? Why would he lose them?

She shook her head.

A man's legs would snap like barley sugar under the weight of a tree like that.

It took all of them – Isaac Roper and my father, with Frank mostly just getting in the way – to bring him inside. My mother spread a blanket on the floor and bunched some straw under for his head and they laid him down.

Just look at that hair, she said.

We looked. His hair was bright red, the reddest I'd ever seen on any person. Thick on top, but shaved short around the sides and over the ears. His face was rough and bitter. He had the look of someone who'd just walked out of a room where bad things had happened.

Not a farm boy, Isaac Roper said. Not from round here.

He's got city written all over him, my mother agreed. But how come the boots are so clean?

I looked at the boots. They were brand spanking new without a doubt. Not a speck of mud on them.

He stole them, I said before I could stop myself.

My mother gave me a sharp look.

How ever could you know that, Eliza?

I don't know it, I said, blushing to my roots. But anyway he might have.

Later, he lies down on his back in the long, pale grass. Two or three cups of Prosecco in him, face already pink from the sudden warm sunshine – arms spread out, fingers loose.

'Come here,' he says. 'Please. Come over here right now and kiss me.'

He does not look at her, he stares up into space. She watches his face. The words floating upwards into the bright blue air. She hesitates.

'Come on,' he says again, laughing.

She shakes her head. She says his name. But she does not get up. She sits there on the bench in the sunshine looking at him. His body so familiar, so known to her, so loved. It ought to be possible, she thinks.

'I want to hold you,' he says. He laughs again. 'There's no one around, so why not?'

Why not? she thinks. Trying to remember how it used to feel to want to do such things. The warmth of sudden hugs, the way you could twine yourself around the flesh and blood of another human being just like that, as if it was nothing.

He sits up, putting his hands to his face now, laughing. And she starts to speak to him but he stops her.

'It's all right,' he says. 'It was a joke. I was joking. You don't have to.'

She watches as he gropes in his pocket for a handkerchief.

'I'm so sorry,' she says at last – seeing that he isn't laughing at all, but crying.

Jazzy had crept down the stairs. So had Lottie, barefoot and half-undressed as usual, followed by the twins, Minnie and Charlie. I think Frank was with them. Honey came behind, holding onto his knees.

Jazzy was ten years old and Frank was seven. The twins were five and Lottie was only four. Nobody could remember how old Honey was but she used to be the baby until the new one came along, so she wasn't that old. Our mother had had some other children too after I was born, but they had died and these were the ones that were left and what with the new baby to boot, she said it was quite enough.

The dog saw the kiddies and wagged her tail and rushed around trying to nip at their hands and feet while they laughed and screamed. At last Frank caught hold of her. But when she saw the man she went stiff all over and began to growl.

What's up with her? my father said, because our dog was the least suspicioning animal you ever met.

She's afraid, said Frank. Who's that man on the floor?

Yes, Jazzy said. Who is it?

I'm afraid! said Lottie and she looked at Minnie to encourage her and then they both lifted up their skirts and jumped up and down on the spot, laughing and squealing.

Be quiet, all of you, my mother said.

My father bent down to the man and asked him what his name was. The man groaned.

I knowed his name, Lottie said.

No, you don't, said Jazz.

I did! I used to know it when I was a little bit dead.

Can you move your legs? my father said to the man.

The man tried. At first he couldn't do it, but then he could. He moved them a little bit.

Jazzy looked excited.

Are his legs broke?

Not if he can move them, my father said.

My mother was shaking her head and looking at Isaac Roper.

I thought the tree was on top of him, she said. Right on top of his legs, I honestly thought it was.

Well, it wasn't, my father said.

All the same, she said, still looking at Isaac, I can't believe it. How is it possible? How can no bones have broke?

What's broke? said Charlie.

I want it! Lottie shrieked.

It's a miracle, Isaac Roper said.

Merricales! Lottie said and then because she couldn't think of any more stupid things to say, she began to cry.

My father's face didn't move. Anything to do with Isaac always washed straight over him.

It is what it is, he said.

The dog was still growling. I put my hand on her. The growl went down through my hand and into my bones.

Can't someone shut that animal up? my father said.

She's afraid, Frank told him again.

She doesn't want to be killed, sobbed Lottie, even though she was under the table now and no one was listening to her any more.

Look at the poor lad, my mother said. What ever on earth is there to be afraid of?

I did look at him then. I looked at him and I knew straightaway that he wasn't a poor lad. I looked at the dirty face and the bright hair and the eyebrows that met in the middle. I looked at the blue and black tattoo of something that went curling right down his neck.

He hadn't any jacket and his shirt was half open. You could see a nipple and some reddish hair. I didn't want to look, but I couldn't help it, I did look.

Something cold crept through me.

I don't like him, I said.

They leave most of their things in storage, moving in with the barest minimum, just a few pieces of furniture and the stuff they can't do without. Kitchen equipment. The sofa and armchairs and the TV. Their bed, of course, and towels and linen. Not even all of their clothes.

They don't bring their books or CDs. We'll get new ones, Graham says, though neither of them believes it. They both know it's going to be a while before they can face reading or listening to music.

Even though it's late spring, the house is dark and cold. Some of the plug sockets don't work and the bath takes half an hour to drain. They find mouse droppings in the kitchen cupboards and the curtains they got for the bedroom window don't fit so they're woken at dawn with the sun in their eyes.

'It feels like being on holiday,' Mary tells him, when he apologises for everything that's wrong with the place. 'Except that I don't quite know what to do with myself.'

His face softens.

'You don't have to do anything.'

'I know that.'

'It's all going to take some getting used to.'

'I know.'

She watches his face as he comments on the beauty of the old flagged-stone floors, the huge brick fireplace, the sturdy whitewashed walls with their original thick wooden beams.

'It's all just as it would have been,' he says. 'No one's gone around ripping out the period detail. It's all here. Even these little latches on the doors, for instance.'

Mary raises her head from the peas she is shelling and looks at the narrow wooden door that leads to the stairs. The stripped pine with its iron latch. The steep, shadowed staircase just visible through it, the pale, grubby whiteness of a child's bare foot as she comes bumping downstairs on her bottom—

Her heart twists. She takes a breath, blinks. Looking back down at the colander of peas. Inspecting the green pea sludge under her fingernails.

'Oh,' she says, 'Ruby rang.'

'Ruby? What, here on the landline? When? You didn't tell me.'

She glances at the stairs again.

'It was only just now, about ten minutes ago.'

He sighs, muttering something under his breath.

'I'm not going to rush around after her all the time as if everything's an emergency,' she says.

He looks at her.

'Quite right. Of course not. No one expects you to.'

'She expects us to. And so does Veronica.'

He sighs again.

'All right. I'm sorry. I'll deal with it.'

'You don't have to apologise. And I'm not sure there's anything to deal with anyway. She said she just wanted a chat.'

'A chat. It's never just a chat. How did she sound?'

She hesitates.

'OK. She was perfectly polite, if that's what you mean.'

'Did she ask how you were?'

Mary laughs. 'Of course not.'

'And sober? Did she sound sober?'

'You mean not drunk?'

'I mean not under the influence of anything.'

She thinks about it.

'I don't know. I think so.'

'You think so?'

She lifts her head.

'I didn't know it was my job to police her.'

'I didn't mean it like that.'

'I know you didn't.'

He sighs.

'All right. I'd better go and call her.'

It was nearly morning. The storm had worn itself out. All that was left was a sour yellow flashing in the sky over towards Laxfield.

The man was lying on the floor with his eyes closed. Isaac Roper and my mother were smoking and laughing and passing the time together like they always did. I saw my father noticing and as usual I felt my stomach bunch up. The dog was still growling and my father told Frank to put her in the cupboard. He didn't want to do it, but he did.

Why doesn't she like the man? Minnie said.

Is it because he's bad? said Charlie.

Of course he's not bad, my mother said.

We don't know the smallest thing about him, Isaac Roper pointed out. He could be a felon or a murderer.

Well, the dog doesn't like him, Frank said.

She thinks he's bad, Minnie said.

Bad! shouted Honey, as she pulled herself up to stand, holding onto the arm of the chair. Ba – ba – bad.

Lottie had crept out from under the table. She had her eyes on the man. She was sucking her thumb and fidgeting with her chemise, which only half covered her.

I used to be a dog, didn't I? she said.

Lottie, I said when I saw that she couldn't keep still and kept on twisting about and clutching at herself, do you need the pot?

She blinked at me as if I wasn't there.

All right, but a long time ago when the bad man came and he kicked the door down and he stamped all over my head, I did?

Did what?

Used to be a dog.

You were never a dog, my mother said. You're talking nonsense, Lottikins. And Eliza's asking if you want the pot.

I was about to get it but then there was a quick wet spattering on the floor.

Oh Lottie! my mother said.

Lottie looked down at what she had done. She blinked.

But later I will be, won't I? she said.

Minnie and Charlie picked up feathers from the floor and blew them around while I mopped up Lottie's mess. Jazzy was sat under the table singing to herself and undoing the tassels of the big heavy cloth.

Honey was on Frank's lap though he kept trying to push her off. He asked if the dog could come out of the cupboard yet and my mother said yes.

But what if she bites the man? Jazzy said.

She won't do that.

But what if she does?

Look at her. She's afraid to go near him, I said.

I was right. The dog went straight over and sat by the door with a rattled look on her face. My father had to go and do the animals. He was getting his boots on. My mother looked at him.

We should get the doctor, she said.

He doesn't need a doctor.

Why? said Jazzy. Is he going to die?

We're all going to die, said Isaac Roper. Praise Jesus but it's the truth that we will all die.

Like me, I died, Lottie said, but no one was listening because we all knew it was a great big booming lie.

My father left the room, slamming the door behind him. A quick, unhappy silence, then the air closed up around it.

Well, if you want my opinion, I reckon we should get the constable, Isaac Roper said at last.

My mother cupped the baby's head in her hand as if it was the softest piece of fruit she had ever held.

The constable? Whatever for?

Isaac scowled and rubbed at his chin. The rasp of his night-time beard made my teeth hurt.

Who is he, Sally? What do we know about him? How do we know he's not escaped from somewhere? He could be a murderer. A swindler. A housebreaker.

Oh, come on, my mother said.

How do you know he's not dangerous? We've no idea at all about him.

My mother yawned.

He's just a young man, she said. I don't think we need to worry about him. I'm sure he'll be on his way in the morning.

I looked at the man. His eyes were shut, but he had the fierce tight look of someone not asleep.

The baby was whickering and my mother began to undo her chemise. Isaac Roper watched her. Honey, too, seeing it was undone and wanting the milk, got up off the floor and lifted her arms in the air and started to cry. My mother ignored her and at last she stopped her noise and fell asleep on the rug.

The night was almost over, but the blackness was still there, it wouldn't be light for a while. Apart from the sound of the cows across the yard, the kitchen was quiet. My mother changed the baby over to the other side. His small hand stayed up in the air while he sucked.

All you children should be in bed, my mother said.

Isaac Roper was filling his pipe. I watched him: a quick bad memory of walking past the scullery door on a hot afternoon and seeing my mother with her face buried in him. His hands strung through her hair, pressing her down against the flap of his breeches.

I don't like the look of him, Isaac said. If it was my house I wouldn't want him in it for a moment longer than was necessary.

The next day on his way to Blaxhall, Isaac Roper was struck by a train and died on the spot. No one expected it. But lots of things happen in this life that are not expected.

It was easy enough to look for reasons. Maybe we should have covered up the bedroom mirrors during the storm as Mrs Narket's married niece later suggested. Or maybe Isaac should not have been in such a hurry to cut down the old holly tree in Glebe field that winter, since it had been there for fifty years and everyone knew that felling a holly could change a person's luck.

Maybe we should have listened when Jazzy said she'd seen a single magpie shrieking and hopping like a mad thing in the lane that morning. And maybe we should have sent one of the kiddies to seek out another one quick before the bad luck of the singleton could take root.

Or maybe, it occurred to me later, Isaac should have thought twice before he accused a perfect stranger who was lying on our kitchen floor of being a housebreaker or a murderer when he didn't know the smallest thing about him.

2

The first time Graham leaves her alone there, Mary is lost. She does what is necessary. Puts the breakfast things in the dishwasher. Wipes the table. Stands looking at the crumbs sticking to her hand, then goes over to the tap and rinses them off.

Drying her hands on a tea towel, she finds herself opening the front door. She stands there, looking out, feeling the heat on her face. Not unpleasant. Sunlight and warmth pouring in, showing up the dirt on the old stone floor.

In the lane, birds are singing. A white van goes past. A kid on a bicycle, shouting. Somewhere far off across the fields, a dog barking. A little way away she can see a man. Red-haired. Young. Her heart stirs at the sight. His lean, quick shape moving along the hedge.

She comes back in and shuts the door. Standing there, waiting, she doesn't know for what. After a moment, without knowing why, she bolts the door. A sudden, velvety silence. She likes it.

When the landline rings, she jumps. Her mother.

'I wanted to see if you were all right.'

'I'm all right. How are you?'

Her mother hesitates.

'Really? You'd say if you weren't?'

'We are. We're fine. We're doing OK.'

'Really? What are you up to?'

'Well, Graham's at work.'

'And you?'

'I'm just here, sorting things out.'

'And the house?'

'It's fine. It's good. A bit of a mess still. You'll have to come and see it.'

'I will. I'd like to do that. Maybe without your father. If you don't mind looking into trains and having me for a night or two—'

She is about to tell her mother that would be fine and then try to fix a date as far in the future as possible, when her mother's tone changes.

'I'm sorry – I'm so sorry,' sobbing now, 'I've been trying not to ring you. Your father told me off. He was really quite angry with me. He said I should wait. You've no idea. I've been trying so hard to leave you alone.'

Mary stares at the old pine kitchen table with its marks and its knots and whorls. Placing her hand on its rough, cool surface.

'You don't have to do that. I never said you had to do that.'

'Do what?'

'Mum. Come on. You're allowed to call.'

She is about to continue when something – a sound from upstairs, a sudden heaviness on the floorboards, the quick shudder of a door closing – makes her stiffen and turn. Her mother sniffs.

'It's a new life for you, darling. I understand that. I do, you know. I know you both want a fresh start.'

Holding the phone, Mary walks to the bottom of the stairs, pulls open the door. Staring upwards, eyes on the shadows.

'That doesn't mean not talking to family.'

She hears her mother take a quick, wet breath.

'But we don't really talk any more, do we? Not the way we used to. It's not that I expect you to call me. I know how busy you are. But this is very difficult for us too, you know. Your father said—'

Mary shuts her eyes. She sees her father's long, pale face, his hands, his trousers belted a little too high. The raw, bloody, animal sound he made when they sat him down that rainy night and told him.

She gazes at the staircase, straining to listen. Thinks she hears a tap dripping in the bathroom. She tells her mother that it's not a good moment, that she'll call her at the weekend.

There's no one upstairs. This becomes very clear as she wanders quickly from room to room, her own bare feet sticking to the dusty boards, the sound of her own breath in her chest, her throat. Throwing a pile of towels onto a chair, she kicks off her shoes and lies down on the bed. She lies there and watches the sun make its slow way across the walls. Reaches out and flicks the radio on. Hears a man's voice going on and on. Flicks it off again. She feels very calm. She realises without much surprise that she has been crying.

Outside, she can hear children shouting, playing. Several of them, two or three at least, maybe more. A whole crowd of little children. The sound comes and goes, very loud sometimes and then for a while barely audible. She thinks that one of them seems to be crying. Nothing dramatic – more a toddler's fed-up chuntering. Silence, then a shout, and then laughter again.

She holds her breath, not upset, just mildly curious, wondering whose kids they can be. Their nearest neighbour who they've nodded at once or twice, is an elderly man, apparently alone and without children or grandchildren, and she remembers how heartened she was to discover that. The shouts grow louder, though the crying has stopped. Mary waits, listening. At last, unable to resist, she gets up and crosses the room, floorboards creaking under her bare feet, and goes to the window to look.

Out in the sunny lane, there is no one, nothing. Only a very large magpie, wings half-spread and dragging in the dirt, hopping backwards and forwards, clucking and screeching.

She watches it for a moment and then she walks back across the room and lies down again on the bed.

He comes home to find her there. Six hours at least have passed, maybe seven.

'Darling?' His voice on the stairs. 'Didn't you hear me? I was knocking and knocking. The door was bolted. I couldn't get in. I had to go round the back.'

She does not speak. Something heavy and warm in her arms. Not wanting to wake. Trying as hard as she can to hold on to it.

'Why on earth did you bolt it? What's going on? Did you realise you'd done it?'

He comes and stands over her. Keys in his hand, his jacket still on. She hears his worried breath.

'Mary? Are you all right?'

She says nothing. Lifting her hands to cover her eyes. He stands looking at her for another moment, then she feels the bed sinking as he sits down. His arms around her. His face on her neck.

'You've been here all day, haven't you?'

When she still doesn't speak, he lets go of her. Twisting around and sitting up. His head in his hands.

'I heard someone say my name,' she says, realising only as she says the words that they might be true.

He looks at her.

'What? You mean like before?'

Mary blinks. She's almost forgotten that odd, shrill morning with the estate agent.

'Yes. Like that. I heard it again. The same thing. Like someone calling out – they called me.'

He shakes his head.

'I don't know what you're talking about. Where?'

'I thought there was someone in the house.'

'What? It's not possible.'

'I know. It's not possible, is it? It was weird.'

Graham puts his head back in his hands.

'There's no one here.'

'I know.'

'So what are you talking about?'

'I don't know.'

He is silent for a moment.

'I thought you were better,' he says. 'I thought you liked it here. I honestly thought you were getting better.'

She looks up at him with interest.

'I do like it here.'

His eyes back on her.

'You do?'

'I do.'

He sighs.

'I think you need to see someone. Just an hour a week or some-thing. What do you think? I could ask at the clinic.'

'The clinic?'

'The doctor's surgery. In the village. I'm sure if we asked they could fix you up with something.'

She thinks about this.

'There's nothing to talk about,' she says.

He makes a noise of impatience.

'For Christ's sake. You need to tell someone about this. Talk about how you're feeling.'

'I'm not feeling anything.'

He takes her hand. Her warmth in his cold one. She can feel him thinking. Hears him sigh.

'Darling. My darling. Look at me.'

'What?' She looks. His face – once so alive and familiar to her, now alien with worry and sadness. He shuts his eyes for a moment.

'I can't live like this. Neither of us can. We can't live like this.'

She blinks at him. Pushing herself up on her elbow.

'But we are.'

He reaches out and lifts her hair, holding its dark, hot weight in his hand, looking at her.

'Are what?'

'We are living like this.'

He lets go of her hair and looks at her, exasperation – or is it relief? – in his eyes. I can't read you any more, she thinks. She knows it's what he's thinking too. She almost smiles.

'You're cold.'

'What?'

'You're cold. Come here. I'll warm you up.' She laughs, taking a breath – reaching out with her other hand. 'Come here,' she says, trying to pull him onto her, tugging at his belt, beginning to undo him.

He hesitates, still looking at her, then he lets her pull him down. She smells the warmth of him, his skin, the roughness of his chin and jaw, his neck.

'I don't understand you at all,' he says.

She says nothing, laughs to herself.

'I'm concerned about you. You can't lie in bed all day. Am I crushing you?' He tries to shift his weight off her.

'No.'

'No?'

'I like it. Crush me.'

He sighs.

'What are you doing now?'

Mary does nothing. Says nothing.

'Seriously, darling, what are you doing?'

She shakes her head. Lies there. Feeling him on her. His warmth. The crushing of her. Tears at last beginning to come.

His name was Dix. James H. Dix. We knew because he had it written on a small silver box that he kept in his jacket pocket. The box was in the shape of a diamond and the name was carved into the metal with some very fancy slopes and flounces.

When Jazzy tried to ask him what the box was for, he wouldn't say.

It's just a box, isn't it?

He turned it over and over in his hands, looking as if he'd only just laid eyes on it for the first time himself.

All right, said Jazzy, but what do you keep in it?

He scowled.

None of your bloody business.

Then what's it for?

He made a face.

You don't give up, do you?

Jazzy smiled. The smile was wobbly because of all the teeth she'd lost. Our father said she looked like a bat and had the habits of one, too. Hanging upside down by her legs at dusk from the nut tree by the hen house, or climbing the old metal gate and tipping herself upside down till her hair hung in the dirt.

Is it for pennies? she said.

Pennies? Ha!

Snuff, then?

Snuff? James reached out with his finger and thumb and tweaked the end of her nose.

Ouch, she said. That hurt.

That'll teach you to talk about a man and his snuff, he said. And he pushed her down on the ground and tickled her till her legs flew up in the air and she kicked him in the teeth.

When he'd stopped cursing and she'd got her breath back, she asked him what the H was for.

H?

James H. Dix. What's it for?

Hargraves, he said, still rubbing his face.

Hah – what?

Graves. Hargraves. You know? Like the big dark hole where they chuck you in when you're dead.

Jazzy's eyes grew large.

But is it yours?

James snapped the box open and shut.

What d'you mean, is it mine? What kind of a question is that? Why wouldn't it be mine?

She rolled her eyes.

I mean the name. Is it really your name?

Now he looked very angry.

What is it that you're accusing me of now? he demanded to know, and he fixed his eyes on her as if he was considering whether he should box her ears.

But then along came Frank, who punched her so hard on the arm that she forgot all about James and got into a fight with him instead.

Next time I saw them together, James was back to being all soft and smiles. But when she asked if she could have a go at holding the box, he wouldn't let her.

You ask a lot too many questions for a little squitty nothing of a girl, he said as he tucked it back in the pocket of his jacket and patted it to make sure it was there. You need to learn to shut up. Be a nice quiet kid who lets others get on with their business. Like your smart big sister over there.

Jazzy looked over at me.

She's not smart.

Oh yes she is. Smarter and a whole lot prettier and if I had to bet, a whole lot more difficult too.

When he lifted his eyes to see if I'd heard, I looked away. And when he seemed like he might be working up to say something else, I turned on my heel and walked out the door.

Mary gets an email from Lynn Markham. Carefully worded, upbeat, generous, kind. It has a PS.

'It goes without saying that if you ever find yourself missing the good old, permanently thankless world of PR, we could fling something your way. Rufus never stops moaning about his workload and Fiona has a couple of little projects coming up that would hardly involve any meetings in London. Just a thought, in case you want to give me a ring once you're settled. I'm pretty sure we could set you up with something.'

She knows Lynn only means to be kind. She imagines her sitting there at the desk in Holborn covered in all her silver and turquoise Moroccan jewellery and thinking, What could we do to draw Mary back into things? But the idea now of putting any kind of passion into a job that involves persuading journalists to write about old paintings or vases, well frankly it makes her want to laugh.

When she tells Graham about the email, she expects him to laugh too. But he doesn't. He tells her she should consider taking Lynn up on it.

'Isn't it time you started to think about doing something?' he says.

She stares at him.

'You want me to go back to work?'

'Don't say it like that.'

'All right, but you do?'

He holds himself still for a moment. Then, as if this is a moment he's been building to, he gets up and goes over to the sink, fills the kettle.

'I suppose I worry that you're spending too many days alone. You're giving yourself too much time to think.'

'You think I'm being self-indulgent?'

'Of course I don't think that.'

'Soft on myself, then?'

'I didn't say that either. I just wonder if you'd feel better if you did something.'

She thinks about this.

'I told you I might think about doing something in September.'

'Why wait until September?'

'I feel I need the summer to—'

'To what? To lie on the bed all day and cry?'

Mary says nothing. He sighs.

'Look, it's only because I care about you.'

The kettle boils. She watches as he makes her a cup of tea. Hooking the tea bag out at the exact right moment, getting the strength and colour just how she likes it. She notices that he hasn't shaved. She thinks that he looks tired, his eyes pouchy and grey.

'All right,' he says, 'forget Lynn, forget PR or whatever. Why don't you just go out and get yourself an ordinary job?'

'Ordinary? What kind of job would that be?'

'I don't know, a shop, a receptionist or something. You could look at that little library in Framlingham.'

'I'm not qualified to work in a library.'

'Stop looking for obstacles. You could at least enquire.'

'I don't think I'd earn very much in a library.'

He looks at her.

'It's not about the money. You know it's not. I just think it would be good for you to get out of the house, go out into the world.'

'The world?' She makes a face.

'All right, I'll be honest. I think you need something where you'll be forced to talk to other people.'

People. The idea fills her with horror.

'You've been thinking about this,' she says.

'I just can't bear to see you like this.'

'Like what?'

'Hiding yourself away. Losing your confidence.'

'I'm not hiding.'

He says nothing. She looks down at her hands on the table. The rough old pine table, the one that came with the house. Sometimes she thinks it looks like it has teeth marks on it.

Though she could never have faced their own table with its dents and scratches and crayon marks and ancient Weetabix encrusted around its edges, though she's glad that one's still safe in the cool, untampered darkness of Big Yellow Storage, still she's not sure about this one.

'Just pick up the phone,' Graham says. 'I'm not saying it's easy, God knows, I know how hard it is. But I think that once you do it, you'll start to feel a little bit better. Work is the saving of me. I honestly don't know where I'd be without it.'

Mary believes him about this. She knows that every weekday, and sometimes on a Saturday too, he walks out of the cottage and gets in the car and drives to his small new office in Ipswich. She knows what he does there. She knows that he parks in the neat, gravel parking space at the back by the bins, then goes around and puts his key in the door and, bending to pick up the post off the transparent plastic mat, walks into the single large room with its glazed partition and its forlorn smell of paper and cartridge and desk and new beige carpet.

She knows that he throws the post on the desk, his jacket on the chair, then goes into the tiny kitchenette with the small carton of milk he's bought on the way in. Placing the milk on the counter, he fills up the glass jug and turns on the coffee machine. Beginning, as he waits for it to bubble through, to rip open letters, bills mostly – gathering envelopes and fliers for recycling.

After that he checks emails, sends texts, drinks coffee. A bit too much coffee, he said recently. It's making him jittery. He probably needs to cut down.

'It's not the coffee,' she told him.

He looked at her for a second.

'Still. I need to cut down.'

All day he works there in that small room. All day, at his drawing board or his desk, making calls, costing jobs, talking to site managers, drawing up plans, drinking coffee, tapping the keyboard, sharpening pencils.

Stopping briefly at lunchtime to get a turkey or a tuna-salad roll from the deli. Taking his place in the queue and talking pleasantly to the girl with the long dark hair and the nose-ring who knows nothing whatsoever about him and is therefore one of the most engaging and heartening people he knows.

Taking the roll back to eat at his desk or the drawing board, before going on with his work. He might pop out again later and get a Bounty or a Twix. But he tries not to. It's not a great habit to get into, is it, a chocolate hit at four o'clock.

All of this he has told her. Or else she has imagined it. Or else he has told her the bare bones and she has filled in the details for herself.

She knows that he works there in that office all alone, earning the money to keep their lives rolling along. She asked him once if he ever got lonely, and he looked at her with a relaxed kind of interest, as if she were asking him to think of his favourite colour or a number between one and seven.

She knows that he did once relent and have an assistant for a bit, the son of a man he used to play squash with – straight out of university, thinking about doing architecture, keen for workplace experience.

But he wasn't keen enough apparently, always watching the clock, bunking off early. And his personal hygiene wasn't great. And then someone complained about his phone manner so in the end – embarrassed, reluctant – he had to let him go. (She still can't think about this episode without a twist of pain because she knows how Graham placed his trust in that boy, how much he wanted to help, how little he deserved the discomfort that the situation caused him.)

But he likes working alone, he says. In fact, he prefers it. He does his best work when no one is watching over him, when he can think freely, without anyone making suggestions or bothering him with questions. He is very happy on his own, deep in his work. It's a comfort to him, a solace and sometimes even now, an unexpected source of pleasure and satisfaction.

This is what she knows. Sometimes, though—

Sometimes he comes home and his eyes are baggy and tired as if he's been punched or beaten. Not work-tired, but sad-tired. The skin of his face smelling of old man and solitary sandwich lunches. Or maybe he can't face the cheerful, unknowing girl at the deli and he doesn't eat at all. She worries about that.

Or perhaps it's worse than that. Maybe sometimes he doesn't do anything. How does she know that he doesn't just drive there and hang up his jacket and lock the door and sit there all day with his head in his hands? How does she know that he doesn't simply wait in that place, counting the minutes, staring at the smooth, dead-wood veneer of the desk, marking out time until it's the hour when he should return home?

Sometimes she thinks he looks like he hasn't eaten or breathed or done a stroke of work. Sometimes he looks like he's spent the day weeping.

After Isaac Roper was put in the hard and frosty ground, our mother took the baby and went to bed. For a few days or maybe it was about two weeks, we did not see her.

Our father was very patient. He went up and down the stairs taking her things. Cups of water and pieces of bread and cheese and eggs boiled in their shells and a jug of milk. He took her dinner up but she would not eat it. He brought the plate back down with the food still warm on it and when Frank asked if he could have it, he said he could even though Lottie had already taken the potatoes off.

Once, I saw my father with his head in his hands. I don't think he was crying but there was noise coming out. Another time I saw him standing in the yard and staring and staring at the wall as if it might tell him something worth knowing. Sometimes I heard them yelling and screaming at each other.

Don't you tell me what to do! she was saying. Don't you talk to me like that! Don't you dare give me orders!

And my father said something back but it was quieter and I couldn't hear what it was and then the baby started crying and it felt like the house would explode with so much noise and kerfuffle going on.

Meanwhile there was still the problem of the old elm that was laying right in front of our house. Our front room was in darkness because of the leaves and branches squashed up against the window. They brought two cart-horses up from the village to try to shift it. But even though the beasts got down on their knees, they couldn't make the thing budge even half an inch and a third one had to be fetched. In the end, the tree was got no further than the bottom of the orchard, where it lay on its back in the long grass just as if it grew that way.

The day after that, I found my mother down in the kitchen. The baby was cooing and kicking on a shawl on the floor and Honey was tied in the chair next to her while Ma kneaded the dough for the loaf, banging it and turning it as if she intended to beat the dear life out of it.

The baby looked as if it too had risen like a loaf and doubled in size but maybe it was just because I hadn't seen him in a while. But most of all I was shocked by my mother's face. It was shrunken and loose, as if someone had ripped her open and shaken all the feathers out.

She didn't say much but she asked me if the young man was still with us.

What? I said. You mean James?

I thought that Father would have told her that when James Dix had been with us about a week and showed no signs of moving on, he'd told him that if he had no particular plans and wanted to stick around, he could set him to work.

I'd looked up at James to see what his face did at this news. Just as I expected, it sprang to life. He said that he would like that very much.

You've really got nowhere else you need to be? my father said. No folk missing you or whatever?

James shook his head and scratched at his hair. I saw that there was a big bulge in his neck when he swallowed.

Not that I can think of, he said.

My father frowned. Coming from a big family himself, he probably couldn't imagine being alone in the world.

A few weeks, he said. We'll see how it goes. After that, I can't promise anything. You happy with that?

James was happy with that. He was very happy indeed.

He walked around whistling for the rest of the afternoon and when he saw Lottie pulling Honey along in the old dog-cart, he took it out of her hands and bumped it so fast along the brick path that the chickens flew up in all directions and Honey screamed at first with laughter and then with something more like fear.

Mary hears the car door slam. Graham throws his jacket and briefcase on a kitchen chair and drops a white plastic bag on the table.

'Sausages. From the Farm Shop.'

'Oh,' she says. 'That's nice.'

'That's the good news. I'm afraid the not-so-good news is that I'm picking a certain young lady up from the station in a minute.'

Her face falls.

'Ruby?'

'That's the one.'

'What, she's coming here?'

'Don't panic. I said she could stay one night and that was it.'

She says nothing. Picks up the bag of sausages and puts it by the cooker. He walks over to the sink to wash his hands.

'I don't actually think she wanted to come, but her mother gave her no choice.' He picks up the tea towel to dry his hands. 'I'm afraid the even worse news is she's been excluded for a few days.'

Mary catches her breath.

'What, you mean from school? My God. What's she done?'

She hears him sigh.

'Something to do with hanging around the town centre after school or maybe it was the lunch hour. The word shoplifting was mentioned. I don't know if it was her or another girl. She was certainly involved. Don't worry, I've promised her mother I'll have serious words with her.'

Mary looks at him.

'Why you?'

'What?'

'The serious words. Why do they always have to be done by you? Why can't she do it for once?'

She watches as his face changes. The sober, slightly flinching look he reserves for anything that has to do with Veronica.

'It's not easy for her, darling.'

Mary looks at him, sees pain on his face.

'What? What's not easy?'

'Doing all of this all on her own.'

'All of this?'

'Ruby's not easy.'

'It was her choice—'

'That doesn't make it any easier.'

'What, you mean she can't deal with her own daughter?'

She hears Graham let out a quick breath.

'You don't have any sympathy for her?'

Mary says nothing. Thinking about the day many years ago when she was finally allowed to meet this child – this little girl who seemed to be the cause of perpetual heartbreak and long telephone conversations – and her heart jumped. Not because of what she saw in Ruby, but because of what she knew she would now always see when she looked at Graham. Chaos in waiting. The dark-eyed stroppiness of an abandoned five-year-old, biding her time, waiting to make him hers again.

Now he comes over, touches her arm, her shoulders, pulling her to him.

'Look, I don't want to fight about it. All I'm saying is we've no idea what it's like to live full time with a hormonal teenage girl.'

Mary blinks.

31

'And we never will.'

He stares at her. For a moment neither of them can speak.

'I'm sorry,' she says, her voice a whisper now.

He pulls out a chair and sits down.

'It's me. I'm the one who should be sorry.'

'Don't be silly.'

'I should have asked you. I wanted to. It was Veronica. She's in a state. I had to think fast. She put me on the spot, if you really want to know.'

Mary tries to breathe.

'You don't have to do that.'

'Do what?'

'Blame it on her.'

'I'm not blaming it on anyone. I'm just saying it's what happened. She was quite upset. I suppose I felt responsible. But I shouldn't have sprung it on you. I should have asked you first. I'm sorry.'

'It's your home. You can do what you like.'

'It's your home too.'

Home. Mary shivers. She feels him looking at her.

'What? What are you thinking?'

'Nothing,' she says. 'I'm not thinking anything.'

Her first thought when Ruby walks in is that she's put on weight. She's never been slender the way Graham is slender, and even as a child she wasn't exactly skinny, but there's an all-over heftiness to her now – face, neck, jaw, bust, wrists – which you might, if you were pushed, have to call fat.

'Hi, Rubes – what a nice surprise.'

She holds out her arms and, after a quick, sullen moment of hesitation, Ruby comes over and lets herself be hugged. The hug smells of exhaust fumes and cigarettes and something else faintly medicinal that Mary can't place. As usual, Ruby's hair is dyed the blackest black. Her clothes are black. Her unravelling fingerless gloves are black. Her skin isn't good and the dried-up smears of concealer do her no favours, but Mary notices that her eyeliner, two perfect inky wings of black, is gorgeously done.

Ruby plonks herself down on the bench and, frowning, starts to unlace her shiny maroon Doc Marten boots.

'You don't have to do that,' Mary says. 'We're in the country now.'

Ruby looks up, caught out for a moment. As a little girl in London, they always made her take her shoes off at the door.

'The floor,' Mary says. 'Look at it, it's filthy. You can keep your shoes on if you want.'

'I don't mind,' Ruby says, pulling the boots off anyway, revealing lacy tights with plenty of ladders and a hole in the toe.

'But your feet will freeze.'

'I don't mind.'

Ruby picks up the DMs and places them carefully side by side on the mat.

'Great boots,' Mary says. 'Are they new?'

Ruby looks at her, says nothing.

They eat the sausages. Green beans and early new potatoes, which Ruby leaves. She leaves everything except the sausages, which she has second helpings of. She eats in silence, batting away all of her father's bright, careful questions with shrugs and sullen looks. But when he asks her to clear the table, she does it without argument, scraping and stacking the plates with a solemn kind of care and carrying the big, heavy frying pan with its pure white layer of congealed fat, through to the back sink.

After that she stands by the door to the stairs and tells them she's going to the loo. Mary asks her if she needs to be shown where it is. She says she knows.

'Don't disappear,' Graham tells her. 'There's pudding.'

'I don't want pudding.'

He makes a silly face.

'What, not even chocolate ice cream?'

'Not chocolate. The chocolate's gone. It's cherry something,' Mary says, suddenly embarrassed for him.

Ruby blinks at her.

'I don't want it.'

'All right, but anyway don't disappear,' says Graham. 'You and me are going to have a serious talk.'

Ruby is gone for at least ten minutes. Graham looks more and more bothered.

'What on earth's she doing up there?'

'Leave her. What does it matter what she's doing?'

'You think she's hanging out of the bathroom window smoking or something?'

This hadn't even occurred to Mary. She realises how unfit she is to be the parent of a teenager.

'What, weed?'

'No, I meant cigarettes but I suppose now you say it, yes, weed.'

'Wouldn't we smell it?'

'I don't know. Probably.'

They can smell nothing. Faintly, Mary thinks she can hear the creak of the boards upstairs. She catches herself hoping that Ruby isn't in their room.

'Maybe she's worried about what you're going to say,' Mary says at last. 'Maybe she thinks you're going to tell her off.'

'I am going to tell her off.'

'Then she's not going to come back down in a hurry, is she?'

Graham looks at her.

'Well, she's not getting out of it either.' He drains his glass and gazes at the narrow door that leads up into the shadows of the stairs. 'Oh, this is getting ridiculous. Shall I go and give her a call?'

Mary puts a hand on his.

'Don't hound her. You've got to stop treating her like a child,' she adds, when Graham continues to watch the stairs.

He looks at her.

'What do you mean? I don't treat her like a child. Anyway, she is a child. She behaves like a bloody child. I'm furious with her, if you really want to know.'

Mary sighs. He pushes his chair back, throws his napkin on the table.

'All right, all right. I get it. You're right. She's a big girl. I just wish she would act like one, that's all.'

When Ruby reappears, her face is flushed, her eyes bright. She's tugging at the black and ragged sleeves of her pullover, pulling them down over her hands.

'You OK, darling?' Graham asks her.

Ruby sniffs and looks past him at the dark windowpane.

'I don't want to stay here.'

'What?'

'I can't stay in this house. I want to go home.'

Graham flicks a glance at Mary.

'Rubes. For God's sake. It's nine thirty. You can't possibly go home now.'

'Why not?'

Graham begins to laugh. 'Well, there's no trains for a start.'

'Why not?'

'This isn't Camden. We're in the countryside. The last train went at about eight.'

'Can't you drive me?'

'No, honey, I can't.'

'I'll call Mum.'

'What? And ask her to do a four-hour round trip to come and collect you in the middle of the night? I don't think so.'

'I'll hitch then.'

'Don't be so bloody ridiculous. For goodness' sake, Ruby, what is this? What on earth's got into you?'

Mary looks at Ruby. Seeing something blurred and wobbly and on edge about her and wondering for a moment if she's been crying. She hasn't seen her cry for many, many years, not since she was a child of ten or eleven, certainly not since she's been a teenager.

Even when they told her what had happened, even then, she didn't cry, but stared dry-eyed into space and then brought her fist down so hard on the table that a glass rolled onto the floor and smashed. 'That girl needs anger management,' Mary's mother had said, forgetting that she herself was existing on a diet of rage, Scotch and diazepam.

'What is it?' Mary says now as gently as she can. 'Why don't you want to stay?'

Ruby pulls her attention away from Graham and squinches her eyes at Mary.

'What do you mean, why?'

'Well, you were perfectly happy to stay a while ago. So what's the matter? What's changed? Has something changed?'

Ruby looks at the ground. Graham makes a noise of exasperation.

'Come on, Rubes, we haven't got all night.'

Ruby looks at him.

'You're not going to like it.'

'Try me.'

Ruby draws her cuff further over her fist and brings it to her mouth.

'It's this house.'

Mary feels her heart contract.

'What?'

Ruby looks at her.

'I don't like it.'

'What do you mean, you don't like it? What don't you like?'

Ruby doesn't move. Her eyes flicking over to the windowpane then back to her father.

'I just don't like it, that's all.'

Mary looks at Graham. His face is calm.

'You're just not used to it,' she tells Ruby. 'I know it feels very quiet after London. But that'll change, you'll see. You'll be all right when you've stayed here a few times.'

Ruby gives her a quick, startled look as if she'd forgotten she was there.

'No,' she says. 'It's not that.'

'What is it then?'

'You wouldn't understand.'

'We might.'

'I don't want to talk about it.'

There's a brief silence, then Graham laughs. He picks up the bottle, pours more wine.

'Oh, I see. I get it. I know what this is. Look, my darling, I don't care whether you like this house or not. I don't care how many little distractions and red herrings you decide to chuck at us. You're not getting out of this talk.'

Ruby says nothing. Mary thinks she sees tears in her eyes. She gets up, heart banging, her chair scraping the floor.

'I'm going to leave you two to it,' she says.

Ruby turns her head and looks at her. Mary notices that her pupils are enormous. Dilated and black as her clothes.

'Sit,' Graham says to Ruby.

With surprising meekness, she obeys. As Mary leaves the room she hears her sniff.

'I don't want some great big lecture, all right?'

*

But later, much later, getting ready for bed, he stands there frowning, unbuttoning his shirt.

'She says she saw a man out there.'

Mary sits up in the bed.

'What? What do you mean, a man? Out where?'

'In the lane. Outside the house. She was very definite about it. A tall young red-haired guy, she said. Smoking a cigarette and standing looking up at the house. She says she saw him when she was in the bathroom. She says that's why she was gone so long.'

Mary stares at him.

'She was sure he was looking at this house?'

'Apparently.'

'But – my God – who would be looking at this house? And anyway why didn't she come and tell us?'

'Exactly.'

'What? You don't believe her?'

'I don't know.'

'I don't see why she'd make up something like that.'

Graham laughs.

'She makes up almost every other bloody thing. Seriously, she lies about everything. I'm frankly disinclined to believe a single word she says. Do you know what she told her mother? That we'd moved here because we wanted to hide ourselves away from everybody, including her.'

Mary looks at him.

'She's right about that.'

'What?'

'Well, it's true, isn't it?'

'What do you mean, it's true?'

'Not to get away from Ruby, obviously. But everyone else.'

Graham's face is perplexed, cold. She sees that she's upset him and she realises that in some haphazard way she meant to.

'That's really what you feel?'

'Don't you?'

'No, I don't. But you clearly do.'

'Sometimes that is what I feel, yes.'

He takes off the rest of his clothes and chucks them on the chair. Standing there naked and sad, looking at her.

'I thought it was the opposite,' he says.

'The opposite?'

'I thought it was supposed to be the start of not having to hide. Of being able to do normal things again.'

Mary says nothing. She looks at her hands, thinking that they look like the hands of a very old woman.

'I don't know what normal things are any more,' she says.

Graham looks at her. He goes into the bathroom.

'Is that what frightened her?' she says when he returns, toothbrush in his mouth.

'What?'

'The man. Was that why she didn't want to stay?'

'I don't know. We didn't really get on to that. Anyway, she's here now, let's not worry about it.'

'She didn't ask to leave again?'

He shakes his head.

'And is she OK?' she says, picturing Ruby in the still undecorated spare bedroom with its two creaky single beds and pictures stacked against the wall and a single light bulb hanging from the ceiling. At least it looks into the garden and not the lane, she thinks.

Graham shrugs.

'She got a police caution and she's not allowed back to school till Monday. And she doesn't seem the least bit bothered about any of it. Still, there don't seem to be any substances involved, which is what Veronica was most worried about.'

Mary stares at him.

He goes into the bathroom and spits. When he comes back in and gets into bed, he tries to put his arms around her. She hesitates and then she lets him.

'I don't want Ruby to be frightened of the house,' she says.

'Don't be silly. Of course she isn't frightened. She just said the first thing that came into her head.' He looks at her. 'I don't like you saying that, you know.'

'What?'

'About us hiding ourselves away. It's not true. I'm not going to let you say it. Who do you think you're hiding from?'

Mary says nothing. She thinks of her mother and father, her sister, Lynn Markham. She thinks of all the friends who said they'd get in touch and never did. Then she thinks of all the ones who did, whose cautiously upbeat and determinedly newsy emails she could never quite bring herself to reply to.

She sighs.

'All we ever do is watch TV.'

'What?'

'In this new life of ours. Haven't you noticed? It's all we ever do.'

He sits back in the bed. Picks up his watch off the bedside table. Puts it down again.

'I thought you liked it. I thought it kept your mind off things. All that rubbish. All those property programmes.'

'That's the day. When I'm on my own. And anyway I don't really bother with them any more.'

It's true. She doesn't. Last time she tried to watch daytime TV, she flicked on CBBC by mistake and broke out in a sweat.

He leans over and puts one of his pillows on the floor.

'I don't know what you want to do,' he says. 'I thought you didn't want to read. And you've no idea, when I try to suggest things—'

'What? When you try to suggest things, what?'

He sighs.

'Nothing,' he says. 'Forget I said that.'

She looks at him. The side of his face. Thick grey hair cropped short. When she met him it was down to his shoulders. He wore a funny kind of hat – was it a fedora? She cooked him beef stroganoff and she burnt it so it was inedible and he said don't worry I'm not hungry and he kissed her for an hour instead.

He yawns, reaches to turn out the light on his side.

'Some people would go to the pub,' he says. 'Get drunk and stagger home and never have to think at all.' He kisses her shoulder. 'Well, they would, wouldn't they?'

'You want to do that?'

'No. I'm just saying it's what a lot of people would do.'

A silence while they both think about this.

'You feel like reading?' he says.

She tries to remember what a book felt like.

'I don't know. Maybe. I don't know.'

'Order some books,' he says. 'Why don't you? Go on Amazon.'

She says nothing.

'Anyway,' he says as he punches his remaining pillows and turns over on his side ready for sleep, 'the days are getting longer. We can have evenings outside soon. We can do the garden, stuff like that. That'll pass the time.'

So even though he came from under a lightning tree and no one knew the smallest thing about him, James H. Dix slept on a pallet in the barn and washed at the tap in the yard and spent his days among us as if it had always been this way. As the weeks and then the months passed and winter turned to spring and the days got longer and softer and brighter, it was hard to remember that we had ever been without him in our lives.

The little ones were mad for him. Jazzy trailed him around the place from dawn to dusk, asking him so many questions that in the end, instead of getting angry with her, he took the easy way out and simply stopped listening.

Lottie stuck on like a limpet, not giving a scoot what he said or did as long as he said and did it to her. Even the twins, normally so thick with each other that no one else could get near them — let alone a stranger with thick red hair and staring eyes and a snake tattooed on his neck — they couldn't get enough of him either.

He chased them round the yard till they wept with excitement. He hid behind trees in the orchard, jumping out on them like a bogeyman, slicing through the air with his imaginary sword. He put them both in the wheelbarrow and gave them a fast, rough ride, threatening to tip them into the water trough at the last moment. They shouted so loud that our mother had to come out and tell them to be quiet, but she softened as soon as she saw James. It was like he was a saint or something. Nothing about him ever seemed to vex her.

He taught them to dab poppy seeds off the kitchen table with a wet finger.

But don't eat too many, he said. Because they'll give you wild dreams.

And Minnie asked him what a wild dream was and he made his eyes into slits and told her it was lions and tigers and crocodiles chasing you all night long and not giving up till morning.

She threw me a worried look.

What and biting you too?

James laughed. One moment he'd look very happy and alive but the next his face would be sweating and he'd look like he didn't know what to do with himself. He set his teeth on the edge of the table and pretended to gnaw it.

What else would wild animals do? he said and, keeping his eyes on Minnie, he wiped his face on his shirtsleeve.

It's not true, I told the twins. Don't listen to him. He's just making it up to frighten you.

I want a wee, Minnie said and she ran out of the room.

I wasn't afraid, Charlie said, but he slipped his hand in mine and kept it there.

Another time, James put Frank and two other boys from the village up against the wall in the yard and made them wait with their hands shoved down their breeches while he threw punches at them – left, right and centre – teaching them how to dodge and duck and slide so they could look after themselves if ever they got in a tight spot on the road.

He explained that this was what his own dear father had done for him and hadn't it always stood him in good stead?

And where is your own dear father? said Jazzy, who was sitting on the wall with Lottie, kicking her feet and watching.

James laughed and told her to mind her own business, but I could see that he was annoyed. He was dark as a pocket, when it came to his own personal history.

Is he in heaven with the angels? Lottie asked him.

Maybe, he said.

And are they poking pins in him because he tried to kick the door down?

James gave her a quick, black look.

What door? he said. I don't know what you're on about. My pa never kicked any door down.

Jazzy looked at her and laughed.

Angels don't have pins, you nonny. They don't have any sewing in heaven. Only clouds and stars and great big golden thrones.

They do have pins! Lottie shouted at her. They do! I seen it when I was sleeping.

Jazzy looked at James.

41

Ah, when you were sleeping, was it? Well, that's what we call a dream, you little goose.

A cloud went over Lottie's face.

It wasn't a dream.

Then how did you see it? Jazzy said and she folded her arms and waited, still looking at James.

Lottie stuck out her lip.

When I was in heaven, I saw it.

Jazzy frowned.

But only dead people go to heaven, Lottikins.

That's right. I died.

You didn't die.

I did.

Don't lie. Of course you didn't.

Now Lottie began to cry.

I did! After the bad man hit me with the knife, I did.

James looked at her now and clenched a fist.

What bad man was that, Lottie? If a man hits you, you take me to him and I'll give him something to think about.

Lottie's whole face was trembling and the tears were falling out of her eyes now.

I can't, I can't. I can't take you to him.

Why can't you?

She shook her head and held out her hands.

Because I just can't.

I was scrubbing pots in the back sink when he came up behind me. I smelled him before I heard him. Tobacco. Onions. And something else more alive. The bright, raw smell of a young rabbit when the skin's come off.

He touched my shoulder and I swung around. He was smiling like a lunatic. His teeth were strong and white and only one missing, towards the back. His breeches were ragged and his shirt was untucked and you could see the inky swirling point of his tattoo.

Did I frighten you? he said.

No.

I didn't mean to.

Well you didn't.

He stood there not moving, looking at me. I felt my cheeks start to burn so I turned back to the pans. My hands were sore and stinging and I was in a hurry to get the job done. I tipped the heaviest pan over onto the wooden board to drain. He folded his arms and leaned up against the wall next to me. I didn't look at him but I felt my skin start to prickle with his closeness.

What's the matter? he said.

Nothing's the matter.

Don't you want us to be friends?

I took a breath.

Not really, I said.

Why? What is it? Don't you like me?

I don't know, I said and I rinsed another of the big pans and turned it over to drain.

I felt him staring at me.

You're a bit of a princess, aren't you?

No, I said.

Oh, but you are. It's on your face. Princess Eliza. Look at you – you think yourself so very high and mighty and fancy and fine.

And he looked at my face and laughed to himself as if there were something secret and interesting there that only he could see. I wanted to say something but I knew it would be no use so I buttoned my lip. But I couldn't help glancing at him and as I did so, the look on his face made my blood freeze.

What? I said.

He shook his head.

You don't know it, do you? he said, laughing again. You've not found it out yet, have you? You've no idea.

I knew he wanted me to ask him what he was talking about, so I didn't. But I could not easily turn my face away and he looked straight into the very centre of my eyes and he smiled as eerily as if he had just turned over a card and found he'd won a great fat prize.

You're mine, he said. It's you I came for. It's why I'm here. I can do anything I want to you, Miss High and Mighty Princess Eliza.

Her birthday. Forty-two years old. A cool grey day, her heart so small and dry and tight she can barely feel it beating inside her. She wakes

43

and tries not to think of other birthdays. Tries not to think of anything. She stays very steady. She does not cry.

Graham brings her breakfast in bed. Coffee and croissants and damson jam with a little gingham cloth on the lid. She expresses surprise. And pleasure. Tells him he didn't have to do it. He tells her of course he did. Adding that she needs to hurry up and get dressed because they've got to go and pick up her present.

'What?' she says. 'What do you mean, pick it up? Pick it up from where?'

She goes into the bathroom and washes herself. In the mirror these days, what is it? Her face, slowly disintegrating. Lines where there never were lines, shadows where once there was nothing but light.

'What are you doing in there?' he calls. She can tell from his voice that he is on edge, excited. 'We've got to get a move on, hurry up!'

He looks almost nervous as they drive out of the village, up the main road to the T-junction where he turns left. After fifteen or perhaps twenty minutes on the fast grey road, lorries thundering in front and behind, he turns off. Following a small country lane until it narrows and then peters out and becomes a track.

'I thought about getting it without you,' he says as they bump along the dusty track, birdsong loud in the air around them. 'Having it all ready to surprise you when I came home. But then I thought that would be no fun. And anyway, the truth is I think I might need your help bringing it back.'

Fun? Help? She looks at him, suddenly afraid of what the present might be.

They park outside a low, squalid-looking bungalow. Empty plant pots and broken plastic chairs piled outside. He tells her to stay in the car and he goes across the white crazy paving and knocks. After a few moments he bends and looks through the letterbox. A lot of dogs start barking.

A fat, elderly, grey-haired woman in a tracksuit comes out. Mary watches from the car as Graham talks to the woman for a moment and then they disappear together through another metal gate around the back.

She does what she is told. She sits in the car, her hands in her lap, and she does not move. Sun spills from between the clouds and for a moment she is blinded. Then it slides away and she can see again. She thinks she sees someone at one of the windows, lifting a net curtain. Still she does not move. Her eyes straight ahead, her limbs like water. She wonders what would happen if Graham never reappeared, if he never came back at all. Would she just sit here, melting into the car seat, dissolving to dust as the years passed?

But a few minutes later, he does appear, followed by the woman who turns back briefly to secure the gate. Mary sees that in his hand is a lead and at the end of the lead is a small black and white dog. Jesus, she thinks, oh God, oh no. He approaches the car, smiling in a careful, bunched-up way as if he is about to introduce himself to her for the first time. He pulls open her door.

'Happy Birthday,' he says.

She stares at his face and then at the dog's white whiskery muzzle.

'We can't have a dog,' she says.

He seems ready for this.

'It's all right.' He holds the lead out to her. 'That's fine. I knew you'd say that. It's on approval anyway.'

'It?'

She looks at the lead but she does not take it.

'She. Little collie. Four months old.'

Four months. The dog looks frightened. Graham pushes the lead into her hand.

'I don't want a dog,' she says. 'You're not listening to me,' she adds when he just smiles. 'I mean it, Graham. I don't want a dog.'

He hesitates, still smiling, his eyes on her.

'It's all right. Like I said. We've got a bit of time to decide.'

He lifts the dog and puts it in the car. The lead is loose in her hand. The dog gives her a quick, startled glance then lies down, its body heavy and warm against her feet. It tucks its nose into its tail and holds very still.

'Look at that,' Graham says. 'Settled already.'

'It's terrified,' she says.

Our dog hated James Dix. She would not go near him. She made sure to move out of his way if he came too close and she would not even eat the scraps we threw to her if James was in the room. If, out of nowhere, you saw her ears flatten and you heard her growl, you could be sure that seconds later his bright, unmistakable head would go bobbing past the window.

When he found me in the darkness of the scullery, she was stretched out asleep on the floor, but as soon as she felt him, she jumped up and ran off.

I would have run off too, but I knew it would just have excited him. Instead I made a point of staying level and tight and calm.

What is it now? I said. What do you want?

He looked at me.

Oh, Eliza. Do I always have to want something?

I said nothing. He began to smile.

I could buy you some boots, if you want, he said.

What?

Boots. Boots for your pretty little feet.

I looked at him.

I know what boots are.

Well, then?

No thanks.

You don't want them?

No.

His face went soft and sad.

But look. Look at what's on your feet, Eliza. I'm telling you, you do need some.

I didn't need to look at my feet. I knew what my boots were like. I knew that they were torn and scuffed and muddy and coming apart so they flapped wide open at the toe and heel.

They're not my Sunday ones, I said.

Still, he said. I could get you some.

I stared at him. The house was empty. Everyone was either at school or else out in the fields. He should have been there too. I knew he'd come back on purpose. There was no sound but the clock ticking.

I wish you'd go away, I said.

I heard him suck his teeth.

Where are your manners, Eliza?

It's the truth.

It's very rude when here I am offering to get you some boots.

You can't get me boots, I said.

I can. I can get anything I want. You'll see.

You've no money.

Who said anything about money?

I looked at his eager dirty face and I remembered the new boots he'd had on that first night, the night of the storm. Boots that no man had ever walked anywhere in. I looked down at his feet. They were old now, those boots, old and worn as if he'd been wearing them for two years or more.

What? he said. You won't let me get you some? You won't do me the honour?

No.

All right, then, Princess Eliza. Have it your way.

I will, I said.

He stuck his hands in his pockets and he didn't say anything and when I didn't either, he turned and walked away.

But a moment later, he was back.

I could take you to the sea, he said. What about that? I bet you've never seen the sea. Tell me right now, have you ever seen the sea, Eliza?

I have seen it, I said.

I don't believe you.

Three years ago. We went to the sea at Yarmouth. Father took us. We took the kiddies in the cart.

It was true. I remembered it well. The loud excitement of the kiddies and the wild, smashed feeling I got as my father drove the cart around a narrow bend in the road and there it was in front of us, glittering and vast, the boldest, most astounding thing you ever saw.

Well then, said James Dix. How about I take you there again? We can make a proper trip of it this time.

It was a proper trip last time, I said.

All right, but this time we can ride on a donkey and dip our feet in the cold water and walk on the promenade and look at all the fancy tricks on the pier.

We did all of those things last time, I said, even though I knew we hadn't.

What, even the pier? You went on the pier?

I looked at him and I said nothing. And I thought of the pier at Yarmouth that I hadn't ever been on and how much I would have liked to do all of those games like the one where you brought the hammer down as hard as you could and the thing slid up and hit the bell and showed how strong you were. I also thought how frightening James Dix looked when he talked about wanting to make me do things.

Well, we had to come home, I said at last. Because Lottie fell in.

James smiled.

Fell into what?

She fell in the lake. The boating lake. She walked right in and the water was higher than her head and she got a mouthful of tiddlers and our father had to pull her out. She was ever so upset and her clothes were sopping wet. Father put his coat around her but we had to come home in case she got a chill. She was only one year old at the time, I added. It wasn't her fault.

James laughed.

Maybe I'll take young Lottie to Yarmouth, he said. If you won't come with me. Maybe I'll take all the little kiddies and show them what a good time really is.

I looked at him. I realised I didn't like the way he talked about the kiddies.

How long are you staying here? I asked him. What I mean is, when will you go?

He was still laughing about the kiddies but that stopped him. So as not to look surprised, he stuck his hands in his pockets. I saw him shrug.

I don't know how long. What does it matter? Just as long as your father wants me, I suppose. Why, Eliza? Why do you want to know?

I felt my heart start to race.

He doesn't want you, I said.

What?

He doesn't want you here, James. Don't you see? He's just being kind. My father is a very kind man and he feels very sorry for you, that's all.

Now at last he looked quite angry. His face grew pale and I saw him swallow hard.

Why would your father feel sorry for me?

I tried to shrug.

Because of how you've no family or work and you're all alone in the world and all that.

He rubbed at his hair. He seemed to be thinking hard about this.

I'm not alone in the world at all, Eliza. You're quite wrong about that.

Who's your family, then? Where are they?

That's none of your bloody business.

I wanted to laugh then but I decided not to. I thought again of that day by the sea at Yarmouth and how happy we'd all been even though we hadn't gone on the pier. And I thought that even if I didn't like James very much, I ought to feel very sorry that he didn't have any of what I had – family and memories and small brothers and sisters and always the happy possibility that one day something good or interesting or new might come along.

But still my heart was thumping.

We don't know anything about you, I said.

His face grew careful.

Who is it that says that? Does your father say that? Does your mother?

I shook my head.

It's only me who's interested. And I suppose Jazzy and Frank and Lottie are quite interested too.

Not the twins?

The twins are only interested in each other.

And Honey?

Honey? It made me shiver that he knew all our babies' names.

Honey's just a baby, I said. She doesn't even know to be interested in things yet.

He seemed to relax.

One day, Eliza, I'll tell you my whole life story and then you'll be sorry.

Why will I be sorry?

Because it's a very sad one and if you've any heart at all inside that pretty little breast of yours, it will make you feel ashamed to have been so unkind.

I looked at him. I didn't know if I was being unkind or not and I wasn't sure that I cared.

I'm sure your life story is very sad indeed, I said. But I'm also sure that it's none of my business.

And because I'd had enough, I began to walk away. But as I walked, he called out to me and what he said next made my heart jump.

It's called the High Striker, by the way, Eliza, he said.

I stopped.

What? I said, blushing to my roots. What is?

That thing.

What thing?

The thing that you hit with the hammer to show how strong you are.

Back home Graham shows her the things he's got for the dog, things he's been hiding in the old apple store at the bottom of the garden, a place where he says he knew she would never dream of looking. There's a bed made of soft brown furry fabric. Metal bowls. A bag of dried puppy food. A plush toy that is supposed to be in the shape of a bone, but which they both agree looks more like a legless rat.

For a quick moment this makes her laugh and she sees how eagerly he jumps on that fact, his whole face brightening.

'Look,' he tells her as they sit together on the bench in the kitchen and watch the little dog potter around on the sheets of newspaper they've had to put down. 'I knew it was a risk, obviously I did. But I also knew that if I asked you, you'd say no before you'd even thought about it.'

Mary says nothing. His arm is around her. He squeezes her shoulder.

'Well?' he says. 'Isn't it true?'

She doesn't look at him. Is that what she's turned into, she wonders, a person who says no to everything without even thinking?

She holds out her fingers to the dog, who sniffs at them, tail moving gently from side to side. Feeling Graham watching her.

'But you were right,' he goes on, 'the other day. When you said all we do is watch TV. It's true. It is all we seem to do. We need to do other things. We need stuff in our lives, even difficult stuff. We need to start living again.'

Mary looks at him.

'By getting a dog?'

He glances back at the dog for a moment as if he expects it to answer the question.

'Well, it's a start, isn't it?'

Mary says nothing. She allows herself to touch the animal's dark head. The softness behind its ears, the sprinkling of dark freckles on its white nose. Two black patches around its eyes.

'Has it got a name?'

Graham shakes his head, but she can feel his delight at the question.

'She said they've never called it anything. What do you think? What should she be called?'

Mary hesitates.

'We can't keep it. I mean it. We just can't.'

He keeps his eyes on her – soft, apologetic.

'Just give yourself some time, darling.'

She shakes her head. 'I won't change my mind.'

Graham sighs. He passes his hand over his face.

'All right. Three days. Can you just give me three days? Will you do that for me? I told her we'd decide in three days.'

He says he'll take the dog for a walk around the garden. She watches them both go, the little dog leading him as it sniffs and pulls and wanders. She thinks that they both look very content.

But ten minutes later, glancing out of an upstairs window, she sees him sitting on the white bench with the dog at his feet. His head is in his hands. She watches him for a few more moments, then she moves away.

That night in bed, he turns to her and for the first time in as long as she can remember, she lets him in. He does what he hardly ever does these days: holding her to him, kissing her, putting his lips on the parts of her that are nearest to his mouth. She hears him telling her he loves her. He licks her bottom lip, tasting her, and then she feels him nudging at her, pressing and parting, gaining ground. A sigh, a little moan – the old familiar sounds and rhythms, breath and body, skin and hair, fingers, lips, tongue. The bright, warm taste of his saliva. The skin of his thighs, his belly, hot against her. A quick nip with his teeth.

Afterwards, she lies there. Calm. Wet. Breathing. Thinking that perhaps she won't take a pill tonight. She'll just stay very still and see what happens without.

She gazes at the slit of sky just visible under the blind – put up recently to replace the too-short curtains. Navy blue, edged with something. Past ten o'clock and the sky not yet black.

His hand comes over, reaching for her, coming to rest on her thigh. His breathing tells her that he's not asleep.

Next time she opens her eyes, the room is dazzling, alive with sunshine. At first the voices are very quiet, a man and a woman, coming from somewhere else, close or far away, she can't tell, not in the room, maybe the lane –

What you don't think about, you don't know.

But I do know—

You need to forget what you know – if you value this little beating heart—

Mary tears herself from sleep, sitting up, crying out, hands clenched as she grabs at the sheets, eyes wild, heart banging.

'What?' Graham, eyes still closed and clutching at her, putting his arms out. 'Darling – what? What is it? What's the matter?'

She stares around her. Trying to breathe.

'It's that place.'

'What? What place?'

'The shed. Where you put the dog things.'

She stares at him, her throat hot and tight.

'The apple store? What about it?' He's sitting up now, eyes open, looking at her. 'Mary, wake up. You're making no sense. I've no idea what you're talking about. Seriously, what's the matter?'

She gazes at him.

'I don't know.'

'What?'

'I don't know what I'm talking about,' she says, beginning to cry.

His arms now, coming around her, closing around her, shushing her. He holds her.

'Darling, my darling – you were asleep – open your eyes now – I mean it – look around you. Open your eyes and look at me. Look at where you are.'

She does it. Still clinging to him, she opens her eyes and she looks. Sees the old chest of drawers, the brown cardboard boxes still to be unpacked. Her jeans and bra flung on a chair. Yesterday's scrunched-up newspaper and his bottles of pills, a comb, his loose change. The wavy light coming in through the window.

He kisses her head.

'There,' he says. 'All right now?' And when she still doesn't speak. 'That hasn't happened in a very long time, has it?'

3

It was May and in the lanes you couldn't move for folk going on about how overjoyed they were to see the blossom and the sunshine and the birds and the bees and so on. The lambs were growing fat on clover. Mother did all our beds with turpentine and salt to get rid of the bugs. The days got longer and the night frosts stopped and small brown birds bathed themselves in the dust pockets in the lane where the puddles used to be.

A wren started to build her nest under the eaves of the shed and as usual the cat sat and watched, waiting to kill the fledglings just as soon as they hatched. And as usual Minnie and Charlie moaned and cried about it and said it wasn't fair and why didn't God stop it? Maybe God has better things to do, our father said.

Bees drifted over the garden and hollyhocks unfurled their hairy buds and stood in their lemon and salmon rows. Slowly, our mother seemed to wake up and start eating and thinking and talking again. She took the baby into the garden and laid him on a piece of sacking under the apple tree, where he kicked and cooed and watched the light flicker around in the leaves. She sat and watched him and I saw our father watching her very hard – careful always to glance away the moment she saw his eyes were on her.

Honey found a dead rat lying by the tap in the orchard, its pale, hairless feet curled and flies crawling over its face and we told her not to touch it and she didn't. The air was full of mown grass and the ripe, baked scent of the wallflowers that grew by the back door. One day Jazzy's freckles weren't there and the next day they were, as if someone had crept up in the night with a paintbrush and done them while she slept.

Each warm morning the Narkets hung their birdcage outside so the parrot could bask and preen in the warmth of the sun, except that this year old Mrs Narket, who had died at Christmas, wasn't around to see it.

But it doesn't matter, Lottie said, waving her fingers around as if she was enjoying a merry tune that no one else could hear. Because she's coming back and she's on her way right now!

I was darning Frank's socks. I pulled the thread from my mouth and held it up, stiff and wet, in the air. I looked over at our mother, who was sweeping the floor.

Coming back? What do you mean, Lottie, who's coming back?

Lottie blinked at me.

The old lady. The one that was dead. She's coming back. She says we don't need to worry about anything, cos it won't be long now.

Lottie always did have special ideas about the dead. Once, when she was two or three, she pointed, laughing and smiling, to the darkest corner of the room and shouted 'Man, man!' in her loudest voice. When we asked her what man she was talking about, she said it was her friend who'd come looking for his old family.

What old family? we said.

His old family from when he used to be alive, of course!

Another time she insisted that a dark-faced hawker that came to the door selling tin toys was a little boy she used to know.

How ever could you possibly know him, Lottie? You're only three.

I knowed him when I was his age, she said.

His age? But he's even older than Father.

Lottie smiled, but something about her face didn't look quite right.

Just like I used to be, she said.

Sometimes weeks or months went by and Lottie seemed to forget her queer ideas. Now and then she'd just be a plain old ordinary little child for a while, larking around with Honey or the dog or the twins and playing Susie Go Round the Moon and fighting and shouting and stopping all the nonsense about dead people. But something about James Dix's arrival in our lives seemed to have stirred it up again: as if the simple sight and sound of him had rattled some sour old memory in her and got her going.

You mean old Mrs Narket? I said now as I tried again to thread the needle. Poor Mrs Narket's in heaven, Lottie. Even if she wanted to, she couldn't come back here.

Lottie shot me a look. Her face said I didn't know a single thing.

She's comin'. She says that nothing's going to stop her because – because – because she misses her parrot too much. She don't much care for it there anyway.

I smiled, twisting the thread and pulling it through the needle's sharp slit.

Doesn't care for it where?

Lottie narrowed her eyes.

In heaven! She don't like the colour of it and she don't like God one little bit and anyway she says the poor parrot is very sad without her.

Our mother stopped sweeping. Leaning on her broom for a moment, shaking her head.

What a lot of nonsense, Lottikins. Since when were you talking to old Mrs Narket, anyway?

Lottie frowned and tapped her finger on her forehead.

Um, let me see – I think it was when she was crawling on the floor under my bed.

Now I couldn't help laughing. It was hard to think of old Mrs Narket who had never been the sprightliest of persons at the best of times crawling around on her hands and knees on the floor under Lottie's bed.

Our mother picked up the broom again.

Now you just stop telling boomers, she said. And you too, Eliza; you ought to know better than to laugh about the dead. Poor Mrs Narket was put in the ground on Christmas Eve and everyone knows she's with her Maker now and God bless her.

Lottie frowned.

What's her-maker?

It means the same as heaven, I said.

Now Lottie stamped her foot and shook her head, blowing air out of her mouth.

Not in heaven, she ain't, not any more – I told you! She only went there for a little bit of time and that was only because she wanted to see her boy.

What boy? I said.

Lottie shut her eyes and opened them again.

Let me see: I think it was the one that was hit by the cart.

Now our mother straightened up and stared at Lottie.

How do you know that?

What?

About Mrs Narket's lad. How do you know it?

Lottie yawned.

I don't know how I knowed it. I just did know it.

I looked at my mother who was still gazing at Lottie with her mouth open.

I didn't know Mrs Narket had a lad, I said, because as far as I knew all the Narkets since way back had been girls.

My mother stood the broom up against the wall and took her shawl. Winding it around herself. She seemed to shiver.

He was hit by a hay cart when he was small. Years ago. I was only a girl myself. She never spoke about it. She didn't like to. No one in the family did. It's been years since I heard anyone speak about it.

My mother sat down by the hearth. Shock all over her face. And I looked at my naughty sister, who was bobbing around the kitchen now, lifting her petticoats and jigging around on the spot and looking a bit too pleased with herself. She glanced at me then and a quick blast of surprise shot across her face and she started to laugh. Pointing her finger at me. I felt my skin grow cold.

What? I said. What's the matter, Lottie? What is it?

Lottie nodded at something just past my shoulder.

There, she said, and she narrowed her eyes as if she was staring at something.

What?

Eliza, look! There. It's her – she's just behind you.

I couldn't help it. I shivered.

What do you mean? I said. Who's behind me?

Her. The lady.

I tried to look behind me. Lottie was laughing, very amused now. There's no one there, I said.

Yes, there is.

Where?

I watched as Lottie's face went cool and intent, as if she was trying even harder to look at something.

There! By your neck—

My neck?

No, your hair. Oh no, now she's right by your hand!

57

I pulled my hand back sharply and looked at our mother. I tried to laugh.

What? Now you're saying you can see old Mrs Narket standing next to me?

Still gazing at the space around me, Lottie shook her head.

Not Mrs Narket, no. The other lady.

What do you mean? What other lady?

The one with the long black hair. The one that cries all the time and doesn't have any skirts.

Our mother seemed relieved that it wasn't Mrs Narket. She let out a laugh.

No skirts? A lady in the altogether? Now that would certainly be enough to make anybody cry.

Lottie gazed at our mother and chewed her lip as if she was considering this. Then she shook her head.

No, she ain't in the altogether. She don't mind about the skirts. She has other clothes. She has breeches.

A lady in breeches?

For a moment Lottie looked upset.

And she's crying because of the man.

What man?

The man that took her little girls away and did – this! – to them.

Lottie raised up her hands and brought them down so hard on the table that the spoons and knives rattled in the drawer. I gasped. I saw a flash of fear go across our mother's face.

Don't do that, Lottie, she said. I mean it. You just stop it right this minute or you'll break something.

Keeping herself very still, Lottie blinked.

It's what the man did.

The man. A cold, dark pain in my chest. For a quick moment I couldn't breathe.

What man? I said. What little girls?

Lottie didn't look at me. She had a look on her face that I didn't recognise: you would think she was staring at something that was going on a very long way away from us.

I don't know if they're in heaven or not but I don't think they're coming back ever again.

*

It's May. The skies are blue and the days are lengthening. They had a week or two of coolness and cloud, but now every morning they wake to the same wide, steady sky, the same swelling promise of heat.

Leaving the back door open, Mary walks down the garden to hang the washing. The dog follows her, bobbing in and out of the flower beds, sniffing at leaves and shrubs, squatting always to pee in the exact same, yellowing place on the edge of the lawn where the grass is mostly moss and scrub and dandelions.

She hasn't named it yet. But for Graham just the fact that she hasn't made him take it back is enough. Three weeks now they've had it.

A week ago, Ruby phoned up and said if they didn't want it, she'd take it. She said that her mother had agreed to seriously consider it if it would make her work harder at school.

Mary heard Graham laugh.

'If she really said that, then she's an even bigger fool than I thought she was. The only thing that's ever going to make you do any work at school is you, Rubes. And anyway that dog was Mary's birthday present and we're keeping it, thanks very much.'

Ruby must have asked if Mary really wanted to keep it, because she heard Graham hesitate.

'Yes. Yes, she does. She's coming round to it anyway.' He paused, listening. 'Oh, she did, did she?' Then he laughed. 'And anyway I seem to remember that you don't have the best track record when it comes to looking after animals,' he added, reminding Ruby of the hamster that she took to school, which drowned in a bucket of glue.

When he came off the phone, he looked at Mary.

'She says it wasn't her fault.'

'What wasn't?'

'The hamster and the glue. She says she was seven years old and the supply teacher left the cage door open.'

Seven years old. Feeling Graham watching her, she tried to smile. Heard him sigh.

'Did you tell her you didn't want the dog?'

Mary remembered the phone call. Ruby, clearly put up to it by her mother, ringing to wish her a sullen happy birthday.

'I didn't say that.'

'But you said something?'

Thinking about that morning, something inside Mary seemed to collapse.

'Oh God. I don't know what I said. I can't remember. You know what she's like. She hears whatever she wants to hear.'

Graham looked at her with pain in his eyes.

'I don't mind. It doesn't matter if you said it or not. I was only making conversation.'

'All right.'

'I was, you know.'

'I know you were.'

He took a breath.

'She's not having it anyway. I'd rather take it back to the breeder than let her and her mother get their hands on it.'

'Come on,' Mary says now to the dog as she makes her way down the garden with the washing basket. 'Come on, let's go and hang up the washing.'

They thought about having a line in the yard – there's even a handy iron hook on the old brick wall. But she's come to rather like this short walk – down the shallow stone steps, brushing past the tired and leggy old lavender and on through the long, unmown grass, down towards the huge old tree trunk that looks as if it's lain there for a hundred years or more.

The line is strung between two apple trees. On a hot day, the washing is dry in less than half an hour. She can get a couple of loads done before lunch.

They haven't done anything to the garden yet, though they keep on telling each other they will. In the old house, she grew anything and everything. Lupins, delphiniums, hollyhocks, sweet peas, anything she could get past the slugs. She used to say it was her passion, gardening. She meant it, too. She'd lie in bed reading gardening books and fall asleep dreaming of chitting potatoes and digging rich manure trenches in which to sow broad beans. Graham has said he wouldn't mind making a cut flower patch, robust, old-fashioned blooms like dahlias and chrysanthemums. She likes that about him, that he can talk about flowers. And yet it's May and neither of them has lifted a finger.

He did at last clear an area around the old white bench so they could sit with a drink in the evening. But that was weeks ago and the weeds are already knee-high again. Most mornings she sits here with her tea among the giant nettles and the henbane and the other tall, springy plants she cannot even name and she can't see more than a couple of feet in front of her. She has to take it on trust that the cottage still exists on one side, the seemingly endless, bottomless garden on the other.

She pegs the washing out quickly – his socks, his pants, a couple of shirts and a worn and faded T-shirt with holes under the arms and some French ski resort advertised on it. Two of her bras. The jeans that used to be tight but hang so stupidly loose on her now.

Once she's finished, she makes sure not to glance at the line – one half of a family blowing there – but turns away quickly, bending for the basket and calling the dog, ready to head off back across the wavy, sunlit grass.

And the very moment she straightens up, there he is.

I didn't think James Dix would be much of a worker. I thought he would kick up a rough if he had to do half of what my father managed each day. But I was wrong. He got on with it. He did everything he was told to do and more.

He helped with the hay harvest and he raked up the cuttings and he lifted and turned the compost and helped to get the piglets away from the sow for weaning. He watched my mother as she soaped the gooseberries to keep the sawfly off, and all by himself he earthed up the potatoes we'd put in at Easter.

My father showed him how to go on the common and tell which cows were ours so as to bring them in for milking. He made Frank take him into the fields and teach him to use a weed-hook and how to recognise sorrel and megbeg and field vetch and hensfoot and all the other sly and creeping weeds the crops didn't get on with.

You could tell he wasn't from the country. He had to be shown just about everything. He didn't know the first thing about grazing, or where a cow's teat was or which part to pull so the milk came down. He didn't know a thing about growing or corn or what was in the earth or what animals could understand or do for themselves. He didn't know which tools were for what or when you should plant things or how you kept the crows off or why you had to take notice of the rain and the wind or the sun and moon or do things in a certain order according to the seasons.

But he didn't shirk. He put in the hours. And he was handy when he wanted to be. At his own suggestion, he patched up the chicken coop with some planks he found in the apple store and my father – who'd been grumbling for months that it was a job that needed doing – was very happy indeed with it. And after Frank had showed him how to go over the dry earth between the corn rows with a daisy-rake, he prepared the ground as good as anyone could have, and then organised hours of stone picking in the turnip fields with the little ones.

My mother, who was growing stronger with every day that passed, stopped pounding the washing and looked up from the tub to watch.

Look at that, she said, wiping her raw, sudsy hands on her apron so she could shield her eyes against the sun. Whatever is he up to with all those kiddies?

I looked. The little ones were staggering up and down over the brown earth behind him with their buckets and baskets. Even Lottie, who could never usually be got to do anything halfway helpful or useful, was managing perfectly well with a small basket all of her own.

He's got a way with him, hasn't he? my mother said. He can get anyone to do anything, that one can.

And I looked at her and I saw that there was a flush of brightness on her cheeks for the first time since Isaac Roper died.

'The dog didn't even growl,' Mary tells Graham later when trying to describe what exactly she saw. A slender, red-haired man, crouching at the bottom of the orchard and looking at something in the long grass.

'Looking at what?'

'I don't know. I couldn't see. And then the next moment, I don't know what happened but he just wasn't there at all.'

'Well, you must have looked away for a second.'

'And what?'

'And he ran off.'

'But I didn't. I didn't look away. I was so shocked.'

Graham smiles.

'OK. So he dissolved.'

Mary says nothing. Already in her mind the moment is less certain, more indistinct. She remembers some things. The sun hot on her shoulders, the creaky lightness of the empty basket in her arms. She remembers the dog idly sniffing at a clump of lemon balm. A bee floating past. The sudden shock of understanding she was not alone.

'Maybe I imagined it,' she says.

Graham's face tightens.

'Either he was there or he wasn't.'

'He was. It's just – well, it only felt like a split second.'

He takes a breath.

'Do you think it was the same man Ruby saw?'

'What?'

'You know. Red hair. In the lane.'

Ruby. The man in the lane. Mary realises she'd forgotten all about that night. She looks at him.

'I thought you weren't sure that was true?'

'I didn't say that exactly.'

Mary hesitates.

'There was smoke,' she says, remembering all of a sudden the thin wisp of white she saw, rising up from the long grass.

'Smoke?'

'Didn't Ruby say the man she saw standing there and looking at the house was smoking? Well, so was this man. I'm sure he was smoking.'

'A lot of people smoke.'

'But the hair as well.'

Graham looks at the dog, who is sniffing at his shoe.

'Ah well, we probably need to have a look at the fence, don't we?' he says.

'What fence?'

'At the bottom of the orchard. There's almost nothing left of it. At the moment anyone's free to wander straight in from the fields.'

Mary stares at him.

'Does it matter?'

'Well, it clearly does, doesn't it? Don't worry, I knew we needed to do something about it. It's just not been high on my list, that's all.' He bends to the dog again, pulls at its ears. 'Rotten bloody guard dog you turned out to be,' he says.

*

Frank wanted to know if I thought James Dix was a good sort. He went on and on about it as if it was the most important question in the whole world.

I don't know, I said. I don't know what I think. Why do you want to know?

He scrunched up his nose.

Well, you see, sometimes I think he is and sometimes I think he isn't.

I kept my eyes on Frank and tried to stay steady.

And why ever would you think he wasn't?

Now he looked uncomfortable.

Well, I do like him a lot—

But?

But what?

That's what I'm asking, you idiot. What don't you like about him?

I do like him!

I thought you said that sometimes you think he isn't such a good sort.

Now Frank looked quite troubled. He licked his lips. Then his face brightened.

I like how he lets us punch him in the stomach and he's brazen and not afraid of anything and he shows us how to fight—

Fight? You think fighting is good?

Frank looked at me, his eyes uncertain.

Well, I don't know, but he says he's going to teach me to ride a bicycle—

You haven't got a bicycle.

He says he can get one and anyway I like his snake tattoo and—

I laughed and I saw that his ears were turning red. Frank could never hide his feelings. He looked away quickly.

I hate his tattoo, I said.

Why?

I shrugged.

It's a snake, isn't it? Who would want a snake on them? Snakes are wicked and slimy things.

Frank looked at me as if he was thinking hard.

Why don't you like him, Eliza?

I never said I didn't like him. I said I didn't like his tattoo. And anyway you're blushing. Why are you blushing?

I'm not blushing.

Oh, Frankie. Your ears. They're on fire, look at them – you'll die from the heat.

Even though he was only seven, Frank was my favourite brother. My only brother, really, because Charlie was more like a girl and the new baby didn't count. I decided to stop tormenting him.

Why do you think I don't like him, anyway? I said.

He blinked at me.

Lottie told me.

Told you what?

She told me that you didn't like him.

This made me catch my breath. Lottie could be the limit sometimes.

But how ever does Lottie know?

Frank shrugged.

Well, I think James told her. He tells her everything. Him and Lottie are always talking. They're very thick together, you know.

Even though I hadn't really thought about it, I realised I did know this.

Lottie's just a baby, I said at last. I wouldn't worry about what Lottie says.

And anyway, I do think he likes boys as well, Frank said at last.

As well as what?

As well as little girls.

Mary goes to the Farm Shop to get bread and milk and to see if they have any minced beef or lamb. Most of the meat there is frozen, but at least it's local and anyway she can't be bothered to drive to the nearest proper butcher's, which is a good five miles away at Hinton.

She picks up a couple of pints of milk, a loaf, some Cheddar cheese and decides in the end to get chicken breasts instead of mince. She also picks up two bunches of local asparagus, their fat stalks held together with blue rubber bands. She goes to the counter to pay.

The woman – she's spoken to her once or twice and thinks her name might be Rose – is on the phone, but she hangs up quickly when she sees Mary waiting. Starting to ring up the items on the big, old-fashioned till. She smiles at her.

'Seen your daughter recently, then?'

Mary freezes, her whole body suddenly rigid.

'What?' She chokes it out, barely even a whisper.

The woman doesn't look at her. Pulling a white plastic bag from under the counter, shaking it open.

'Didn't she come and stay the other week? My other half says he saw your husband at the station, getting her off the London train.'

'Oh.' Mary can hardly speak, relief like warm water flooding through her. 'Yes. That's Ruby. My stepdaughter.'

The woman, Rose, puts the things in the bag. Shaking her head, gold hoop earrings catching the light.

'Ha, that's funny. Reg only mentioned it because he said how she was the spitting image of you. All that lovely dark hair. Mind you, proper handfuls, teenagers, aren't they? Bet you're glad you've only got the one.'

Mary manages to say that she is glad. She asks Rose then if she has kids. Rose throws her head back and laughs, fiddling with one of her earrings.

'Six! At the last count, anyway. Four boys and two girls. And do you know, the last two were complete bloody accidents. Welcome accidents, but all the same. I guess you never know what life is going to dish up, do you?'

She walks home through the lanes with her white plastic bag. The hedgerows are scented, humming with smells and sounds. She passes the dried-out, zigzag skin of a snake flattened into the asphalt and stops for a moment to look at it. She sees no one except a youngish, dirty-faced boy on an odd, old-fashioned bike, fair hair lifting as he pedals past.

She gets back to find Graham in the little room that, partly as a joke and partly not as a joke, they call the snug. A dark space off the kitchen with one small window, it contains most of the boxes that they could not bring themselves to leave in storage but have not been able to face unpacking either. He is hunched in the collapsing old armchair, piles of photographs spread out before him on the low coffee table.

She gasps.

The sudden sight of those pictures – the precise, agonising colours of her old life's happiness – almost knocks the breath out of her.

66

Standing there in the doorway, fingers gripping onto the frame, her voice seems to slide away from her.

'What are you doing?'

He glances at her, his face alert, different, feral almost. She sees that the dog is curled at his feet.

'Nothing. Having a bit of a sort-out, that's all.'

She stares at him: a prickle of something like fear creeping over her.

'Why?'

He turns to look at her again.

'Because this room is a mess. Because we've been here almost two months and it still feels like some kind of a dumping ground. Because—'

Because. Mary's eyes dare not go to the other things that may or may not rest in the darker shadows of the room. She has not yet given herself permission to remember what they stored, what they brought. Decisions made with her eyes, heart and mind half-closed. There is a photograph in Graham's hand. She is not able to let her eyes go to it.

He is silent and she swallows, waiting. He takes a handkerchief from his pocket, one of his great big white cotton handkerchiefs. He does not do anything with it, just holds it. She watches and as she does so, she feels her heart leave that small dark room and fly back out to the lanes, to the recent bright hedgerow, the dizzying smells, the boy on his bicycle. She thinks of the snake, sliding along smoothly on its belly one moment, stopped and flattened by the car tyres the next.

Graham looks at her. So does the dog, lifting its head briefly from sleep, looking at her.

'Because I don't want not to be able to,' he says.

How old is this girl of yours? James asked my mother even though I was sat right there in front of him mending Lottie's petticoat.

My mother's hands were covered in flour. She rubbed her nose with her wrist and blew some hair out of her face.

Eliza? She's thirteen.

Thirteen and a half, I said.

She's fourteen in November, my mother said.

James didn't look at me. He kept his eyes on my mother.

I didn't know she was that old. You must have been quite a child yourself when you had her.

My mother laughed but you could see that she was pleased.

Not far off, she said. Seventeen.

James looked at my mother. I didn't know what he was thinking. I saw that there was sweat on his face and his eyes were unsteady, darting all around.

Anyway, I don't think she likes me very much, he said.

What? said my mother.

Your girl Eliza. I don't think she likes me at all.

It's true, I said. I don't like him.

My mother wasn't listening. I could see that her mind was elsewhere as she punched and kneaded the dough. I looked at James and saw how hard he watched her. I didn't know if she was beautiful or not because to me she was just my mother, but I saw how long and wavy her hair had grown and how it never stayed in her cap, but fell in curls down her back and over her bosom. I saw how lithe and skinny her bare arms were, right up to the elbows in flour. I saw James noticing all of this.

But you like me, don't you? he said at last.

What? She lifted her head.

We get on like a house on fire, don't we, Sally, you and me?

I thought he was being very fly and fresh with her but maybe she was used to it, for she just shrugged and smiled.

I think you're a rascal and a half, she said. But you're all right, I suppose.

Later, though, when she'd put a cloth over the bread and gone out of the room to go and see to the little ones, he put his feet up on the table and grinned.

She's a right bit o' raspberry, your ma.

What? I said.

He kept on laughing, running his hands through his hair.

As in jam. As in, she's the real raspberry jam.

I said nothing. He burst out laughing – an annoying laugh as if he had forced it – then he stopped and looked at me harder.

Really, Eliza? You don't get it?

I shook my head and he put his feet back down on the floor and turned to me.

Well, Eliza, you're very young and innocent. Not to mention being a royal princess. I don't really know if I should tell you what it means.

Don't then, I said. I'd rather you didn't. I don't very much care what it means anyway.

And I put down my sewing and I tried to pick up the washing basket and walk out of the room but in that instant he struck, quick as a snake, catching hold of my arm. The feel of his hands on me made me hot to the centre of my bones.

He pulled me to him. So close that his breath was moist in my ear. I shivered.

It means she's a right one. A real stunner. A goer, it means she's a—

Shut up, I said.

I pulled away as hard as I could and at last had to smack at his wrist. After a second or two of struggling, he let me go. There was a long silence while we both got on with disliking each other.

Then in an instant he was all soft and smiles again.

Come here, he said.

No.

I said, come here.

I said no.

Please, Eliza?

No.

You don't want to?

No.

All right then, he said. Do as you please.

And I did. I did do as I pleased. I picked up the basket of washing and I walked out into the yard to hang it and I thought how stupid people like my mother were to fall for James and his wheedling and flattery and lies and how glad I was that I had a calm head on my shoulders and could see straight through him and out the other side.

I thought all of these things. But as I leaned down to pick the wet things out, my heart felt ready to jump out of my chest and I saw stars.

They accept an invitation to supper in the village. The couple who live next to the post office. Deborah and Ted, Graham thinks. Or maybe it's Ed. Yes, that's it. Deborah and Eddie. He got talking to her in the Co-op. Blonde woman, very chatty and rather pretty. She seemed nice.

Mary stares at him.

'You mean tonight?'

'It's only supper,' he tells her before she can say anything or start offering up objections.

She is full of questions. How old are they? What are they like? What do they do? Have they got children? Do they know about us?

He lifts his eyebrows.

'A bit younger than us, I'd guess. I told you, she was nice, very friendly. No idea. Haven't a clue. Don't think so.'

And then the last question: do we really have to go?

He straightens up from clipping the lead on the dog, looking around for his keys. His face is careful.

'I suppose the reason I said yes without even asking you is because I thought it would be good for us.'

'Good for us?'

He sighs.

'Darling. We never see anyone. We never do anything.'

She looks at him. Her heart turning over.

'I'm just not in the mood for talking to new people, that's all.'

'You never seem to be much in the mood for talking to anyone.'

Mary hesitates.

'It's the whole thing of getting to know someone,' she says. 'It's almost like I've forgotten how to do it.'

He smiles.

'You haven't forgotten.'

'All right then.' She feels herself suddenly close to tears. 'I'm just not sure I can be bothered to try any more.'

He goes to her. An arm around her, lifting her hair off her shoulders. He kisses her neck. The dog gives a little whine and he hushes it.

'I know that. Of course I do. And it's exactly why it's a good idea to go.'

She leans against him, the dog tangling itself around their feet.

'You don't understand. I have nothing to say to anyone. Literally nothing.'

'No one expects you to say anything.'

'Come on. Of course they do.'

He looks at her.

'Anyway, they seem like very nice people.'

'What?'

'Well, she did. This Deborah.'

'What's that got to do with it?'

He looks down at the dog who is whining again and pulling on the lead.

'No one's going to make you do anything you don't want to do.'

She sits down.

'Then I'm not going. You go.'

'I'm not going anywhere without you.'

'Why not? Why can't you?'

He sweeps some loose change off the dresser and puts it in his pocket. Wrapping the lead around his hand. Before he opens the door, he turns to her.

'Does it ever occur to you that I might not really be in the mood either?'

Mary showers, then spends half an hour or more trying on clothes – odd, frantic garments with zips and pleats and tucks, things that she hasn't touched in a very long time and which, when she puts them on, make her look like she's going for a job interview. At last she pulls back on the tired old jeans she's been wearing all day. Adding a silky T-shirt. Pumps. The first earrings she can lay her hands on. Perfume.

'Mary Coles,' says a faint, half-childish voice. She ignores it. It's happened too many times now for her not to know that it must be in her head. 'Mary Coles, Mary Coles.' When she was a child, her mother says she would lie awake in the mornings and talk to herself in a language that sounded like Greek.

'It couldn't have been Greek.'

'That's exactly what I'm saying,' her mother agreed. 'You were seven or eight years old. How could you possibly know any Greek? It must have been some kind of gobbledygook.'

Her mother also told her she once said she saw a man hanging from the ceiling in the corner of her room.

'You were terrified. You described it perfectly. His neck in the noose, everything. It really gave us the willies. You were far too young to know anything about hanging.'

Mary thinks that she must ring her mother. She knows that she's been putting it off and she doesn't want to think about why.

Downstairs, Graham's waiting for her. He's shaved more carefully than usual and is wearing a bright shirt which she hasn't seen in a long time. He looks up from his paper.

'Can't think when I last saw you in earrings.'

'What?'

She touches them, still struck by how pointless it felt to push a metal hook with an ornament hanging off it through a hole in her ear.

'It's nice, that's all.' He glances at her legs. 'But jeans? You really don't have anything else?'

'I thought you said it was just supper.'

'But you've been wearing those jeans all day.'

She says nothing. She does not speak. Turning from him and going back up the stairs as fast as she can.

'Just the trousers,' he calls after her. 'The rest is great. Seriously. You look great.'

She pushes the bedroom door shut and stands for a moment – the room suddenly softer and less rigid, seeming to exhale as it tilts around her. She tears off the jeans. Sitting on the bed in her knickers, gazing in a kind of desperation at the paleness of her thighs, knees, feet.

Outside the light is going, birds growing quieter, sky velvety. She imagines herself sitting around a table in some kitchen with a pair of strangers. I can't do it, she thinks, I don't want to.

She thinks about getting back into the bed, drawing the duvet up and lying there, waiting for Graham to find her. She can hardly breathe, every breath she takes is an effort and she covers her face now with her hands, a sensation slowly building that she is not quite alone in the room.

When she takes them away, the little brown-haired girl is pointing at her, her eyes black and sly and furious. She has no voice, there is no sound at all, the lines all around them and between them wavy and silent and stopped up, the girl still pointing – she can barely see more than a finger, the babyish curve of a top lip, a twisted top-knot of hair – but she knows what she's saying, it's something about skirts: where's your skirts?

Skirts!

The room properly altered now – somehow frayed and odd and dirty – Mary tries to get herself up off the bed and move away. Her limbs slow, the air thick, resisting her. She thinks about crying out for Graham, but before she can make a sound, something unravels and relaxes and the idea of the girl is lost, the sensation gone.

Nothing.

All she can see is what was there before. Chest of drawers, pine mirror catching the evening light, the chair covered in all her familiar, flung-off clothes. And the room absolutely itself again – corners tight and sharp, birdsong shrill and certain, ordinary evening shadows moving over the white walls.

Then, just as she dares to take a breath—

'Mary Coles.'

A flush of heat goes through her.

'Go away,' she says. Then: 'I mean it. Just fuck off.'

Pulling tissues from the box, she blows her nose, wiping at her eyes. She puts on the very first thing that comes to hand – some old red velvet trousers that always used to make her feel fat, hanging off her now.

Going back downstairs, her whole self oddly steady, buoyant, light.

'That's more like it,' Graham says and he smiles at her with genuine pleasure and putting down the paper, he gives her a kiss.

Deborah and Eddie are all right. Mid to late thirties. Friendly, pleasant, pleasantly dull. And Graham was right, Deborah's very pretty. A perfect swing of long, blonde hair, big eyes, lips that look like someone has drawn them on. Eddie is unremarkable. Boyishly timid, greying hair, glasses. They've only been married three years. 'Leather anniversary!' says Deborah. 'Let's not go there,' says Eddie. It quickly becomes clear that they have no children.

The dinner passes easily. Mary is glad that the conversation wanders around, snaking back and forwards and looping itself around a great many not very interesting subjects, but never once coming anywhere near them.

They talk about the village, Eddie's apparently tiresome commute to his business, which assesses the infrastructure of software companies. His interest in fine wines and in local history. His many unsuccessful attempts to stop smoking. Deborah's passion for interior design and her hobby of jewellery making – 'not silver or anything, just some beading, though I would quite like to get into the silver'. Her book group, which meets once a month. Their elderly Siamese cat who is diabetic and who needs daily injections – 'I know, you don't need to say it, we're completely mad'. The extension they're planning so as to create a third bedroom which could also serve as a study for Eddie.

'I do feel a bit guilty,' Deborah says, tucking her hair behind her ear. 'I mean, look at this house. You'd think it was more than big enough for just the two of us, wouldn't you?'

And Mary waits, her face hot with dread, waiting for the fateful words. Having a baby. Planning a family. Pregnant. Trying for a—

'We're just two people who rather like our space,' Eddie tells them cheerfully as he nips out of the back door for a cigarette.

Mary goes upstairs to the bathroom.

'Straight up the stairs and on the left,' Deborah says. 'Don't trip over the cat. He sometimes forgets where he is and falls asleep on the landing.'

'Sounds a lot like me,' says Graham and they laugh.

Safe behind the locked door, Mary looks around the large, immaculate bathroom. The claw-foot bath, the piles of thick towels, the basket of loo rolls, the rows and rows of bottles. Mary undoes her trousers. A small, dragging ache as if her period might be starting, but when she wipes herself there's nothing. She pulls the chain on the big, old-fashioned toilet and the paper doesn't quite go down so she does it again.

Coming out, she finds Eddie standing there on the landing, arms folded. He grins.

'Sorry. Didn't mean to scare you.'

'What?'

'I made you jump.'

'No you didn't,' she says, though he did.

She waits for him to say something else, but he doesn't. He stands there. She doesn't know what he wants. She tells him she loves the house.

'I can't believe how big it is,' she says. 'It's lovely.'

He makes a face.

'Well, I guess it ought to be, the amount we've spent on it.'

Feeling his eyes on her, Mary looks around. She looks at the pastel wall, cream carpet, the antique grandfather clock made of some shiny dark wood. None of it tells her anything.

'It's got a good feeling,' she says, struggling now, but feeling it would be too rude to turn and go downstairs. 'The atmosphere, I mean. It's nice.'

He looks at her.

'I wish you'd tell Deborah that.'

'What? She doesn't like it?'

'Not quite that but – well, itchy feet, you see. She can't stay in one place for very long. Or won't. It drives me mad. Wanting to move all the time.' He keeps his eyes on her. 'So, you notice these things, then?'

'What?'

'Atmospheres. In houses.'

'Doesn't everyone?'

'I don't know. Do they? I don't think most people even know what time of day it is. And it's just that you seem very – I don't know – alert to these things.'

Now Mary smiles.

'Don't be silly.'

'I'm not being silly. I'm being deadly serious. I noticed it the moment you came in – the first thing I noticed about you, in fact.'

She feels him staring at her, wishes he wouldn't.

'What? What did you notice?'

'I don't know. It's not a precise thing. Just call it a feeling. You seem – attuned.'

Attuned. Mary thinks about this. A sudden memory of the bungalow they lived in when she was seven. The smooth, paved patio, the wrought-iron gate, monkey puzzle tree outside. And, layered on top of all of these things, the certain knowledge of a fire breaking out. It would wake her at night, this fear, make her cry out, the sheer anticipation – the fire, the fire – she was terrified, too afraid to go to sleep.

Except there'd been no fire, there definitely was no fire, as her parents constantly tried to reassure her. And they were right, of course. It was true. She was safe, they were all safe. The fire, it turned out, was later – long after they'd moved, in fact – an electrical fire that killed some people. Four people dead in that house in the night.

75

She feels Eddie looking at her.

'What? What are you thinking?'

She shakes her head.

'You have a back-to-front memory,' her mother had said when they found out about that later fire, reading in the *Echo* of the man, the two women, the little boy. 'Or do I mean front-to-back? You remembered the future.'

As if it was a good thing. Trying to normalise it, trying to fob her off.

Mary thinks about how none of it matters now – past, present or future, what does it matter? She turns back to Eddie.

'I'm not attuned,' she says. 'Or not in any useful way, anyway.'

Eddie looks interested.

'And what does that mean? What would be useful?' He takes a quick breath. 'Sorry. Forget I said that. You don't have to answer, of course.'

Mary is silent.

'I'm sorry,' he says again. 'I didn't mean to – what I mean is, that was too much.'

Mary takes a step back, away from him. She tries to laugh.

'I honestly don't even know what we're talking about,' she says.

He smiles at her.

'Quite right. You're right. Neither do I.'

She hesitates then turns to go downstairs, but he stops her, touching her briefly on the arm.

'Want to see something?'

She doesn't know if she does, but she follows him across the landing, into what she assumes is their bedroom. Low ceilings and creaky boards. A faint smell of sweetness, old sheets and scent, a mess of thrown-off clothes implying that Deborah may have gone through as many changes as she did. She notices a pile of interiors magazines falling all over the floor by the bed. A pair of tweezers, a box of tampons. She looks away. Sensing that Deborah wouldn't want her coming in here.

Eddie leads her across the room to the wall by the dressing table. An old photo, Victorian probably – old glass, thin black frame.

'Have a look at this,' he says.

Mary looks. A country lane, brick cottages, trees, long grass, a huge dark cartwheel leaning up against a fence. In the far distance, what look like some ducks or chickens and, standing against a tall hedge, a group of young children: white pinafores, bare legs, heavy boots. A boy and a girl standing hand in hand, one of them holding a piece of rope. A toddler, maybe one or two years old, arms outstretched and her face a white blur as she moves or turns. Another small girl, her hair tied in a top-knot, chubby and serious, holding a stick, scowling and looking down. And the oldest one, maybe nine or ten, her legs hooked over the gate so she's hanging upside down, long dark hair sweeping the ground.

She feels Eddie breathing over her shoulder.

'Recognise it?'

'What?'

'The place.'

Mary feels herself go still.

'Is it here?'

He smiles.

'This village. End of the nineteenth century. You can't see our house, but if you look just past there, you see that long shadow? Well, if you could go round the corner, which you can't, of course, that's your place.'

Mary looks again. For a few quick seconds feeling herself right there in the lane, walking around that corner, dust underfoot, sun in her face, the shrill clatter of birds in her ears, the long shadow—

'There's someone else there,' she says, hearing the words come out before she can think about them.

'Is there? Where?'

Mary moves her face closer.

'Around that corner. That's what the shadow is. Look – you can see, there's someone standing there.' Mary points with a fingernail.

He leans in closer. His body so close to hers for a moment as he stares into the picture that she catches the cigarettes and clean laundry smell of him.

'I can't see anything,' he says at last.

'You don't see the shadow?'

'I think so but – that's just a shadow.'

Mary's heart is thudding. Blood in her ears.

'You can't see him,' she says. 'But he's there.'

'He? How do you know it's a he?'

77

Mary looks again at the skinny, upside-down child, whose face she can't see. The blurred baby. And the one with the stick, only about four or five years old, gazing at the ground – she sees that her fists are clenched.

She turns away, unable suddenly to bear it.

'I don't recognise the cottages,' she says.

Eddie takes off his glasses, cleans them on his untucked shirt.

'What, those two? Pulled down, I think, don't know when. There's a bungalow there now. But you see that one?' She looks again as he points to the rickety tiled roof just behind. 'That's still there. I don't know who lives there now, but it's much the same.'

Mary looks at him.

'Where did you get it?'

'The picture? A junk shop somewhere on the way to Kessingland. I don't think it's there any more. I got two more as well – look.'

He goes to the bottom of the wardrobe and pulls out a second picture: a young boy pushing a girl along in a wheelbarrow – blurred again, her bonnet flying behind her, laughter. The glass is cracked. Mary looks at it.

'The same children?'

'I think so, don't you? Aren't they the two holding hands in the other picture? The same family, anyway.'

Mary takes it from him. For a moment she can't look at it, and then she can, she has to, she does.

'And this one – look, don't you love it?'

He holds out a smaller picture, the glass also broken: a pair of grubby childish hands holding an old wicker bicycle basket, a brood of chicks nestled inside.

'They need new frames,' he says. 'I need to get them fixed – then I'll put them up.' He looks at her. 'Local history. I love it, don't you?' He puts his glasses back on, smiles. She notices for the first time that he has a dimple.

'Why?' says Mary.

'Why what?'

'Why do you love it?'

He takes a breath, looks surprised.

'Well, I suppose it's proof, isn't it?'

'Proof?'

'That they were here. That we're all here. Even that you and I are here right now. It seems to fix things somehow.'

'Does it?'

'I think so. Yes.'

Mary looks again at the first picture. Chubby bare arms, small, scowling faces. The sun is bright, the air hot – a hot day, she thinks. Someone has lined them up for a reason. Why? She turns away, not wanting to look again at the shadow.

'Do you know anything about them?' she says.

'What?'

'The children. Do you know who they were?'

'No, I don't.' He looks at her. 'Do you?'

They eat pudding, ice cream from the Farm Shop – 'I tell you, everything we bloody eat comes out of that Farm Shop freezer,' Eddie says, laughing – and then they have coffee and chat some more and Graham looks at his watch and says it's late and they really ought to go home and see to their dog.

'A dog!' says Deborah. 'You never said you had a dog!'

Graham looks at Mary.

'Just a puppy,' he says. 'Which is why I don't think we can leave her too long.'

'A puppy! But that's adorable,' says Deborah. 'You should have brought her.'

'You're not a dog person,' Eddie points out in a way that Mary finds unnecessarily mean.

Deborah looks at him.

'Everyone's a puppy person.'

Mary thinks of the little dog who will almost certainly be curled on the brown blanket on the chair in the kitchen instead of in her bed.

'I suppose we should get back to her,' she says, trying not to notice the look of appreciation on Graham's face.

Before they go, Deborah insists on taking them outside, walking them down the steps towards the dark lawn, the air around them dewy and fast-cooling.

'It feels like we have a proper home at last,' she tells Mary as she takes her arm and makes her sniff at the air to take in the scent of jasmine and tobacco plants. 'I'm really hoping I can finally get Eddie to settle down.'

Mary looks at her, surprised.

'But I thought it was you?'

'What?'

'Eddie told me you were the one who liked moving house?'

Deborah laughs, shakes her head.

'God, no, not me. I'm a bit of a homebod really. I try not to be. I mean, it was fun, moving around and all that, but I suppose I really long to put down roots.'

'And Eddie doesn't?'

Deborah thinks for a moment. When she speaks, her voice is careful.

'He's one of those people who's always on to the next thing, I guess, the next project, you know? His energy is unbelievable – and I mean that literally. You have to see it to believe it. And I know you can't really ever hope to change people and of course I wouldn't want to change him, not at all but, well, I suppose it just got a little bit tiring, moving around all the time.'

Walking back home under an almost starless sky, Graham squeezes her arm.

'Well done.'

'What do you mean?' she says. 'Well done for what?'

He breathes out a long breath.

'I know you didn't want to do it.'

'It was OK.'

'All right but I know it cost you something.'

'It didn't cost me.'

'You know what I mean.'

She's silent a moment.

'It was all right,' she says at last. 'I liked it more than I thought I would. I liked Deborah. And he's OK. And it was a nice dinner. And at least they didn't know anything.'

'Know anything?'

'About us.'

He turns to her.

'Oh,' he says. 'Oh, but they did. They'd worked it out and of course they'd Googled us. And when you were upstairs, well, Deborah said some very kind things. And then just now in the garden, while you were talking to her about the roses or whatever, well, Eddie was the same. He was really very sensitive, careful.'

She stares at him. Thinking about finding Eddie waiting there for her on the landing.

'I was glad actually,' Graham says. 'If we're going to get to know them, I mean. Far better to get it out of the way now. I don't think I could bear to have them discover it and then for us to have to go through it all with them, could you?'

4

Phoebe Harkiss, an unpleasant, pingly, freckle-faced girl who lived down the lane, came round with an apronful of kittens. And because Jazzy won a badge at school for helping with the smaller kiddies and laying the fires and fetching the mistress's bread and so on, she was allowed to choose one to keep.

But that's not fair! Minnie screamed.

And who the hell ever said life was fair? our father shouted so loud in her face that she burst into tears.

While Minnie sobbed and Honey, helped by Charlie, crawled around on the floor trying to grab at the little, sticky-up tails, Jazzy sat with her skirts bunched up around her knees and examined the kittens carefully one by one.

What are you going to name it? Lottie asked her, as Jazzy lifted each one and kissed its warm belly and breathed in the smell of its fur.

I haven't decided which one it's going to be yet, have I? Jazzy said. How can I know what its name's going to be?

Lottie thought about this.

But when you do decide, what will you name it?

I laughed.

Give her a chance to choose one first, Lottikins, I said.

Lottie ignored me. She kept her eyes on Jazzy.

I think you should name it Miracles. That's a very pretty name, don't you think?

Jazzy laughed.

That's not even a name. That's just a word. No one in the world's called Miracles.

She carried on looking at the kittens and saying it was awfully hard to choose and she wished she could take them all. But since she couldn't, and since Phoebe was standing there in the doorway sighing and tossing her hair about to make it quite plain she did not have time to wait around, she chose the smallest, a flimsy grey thing that barely made a sound when she lifted it up, but instead just hung there and returned her solemn gaze.

The sweetest and the saddest, she announced, as if that settled it.

Lottie stepped in closer, her eyes on the kitten.

And what are you going to name it?

Jazzy blinked.

I've got to make friends with it first and see what kind of a kitten it is.

Lottie blinked.

I can tell you a good name for it.

Didn't you hear me the first time? Jazzy said. I don't want your piddling names. Anyway, I need to ask Father to look if it's a boy or a girl.

It's a girl, Lottie said.

Jazzy looked at her.

You don't know if it's a boy or a girl. You don't have any idea at all, so stop making things up. And whatever it is, I promise you I'm not calling it Miracles.

Lottie carried on looking at her with hard dark eyes.

Not Miracles, she said. Merricoles.

Ruby comes for half-term.

'It wasn't my idea and I don't want to be here either, so please for God's sake don't go blaming me,' she tells them as she slams the door and throws down her rucksack and marches straight to the downstairs toilet.

But coming back out, she sees the dog.

'Oh my God.' She drops down on her hands and knees on the floor. 'You never told me it was this cute! Why didn't you tell me it was a Babe dog?'

Graham laughs.

'I'd forgotten all about Babe.'

Ruby looks up at him from where she's sitting on the old stone floor as the dog jumps and snuffles and licks her fingers and tries to nibble her jumper, which is already full of holes. Her eyes are shining and she looks so like the little girl that she used to be, that for a quick moment Mary has to look away.

'Hey, I've got it, maybe that's what you should call her – it is a girl, right? – Babe!'

Graham looks at her.

'Babe? Is that the name of the dog in the film?'

'For God's sake, Dad, Babe's the name of the pig. Don't you remember, the dog's called Fly? But it's such a cute name, don't you think, Babe? Or Fly? Fly's nice too. Oh look, she's trying to lick me through the holes in my jeans,' Ruby says, laughing.

'Don't let her eat the pins,' Graham says.

'What pins?'

'You've got about a hundred safety pins holding those jeans together.'

'Oh,' Ruby says. 'Yeah, don't worry, I won't let her get them.'

She goes up to her room and is gone for an hour.

'Do you think she's all right?' Graham says.

'Please,' Mary says. 'Don't start that again.'

'But she's always disappearing.'

'She's a teenager. She's allowed to disappear. Seriously, we'll never get through a week if you keep on wanting to check up on her.'

He opens the fridge, takes out a Coke.

'Veronica says she's worried about her.'

'In what way?'

He sighs. 'I don't know. School say she's been OK. But there's something.'

'Something?'

'Veronica says she stays in her room all the time and she hardly ever eats.'

'She looks like she eats.'

'What, you think she's overweight?'

Mary looks at him.

'Seriously, I wouldn't worry about her not eating.'

When Ruby comes back down, she's tied her hair up in a single bunch on top of her head and changed into another jumper with even more holes than the last. Graham looks at her.

'Goodness, Rubes, aren't you hot? It's almost summer outside, in case you hadn't noticed.'

Ruby looks at him and pulls the sleeves over her hands.

'I'm never hot. I'm always freezing. I get it from Mum.'

'I don't remember your mum ever being cold.'

Ruby blinks.

'She is. She's always cold. Even in summer. And I'm the same. I don't mind – it's better than being hot all the time. It means you don't sweat.'

The sadness in Jazzy's kitten turned out to be a bad sign. Soon after Phoebe Harkiss went home, it started to cough and even though Jazzy was allowed to keep it in her bed all night, by morning it was cold as stone.

Jazzy wept and wept, holding onto it with both hands and refusing to give it up, swearing that she could still see some life left in its eyes. In the end we had to prise it from her and send Frank off with a shovel to put it in the ground before she changed her mind.

All that day she took the loss very badly, staying hot and sad and becoming so feverish that our mother worried. It seemed that only another kitten would console her, so in the end Phoebe was fetched back so that she could choose another one. This time the girl emptied the kittens out on the kitchen floor a bit too roughly and then waited by the door with folded arms and a sullen look on her face.

You picked a wrong'un, she told Jazzy. I could have told you that one wouldn't make it. Don't you know the last one born is always the runt?

Jazzy gazed at her.

It was a dear little thing, she said. And I didn't know it was a runt, but I loved it all the same.

I looked at Phoebe. The freckles went all over her face and mouth and neck and even right down under her dress. I thought that they made her look dirty. Her mother, the widow of the Smithy, was well known to be proud and miserly. The type that would go to bed with the sun most of the year to save candles, and would make her children shake the tablecloth out in the garden in the showiest manner possible, even if they'd had no dinner.

If you could have told her, I said, then why didn't you?

Phoebe shrugged and chewed on a nail. All her nails were bitten down to stumps. You never saw her without a finger in her mouth.

But she shrugged and did not look at me. You could tell she didn't care a scoot what I thought about anything.

But then James came in the room and her face changed. She was all smiles, wiping her wet fingers on her skirt and gazing up at him with all the measly trappings that her eager piggy face could muster.

He paid no attention, of course. He put out his cigarette and crouched down on the floor with Jazzy to look at the kittens. He sat and watched them for a long time, careful as anything, putting out a hand to stroke them as they stumbled around, mewing and pawing and falling over each other.

He sat there so still and gentle that Honey crawled over and sat herself down between his legs and Minnie and Charlie snuggled up to him and even Lottie came over, standing there calm as anything with her small hand resting on his shoulder.

Get a girl, she whispered, not to anyone in particular. Pick a girl. I want you to get a little girl cat.

Jazzy ignored her; in fact, everyone ignored her, but still Lottie carried on.

You've got to get a girl and call it—

Shut up, Jazzy said and she put her hands over her ears. I'm not listening to you, Lottie, so just shut up!

Lottie stuck out her bottom lip.

I think the little tabby looks quite hale and hearty, James said at last.

That's a girl, Lottie said.

Jazzy ignored her. She looked at James.

What, the one with the white paws?

That's Merricoles, Lottie whispered in a naughty voice as Jazzy scooped it up, but no one paid any attention. The kitten hung there for a moment, its tail stretched in the air as it tried to balance.

That's the one, James said. That's your cat.

Jazzy looked at the kitten and looked at James. And that was that. It couldn't have been clearer if God Himself had groped His way down from the skies and made His choice.

Mary drives six and a half miles to a place where she's heard there's a Wednesday market. A small enough expedition, but she has not been out of the village without Graham since they moved in.

She asks Ruby if she'd like to come.

'Come where?' says Ruby, craning her neck around from the sofa to look at her. Mary's eyes go to the TV screen, where some loud, groomed characters in an American sitcom have been paused mid-joke.

'I'm going to a market.'

'What kind of market?'

'Flowers. Fruit and veg. Stuff like that.'

Ruby blinks.

'I'll be all right, thanks.' She turns back to the TV and presses a button and the beautiful people jerk back to life.

Mary knows that if she thinks too hard about what she's about to do, she won't do it. But when she gets in the car, she's surprised at how easy it feels to speed along the hard grey country roads, bright, sunlit fields slipping by on either side. Corn, rape, something that might be potatoes. And cows. She slows to go over a metal grid. Stops at a railway crossing, winding the window right down and breathing in the musty green of cow parsley as the train rattles by.

She drives past a pub, a bunch of pink cottages with For Sale signs, a trestle table with flowers and vegetables on it. She sees thick dark hedges, a black smudge of woodland, a man walking his dog. She notices some kind of a bloody mess at the side of the road and is pleased with herself for not minding it. Just a rabbit or a fox, she thinks, driving on.

She parks near the market. Gets out of the car and makes herself walk around. It is midday, the sun high and hot. She looks at cabbages and cauliflowers, punnets of strawberries and plastic buckets of every kind of summer flower.

She knew that there might be children – and sure enough, a mother with a baby in a sling on her chest is bending to speak angrily to a three-or four-year-old boy in a T-shirt with a TV character on it. With one hand cradling the infant head as she bends, the mother uses the other to grab the child's arm, pull his hands down and make him look at her.

'You think it's good?' she says. 'Tell me? You think fighting is good?'

The child sobs loudly and the mother keeps on talking and Mary, realising she is staring, looks away.

She doesn't want or need anything from the market – their fridge is already crammed with food – but she buys things anyway. Beetroot, onions, pleasingly muddy bunches of carrots, a glass bottle of apple juice, strawberries. Just as she is taking the plastic bags from the tall, long-haired market guy, she feels a hand on her elbow.

She turns a bit too quickly and sees a grey-haired man in glasses smiling at her.

'Eddie.'

'What?'

'As in, Deborah and Eddie? The other night?'

'Oh, I'm sorry.' She takes a breath, noticing the dimple as he smiles at her.

'I knew you wouldn't recognise me.'

'I do,' she says. 'I mean, of course I recognise you.'

He laughs. 'It's OK. I've been told before. I've got one of those faces.'

'What?'

'You know. Unmemorable. Without any distinguishing features.' She stares at him and sees that he is smaller than she remembers, slimmer perhaps, and more dishevelled. He points to his jeans. 'And I was all dressed up the other night. This is the real me, I'm afraid.'

He laughs again, looking at her.

'I'm off work today. On holiday. A rare event. You got time for a coffee?'

The kitten that James chose ate and slept and thrived and grew. After about a week it was twice the size. It was supposed to have just water and scraps, but when our mother wasn't looking, Jazzy would put a plate of warm milk on the floor and the kitten knew to run over and lap at it with its tiny pink tongue until the plate was as clean and dry as if there'd never been anything on it at all.

Lottie was right. The cat was a girl. But Jazzy didn't call her Miracles as Lottie had suggested, but Lupin.

I would've called it James if it was a boy, she said.

Phoebe Harkiss called round at least three times that week to see how the kitten was doing. At first I was surprised. It didn't seem all that likely that she would give a toss whether it was alive or dead. But then I saw how carefully she'd tied her hair, fixing it with pins and a velvet bow, and how she swished herself around just like a dancing lady at a fairground, and I realised.

She must have been disappointed, because often James wasn't there at all. Another time he was there, but he had to leave after just a minute to go and do the cows. And even when he was there, he only gave her the briefest of glances before picking Honey up off the floor and throwing her in the air till she screamed and then playing horsey-horsey with her on his knee while Phoebe squinched up her freckly face and watched and smiled, pretending she had an interest in babies, which it was very clear she did not.

The coffee shop is one small room with no one in it. Framed pastels of dogs and cats on the walls. A window with a view onto a well-kept garden with a blue and yellow children's climbing frame in the middle of it.

They can hear the noises of a kitchen, but they wait for a long time and no one comes. At last Eddie gets up and goes and shakes the old-fashioned bell that hangs from the wall. A waitress appears. She can't be more than fourteen. Eddie picks up the laminated menu, turning it over and over. He looks at Mary.

'Cappuccino? Espresso? Americano? What do you want?'

'We only do cafetières,' the girl says.

He gazes at her for a moment, bewildered.

'It's fine,' Mary tells her. 'Whatever you have.'

The girl goes away. Eddie seems to relax.

'Well,' he says, 'it's not exactly jumping, is it?'

'What?'

'The joint.'

She tries to smile. Glancing over at the window, where the climbing frame gleams bright in the sunshine. She does not want to look at it but there is nowhere else to look. She can feel his eyes on her.

'You're wishing you hadn't said yes, aren't you?' he says.

'What?'

'To coffee. I rather crept up on you, didn't I? You didn't have time to think of an excuse.'

She looks at him in surprise.

'Of course I don't think that,' she says, even though a part of her definitely does.

He grins.

'And you could even have escaped just then. Before the girl came. Come on, admit it, I know that's what you were thinking.'

She feels herself flush.

'I wouldn't have dreamed of doing that,' she says.

He lowers his eyes.

'Ah well, that's only because you're a nice, well-brought-up girl, you see.'

She can't help it, she laughs.

'It's a long time since someone called me a girl. Never mind well brought up.'

He blinks and suddenly she understands. He's nervous.

'Well, you are. You're both. I'm an expert. I can tell. You're very polite, very restrained.'

'Restrained?' Mary makes a face.

'It's a good thing. Trust me. Not enough people are restrained these days. No one has any manners any more. And as for being a girl—'

'I'm forty-two,' she says.

He glances at her, caught off balance.

'Well, that's young, isn't it? It's very young indeed. And take it from me, you're very youthful, very girlish.'

The waitress brings the coffee and they both sit in silence whilst trivet and pot and spoons and cups and sugar are all laid out. Once the girl's gone, she asks him what he's doing at the market.

He makes a gesture of defeat.

'I was sent on an errand. By the wife. To buy veg. She was not very specific. I have no idea what she wants. Help me. Please. Tell me what I should get?'

She looks at him.

'Why don't you just buy what you want?'

He makes a face.

'I'm not a great fan of vegetables. Wouldn't mind if I never saw another green thing as long as I live. I expect that puts you off me, doesn't it?'

Mary looks at him.

'So what do you eat?'

'Anything that's not green.'

His face is solemn, but Mary sees that his eyes are smiling. She can't tell if he's teasing her or not. She looks down at her coffee.

'People are allowed not to like vegetables,' she says at last.

He sighs and takes off his glasses and wipes them on his shirt. For a moment, without them, he looks like a teenager. Glancing at her with his raw boy's eyes.

'I'm sorry,' he says. 'Listen to me. Talk about a boring conversation.'

She smiles.

'It's fine.'

'It's not fine. Now you're really just being polite.'

'I thought you said manners were a good thing?'

He laughs, caught out.

'You're only trying to be friendly,' she says more gently. 'I appreciate that. I appreciate that you're making an effort.' She looks away, briefly, out of the window. Suddenly exhausted. 'It's been a while since I did anything like this.'

'Like what?'

'I don't know. Just sat and chatted over coffee about nothing in particular with someone I hardly know.'

Now he puts down his cup.

'You do know me.'

'No, I don't.'

'Well, I'd like you to know me – or what I mean is, I'd like to get to know you better.'

Mary looks at her hands.

'Well, me too. That would be nice. We had a great time the other night. We'll have to get you back to ours.'

She feels Eddie looking at her.

'Tell me honestly: what do you think of me?' he says.

She shakes her head. Laughs.

'What do I think?'

'You can be honest. Say anything you like. I won't be hurt.'

Mary glances at him.

'I don't know what I think.'

'Yes, you do.'

She takes a breath.

'Well, I suppose I think you're quite – direct.'

His eyes light up.

'Direct? Really? You think I'm direct? But is that a good thing?'

'Does it have to be good or bad?'

'All right, but what do you think?'

'Me?'

'Do you mind it? That I'm direct?'

Mary says nothing. She looks down at her cup on the table. Remembering her car waiting for her, parked in the sunshine. Five minutes, she thinks. Looking at Eddie.

'Why do you have such a low opinion of yourself?'

He lifts his head.

'You think I do?'

'I'm pretty sure you do, yes.'

He says nothing. He looks at her steadily for a long moment and then he smiles.

He walks her to her car. She doesn't want him to, but he seems to want to insist and in the end it's less trouble than the larger effort of pushing him away.

'Do you mind?' he says as on the way there he pulls out his cigarettes and, stopping briefly to light it, smokes half of one very quickly, before chucking it away.

At the car she is surprised to find herself offering to give him the two bags containing just about everything she bought. Beetroot, onions, carrots, strawberries. Everything apart from the apple juice, which she thinks Ruby might enjoy.

'You can tell Deborah you chose them all,' she says and she makes him look at how beautiful the carrots are, with their bright fronds of green and the mud caked into their little bumps and veins.

'What?' he says, still gazing at the carrots. 'You want me to lie?'

She laughs and holds them out to him.

'I don't care what you do. I'm just saying that you can take them, that's all.'

Standing there by the open car door, he stares at her.

'I can't take them.'

'Of course you can.'

'But you bought them. They're yours.'

'I don't want them. Honestly. I wouldn't offer them to you if I did. We don't need them.'

He puts his hands in his pockets and shakes his head.

'I can't possibly take them. Not without paying you.'

'Don't be silly. You had us to dinner.'

'That's not the same.'

'All right, then. You paid for the coffee.'

'What, one lousy cafetière?'

She looks at him.

'Come on, Eddie. They're only bloody vegetables.'

He laughs as he lets her give them to him, holding out his hand to her, the wrong hand because the other one's holding the bags. She shakes it awkwardly, then he pulls her to him and seems to be trying to kiss her on the cheek, but she moves away just in time and gets in the car and drives off.

She doesn't look back. Only when she's almost out of the village on the dual carriageway does she realise that she didn't say goodbye.

Less than a mile from home, she pulls off the road and onto a bumpy, dusty track by a metal farm gate. Turning off the engine. Silence. Insects. A tractor somewhere far off.

The pain she feels is beyond pain. Not even properly detectable any more – a blur, a wall, a kind of grey desperation – a sense that nothing she can think, feel or do will ever take it away. Here in this world without them, always – always. She would like to cry, but she cannot cry. Not even that much comfort or relief available to her any more. Her mouth is dry, her breath sticky. She loathes every part of herself. She lays her head down on the steering wheel and waits for the moment to pass.

When at last she lifts her head – it could be minutes, it could be an hour – there they are. Quite unsurprising – as if she'd expected them, as if she'd always known they were coming – a small crowd moving through the field in front of her. The man and an older girl in front, followed by the younger kids, four or five of them at least, one of them tottering along on the smallest legs, no more than a baby.

That's right, she thinks, unable to understand why it makes a kind of sense. Of course. That's right.

She cannot hear them – a deadness and softness stopping her ears – but she knows all the same that they are chattering, laughing. Each child is carrying a small bucket and now and then they stoop to pick things up. Stones, she thinks. They're collecting the stones.

She has no idea how long she watches them for: time stretches and contracts, darkening and then turning light again. All she knows is that for the whole time she keeps her eyes on them, a warm steadiness comes over her. She feels quite tied to this moment – fixed and safe, unwilling to move away.

She watches them until the sun disappears behind a cloud and by the time it comes out again – bands of light rushing over the fields – they're gone and all she can see is the metal gate, the far-off smudge of woodland and the great black crows swooping up and down over the hazy, lilac-brown clods of muddy earth.

I didn't mind the slightest bit if James Dix wanted to give his attention to Phoebe. She wasn't much more than a child, a silly, piggy girl with thin lips and bitten-down nails and I did think she'd been very unkind to Jazzy about the first, dead kitten. But apart from that I had nothing particular against her and anyway I couldn't have cared less who James chose to blow around with.

Still, I was surprised when, looking out of an upstairs window one morning, I saw them standing together in the lane. Their heads were close, their eyes intent. Phoebe Harkiss and James Dix. He was talking and she was gazing up at him. I didn't know what he could be saying. Both of them looked very sly and serious.

As I watched, Phoebe hung her head and her lips and eyes moved as if she was saying something and I saw James put his hands on his hips and take a step back. He looked very angry for a moment, but straight after he seemed to be laughing at her. Phoebe looked forlorn then, her face sad and sullen, her fingers going up to find her mouth. I wondered what James could have said to upset her.

I didn't have to wait long to find out. An hour later, he came and found me. I was in the yard. Everyone else was out in the fields and I was doing my jobs, sweeping with the big hard brush, thinking my thoughts and enjoying the bright bubble of silence that always came from being alone.

He came up behind so quick and quiet that I caught my breath.

I'm sorry, Eliza, he said, but I swear it won't wait any longer. I must talk to you.

I made a point of not looking very interested.

Talk about what?

He gazed at me for a moment, the same slightly furious look I'd seen him throw at Phoebe. Then he sighed the longest sigh.

Eliza. Oh, Eliza.

What? I said, feeling a bit more irritated with each second that passed.

He shook his head and ran his hand over his face.

Can you really not see? Must I explain it all to you? Are you really such a child that you have no idea what's happening?

I looked at him. I saw that his eyes were pink where they should have been white and that there was a white crust of dried-up spit at the corner of his mouth. Also that he needed a shave.

I turned back to my sweeping, hoping he would think better of it and leave me alone. But he thrust his hand out in the air in front of him.

Look! he said. Look at that.

Look at what?

My hand, Eliza. Look at how it's trembling. You've made me into a lunatic. I have no control over it. That's you, Eliza. You did that.

I couldn't help it. I started to laugh.

I've done nothing at all to you, I said, because I was very certain that I had not.

He let his hand drop and he smiled at me.

Ah, Princess Eliza. Innocent as ever. You really are innocent, aren't you, Eliza?

I don't know what you're talking about, I said.

He shook his head.

You really do believe it, don't you? That you've done nothing.

He sat himself down on the edge of the trough then, arms on his knees, his head hanging. I'd had enough now. I leaned the broom up against the wall and I folded my arms.

I saw you in the lane, I told him. I saw you there with Phoebe Harkiss.

I thought this would unsettle him, but he just lifted his chin.

Don't go thinking she's innocent. Do you know what it is that Harkiss girl wants from me? Do you know what it is, Eliza, the thing that men and women do together?

My mouth fell open. I did not know. And then for a few bad moments, I worried that I did.

I felt my cheeks get hot. I picked up the broom.

Do you know what I'm talking about, Eliza? he said.

My heart was racing. My chest felt like sand sinking down into my knees. A hot, slipping feeling that I hadn't felt before.

Go away, I said. I mean it, James. Just go away.

He looked at me.

I wish I could do that, but I can't. I can't go away from you, Eliza.

Please, I said.

He shook his head.

It's your fault, Eliza. You've brought it on yourself. You are just too quick and too beautiful. Look at me, look at what a state I'm in, I can't take my eyes off you.

My whole body felt quite wild with shock and worry, but I turned my head away as swiftly as I could and began to sweep. I didn't know what James was going to do next but at that moment the gate opened.

It was Lottie. Lottie running and screaming and crying her eyes out. I dropped the broom and took her in my arms.

What is it? I said. Whatever's the matter?

I sat down on the ground and pulled her on my lap. She was heaving and gasping out the sobs. Her skin smelled hot and I laid the back of my hand against her head to check for fever.

James was still sitting on the edge of the trough and watching us both.

What is it, Lottie? he said, but she would not look at him and I did not blame her.

Leave her alone, I said, but he didn't look at me, just patted his knee.

Do you want to come over here to me? Do you want to play horsey-horsey or leader in the trap?

Leader in the trap was a made-up game they had, just the two of them. Lottie had been quite mad for it recently.

Do you want to? I whispered in her ear, for I thought maybe he had the right idea and it would lift her out of her grumps and fears. James will play it with you if you want him to.

But Lottie lifted her head and she looked at him and her whole face wobbled and then she buried her head in my dress and clung harder to me.

Some moments passed. I did not know what to do about Lottie so I decided to do nothing. I moved to sit more comfortably in the sun against the wall and, keeping her on my lap, I rubbed her back in little circles, soothing her.

At last she grew still. I hoped James would go, but instead he came over and slid down the wall and sat beside the two of us on the ground amongst the clover that grew between the stones and the straw and droppings that I hadn't yet swept.

I stretched my legs out and took hold of Lottie's hot head and held it so that I could look into her eyes.

Now are you going to tell us what the matter is? I said, but she just shut her eyes and kept her lips tight and shook her head.

Are you hurting somewhere?

She shook her head.

Did something hurt you?

No.

Someone?

Again, she shook her head.

What, then? I said. Were you afraid? Did something frighten you?

Now she nodded hard.

What? I said. Something frightened you? Did it really? What was it?

Tell us what it was, James said. And we'll deal with it. Me and Eliza will deal with it for you, won't we, Eliza?

I did not look at him, for I knew he wanted me to. Instead I held Lottie so tight against me that I felt the fizz of her small body in my own chest.

Tell me, I whispered in her ear.

I waited, but still she did not speak – just let out another small sob. I sighed and I kissed her head. Breathing in her hair that smelled of apples and crusts and the hot, damp earth under our doorstep.

Was it a dog? I said.

I felt her hesitate. She bit her lip.

Not a dog.

A cat?

Not a cat.

A lion? A tiger? A grizzly bear?

She giggled.

Stupid! she said.

Was it a teeny tiny little mouse? James asked her in the smallest squeakiest voice and as he said it, he crept one hand, mouse-like, around Lottie's neck and slid the other one round and laid it on my knee. I tried to shove it off but he put it straight back. Its warmth and keenness seemed to set my leg on fire.

Not a mouse! Lottie said, half-laughing and half-crying as she tried to slap him away.

The feel of James's fingers on my knee was creeping up my whole body and making my cheeks hot. I didn't know whether I minded it or not. My eyes caught sight of the broom, lying on the ground where I'd dropped it.

Lottie, I said. I need to finish all the jobs before Mother gets back. If you can't tell us what it is that frightened you, then I think it's going to have to stay in your own head.

Straightaway, Lottie began to cry again. Sobbing and wailing just as bad as before. She put her thumb in her mouth and then she took it out again. There was wet and tears and dust all down the front of her pinafore.

Upstairs, she said, jerking her thumb towards the house. It was upstairs.

Upstairs?

Yes, I went up the stairs and in the room where we sleep there was – there was – a great big witch with a white face and black hair all tatty and big black boots like that.

She pointed to James Dix's feet. His dusty black boots. He looked at his boots and then he began to laugh.

What? he said. You saw a witch and she had on my boots? Now that's what I call a proper cheek.

Lottie looked straight into his face. For a moment she looked at him very hard as if she'd never seen him before. Then she shook her head.

Not your boots, she said. Not those. Other boots. Not yours.

Ah, James said. Well, that's all right, then.

Lottie ignored him. She put her thumb back in her mouth and she pulled the sleeve of her dress up and held it against her nose.

98

Tell me more about the witch, I said.

Can't.

Lottie, come on.

Lottie sucked her thumb for a moment. When she spoke at last, her voice was muffled.

Well, she was sticking the knife in, wasn't she?

I caught my breath.

A knife? You're saying the person you saw had a knife?

Lottie nodded.

And she kept on doing it over and over.

Doing what?

Sticking it in! And I cried at her to stop but she wouldn't stop and – and – I didn't like it, not at all I didn't – look Eliza, she was doing it like this.

Very slowly and carefully, Lottie made a claw of her hand and drew her fingers down her arm as if she meant to slice through her skin and open herself up. A chill went through me.

That's horrible, I said. You shouldn't talk about such things. I don't understand you, Lottie, not at all. I don't understand where you get these horrible ideas from.

James reached out and ruffled Lottie's hair.

Ah, come on, it was a dream, he said. There's no doubt about it. You must have laid down there on the rug and nodded off.

And I thought that Lottie would turn and shout at him for accusing her of dreaming, but instead she turned her eyes on him again very carefully as if she was looking for something.

Was it a dream? she said. Was it? That means it wasn't real.

It wasn't real, James said.

Lottie screwed up her eyes.

Do you swear on the angels' life that it was?

A dream? James said. Yes, indeed. I swear it, little one.

I felt Lottie relax in my lap. But he did not look at her, turning instead to me and squeezing and rubbing my knee with his fingers.

Get off me, I said and I pushed his hand off as hard as I could and this time I succeeded because he did not put it back and I was surprised at how sorry and cold and forlorn it felt without it there.

*

Mary says she'll take the dog for a walk. Graham can't hide his pleasure.

'Take some treats,' he says, thrusting a small plastic bag at her. 'You can let her off when you get to the path along by the woods. But keep making her come to you and if she doesn't come back the minute you call, then use this.' He hands her a chewed rubber ball. 'You only have to hold it up and she'll be at your feet. Trust me. She's obsessed with it.'

Mary goes. But they're barely into the lane before the dog starts to drag and pull, yanking on the lead and panting in an effort to propel herself forward. Before Mary can even react, she hears a shout. Graham has come out of the house and is waving at her.

'Don't let her pull,' he says. 'Tell her to heel.'

She raises her hand to show she's heard and then, as Graham gives her a thumbs-up, she turns the corner.

She lets the dog pull. Liking the feeling of being rushed along, her arm tensing with the force of it, her feet moving with unaccustomed speed over the grey pavement with its weeds and dandelions and clumps of overgrown grass. She almost starts to run.

They go past the post office and the doctor's surgery and over the little bridge and past the allotments with their hazel wigwams and pieces of coloured cloth to scare the birds and on up the road until the gaps between the cottages grow longer and the hedgerow more tangled and unkempt and then, finally, nothing. They pass one man with a small dog and then nobody. Still moving at a brisk pace, they turn off the lane and up the silent track that leads to the woods.

Mary stops for a moment, the dog still tugging and panting. On one side, flat blond fields stretching into the distance, on the other the darkness of the woods. In that darkness, on the other side of the field, she knows that she can see something – even without looking she knows it's there. A sudden, vivid shape moving between the trees. A flash of bright hair. A pale face. She doesn't want to think about it. She moves on quickly, the dog still pulling her.

Once she gets to the path along the edge of the woods, she does not let the dog off, but stands for a moment, uncertain, her breath ragged in her throat. The village is still behind her. She glances back for a moment at the clutter of cottages, the pale brick of the estate, the spire of the church. The dog whines and pulls and so she gives in and they walk a little further. But once they go around the bend and the village is lost and all that lies ahead is the wide loneliness of field and woodland, she stops again and looks at the dog, who is suddenly motionless.

'What?' she whispers. 'What?'

She looks at the woodland then back at the dog. It whimpers.

She gets back to find Graham staring into the fridge. Behind him on the old pine table, a brown pottery dish with a blue-painted edge, full of olives. Mary gazes at it, her whole body stilled.

'Where did you find that?' she says.

'The dish? In one of the boxes. I thought we were a bit short of things to put nuts and stuff in.'

She gazes at him.

'It's the one from Elba.'

'Yes.'

'I thought we agreed. All that stuff.'

He throws her a quick, exasperated look.

'All right, I'm sorry' – grabbing the nearest plate, tipping the olives onto it. 'You're right. I should have thought. I didn't think.'

He rinses the dish a little too quickly under the tap, rubs a tea towel over it and puts it in a cupboard. Looks at her. Mary still doesn't move. She doesn't know what to do. She doesn't do anything.

'They're just coming round for a quick drink,' he says, turning back to the fridge.

'What?' she says. 'Who?'

'Deborah and Eddie.'

'What, now?'

He glances at her.

'I said any time after six. Don't worry, they won't stay long. They know we've got Ruby here.'

He pulls out half a lemon. Holds it in the air.

'Is this all we've got? I suppose it's enough.'

'Enough for what?'

'I don't know. Gin and tonic. Vodka. Whatever.' He puts the lemon down on the counter. 'Oh darling,' he says, 'come here.'

Still thinking about the dish, she comes. He takes hold of her, kisses her hair.

'I felt it was the least I could do, to offer them a drink. I found him in the lane. Eddie, I mean. He seemed very keen to see us, all of a sudden.'

'All of a sudden?'

'He more or less invited himself round. Wouldn't really take no for an answer.'

Mary takes a breath.

'You're acting as if we have some kind of a duty to them.'

'Come on. You're making too much of this. They're only trying to be friendly.'

She shakes her head.

'I'm tired, that's all.'

'I know,' he says. 'I know you are. So am I.' He reaches out, touches her face. 'I'm really sorry,' he says, 'for not thinking.'

'Not thinking?'

'About the dish. I'm sorry.'

She goes up to change. Pulling off her T-shirt as she crosses the landing, she stops for a moment at the window and glances down. In the lane, a man and a youngish girl, standing close together, deep in conversation.

She can't see the man well – he has his back to her and the hedge half-obscures him – but she is certain about one thing: his bright red hair. The girl is less clear – no more than eleven or twelve, maybe younger. An odd-looking girl – too young to be a girlfriend, not young enough to be a daughter – with her long hair and limp, colourless clothes.

As Mary watches them she feels a kind of exhaustion sweep over her. As if the sight had somehow touched her physically, sucking all the life out of her.

She moves herself away and goes to the bathroom, a loose floor-board creaking under her feet. Chucks the T-shirt in the basket and squeezes toothpaste onto her brush. Staring at herself in the mirror, she wonders what it is she just saw. But when she returns to the window, it's already too late, they've gone. A young boy in a football strip cycles past.

She stands there for a moment, brushing her teeth – a mouthful of toothpaste, hand cupped under her chin. Looking up and down the lane but there's no sign of either of them. They couldn't walk that fast, so they must have got into a car, she thinks.

They leave the front door open so that Deborah and Eddie can come straight in, but instead they go around the side and rap on the thick, old glass of the back window. Mary gasps at the sight of their dark shapes, sudden and close in the bright evening sunshine.

'For goodness' sake,' Graham tells her, 'you're unbelievably jumpy tonight.'

In the kitchen, he offers them gin but Eddie produces a bottle of red wine with such a flourish that he is forced to open it.

'I think I might actually prefer a gin and tonic,' Deborah says, picking something that looks like cat hair off her pale linen trousers. 'I'm feeling a bit rattled. Just now in the lane, we passed this poor dead dog.'

'A dog?'

Deborah nods.

'Just down the road from here. By the farm track. Some kind of a sheep dog. Isn't that what you said you have?'

'It's not yours, is it?' Eddie says.

Graham glances at Mary.

'The dog's with Ruby, isn't she?'

She nods, indicating the sitting room.

'They're in there, watching TV.'

'Oh,' says Deborah. 'Your daughter's here? Of course. Graham said. That must be nice.'

Mary smiles.

'But you're sure this dog was dead?' Graham says.

Deborah looks at him.

'Well, I won't go into the gory details, but yes. Knocked over by a car or something, I imagine.'

'It didn't seem right to leave it there,' Eddie says. 'But I don't know what else we could have done.'

'It had no collar?'

'Nothing. I suppose it must have been a farm dog.'

'Farm dogs have collars.'

'Do they?'

'I don't know, but surely they do?'

'Well, it had nothing, so what could we do?'

They walk down the garden, towards the apple trees. The sun is low, the shadows long. Mary hears Graham explaining it all to them, telling them how the place started off as a small farm, hence the yard and the outbuildings. Though he imagines there was probably even more land here once upon a time.

'It's a magical place,' Deborah says. 'It really is. And your garden's enormous. Look at it, it goes on for ever.'

'We haven't really tamed it yet, as you can see,' Graham says, as they go down between the apple trees and on through the long grass. 'It's all still a bit of a wilderness.'

Deborah tells him she loves wildernesses and he laughs.

'No really,' she says. 'Don't you get sick of all these over-planned and over-primped gardens?'

They come to the washing line, where Mary grabs a couple of tea towels which are hanging there, forgotten and stiff and warm. She feels Eddie looking at her, cigarette packet in one hand, glass of wine in the other.

'Look, this is going to sound incredibly stupid and embarrassing. But if you can forget we ever met. At the market, I mean.'

She turns and looks at him. His glasses catching the evening sunlight. She notices that he seems tense. He looks at the cigarette packet then puts it back in his pocket.

'You can smoke,' she says. 'If you want.'

He looks at her for a moment as if he doesn't know what she's talking about.

'It's just that I never got around to telling her,' he says, batting away the small clouds of midges. 'About the market. Stupid, I know, but it never came up and then – well, if you say anything now, it's going to look a bit odd, isn't it?'

Mary holds the tea towels against her, lifting the other hand to shield her face from the sun.

'Of course,' she says. 'Whatever.'

'It's not that I want you to lie or anything.'

She tries to smile.

'I understand. Honestly, it's fine.'

He looks at her for a moment.

'She was very pleased with the vegetables. Deborah was. I never told her you'd picked them. She thought it was all my own doing.'

Mary laughs.

'Oh good. I'm glad.'

'You did me a big favour there,' he says, keeping his eyes on her till she has to look away.

They continue on down the garden, catching up with the others. When they get to the old fallen tree, Deborah gasps.

'Wow, and look at that. How brilliant. For kids, I mean. Our little nephews and nieces would be all over that—'

She breaks off as she understands what she just said. A quick beat of silence.

'It was a proper orchard once upon a time,' Graham says, rescuing her. 'All these trees, you see. Damsons as well as apples.'

'Twenty-three damson trees,' Mary says.

'Twenty-three!'

'And you see the wooden shed?' Graham says. 'An old apple store. That's where they put the apples when they'd picked them.'

'It's still got all the old shelves inside,' Mary adds.

'Old shelves?' Eddie says. 'What, the original ones with slats?'

'Eddie's mad about anything old,' Deborah says.

Graham looks at the shed.

'To be honest, it needs to come down,' he says.

Eddie looks at him.

'Why pull it down? Why not use it?'

'What would they use it for?' Deborah says.

'To store apples, perhaps?'

'It's rotten inside,' Graham says. 'And I don't think I was cut out to be an apple farmer.'

'I'd be an apple farmer,' Eddie says. 'I'd love that. Seriously, I'd give it all up tomorrow to be an apple farmer.'

'Give what up?' Deborah says.

He looks at her for a moment then he laughs.

'Thanks,' he says, 'for the vote of confidence.'

They all stand for a moment, listening to the far-off drone of an aeroplane.

'Well, I think it's all wonderful,' Deborah says at last.

Mary looks at Graham.

'I do feel a bit guilty that we haven't done more to it,' she says.

'Don't be ridiculous,' Deborah says. 'You've only been here five minutes.'

'It's a great place,' Eddie agrees.

'We're very lucky,' Graham says.

Eddie looks at him and then at Mary.

'We're so pleased to have you here. In the village, I mean. Aren't we, Deb?'

Deborah smiles.

'He's right,' she says. 'We are.'

There's a brief silence. Graham turns to Mary, his face a little stricken.

'We're glad too,' he says. 'Aren't we, darling? We're very happy here. It really is the most lovely place.'

I woke at dawn, hearing the voices I often heard as I came out of a dream. Sometimes they frightened me, speaking in languages I did not understand and telling me things that made no sense. But not this time. This time they were telling me to get up and make my way down to the bottom of the orchard, where I would find James Dix doing something with Phoebe Harkiss.

Something? What thing? I could not even let myself think about it.

Pulling a petticoat over my drawers, I hurried across the landing and down the back stairs. I let myself out of the kitchen door, careful not to make the smallest sound. Everyone was sleeping except for my father, who would have been up for hours, the dog with him.

It was the stillest, hottest morning. The long grass wet my feet, my knees. I knew I should have put my boots on, but there'd not been any time. My body was only half awake, my mind too, it felt like a part of me was still in my bed, still away in my dream. And part of me also expected that he wouldn't be there, but he was. And not with Phoebe Harkiss either, but sitting alone on the old fallen-down tree, the same one that had brought him into our lives. I felt myself slow down at the sight of him, my heart, head and blood at a kind of standstill. There was no time to run, I did not even want to run, so why did the thought come into my mind?

He was smoking a cigarette and watching some half-grown fox cubs that had come out into the sunshine to play.

When he looked up and saw me, it was the first time I had ever seen surprise on his face. It made him look younger, kinder. It made him look like someone you might even trust.

He finished his cigarette. Stubbing it out on the tree and flinging it down as quick as anything.

Eliza? he said.

Though his voice was soft, it was still loud enough to send the cubs running off to hide behind the apple store.

I kicked at a tussock of grass with my bare foot.

I thought you'd be here with Phoebe Harkiss, I said.

He frowned.

I don't know what would give you that idea.

I tried to think of an answer but I hadn't one, so I stayed quiet. So did he.

Well, you can see for yourself that I'm not, he said at last. I nodded and he pulled another fag out of his pocket.

Do you want one? he said.

No.

Have you ever tried?

No, I said, though a boy in the lane had once let me suck on his pipe.

James looked at the fag as if he was thinking of smoking it, but then he seemed to think better of it and put it away again.

I don't know what you're doing here, he said.

No, I said. Neither do I.

Some moments passed. He tilted his head to one side and looked at me. He gave a little laugh.

Well, then, Eliza.

Well, what? I said.

What do you think of me?

I don't think anything, I said.

I saw him hesitate.

Do you think I'm handsome?

I looked away quickly. Rolled my eyes.

He laughed.

What? he said. You don't think I'm a handsome bloke?

I felt my face grow hot. I didn't like it.

Why would you even ask such a thing? I said.

He shrugged.

Why would I ask? Well, let me see. I suppose it's because the ladies always tell me I'm a handsome man.

The ladies?

All the ladies I've ever known have said it, and that's the truth.

I stared at him.

I think you've a great big ugly bucket of a face, if you really want to know.

This made him laugh. But after the laugh stopped and his face was serious again, he didn't take his eyes off my face but kept on looking at me.

What is it now, Eliza?

What do you mean, what is it?

What's in your head?

I told you. Nothing's in my head.

Oh yes there is. You're always thinking something.

I shrugged.

Isn't everyone?

No, not everyone, not the way you do. No one has more thoughts flying around in there than you do. My feeling, if you really want to know, is that you think too much.

I never said I did want to know, I said.

He smiled.

And you have an answer to everything, don't you?

I had no answer to this, so I shrugged.

He was silent for a moment, watching me. I didn't like being watched, hated the feeling. It made my whole face – nose, eyes, mouth – feel too big for my skin.

Tell me what you think of me, he said.

I thought you said I think too much?

He smiled.

All right, but I want to know.

I think you're a piece of bad luck, I told him, though it wasn't something I'd known till I said it out loud.

He stared at me.

Are you a virgin? he said.

Now I flushed to the roots of my hair.

What?

He gave me a sly look.

You know, like Christ's mother, Mary. The Virgin Mary. I wondered if you were a virgin like her?

I thought of Mary with her drab blue clothes and her long-suffering face and her arms full of big fat baby boy. A lot like my mother, I thought.

I'm nothing like her, I said.

He nodded and smiled as if it was the right answer. Then he patted the old dead tree trunk.

Come here, he said.

No, thanks.

I could take you fishing, he said. We could catch a fish and maybe make a little fire and I'll cook it for you and then we could get married and—

I couldn't help it. I smiled.

You're off your rocker, I said.

He grinned.

I love you, Eliza.

Don't be a twot.

I wouldn't say it if I didn't mean it. And you like me. Come on, I know you do. Don't deny it. Don't you know it's a sin to lie?

I could have told him it was a sin to talk about virgins and fish fires and getting married to a girl you hardly knew. But I didn't. My heart was beating so hard in my chest that I worried I might faint and I couldn't think of anything worse than falling to the ground in front of James Dix and having to let him carry me home.

I tried to breathe and steady myself.

I don't know what you're on about, I said, and it was partly the truth, because I couldn't decide what I should think about any of the things he was saying.

He was still staring at me, but for once his face was soft and sad, his eyes quite different from how I'd ever seen them look before – in fact, now I thought about it, everything about him was different.

Come here, he said.

No.

109

I heard him take a breath.

Seriously, Eliza, I don't care what you're thinking, just come here.

I can't, I said.

What are you worried about?

I don't know.

Come here, he said again. Come on, sweet Eliza, this time I'm begging you.

I waited for a moment.

Come on, he said, his voice gentler this time.

Still I did nothing.

Come – it was a whisper this time.

Far off somewhere a bird was squawking, waiting to swoop down over the reed beds. I'd seen them hovering there, waiting to drop down and take a fish in their claws, before rising up again, the poor thing wriggling and slapping about and all the water spraying its bright drops into the silver air.

I listened to the bird and I thought of the fish fanning itself all still and unaware in those brown shallows, then I looked again at him, sitting there and begging me. I began to see it through his eyes. What in the world was I worried about? What could happen?

He's only James Dix, I told myself.

Once I was close, he reached down and pulled me up and put me next to him on the tree. The morning sun had warmed it. The wood felt smooth as butter.

Feeling myself slipping a bit against him, I tried to pull away. But before I could do it, he caught me around the waist and yanked me hard, turning me so my back was to him. Then, holding me there tight against him, he picked up the whole length of my hair which was loose down my back.

What are you doing? I tried to say – but already it felt like the words had passed straight through me and into another place entirely.

Still holding my hair, he put his lips to my neck, then my ear. The slowest of shivers went through me.

Shhh, he whispered. I'm tidying you up.

And at first I laughed, but then quite quickly I didn't laugh any more. Feeling myself go still as his hands tugged gently at my head, lifting the hair and sending more and more shivers down me and making my body go sad and warm and tight.

I took a sharp little breath.

What? he said and I tried to say something back but when I opened my mouth, nothing came out.

Mary hears the phone ringing. The landline. It never rings. It makes her jump. She thinks it might be her mother. She would prefer not to pick it up, but she knows that if she doesn't Ruby will.

'It was good to see you,' he says.

'What?'

'The other night. We really enjoyed it.'

She hesitates, feeling herself tense for no reason she can understand.

'Well good,' she says.

'Good?'

'That's good. It was nice to see you too.'

She hears him take a breath.

'Sorry,' he says. 'I began that all wrong, didn't I? I should have said hello, Mary, how are you?'

She is silent.

'You still there?'

'I'm very well,' she says as smoothly as she can, trying to imagine him in that large immaculate house, pink evening light catching at his glasses. 'How are you?'

A brief, cautious silence.

'Look, I hope you don't mind. It's on the spur of the moment, really. I was just wondering what you were up to?'

'Up to?'

She stares at the fridge.

'What I mean is, we wondered if you'd like to come round again. A spot of supper. The two of you, of course. Tomorrow or Saturday perhaps?'

She tries to think.

'I'm not sure,' she says. 'The thing is – I mean, Ruby's still here, you see.'

'Graham's girl? Well, bring her along too. Seriously. The more the merrier.'

Mary hesitates.

'I'm sorry,' she says, 'but I think there may already be a plan.'

'A plan?'

'To do something. I think we might be busy.'

'What? You mean you won't come?'

He sounds appalled. She tries to laugh.

'Another time. Maybe another time you can come to us?'

After she's put the phone down, she looks at it. She looks at it and she knows exactly what's going to happen next and it does. Except that this time she doesn't do anything. This time she just looks at it and lets it ring.

But when Graham gets back with Ruby and Ruby's friend Lisa who she'd forgotten was coming for the weekend, he tells her he just ran into Eddie.

'They've asked us to go over tomorrow, bring the girls as well. He insisted. I said yes, but only if they let us bring something, pudding or whatever.'

She stares at him.

'You really want to go there again?'

'You said you enjoyed it, the other night.'

'But we only just saw them.'

He shrugs.

'Village life.'

'What about it?'

'Well, do we want to be a part of it or not?'

Mary looks at Ruby, who's crouched on the floor with Lisa, both of them petting the dog.

'There's no way those two will want to come,' she says.

Ruby looks up and so does Lisa. Two unearthly, indoor faces, one raven-haired, the other a shock of cropped, peroxide white. Some kind of foetid scent in the air, like stagnant water or rotting flowers.

'Hi, Lisa,' Mary says, looking at the girl, who she's only met once before and who never appears to speak. She takes in the black clumpy boots, fishnet tights, dirty-looking silver bangles, the ring through her nose.

'Hi,' Lisa says.

'You guys don't want to come to some boring dinner party, do you?'

'We're cool with it,' says Ruby, who's trying to make the dog settle on her lap. 'And Dad says we can always come back here and watch a film if we're bored.'

Later, she gets into bed, pulling the duvet up around her, fixing her eyes on a spot just between the mirror and the chest. There's a shadow she's not noticed before, the faint, rectangular ghost of an old picture.

'We should paint this room,' she says.

Unbuttoning his shirt, Graham glances at her.

'You pick the colour,' he says a little too quickly. 'I'll do it.'

Still gazing at the wall, she sighs.

'I suppose I was hoping we might just have a quiet weekend.'

'I didn't mean do it this weekend.'

'No. Eddie and Deborah. I don't see why they're suddenly so keen on us.'

He stops and looks at her.

'Are they keen on us?'

'I don't know. Don't you think so? Wanting to see us all the time. They seem to be.'

Graham sits in the chair to take his shoes off.

'I think they're just trying to be friendly. And anyway, it's not like we're going to have a very quiet weekend with the Morticia twins around.'

Mary sighs.

'Does she ever speak?'

'What?'

'Lisa. I don't think I've ever heard her say more than three or four words in a row.'

Graham looks at her.

'I think she's just shy.'

He drops his shoes on the floor and stands up to go to the bathroom. Mary watches him.

'Shy? That's not the word I'd use.'

'What, then?'

She says nothing. Keeping her eyes on the shadow on the wall. It is smooth and grey and even. And then just for a moment it isn't: it has curves and contours, a shock of light brown hair, the dark gleam of an eye—

Graham is looking at her.

'You OK, sweetheart?'

'I'm OK.'

She continues to gaze at the wall.

'I'm fine,' she says.

He looks at her for a moment. Then he goes into the bathroom and she hears the click of the light and the soft shutting of the door.

This time Mary notices that Deborah hasn't dressed up, though her jeans are tight and expensive-looking and she looks even prettier with her creamy hair twisted up on top of her head. The dishwasher is on when they arrive and so is the radio – some violin concerto drifting out through the back door and off over the lavender-fringed paving stones. The kitchen could even be said to be in a mess.

'She's making her fish pie,' Eddie says. 'Quite a production, I'm afraid. Never have more pans been harmed in the making of one simple supper.'

'Eddie,' Deborah is laughing, 'that's not fair.'

Graham says that fish pie is his favourite, and Mary knows he's not lying but also that even if it wasn't, he would have said it was. She kisses Deborah on the cheek and catches a scent of something citrusy. They introduce the girls. Ruby yawns and Lisa fiddles with the ring in her nose. Mary notices that she has thick false eyelashes on. The effect is to make her eyes seem even heavier and sleepier.

Eddie asks the girls if they're interested in music. For a long moment, neither of them speaks.

'Kind of,' Ruby says at last.

He laughs loudly, rubbing his hands together. Mary notices that his shirt is coming untucked at the back and it makes her feel briefly sorry for him.

'Kind of? Only kind of? What self-respecting, paid-up member of the teenage class isn't interested in rock' n' roll?'

'Can you really call teenagers a class?' Graham says, helping himself to an olive.

'Class of their own, more like,' Eddie says. 'Super classy anyway.'

Ruby rolls her eyes and Lisa looks away and he asks them if they'd like to see his collection of vinyl and Lisa still doesn't speak but Ruby glances at Graham.

'OK,' she says.

Graham laughs.

'I'm afraid OK is the best you'll get from my daughter. Roughly translated, it means yes please, she would like to very much.'

'And you?' Eddie says to Lisa.

Lisa blinks.

'What about me?'

'What are you into, young lady?'

Lisa doesn't answer, but Deborah turns around from the board where she's chopping parsley.

'Please don't pander to him, girls. And don't feel you've got to see his bloody vinyls either. I don't think Eddie realises that not everyone's as mad about old records as he is.'

Mary expects Eddie to argue with her, but he doesn't. He says nothing and then gets busy pouring them all drinks. Lisa refuses wine and whispers a request for Diet Coke. Straightaway Eddie disappears to another room beyond the kitchen.

'You're in luck,' he says, returning with a can, which he snaps open for her.

Deborah turns down the oven and takes off her apron and they leave the girls inside and wander out into the garden with their drinks. The light is brilliant, the air hot and silky. Mary notices the rows of orange flowers. The stone urns, clipped box hedge. The pond with its coating of bright green algae.

Deborah and Graham stand on the terrace and talk but Eddie follows her as she walks further down the lawn, past the clumps of daisies and catmint and the lavender, still alive with bees. He pulls out his cigarettes.

'I'm sorry,' he says. 'I know you didn't want to come.'

Mary flushes.

'Don't be silly,' she says.

'Yes, but I forced your hand, didn't I?'

She says nothing. Looks over to where Deborah is standing on one leg and taking off her shoe and shaking something out of it while laughing at something Graham just said.

'What?' he says. 'What are you thinking now?'

She turns to look at him properly. Smiling as he lights his cigarette.

'Why is it always so important for you to know what I'm thinking?'

He makes a face.

'Sorry. Just interested.'

Mary shivers. She looks back over at Deborah again. She's putting the shoe back on, her hand on Graham's shoulder, steadying herself.

'It's very nice of you to ask us,' she says. 'Very kind of you to include the girls.'

She feels him gazing at her, deliberate and intent. She knows he's waiting for her to say something else but she doesn't, she says nothing and, when he doesn't speak either, she takes it as her chance to move away.

They eat the fish pie and some salad and drink the two bottles of Prosecco that Mary and Graham brought with them, since Deborah refused their offer of a pudding. Graham says it's the best fish pie he's ever had and he asks for seconds and eats them quickly, hardly pausing between one mouthful and the next, and Mary looks at him, his head bent over his plate, and is struck by how suddenly alive he seems, how awake and alert, and she finds herself wondering what it is that she does to him. Does she oppress him, push him down and make him sad? Does her daily presence only serve to continue the misery for him, a constant reminder of how viciously their lives were interrupted?

Graham insisted the girls leave their phones at home and Mary thinks that may be why Ruby can't seem to settle, tapping her foot and nimming her leg and looking around as if she expects at any moment to hear the ping of a text.

Deborah leans across the table and tells Ruby she likes her earrings and are they really what they look like, little animal skulls, or something? And Ruby mutters something in reply that Mary doesn't catch and then Deborah asks her what subjects she's doing at school and Ruby looks at Lisa and again says something quite inaudible and Mary sees that Lisa has picked every single piece of prawn out of her pie and left them around the side of the plate.

'She's allergic,' Ruby says when Eddie asks her if she's not keen on seafood.

Deborah gasps.

'My God, I'm so sorry. You mean properly allergic? My God, Mary, I do apologise. I feel awful, I really ought to have asked.'

Mary looks at Lisa's pale peroxide face.

'Are you allergic to prawns, Lisa?'

Lisa looks at her plate and seems about to speak, but Ruby jumps in.

'She has stomach problems. It was when you had your appendix out, wasn't it, Lisa?'

Graham leans back in his chair.

'Maybe let her talk for herself?'

At last Lisa seems to startle awake.

'It's all right,' she says in a surprisingly crisp and assured voice. 'It's not an allergy. It's a digestion thing. I developed an allergy to something they gave me at the hospital and it's affected my stomach ever since.'

Mary stares at her. For a moment no one speaks.

'Well, I do hope we haven't made you ill,' Deborah says – and she offers to make Lisa a sandwich, but Lisa says she's had enough.

'But you've hardly eaten anything! I feel we haven't fed you.'

'Leave the poor girl alone,' Eddie says and, when they excuse themselves together to go to the toilet, he leans over and pats Graham's arm. 'They're great,' he says. 'Really great. Both of them. She's quite a girl, isn't she, your Ruby? A real charmer.'

Graham laughs.

'Girl may be one way of describing her. Charming, well, perhaps not so much.'

'Well, I think they're great,' Eddie says. 'Both of them. A breath of fresh air, aren't they, Deb?'

Deborah smiles.

'We just don't know anyone with kids that age – teenagers, I mean. It makes a nice change.'

Eddie nods.

'They're welcome here any time,' he says.

'You're very kind,' Graham says.

Still, Mary is relieved when he suggests the girls go and eat pudding at home.

'They need to let the dog out,' he tells Deborah as he hands Ruby a key.

Straightaway, Eddie jumps up.

'Not so fast. I'm sorry but you're not getting away without seeing my vinyls.'

'Really, Eddie,' Deborah says, 'can't it wait for another time?'

He glances at her, rubbing at his hair. Mary notices that he looks quite agitated.

'Not if you're about to make me pack them away ready for the builders to start on the bloody extension, they can't.'

Deborah laughs. She undoes her hair clip and shakes her hair out so it falls all over her shoulders. She looks at Mary.

'You see why we need an extension? Not for ourselves at all, but to house his entire collection of seventies memorabilia.' She looks at the girls. 'You think I'm joking? Go on up and see. You won't believe the amount of stuff he's got up there.'

I did not know what had happened between James and me, but I knew that something had. Even though he was still the same tall, red-haired, annoying person, he no longer affected me in the same way. Something was different. There seemed to be more of him – so much more – as if his eyes now contained a thousand possibilities that I'd never noticed before. His body, too – or maybe it was my own body. Where I'd once been hard and worried around him, now I was liquid velvet, the softest thing.

Next day and the day after, we sat together again on the old tree and he told me all about himself. He said that his mother had died when he was ten years old and he was brought up by an aunt who had thrown him out on the streets when he was fourteen.

I stared at him.

Why did she throw you out?

He scratched his head.

It's a long story and not for your innocent ears.

He told me he had worked as a dustman in London for a time and after that as a fish-gutter in Lowestoft, where he'd had a sweetheart for a short while but she'd died soon after and that was that.

But don't worry, he said. She wasn't as pretty as you, not even the smallest bit, and that's a fact.

I thought it very unkind of him to be so cruel about a person he had once loved, especially if she'd had the awful misfortune to die, and I told him so.

Oh, he said. But I didn't love her.

Then that's even worse! I said.

He laughed and he reached out his hand and touched my hair and then my face and I didn't stop him but I told him he shouldn't be laughing about it either.

What? he said. Am I supposed to lie about it, then?

I had no answer to that, but all the same I couldn't get the idea of the poor dead unloved woman out of my head. I asked him what her name was and what she died of, but he said he didn't want to talk about her.

We weren't engaged or anything, he said. I wouldn't have been so stupid as to promise her marriage.

I asked him why that would have been stupid.

Well, because she was already poorly when I met her. It's like horses, isn't it?

What?

You don't go putting your money on a lame horse, do you?

I looked at him and didn't know if he was joking or not. I said I thought he was being very unkind.

He laughed.

Oh Eliza, I'm only teasing. You think I'd really say that about a poor sick woman?

I don't know what you'd say, I said. Especially since I don't know the first thing about you.

Dearest Eliza, he said. But you do. You know everything about me. Everything that's worth knowing, anyway.

And he tried to take hold of my hand then, tried to pull my face to his so he could kiss me, but I would not let him. And when he wouldn't take no for an answer, I got quite fierce and shook him off. He did not seem to like this very much, telling me that all through his life he'd always been very upset when women pushed him away.

It began with my mother and my aunt, he said. And after that it was downhill all the way.

I pointed out that, whilst it might be all right to say this about his aunt, it was not exactly fair on his poor mother, since she surely did not choose to die?

But he didn't seem to be listening. He stuck out his bottom lip.

She left me to it, he said.

Yes but what else could she have done?

He shrugged.

She did not care what happened to me—

Oh, but I'm very sure she did care! I cried.

He looked at me for a moment.

Well, it was very hard for me, being left. I don't know any other way to put it, Eliza. She left me to it and that was that.

I struggled for a moment with this and I thought about trying to explain his poor mother a little more carefully to him. But I could see there was no use: his face was pinched and sad and hard.

Well, I feel very sorry for you, I said. But that's all in the past. There's no point dwelling on it, is there?

His face seemed to brighten.

You're right. There's not. And anyway, I've got you now, haven't I?

I looked at my boots.

What? he said. What is it?

I don't think I want to be anybody's sweetheart, I said.

He stopped and looked at me and he pushed some hair out of my face. He put his hand on the part of my skirts where my knee was and then he slid it upwards, to my thigh. A little flame-like feeling crept and flickered around there under my petticoats. I took a quick breath.

You don't have to be anyone's anything, he said. You just have to be you. And to know that I like you very much.

I like you too, I told him.

You do?

And he looked as if he was waiting for more. But the truth was I had run out of words. I thought he must think me a very raw, dull child compared to his old dead sweetheart.

I want to be with you all the time, he said. I mean it, Eliza. I'd see to it if I could.

I stared at him, not understanding.

What do you mean? I said. How would you see to it?

He shrugged.

I suppose I'd kidnap you if I could.

I didn't like the way he said it – as if it was the most natural and ordinary thing in the world. I thought about it for a moment and then I pointed out that you didn't have to kidnap a person if they were already there.

He nodded and smiled as if he'd already thought of this.

And anyway I wouldn't want to hurt you, would I?

I should hope not, I said, though I still felt worried.

And I was about to wonder whether he'd thought about kidnapping the poor dead woman, but then we heard the sound of my mother calling the little ones in for supper, so all ideas and questions disappeared from my head.

Before we parted, he put his mouth to my ear.

Shall I tell you what I'd really like?

I laughed.

No thanks, I said.

He looked surprised.

What? You don't want me to tell you? Really, Eliza? You really don't want to know what it is?

I don't think I do, I said.

Why not?

I shrugged. Feeling my face grow tight and hot.

Because I'm afraid.

Afraid? What on earth are you afraid of, Eliza?

I'm afraid of what it is that you're going to say.

He looked at me for a moment.

You're afraid of me?

I swallowed.

I don't know, I said.

Then he took my hand and held it in both of his. He pulled me towards him and he stared into my eyes.

Well, maybe you're right to be afraid. Maybe your instinct is correct, Eliza. But I'm going to tell you anyway—

I tried to turn my head away.

Please, I said.

Please what?

Please don't – and I tugged at my hand, but he would not let go. Instead, he laughed. And when at last he spoke, he lowered his voice to a whisper as if the next part was so secret that even the birds and insects around us should not be allowed to hear it.

What I'd really like is to see you with no clothes on.

I stared at him. I couldn't believe he'd said it. It was the most awful and nerve-racking idea. He smiled.

And shall I tell you the really funny thing? The really funny thing – and I know you won't believe this but take it from me, it is God's own truth – is that one day you'll feel the precise same way. One day I swear you'll take them all off for me – dress, petticoats, even your drawers. You'll take them all off and you'll stand there in front of me as naked as the day you were born and I won't know which part to look at first – your breasts or your belly or your sweet little fanny.

I swallowed and turned my head away. I felt so ashamed I thought I would faint. I began to cry.

But don't worry, he added, letting go of my hand as if he suddenly understood that he'd gone too far. It's only an idea I have in my head. Just a mischievous idea. I'd never do anything to upset you, Eliza, I promise you that, gentleman's honour.

There's a mown path that leads between the reed beds and up to the golf course. On the edge of a wide field, next to the wood. Mary doesn't go as far as the golf course – she never goes up there. Instead, she stops right here in the middle of the reeds where she's never seen or heard another human soul.

Silence.

Cow parsley as high as your head. Nettles. Wild orchids and foxgloves. Lush, damp grass, where it's been flooded and boggy all winter and spring. The occasional molehill. But apart from the squawk of a bird or the sudden eerie splash of something in the water, nothing. Recently, as spring has given way to early summer, she has begun to look forward to coming here.

There's a bench. She knows it wasn't put there just for her. But she can tell, mainly because of the lush, undisturbed brightness of the grass growing up between its slats, that she is the only person who ever sits on it. She did once find the foil from inside a packet of cigarettes here. And another time, a used scratch card, crumpled and soggy and torn. But apart from that.

She comes here often. Every day sometimes. She doesn't bring the dog, even though she knows Graham would expect her to. The dog would want a walk. Or to jump in the ditches. Or to be allowed to go looking for rabbits. The dog wouldn't let her sit alone in silence and think. And this is where she comes to do that. This is where she comes when she wants to think the thoughts that she cannot safely allow anywhere near Graham or her home.

She's sitting here the day after the dinner at Deborah and Eddie's when he rings her mobile. The sound, breaking the warm, green silence of the afternoon air, making her jump.

'Hope you don't mind, I got your number off your daughter.'

Daughter. Her heart flips.

'Why?' she says. 'What is it?'

'Nothing. Just felt like calling. Wondering what you're up to. Wanted to see if you're all right.'

'All right?'

'Yes. Where are you?'

'I'm out,' she says. 'Out for a walk. Why? Where are you?'

He takes a breath.

'Oh, nowhere. Just at work.'

At work. She tries to picture it. A suit, a tie, a computer screen, perhaps some kind of hefty leather office chair. Or else she sees him standing at a window, tie loosened, hair mussed, phone in hand, looking out over something vast and wrecked and urban. A building site. Cranes. Maybe some water or a railway line.

'Are you all right?' he says again.

'All right?' She looks down at the sodden tissue in her hand. 'Why wouldn't I be all right?'

She hears him sigh.

'I suppose you just popped into my head.'

'Did I?'

'Yes, you did. Anything wrong with that?' He laughs. 'I can't tell you how glad we are to meet some interesting people at last. People worth knowing. You've no idea how dull most of the folk around here are.'

Mary tells him that the few people she's come across in the village seem very nice.

'Very nice?' He laughs. 'You mean very old. You should see Deb's so-called book group. I swear there's not a single person under sixty-five.'

She tells him that people can't help getting old and hears him take a breath.

'Well, you're a much kinder person than I am, aren't you?'

She tells him she isn't kind.

'All the same,' he says, 'I mean it. It's good to have some proper friends at last.'

She puts the tissue in her pocket, looks down for a moment at the long grass at her feet.

'But you must have friends.'

'What?'

'You and Deborah. You must have friends.'

He hesitates.

'We don't. Not really.'

'Come on,' she says.

She hears him blow out smoke again.

'You don't understand. We find it hard – I suppose we don't mix that well. We're very shy, Deb and me.'

Mary thinks about Deborah. Her smiling confidence and friendliness, her sheet of long blonde hair.

'I don't think of Deborah as shy,' she says.

He says nothing.

She lets the silence happen while she tilts her head back and watches a bird falling through the sky. About to swoop down on some poor little creature, probably.

'What?' he says at last. 'What are you thinking?'

'Nothing,' she says. 'I wasn't thinking anything. I was watching a bird.'

She hears him chuckle and something about the sound of it makes her look behind her, glancing back at the tall reeds shuffling in the quiet breeze. She tells him she must go.

'Go?'

'I've got to get back. See to the dog.'

'The dog's not with you?'

Mary hesitates.

'I need to take her home and feed her.'

She gets up from the bench, suddenly annoyed at being forced to explain herself.

'You don't mind this, do you?' he says before he goes.

'What?'

'Me ringing you. Just because I felt like it. I suppose I just couldn't stop myself. I hope you don't mind it.'

Mary hesitates then tells him again that she has to go.

Four or five minutes after they say goodbye, walking through the dark copse and back into the lane, she gets a text.

Forgive me! E x

She stares at it for a moment then she deletes it.

Back home, Ruby and Lisa are in front of the TV with their feet on the coffee table and the curtains drawn. Both have cushions clutched against their stomachs. The dog is lying flat out on the rug. The moment she comes in, Ruby pauses the TV. Mary feels a lick of irritation.

'You don't have to do that every time I come in.'

'Do what?'

'Pause the TV.'

Ruby blinks at her. The dog lifts her head.

'It's very hard to concentrate with people coming in and out.'

Mary takes a breath and looks at the screen. The same well-groomed American characters frozen mid-gesture. She looks at the girls' feet on the table – Lisa's blue toenails. Ruby's black leggings and socks with holes in them.

'It's a lovely day outside,' she says.

Ruby looks at her and shudders.

'Well, it's freezing in here. We're really freezing.'

'Maybe you should try going out in the sunshine.'

'We did. We already tried it. We went outside for a bit but we were so cold that we had to come back in. I wish we could put the heating on.'

'Ruby, it's almost June. It's summer. We're not putting the heating on.'

'Mum has the heating on in June,' Ruby says.

Mary is about to say something about Veronica's heating bills being subsidised by Graham, but she stops herself. She's about to walk out of the room when she remembers something.

'Did Eddie ring and ask you for my mobile number?'

Still clutching the cushion against her stomach and shivering, Ruby nods.

'He didn't ring. He came round.'

'What? You mean he came round here?'

Letting her eyes go back to the TV, Ruby sighs.

'Where else would he come?'

Mary thinks for a moment.

'But – so when was this?'

'When was what?'

'When exactly did he come round?'

'I don't know when it was. Earlier.'

'Can you tell me what time?'

Ruby gives a yowl of impatience.

'I don't know what time! What does it matter? A while ago, OK? Anyway, it was Lisa that saw him.'

Mary looks at Lisa.

'You saw Eddie and you gave him my number?'

Slowly, Lisa turns to look at her. Sleepy-eyed, running her hands through her bleached hair – several thin bangles falling down her arm.

'He said he needed to talk to you. Is it OK? Rubes gave me the number.'

Ruby tuts.

'Look, is this important? Have we really got to talk about it right now? It's just that me and Lisa have only got about three more episodes to watch.'

Mary gazes at her for a moment, then she turns and walks out of the room.

5

I did not love James Dix. Not at first, and not in the way he wanted me to. If love meant waking up and letting your thoughts go straight to that one person and then keeping them there. If it meant knowing you had a sweetheart and wanting to be near them all of the time and breathe in every word they said and have their fingers wrapped in your hair, then this was not what I felt.

Sometimes I woke and I was afraid of what had happened between us, of what might still happen.

But James knew a lot. He knew how to entice me. He liked to promise me things and call me his love and his princess and make sure I knew that I now had his heart in my two hands and must take great care of it or else. He said that his heart had been broke in the past – not by the dead woman from Lowestoft but by another one he hadn't even told me about – and he did not think he could take that again.

Who is the one you haven't told me about? I asked him.

He said it was better for all of us that I did not know.

A private matter, he said. Don't get the wrong idea, Eliza. But even though I love you, I would not want you to know the sad and tawdry details of that little romance.

Some of the things he said made me laugh and not always in a good way.

You should have seen me, he told me when he was talking about the one who broke him. I was so mad with love that I used to rage and howl and throw plates around. Once I ran out in the street with no clothes on, I was so very upset at the way in which she had spurned me.

I looked at him and said I hoped he would not do that with me. And he looked very sad and serious then and said didn't I realise that

I was a whole different kettle of fish altogether? Could I not see that I had punctured his soul with my sweetness? And if so, why did I keep on laughing at the things he said, instead of gazing into his eyes with the kind of loving dedication he required?

I reminded him that I was only thirteen.

I thought you were fourteen?

Not till November, I said, suddenly not wanting to be old at all, but to stay as young and safe as possible for as long as possible.

He looked at me.

Thirteen isn't young, he said, as if he could read my thoughts. You're not a kid, Eliza. I've known much littler girls than you who had far better manners.

I didn't like the sound of that and I asked him what he meant by it. He looked bashful.

I had a very young girl, he said. Much younger than you. Tilly, her name was. And we was going to be engaged and all that. And I even got a loan and went and picked out the ring, gold with a single diamond it was, and then she went and changed her mind for no reason at all.

It couldn't be for no reason, I told him – thinking that if Tilly really was so much younger than me, then she must truly have been a child no older than Jazzy who ought not to marry anyway – why on earth would she do a thing like that if she properly loved you?

He threw me a sly look.

Well, but you see, the truth was she didn't love me after all.

Why not? I said.

We fell out about something, didn't we?

What do you mean? What kind of thing?

He kept his head down but he looked out at me from under his gingery lashes.

She would insist on seeing her family. Putting them first, before me. Her friends as well.

What? And you didn't think she ought to?

They were silly girls, Eliza, with nothing to say. Airheads, you might call them. They worked at the dressmaker's. They were always laughing and chattering about this and that. They did her no good at all.

I thought about this. I thought about how it might feel to have some friends that were real girls, people you could chat and laugh with like that. For as long as I could remember – my whole life, in fact – all I'd ever had was Jazzy and Frank and a whole bunch of silly little babies.

I sighed.

Maybe she just liked them, I said.

What?

Her friends. Maybe she liked them. Being with them, I mean.

Straightaway his face went hard and tight.

What? You think she preferred them to me?

She might have, I said, already regretting it.

He shook his head.

You don't know what you're talking about, Eliza.

You're right, I said. I don't.

You don't understand.

All right.

He reached out then and took my hand. I liked the rough hot feel of his fingers on mine, so I let him. Sometimes he squeezed a bit too hard but I didn't say anything.

But is it really so wrong to want to see your friends? I said at last.

He gazed at me so hard this time that it gave me an icy feeling.

I thought if she wanted to be a wife, then she should cleave to me.

Well, I said, taking my hand away now. No man would ever stop me seeing my family and my brothers and sisters who I love so much, and that's a fact.

I know that, he said, though his face told another story.

Not my friends either. Not if I had any, that is.

I folded my arms. I saw him watching me.

But you don't have any, he reminded me.

That doesn't mean I wouldn't want to see them if I did.

He stared at me for a moment.

Let's not talk any more about it, he said.

And that was it. He kept to his word and we spoke no more about it. Except that later I caught him looking at me in a very particular way. His head on one side. A little bit of light in his eyes.

What? I said. What is it now?

Are you my girl, Eliza?

I don't know. Yes. I suppose so.

You suppose so? You only suppose so? You don't love me passionately, then?

Maybe I do.

And would you do anything for me? Would you?

I don't know, James. It's not that I don't want to, but I think it's the wrong kind of question to ask.

What kind of question would be the right one?

I don't know, I said.

And that was when he whispered it. He bent and whispered in my ear that even though he didn't care at all for Phoebe Harkiss, he knew that she would do anything for him.

I looked at him.

Phoebe Harkiss is a child, I said.

No more than you, she isn't.

She is. She's a year younger than me and she's a horrible girl, I said.

He smiled.

Ah, he said. I thought so. Jealousy.

It's not jealousy. I'm just saying you shouldn't go blowing about with a young girl like Phoebe Harkiss.

He took his hands off me and lay back and put his boots up on the kitchen table even though he knew my mother didn't like it.

Then don't make me, he said.

Ruby and Lisa leave and go back to London. Graham drops them at the station on his way to work. Mary, stripping the sheets in their room, even though she had asked them to do it themselves before they left, sees streaks of blood on Ruby's sheets. She stares at them for a moment, then takes them down and sprays them with Vanish before putting them in the washing machine.

On the floor under Lisa's bed are a scattering of the white nubs that she recognises as cigarette filters and an empty pack of Rizlas with strips of the cardboard torn off. On the window sill, hairy brown remnants of tobacco.

Mary sweeps the window sill clean and flings everything into the waste bin and takes it downstairs, but before she can even tip it into the dustbin, she has to prise several pieces of dried pinkish-grey chewing gum off the bottom with her fingers.

She feels like phoning Graham to complain about all of this, but she doesn't. Instead, when Ruby rings from the train to say she left her phone charger, Mary tells her she'll put it in the post first thing tomorrow.

A little later, she comes in from the garden to find him sitting at the kitchen table. His jacket is off. Briefcase on the floor. Head in his hands.

She stares at him.

'What is it?'

'What?'

'What are you doing? I thought you went ages ago.'

He lifts his head and she sees that his face is all wrong. White spaces under his eyes. Has he been crying? It's been a while since she saw him cry.

'I did,' he says. 'I did go ages ago, but—'

'But what? Darling. What are you doing? What's the matter?'

He takes a breath. Letting it out. His hand on his forehead. Looking down at the table.

'I did go. I tried to go. I dropped the girls off and got part of the way to work and then I had to turn the car around and come back. I'm so sorry.'

He lets his hand slide down over his face, beginning to sob.

'What is it?' she says, her voice small and stupid now. She pulls out a chair and sits down next to him, stroking him, touching his shoulder. 'You're hot,' she says. 'You're sweating. Are you ill? Do you feel bad? What is it?' she says again.

He shakes his head, wiping his eyes and swallowing hard.

'I'm not ill.'

'What then?'

He looks at her, then back at the table.

'I haven't been like this for a while, have I? You know I haven't. Seriously. I've been great, haven't I?'

She looks at him, suddenly afraid.

'You have. It's true. You've been great.'

He nods.

'I know. I know I have. To be honest, I haven't even found it very difficult. But then this morning. I don't know what happened—'

He begins to sob again. She holds out her arms to him.

'What? Please – what is it? Did something happen?' She watches, trying to hold him as he continues to sob. 'Just tell me what it is,' she says.

He looks at her.

'It isn't anything.'

'It must be something. Is it because Ruby's gone?'

'No. No, that's a bloody relief, if I'm honest.' He shakes his head, trying to laugh.

'What, then?'

He swallows. Looking around the room.

'I hadn't thought of him in a long time, really I hadn't.'

Mary is silent. She knows who he's talking about. Graham looks at her, his eyes wild and hard.

'But when I woke up today – for no reason at all, don't ask me why – he was suddenly right here in my head. Almost as if he was here in the house with us. I can't get rid of him. Nothing I do—' He gazes at her for a moment. 'I'm sorry, my darling. I'm so sorry.'

She holds her breath, her eyes filling now.

'Sorry? Sorry for what?'

'I didn't mean to say this to you, to talk like this. Didn't want to tell you. I thought – if I could just get myself to work . . .'

Mary hears herself saying something, making some kind of a sound, but she doesn't know what it is. She holds him. Trying to pull him to her. His wet face. Trying to kiss his rough, hot cheek, missing and instead brushing his ear with her lips.

'It's all right,' she says.

'It's not all right.'

'It is, it is. Darling, it is.'

He lifts his head and looks at her.

'I mean it. For so long, I've been absolutely fine.'

'I know. I know you have—'

'And there was I, telling you you needed to talk to someone, when all along—'

'Stop it,' she says. 'Don't.'

He stares at her.

'You see, I really did think I was on the way to – but now, today – why suddenly today after all this time? Why now? Why suddenly out of the blue like this?'

Mary is silent. The cold – it runs from her head through the very centre of her and right down to her feet. Remembering the trial, the shock when he suddenly changed his plea, the brief couple of seconds when she dared herself to look at his dirty, gingerish face and saw how relaxed he seemed, smoothing his hair and pulling down his shirt cuffs and carefully adjusting his collar and tie, as if the only important thing in that moment was to get himself settled and comfortable.

'It's not out of the blue,' she says.

'It is.'

'It's not.'

'But I haven't thought of him in so long.'

He takes another quick, sobbing breath. Mary stands up and gets the roll of kitchen towel from the rack. She hands it to him and he tears off a sheet and blows his nose.

'I love you,' she says.

He tears off another sheet. Holds it.

'I know you do. I know. And the terrible thing is, it means nothing.'

She stares at him.

'What means nothing?'

'Love. Our lives together. This. Everything. He destroyed it all, didn't he?'

'Graham. Please don't say that.'

'Isn't it true? Don't you think it, too? Isn't it absolutely obvious to you? He destroyed us completely, didn't he?'

Mary says nothing. She looks out of the window. Taking her eyes away from him, away from the room, beyond, out. That blue sky out there.

Graham is shaking his head, staring at her.

'I should have killed him. That's what I keep on thinking. Even if I went to prison for the rest of my life, even if it meant my whole life was over – my life and yours together – even if that was it, forever, it would have made us happier. Wouldn't it? Admit it, Mary. Anything would have been better than existing in this – this fucking awful limbo.'

Frank wasn't well. He'd gone too near a horse and it had kicked him in the stomach. The doctor said he might be bleeding inside. But the pain wasn't in his stomach, it was in his chest. He coughed and coughed. All night long he couldn't stop. Afraid he might have the whooping cough, Mother rubbed some pork lard on him but it did no good at all and he kept on hurting.

My mother was worried. She said the doctor should have looked at him more carefully. My father said he would be fine and they should wait. I heard them arguing about whether they could afford to see another doctor. In the end, my mother won and they put him in the cart and drove him into Ipswich. She couldn't take the baby and Honey had a tooth coming through, so I was left with the little ones while Jazzy and the twins went off to school.

I laid the baby on a rug on the floor to kick. And I tied Honey into the big armchair and gave her a crust to suck on. Her cheeks were red and shiny and she kept on dribbling and was properly cranky. Every time I went past the chair she waved the crust in the air and flung back her head and drummed her feet in fury and moaned at me because she wanted to be got out.

Shut up, I said. I mean it, Honey. If you stay there like a good girl, I'll fetch you your raggy to suck on.

I got on with clearing the grate and sweeping the floor, Lottie trailing around behind me and picking up brown feathers and bits of fluff and singing to herself and getting in the way as usual. It was a bright blue morning, the skies wide and not yet too hot. I'd opened all the windows to let the cool air in.

At last, James came back from the fields. He leaned in through the window and told me to make him a cup of tea and put a sliver of bang between two slices of bread.

And put some of your ma's ketchup on it, he said. And don't be mean with it. I want a nice big dollop, if you don't mind.

I told him I did mind. I had work to do. I told him he would have to make it himself.

I want you to do it, he said.

I looked at him.

Can't you see I've got to finish all of this before they get back with Frank?

Keeping his elbows on the sill, he fixed me with his eyes.

I don't think you heard me, Eliza. I'm asking you to do it for me.

Why?

Because you're my sweetheart.

I shook my head.

I'm busy, aren't I?

He seemed to freeze then, staring at me. I'd never seen his eyes so cold and hard.

I beg your pardon, he said.

What?

I said I beg your pardon, what did you say?

I shrugged. He fixed me with the same angry stare, but then his whole face softened.

Come on, Princess. It's boiling out there. I'm parched. I'm asking you nicely now.

I sighed.

I can't.

I'm saying please.

Look, James, how many times do I have to say it? I just can't.

Pretty please—

Look here, I said. Can't you just get on and do it for yourself?

He made a furious noise.

All right, he said. That's it. I'm giving you one more chance. A cup of tea and some bread and bang and make it snappy.

I said nothing. The blood was going round and round in my head but still I kept on sweeping.

The dog was on the floor by the chair that Honey was in. Normally she'd keep her eyes on the broom, hoping to get a chance to rush and nip at it as she did with any moving thing. But now I saw her eyes were on James Dix. And she was growling.

James hitched himself up on the sill and leapt in through the window. I gasped and was about to rush at him, but I hadn't even put down the broom before he was grabbing at my wrist and shouting at me. This was enough for the dog. Before I could do anything, she was on him. I saw her teeth, the white part of her eye, her tongue—

He cursed loudly and I heard his boot cracking down on some brittle part of her. I caught my breath as the dog gave a terrible howl and ran to the wall. Honey began to cry.

James was standing in the middle of the room now. His face was steady and he took very small breaths and he did not move and neither did I.

Put that animal out, he said.

I shook my head.

Put her outside now.

I told him I wouldn't.

Do it, Eliza.

I won't, I said.

He stared at me.

All right then, it's your choice. If you won't do it, I'll do it for you.

He grabbed the dog by the neck and dragged her out of the door and into the lane. I watched him do it. She went quite droopy, letting him move her like a sack of potatoes, just hanging there not like herself at all, making no sound nor the smallest attempt to snarl or nip.

I picked up Honey to comfort her. I rubbed my fingers on her hot wet gums and she grizzled and drooled and I kissed her cheek, which smelled of old milk and piss and all the things that babies who haven't had a wash in a good while smell of.

A few more moments passed and then at last James came back in. He stood there looking at me. His face was normal now, but I saw that the muscles in his arms stood out all wiry and hard.

I'm sorry, he said.

I said nothing.

I'm awful sorry, Eliza, really I am. I shouldn't have spoken to you like that. Will you ever forgive me?

I stared at him and I pulled Honey close against me, cupping her warm head in my hand.

Where's the dog? I said.

What?

James, where is she? Where's the dog?

He blinked at me as if he didn't know what I was talking about.

I think she ran off, he said at last.

What do you mean? Ran off where?

He shrugged. I think she went into the fields. I'm sure she'll come back soon. I didn't go after her. I will if you want. Do you want me to go after her, Eliza?

She wakes in the night and she hears them, back again now and playing with the tap in the yard. It's not safe, she thinks, it can't be safe – it's dark, it's cold, so cold, they shouldn't be playing out there on their own at night. Didn't I put them to bed? Did I close the door? Why can't I remember? Is it my fault? How did they get out? I'm dreaming, she thinks. I'm dreaming. I don't know how this happened. It's not my fault. I mustn't think about it. There's nothing I can do – nothing at all that I can do about this.

But the dream goes on. She's fast-flying now, swooping over the dark, dark earth.

And there's a house – here it is, huge, cold, dark, shuttered, dust sheets over all the furniture – and she doesn't know how, but she knows she's left them there, and now she walks from room to room, looking for them, calling to them, walking up and down those vast curving stairs, straining to hear where the little voices are coming from.

And now this water – what is it, the water? All the taps running, doors shutting, lights flickering on and off, the house alive around them, keeping them from her.

She sits up and the voices are calling to her, she can hear them plainly now. Mummy. Mummy!

She turns to Graham. Sleeping on his side, eyes shut, mouth slightly open. Calling to him, shaking him. When he doesn't answer, she flips back the duvet, struggling to get up, before realising that she is underwater, the water flowing over her, through her, pulling her down.

Gasping for breath. Graham. She tries to shake him awake and he groans. Pushing his fingers into her hair.

'You're dreaming,' he says and he holds out his arms to pull her back to bed but she stops him just in time, crying out, grabbing at him, using all her strength to push him off. His whole face – bristle, flesh, the sharp handful of bloodied teeth – coming away in her hand.

She screams. Opens her eyes. Sun under the curtains. Birdsong. Morning.

He brings her tea. Managing the tray awkwardly, newspaper tucked under his arm. Pushing the door open with his foot and then with his elbow.

'What's this?' she says.

'Waiter service. And it's not even your birthday.'

She sees that he's dressed, shaved.

'I didn't hear you get up,' she says.

'I know you didn't.' He drops the newspaper on the bed, looking at her. 'You had a bad night, didn't you?'

'Did I?'

'You were dreaming. You don't remember?'

Mary thinks about the tap in the yard, the old-fashioned wrought-iron pump. She sits up, confused, the taste of their voices still on her.

Graham picks up his jacket.

'Do you think I need this? So warm out there.' Looking out of the window and then back at her. 'Only dreams,' he says. 'Remember that. What's in your head can't hurt you.'

When he's gone, she falls straight back into sleep. This time she doesn't dream of anything. A blank cold comfortless morning sleep and even though once or twice she has the chance to wake up, she doesn't: she keeps herself down there.

She wakes at last to hear the dog whining to go out. An odd, metallic taste in her mouth, a black dryness that wasn't there before. Picking up her watch, she's surprised to see that it's almost midday.

He came and told me he could not find the dog. I stared at him.

What do you mean, you can't find her?

He shrugged and his face was steady and blank.

Just what I said. As simple as that.

But you took her outside!

Then I suppose she must've run off somewhere, in a sulk, I expect.

I said nothing. He watched my face. And I felt all of my blood sinking, heavy and slick, down, down towards my feet.

What? he said. What is it now?

I'm afraid you've done something to her, I said as I tried to hold back the tears. Where is she? Please, James, tell me you haven't done something terrible.

He shrugged, rubbed at his hair.

Well, I won't lie to you, Eliza—

I stared at him.

What? What did you do? Please tell me she's all right?

He shrugged.

I gave her a good hiding, if you really want to know. And so what? She had it coming, that animal did. She's nipped me before now. Honestly, Eliza, that dog has it in for me. There've been times I

138

haven't even told you about – I kept quiet, you see, and all because of Frank being taken so poorly and all that.

I tried not to listen. I didn't care what he had to say about nipping and Frank and the dog having it in for him. Something cold was in my mouth. I swallowed it back.

So where is she now?

What?

The dog. Where is she?

He blinked at me.

I told you. She wouldn't come out.

Come out of where?

I don't know, Eliza. How do I know where she's gone and hid herself? You calm down now and you'll see, she'll turn up.

Downstairs, the dog is standing by the door, gazing at her, its tail moving rapidly from side to side. It jumps up at the door and the sound of its claws on the painted wood makes her teeth hurt. Mary lets it into the garden. Then she puts the kettle on and while she waits for it to boil, she wanders out there too, still in her T-shirt and pyjama bottoms.

She follows the dog down the wide path Graham has mown between the apple trees, around the washing line and on down to where the old fallen tree lies next to the shed. Leaning back against the tree's rough bark, Mary looks at the shed. The roof quite rotten, the walls covered in yellow-green moss and lichen, an almost neon fluorescence that, as she gazes at it now, makes her feel ill—

Still, when it comes, it takes her by surprise, even though the relief is instant. She stares into the bright, spattered grass for a quick moment, before wiping her mouth with her hand.

She calls to the dog and walks back up to the house, where she sits at the rough pine table and, not allowing herself to think about what has just happened, she drinks her tea.

I thought that was it but I must have rattled him because it was just a matter of minutes before he came and found me again.

You mean the whole world to me, Eliza, he said. I want you to know that. Whatever happens, that won't change. You have no idea how it feels to be a flesh-and-blood man like me and want a girl this much.

I looked at him. The blood was pumping through my head in a dark, blind fury.

Want? I said.

Love, he said. Love. You know I mean love.

I thought about this.

Whatever happens? I said. Whatever happens? What does that mean? What exactly do you mean by that?

He shut his eyes. Opened them again.

No one knows what's coming to them, he said. It's a fact, Eliza. There are things over which we have no control.

What things? I said.

What?

What are the things over which you have no control?

He seemed like he was about to answer, but then thought better of it. He held my gaze for a second or two and then he went out into the yard. Moments later I heard him washing himself under the tap.

She is still sitting there when the dog starts growling. Seconds later, Eddie is leaning in through the open window. Dark T-shirt, jacket, sunglasses.

'Is it a bad moment? Be honest, now. Just tell me to go away and I will.'

She holds herself still for a moment and then the dog begins to bark. Grabbing its collar, she goes over and opens the door a couple of inches.

'I'm not even dressed,' she says.

He looks her up and down.

'Quite fetching, I'd say.'

'I'm sorry.' Trying to smile, she lets the door open a little bit more, the dog still pulling and barking. 'I'm actually not that well.'

He blinks at her.

'Well, how about this for a plan? You go up and make yourself decent and we go down the Queen's Head for some lunch? My treat.'

She looks at him.

'Eddie, I'm not well. You asked me if it was a bad moment. Well, I'm afraid it is. It's a bad moment.'

He smiles.

'Food. That's what you need. You two ever go to that place? I bet you don't. It's a bit microwaved. Deborah won't touch it. But if you order carefully, it's actually surprisingly OK.'

Mary stares at him.

'I don't eat lunch.'

'What, never?'

'Not really.'

'Ha! Well, no wonder you don't feel well.'

She looks at him and sighs.

'So it wasn't true?'

'What wasn't true?'

'That if I told you to go away, you would.'

He holds her gaze for a moment then he starts to laugh.

He carries the metal tray out into the almost empty garden of the Queen's Head. A table with a bench and an umbrella, close to the clean grey gravel of the car park. Next to them, a tap with a hose attached, neatly coiled. Beyond that, several hazel wigwams covered in red, pink and mauve sweet peas, the warm air made exquisite by their scent. She remarks on the scent and he asks her what they are.

She turns in surprise. Watching as he takes off his jacket and puts himself in the sun, unable to stop herself noticing his skinny shoulders and forearms.

'Seriously, you don't know? Sweet peas. They're sweet peas.'

'Ah. You know a lot about plants.'

'Only because I used to grow them. Every year, I grew them from seed.'

He looks at her.

'That sounds difficult.'

She smiles, shaking her head.

'It's not. Not at all. It's unbelievably easy.'

'But not any more?'

'What?'

'You don't do it any more?'

Mary glances back at the flowers.

'No.'

He says nothing. She sips her water. Hears the tinny sound of a radio from what must be the pub kitchen.

'Go on,' she says, 'order some lunch.'

He hesitates.

'You really don't want anything?'

She shakes her head. He picks up the laminated menu, turns it over, puts it back down again. She asks him how come he's not working.

He looks away.

'Day off.'

'You have a lot of days off.'

He lifts his head.

'Do you know, I've actually taken three days off this month.'

'Three?'

'Yes, three.'

'Is that a lot?'

'Not when I'm owed three and a half bloody weeks; no, it isn't.'

Mary thinks about this and asks him to explain what it is that he does. He laughs, looking away down the lawn.

'My work? You don't want to know about that.'

'How do you know I don't?'

'All right, are you interested in software? Systems analysis? Implementation quality? Net productivity?' Mary smiles. 'I thought not.' He pulls cigarettes out of his pocket, places them on the table. 'Look, I had a day off, didn't I? I was passing. I suppose it just seemed like a good idea to ask you to lunch.' He hesitates. 'An impulse. There's nothing more complicated about it than that.'

'All right,' she says.

He looks at her, passing his hand across his face.

'And OK, I suppose I just thought you might need someone to talk to.'

'Talk to?'

'You know. A friend.'

Mary takes a breath.

'I don't need friends.'

'Everyone needs friends.'

'I don't. Not any more.' She stares at him, her good mood suddenly gone. 'Seriously, Eddie. I don't need to talk. If you knew how much money and time and bloody energy we've spent on talking—'

She breaks off, seeing his face. Hurt in his eyes. Looking down at the table. Its rough brown slats. The hole for the umbrella. She runs her fingers round the hole.

'I know you're only trying to be kind,' she says.

'Sorry.'

'You don't need to say sorry.'

'All right, but I can see you must be sick of that.'

'Of what?'

'Of people trying to be kind.'

Mary shrugs. Watches a woman in an apron cross the lawn to the bins. Lifting the lid and putting something in. Coming back again, wiping her hands on her apron.

He pulls a cigarette from the pack and gets ready to light it.

'Can I have one of those?' she says.

He stares at her.

'You don't smoke.'

'Watch me.'

He lights it for her, shaking his head, laughing.

'It doesn't work. You look all wrong with a cigarette.'

She blows out smoke.

'I hardly ever smoke these days. I shouldn't. Graham doesn't like it. For God's sake, even I don't like it.'

He looks at her.

'He's a good man.'

'Graham?' She nods, looking down at the cigarette in her hand. 'Yes. Yes, he is.'

'And she's great, that girl of his.'

'She is. Ruby. She's great.'

'Though I suppose it must be hard for you sometimes.'

'Hard?'

He looks at his hands.

'Well – I mean, that he, you know, that he has Ruby.' He lifts his head and looks at her. 'Oh God. I'm so sorry. That came out all wrong.'

'It's all right.'

'It's not all right. I'm really sorry. Forgive me.'

She looks at him.

'What?' he says.

She sighs. 'Can I be honest?'

'Of course you can.'

She takes a breath. Flicks ash to the ground.

'I think you've got the wrong idea about me, that's all. All of this.' She indicates the pub, the garden. 'Well, it's a kind thought, I know you only mean to be kind. But you see, there's no point. I haven't any interest in any of it. You know – friendships, life, talking to people, whatever.'

'You haven't any interest in life?'

'Not really, no.'

She watches his face, listening to her. Watches as he looks off across the lawn, keeping his eyes away from her. He bites his lip. Looks at her.

'I'm very sorry to hear that,' he says.

'I'm not just saying it. You have to believe me.'

He blinks.

'I do believe you.'

They are both silent for a moment. At last Mary takes a breath.

'That kind of loss – what happened to us – people think it makes you angry, and who knows, I've lost track, maybe it does. I honestly don't think I'm the best person to tell if I'm angry any more.' She gazes down again at the cigarette. 'But more than anything, do you know what it does? It just sucks every single little thing that's interesting out of you. All the life. All the stuff you had before, the stuff that made you worth knowing. It sucks it out. It makes you dull.'

Another silence. She waits.

'Do you know,' he says, 'that's the first time in all these weeks or however long that I've heard you refer to it.'

She puts out the cigarette, half-smoked. Takes her glass and lines it up with the slats of the table. Moves it off again.

'Is it?' she says, knowing that it is.

He says nothing. She doesn't know what he's waiting for. She knows he is still looking at her.

'Can I ask you something a bit personal?' he says at last.

She says nothing. Feeling him hesitate.

'What were your daughters' names?'

Her daughters. She looks up at him. Her face flushed and her heart thudding. She licks her lips.

'Ella,' she says. 'And Flo. Ella and Flo.'

'And how old were they?'

She swallows.

'Seven and a half and almost six.'

It was very bad luck that they found the dog when they did. Frank loved that dog and she loved him. He was the keenest of all of us on animals, always good at using ferrets and setting snares for rabbits and trapping sparrows and bullfinches and even knowing how to creep up stealthily and take a pheasant off the branch of a tree with his bare hands.

And he'd chosen the dog from a litter as a puppy and she was his mate, he said, his chum. She hadn't a bad bone in her body, that dog. And though she was in most ways a working dog, and though our father said it was best to keep it that way, still to our Frank she was a dear and beloved pet. He loved her. She could do no wrong in his eyes.

The doctor at Ipswich had looked him over and said the horse had done no real damage and he didn't think he needed an operation. He said that the cough was nothing much and it would soon clear up and Frank would stop being pingly and poorly if he rested up and didn't go climbing too many trees and was properly looked after.

And this news was so cheering that on the way home according to my mother he already reckoned he felt better and managed to eat a whole sugar bun and three sips of the lemonade they'd got him from the fancy grocer's at Needham Market.

So they got home and put the cart in the yard and our mother called out the good news while our father lifted Frank out and carried him round and there she was. She had crept around behind the hedge to die and was half-hidden except that Frank had spied the feathery white ends of her tail sticking out.

Frank was always a calm boy and it wasn't like him to kick up a fuss about anything, but he screamed. He screamed and he kept on screaming. The kiddies had just come in from school and we heard the screams from where we were indoors and we all came running out. We stared at the dog. Her ears were wet and there was blood around her mouth. Flies already crawling over her eyes.

Our father's face was dark.

Does anyone know how this happened?

No one spoke.

Frank had to be put to bed while our father wrapped the dog in a sack and went to dig a hole.

Where are you going to put her? Jazzy said.

I don't know, he said. In the woods, I suppose.

Jazzy said why didn't he bury her on the edge of the orchard under the hawthorn, like the first dead kitten, so that they could keep each other company – and our father said that he would do his best but I knew he was only saying it to keep her quiet.

When they'd gone, Lottie looked at me.

Where's James?

I don't know, I said.

She stamped her foot.

Tell me, Eliza!

I told you, I don't know where he is. Why should I know? And why do you want him anyway?

Lottie made a face. There were tears standing in her eyes and her chin was wobbling. She glanced back at the kitchen door.

I don't want him to creep up on me.

Creep up on you? What do you mean? Why would James do that?

Lottie shook her head.

I don't know.

Tell me, Lottie. What are you talking about?

She gave a little sob.

I don't know.

Are you scared of him? Are you scared of James?

Lottie uncrossed her arms. I saw that there were scratches all over them. She bit her lip.

When our Frank dies, will there be dirt and blood and flies on him?

I gazed at her and my skin began to crawl.

Blood and flies?

Like our dog, will he be like that?

Her chin wobbled again and she began to cry.

Oh Lottie, I said and I pulled her onto my lap. Frank's not going to die. Didn't you hear what Mother said? The doctor said Frank's going to get well very soon. He's just very sad about the dog, that's all.

*

Eddie orders pie. Pie and chips. The chips are a fatty yellow, crinkly at the edges. He pokes a fork into the pastry lid of the pie, lifts it, steam coming out.

'I've forgotten what I ordered now, the chicken or the steak.'

Mary fingers the plastic sachets of ketchup. Thinking of Ella, turning the bottle upside down and banging it the way she'd seen Graham do it. Ketchup spraying across the table, the wall and onto Flo's face, into her hair. Both of them laughing as she pulled her out of the high chair and carried her straight up to the shower.

'Ah,' he prises the pastry lid further off with his fork, 'some kind of steak. Steak and kidney, was it?'

She takes a breath.

'How's Deborah anyway?'

He picks up a pink paper sachet of salt. Shakes it and tears it. Meeting her eyes.

'Deborah? She's fine. She's at the shop today. Helping that woman Ann out. You know, the antiques place in Wickham Market?'

Mary says she doesn't know it.

'And she didn't want to come out to lunch?'

'Lunch?' He sprinkles salt on the chips, pushes the plate towards her. She shakes her head.

'But didn't she want to come?'

'I told you,' he blows on a chip and puts it in his mouth, 'she doesn't rate this place. She's not a pub person.'

'You didn't ask her, did you?'

He doesn't look at her. Picks up a paper napkin to wipe his mouth.

'Why? Does it matter?'

'I don't know.'

'Well, then.'

'I didn't say it didn't.'

He smiles at her, taking another chip.

'You don't need to worry,' he says.

'Worry about what?'

'About anything.'

After the pie, he orders coffee. She says she doesn't want anything, but he insists, so she orders a Diet Coke. He watches her pour it.

'I thought it was just teenagers who drank that stuff.'

'Teenagers?'

'Little blonde punks. Like your friend Lisa.'

She smiles.

'She's not my friend and I don't think she's a punk.'

'Sorry. Am I in the wrong decade?'

'The wrong century, perhaps.'

He laughs.

'And you don't like her?'

'What?'

'Young Lisa. You don't like her?'

'I didn't say that.'

'But you don't?'

'She's OK.'

'Bit of a handful, are they?'

She glances at him.

'What, the girls? Not really. No more than you'd expect, anyway. I don't think Ruby really appreciates being out of London.' She hesitates. 'You were nice to them, the other night. It was good of you. I know Graham appreciated it.'

He stares at his plate for a moment.

'It was no trouble at all. I told you. I thought they were great.'

'All the same. You went out of your way with them.'

'It's easy for me, though, isn't it? I don't have to live with them.'

'Well, neither do I, most of the time.'

He's silent for a moment and she sees that he's watching her.

'Am I allowed to ask you another extremely personal question?'

'I don't really know how to stop you.'

'I'm sorry. I suppose I shouldn't be so nosy. I keep on forgetting to be careful around you.'

'You don't need to be careful. I'm sick of people always being careful.'

'Are you?'

'For a while people were so careful that they avoided us in the street. People who knew us, I mean. People who used to be our friends. They literally crossed the road if they saw us coming.'

He stares at her.

'You're not serious?'

She shrugs.

'Well, it's embarrassing, isn't it?'

'What is?'

'Grief. Having to deal with other people's grief.' He holds the cigarettes out to her again. She shakes her head. 'All right,' she says. 'So what's the question?'

He bites his lip.

'I don't know if I should ask it now.'

'Come on,' she says.

'All right, it's this. Do you think you'd ever try and have more children, you and Graham, I mean?'

'Children?'

She feels herself flush.

'Sorry,' he says. 'You don't have to answer if you don't want.'

'We can't,' she says, cutting him off before he can say anything else. 'Even if we wanted to, I mean.'

He looks at her. She takes another sip of her Coke, puts it back down.

'After Flo was born, he decided – he was actually very definite about it. He went and had a—'

The word. For some reason she can't bring herself to say it. But he nods.

'And you?'

'What about me?'

'Were you definite about it too?'

She looks away over the grass for a moment. Remembering Graham as he was then. So young, so certain, with his knitted pullover and his jeans and his black curly hair. Standing in the doorway of their old bedroom, sun streaming in through the sash window, the curve of her daughter's warm head at her breast.

'I suppose at the time I didn't feel very strongly either way,' she says, suddenly amazed at her long-ago and mysteriously oblivious self.

You're a piece of bad luck, I told James. I knew it from the first moment I saw you. Lottie knows it too. She's afraid of you, you know.

My heart was thudding. I thought he would yell at me but he didn't – he did nothing. Just stayed where he was and looked up from where he was sitting all lamb' n' lettuce on my mother's creaking rocker.

Did you hear me? I said. Are you listening to anything I say?

He said nothing. I saw that he was smiling.

And I tried my best to look at him with a cold heart – tried to take him in as if I was seeing him for the very first time. The hard brightness of that hair. The dirt on his face. The inky snake of the tattoo that so impressed our Frank. I tried to forget all the love things we had said to each other. The sweet shudders that had run down my whole body when he breathed on my neck.

I waited.

Why is everything always my fault? he said at last.

I stared at him.

Everything isn't your fault. But certain things are.

What things?

You know what things. And that thing that we were doing by the way, it's over. I'm not your sweetheart any more, James, and I don't want to be ever again.

For a moment he was still. Then he raised his eyebrows and looked at me. Pulled out his pouch and began to make a cigarette.

And all because I showed a bad animal who was in charge?

The dog wasn't bad. It's you who are bad.

He laughed.

Good, bad, what difference does it make?

I licked my lips. My mouth was dry.

What difference? What are you saying? You know very well that it makes all the difference in the world.

He seemed to think about this, but then he shrugged.

Do what you want, Eliza, it makes no odds.

I don't care if it makes no odds to you. It does to me. I don't like you and I won't blow about with you any more.

He glanced at me then and I was glad. It meant my words had got to him. He took the cigarette out of his mouth and held it.

You're ditching me?

That's right.

He began to laugh.

Stop it, I said.

I can't. I can't stop it. Because that's very funny.

Shut up, I said. It's not funny.

He leaned across to light his cigarette.

It is, he said. And I'll tell you why. It's funny because I haven't even had you yet. You think you can ditch me before you even know what you're ditching?

My heart was banging.

I'll do what I want, I said.

Do anything you like. Go and hide behind the moon if you want. It makes no difference, Eliza. I'll come and get you when I'm ready.

'But what about you?' She asks him later when the sun has moved into the clouds and out again and he's asked for the bill and the air is alive with the sound of bottles being chucked in a bin.

'Me?'

'You and Deborah. Do you think you'll have kids?'

He sighs. 'She's thirty-eight, you know.'

'That's not old. It's not old at all.'

'All right, but she doesn't want to. Never has. Says she's not maternal, whatever that means.' He rubs at his face. 'And I already have one. So I can't really complain, can I?'

Now Mary stares at him.

'You? You have a child?'

He doesn't look at her. Flattening the curling paper on the metal dish. Peering at it for a moment. Taking out his wallet.

'That's right. I do. A boy. He lives with his mother. In London.'

'You were married before?'

He shakes his head. 'Not married. Just someone I – an accident. Not quite a one-night stand, but, well, I didn't know a thing about it till after he was born.'

She tries to think about this. Watching as he places a note on top of the bill. Pushing it to the edge of the table.

'What? You genuinely had no idea?'

He shakes his head. 'She wasn't someone I – we didn't keep in touch. I found out in the end because she sent me a text.'

'A text? You mean just like that? Right after he was born?'

'He was about four months old.'

'My God.'

He smiles.

'It was a shock, I suppose.'

She shifts on the seat.

'But – so, what's his name?'

He frowns. 'My boy? Ollie. He's called Oliver. Oliver Edward John. Her choice.'

'You don't like it?'

'It's OK. It suits him,' he adds, delight briefly flashing over his face.

'And how old is he now?'

'Ten. He's ten. Well – eleven in October.'

Ten, she can't help thinking. Ten springs and summers, ten Christmases. His mother has managed to keep him safe for a whole decade.

'And what's she called?' she says. 'His mother, I mean.'

'Ollie's mother? Tricia. She's called Trish.'

'And does she – is she a good mother?'

He glances at her.

'That's a funny question.'

'It's the only question.'

He hesitates.

'Yes. Yes, I think so. She wanted him, if that's what you're asking. Why?'

She takes a breath.

'I suppose I'm trying to imagine it, that's all. You with a son. I'm quite surprised.'

'Yes, well, that makes two of us.'

'I didn't mean it like that.'

'I know you didn't.'

'And what's he like?'

'Ollie?' Eddie's face brightens again. 'What's he like? Bloody hell. I don't know. Much like any other ten-year-old boy, I suppose. Noisy. Unstoppable. Impossible. A bit out of control sometimes. Won't eat anything but white food. Glued to a screen for much of the day – far too much of it, in my view, not that I have much say.' He sighs. 'I don't get to see him very much.'

'Why not?'

He hesitates.

'Oh look. It's complicated. It's a long story. And before you go jumping to any conclusions, I should warn you I don't come out of it very well.'

Mary thinks about this.

'But if you didn't even know he existed?'

'I guess what his mother would say is, I didn't behave so very well once I did know.'

'Why not?'

He begins to laugh, stops himself.

'Why didn't I behave well? Oh, I don't know. Why do people do things? It's always complicated, isn't it? I was rattled, I suppose.'

'Scared?'

'It wasn't as simple as that.'

'What, then?'

He is silent.

'I don't know,' he says at last. 'You're the only person ever to have asked me that and I suppose I haven't questioned myself too hard about it.' He breaks off, thinking again. 'I didn't think I'd be any good as a father. I didn't really know how to be one. My own father – well, it wasn't like I'd made a choice—'

'You didn't get on with your father?'

He looks at her, his face softening. 'You don't really want to know all this.'

'Yes, I do.'

He takes off his glasses, rubs at his eyes.

'My mother died when I was ten. A car crash. My father – well, I suppose he couldn't cope. He fell apart. These days I imagine he'd have been offered counselling or whatever. But, well, he was grieving and he couldn't cope so he sent me away.'

She stares at him.

'Away? Away where?'

He sighs. Looking at his glasses, turning them over in his hands.

'His sister. My aunt. A widow, she had no kids. I don't know if she ever wanted any. But she was OK, she was willing enough. I suppose she brought me up, really. And then, years later, my father married again and he sent for me.'

'Sent for you?'

He makes a face.

'I know. It sounds like something out of some novel, doesn't it? Yes, he decided he wanted me after all; couldn't live without me, in fact. And so he had me move back in. But his new wife – she was barely even into her twenties, this young girl – she didn't want some spotty, truculent adolescent boy ruining things.' He looks at her. 'Basically, she made my life hell.'

She stares at him.

'How did she do that?'

He blinks.

'Oh God, Mary. Let's not even go there.'

'I'm sorry,' Mary says.

He sighs.

'It's stuff I haven't thought about in years – don't want to think about. And it was all a very long time ago. Water under the bridge and all that.'

Mary thinks about this.

'And then what?'

'I ran away. Left home, I suppose you'd call it. Well, I was old enough, just about.'

'How old?'

'Seventeen. Just. I lived on the streets for a while.'

'On the streets? But that's terrible.' She takes a breath. Unable to imagine it. 'But what about your aunt?'

'What about her?'

'She didn't want you to come back?'

'Who knows. I never heard from her. In fact, I never saw her again. I don't know. Maybe she imagined I was still with my father. I suppose at that age you don't really think about these things. I was OK, though. I got a place at a hostel. I worked in bars and so on. I was even on the bins for a time—'

'A bin man?'

He makes a face.

'I can tell you it wasn't the worst job I ever did.'

'What was the worst?'

'Yarden's fish factory, down by the docks. Disgusting. Wet and cold, the scales stuck inside your fingernails, you could never get the smell off. Far worse than the dirt of the bins—' He breaks off, smiling at her. 'Anyway, all of this, I suppose it explains a lot about me, doesn't it?'

The sun has moved around the garden and is in Mary's face. She turns her chair, shields her eyes, trying to see him.

'Why? What does it explain?'

'I don't know. What I'm like, I suppose. Why I'm such a waste of space.'

She stares at him.

'What do you mean you're a waste of space? That's a terrible thing to say about yourself.'

He sighs.

'I'm sure it's how Deborah sees me.'

Mary shakes her head.

'Deborah loves you.'

'Does she?'

'Oh, come on. It's obvious that she does.'

'Is it?'

For a moment, Mary just stares at him.

'I can't imagine Deborah ever thinking anyone was a waste of space,' she says at last.

He smiles.

'Well, it's what I'd think if I were her. I'm aimless, aren't I? A drifter.'

'A drifter? What's that supposed to mean? I don't see you like that at all.'

'You don't? You don't think I'm unreliable and aimless and – well, a complete tosser in many ways?'

Mary sits up in her chair.

'Eddie, it's not true. You're not aimless at all. Why are you so hard on yourself? You have a job, for God's sake, a wife, you have a home . . .'

He shakes his head.

'You don't know the truth, Mary. It's not the way it looks. I was always like this, you know, always. I can't really even blame my mother. Even as a young child, I could never settle.'

'Settle to what?'

'I don't know. My concentration span, it was just – zilch.'

'Well, that was hardly your fault—'

'And afterwards, long after I'd left my aunt's, for a long time I did just that. I drifted. From job to job. Even from woman to woman.'

'You had a lot of women?'

He smiles.

'You find that hard to imagine?'

Mary shakes her head, even though she does.

'This whole story, all of it, it sounds so incredible.'

His face tightens.

'It's not a story.'

'I didn't mean it like that.'

'I know you didn't.'

He sighs. Taps his fingers on the edge of the table.

'I'm not sure I should have told you any of it, anyway,' he says.

'It's all right. I promise you it won't go any further.'

'It's not that. It's just – I'm afraid you'll never be able to think well of me again.'

'Don't be silly. This doesn't change anything. In fact, I feel very sorry to think of everything you've been through.'

'I don't want to be pitied.'

'I don't pity you. I'm sad for you. It's not the same at all.'

He lifts his head, looks at her.

'You still like me?'

'For goodness' sake, Eddie. Of course I do.'

'You promise? You're not just saying it?'

Mary laughs, realising that he's playing with her. She looks away.

'But what about now?' she says at last.

'What about it?'

'Your life now. Isn't that what matters?'

'There's only one now I'm interested in and that's sitting here at this moment in this garden with you.'

Mary hesitates, avoiding his gaze.

'But – are you saying you're not happy?'

He sighs.

'I don't know about happy. I suppose I think of myself as pretty lucky, the way things have worked out. But . . .' She watches as he takes off his glasses again, pinches at the space between his eyes, puts them back on. 'Well, there's always some fall-out, isn't there?'

'Is there?'

'I don't get to be with my kid, do I?' He says nothing for a moment and neither does Mary. Both of them sitting there, not speaking. At last he looks at her. 'Once I knew about him, that was it. It was astonishing, how everything changed. It's not that I'm surprised that I love him—'

'Love him?' Mary feels the blood rise in her cheeks. 'Of course you love him.'

'All right, but that it would take up so much of my head, that I would have no choice, that it would be so overwhelming – well, I suppose I never expected that.'

Mary says nothing. Under the table, she knits her hands together. Watching the faint movement of his face as he looks out across the garden, to the fields, the wide sweep of the sky.

The waitress comes, picks up the bill and the money, walks away. He watches her go.

'Every day I feel the loss of him, you know. Every single day— ' He stops, breaking off suddenly and looking at her. 'Oh God, Mary, I'm sorry.'

He puts a hand on her arm. Gives her the one unused paper napkin. She stares at it for a moment, then she puts it to her eyes. She hadn't even known she was crying.

For a moment he just sits there. Then, when she doesn't do anything, he leans forward and touches her hand with his and, when she doesn't pull away, he covers it, puts his whole hand on hers and he leaves it there.

6

Frank died. They thought he was better but he wasn't better. He had a fever and a prickling scarlet rash and the rash got worse in the night and the first doctor was called back and this time he said the Ipswich doctor had got it all wrong. It wasn't because of the horse kicking him or the whooping cough but a bad infection that had got inside his bones and there was nothing to be done.

My mother wept. She'd lost the two or three babies after I was born, but we'd never known them so it didn't matter. And then after that she'd had a lucky run of it and all her children had stayed sturdy and bonny and alive.

Until now.

I don't believe it, my father said after the doctor had packed up and gone. He could be wrong. He's had it wrong before. Remember poor old Mrs Hancy, how he had them ordering up her coffin, but she went along quite well for another two years?

My mother said nothing.

For a while Frank seemed peaceful. His breath went in and out just as if he was having any normal kind of sleep. I began to wonder if my father might be right and he'd recover. But then, as the dawn broke and morning sunshine flooded the room, he seemed to change. His face looked like a stranger's face and his breath came harder and louder and he looked like he was fighting some startling and terrible presence in the room that none of us could see.

My mother covered her face with her hands.

No, she said. No.

Frank's eyes rolled back in his head as if he was just playing a joke on us and then he stopped breathing.

No! my mother screamed.

I stared at him. He still looked like my brother and not at all like a dead person. He looked like he'd just forgotten to take another breath. I found I was holding my own breath, waiting for him to do it.

Is he all right? I said at last.

My father had been swearing and cursing but now I saw that he was crying as well. There was a string of nose-blow hanging from his face. He lifted Frank up a bit and held him and kissed him and rubbed at his chest.

Is that it? my mother sobbed. Is that it? Are you telling me he's gone?

My father said nothing. He lowered Frank back down onto the bed. Upstairs the baby started crying but my mother ignored it. She bit down hard on her clenched-up fist. Her eyes were closed tight and there was a sound happening right in her throat but it didn't seem to want to come out.

I looked at Frank again. It still seemed to me that he might change his mind and take another breath, but he didn't. The more I watched, the more he stayed there just exactly as he was, eyes and mouth open, staring at the foot of the bed.

My father reached out and put his fingers on his eyes to shut them.

He told me to sit with him while he went to fetch the undertaker and my mother went up to the baby. He said I shouldn't touch him and at first I didn't mind because I didn't want to. But then as I sat there with the morning noises and normal sunshine going on outside, my courage began to come back to me. It was only our Frank, after all. Also I was curious to know what a dead person felt like. I stretched out a hand and put a finger on his poor, bare arm.

Hello, Frank, I whispered.

I put one finger on him very lightly and then I put another. He wasn't even cold, but he was hard as dead meat and for a moment the warm firmness of him made me want to heave. I took my hand off and sat there for a moment, taking little breaths and waiting for the feeling to pass.

My father came back in.

He said he'd told James and sent him off to do the animals. He said we weren't telling the kiddies yet, but I was to wake them and make them get dressed and send them into the orchard to play while the undertaker came.

Why? said Charlie when I went up there.

Yes, why? Minnie said.

Because Father says so, that's why.

But what's the reason? Jazzy demanded, picking up her kitten and trying to make it stay in her apron pocket. Why does he want us out of the house? You can't just say that and not tell us the reason.

I know the reason, Lottie said.

You don't know anything, Jazzy told her, struggling with the kitten as it mewed and scuffled to get out. You don't even know how to tie up your own shoe, you little twot.

Lottie looked at me with hard black eyes.

Is it because of Frank?

What about him? Jazzy said.

I looked at Lottie.

We'll talk about it later, I said.

The undertaker came. He was a horrible man. He laid Frank out on the kitchen table because he said he needed a steady surface to work on. The table still had some grease and crumbs on it, so I got a cloth and wiped them away. I didn't think it right that Lottie's mess left over from breakfast should be all over Frank.

The undertaker washed him and cut his hair which didn't need cutting, and he put him in the good Sunday clothes my mother had given him, twisting his poor arms back and forwards a bit too roughly to get them in the sleeves and not really caring that much what he did to him. Then when he'd finished he put the coffin next to Frank on the kitchen table and lifted him into it with our father's help.

Father went upstairs to comfort my mother. They asked if she wanted to see him but she said she didn't and that she would not come down till the man was gone.

The undertaker asked to use the privy then, so I had to take him out the back and show him where it was. He smiled at me a bit too hard and said would I like to wait to escort him back after he'd used it?

No thanks, I said.

And he stood there still looking at me and not going in the privy and saying what a pretty young girl I was, how sweet and fresh-faced, and was I courting any lads yet?

I told him that was none of his business. And he stared at me then and said I had a very overly sharp tongue for someone whose little brother had just died and I ought to have a bit more respect.

Respect for what? I said.

Respect for the dead.

I do respect the dead, I told him. It's the living I don't respect.

He smiled at me as if this was somehow a compliment to himself, and then he turned and went into the privy. I went back inside and looked at poor Frank who lay there in the coffin on the kitchen table not really looking that dead but for all the world as if he might be about to spring to life and chase the chickens around the yard as usual.

James came in. He had on his hat that he wore in the fields, but he took it off and held it to his chest as he looked at Frank.

Don't do that, I said. I mean it. I don't want you here. Just please go away.

He held up his hands.

I only came to look at him.

I don't want you looking at him. You have no right. You broke his heart. It was the last thing that ever happened in his life, the killing of the dog, and the worst thing too.

James looked at me carefully.

I wish you'd stop saying that I killed the dog, Eliza. When you know perfectly well I had nothing to do with it.

I shook my head and pressed my lips together. I wondered where he had learned it from, the knack of always making you feel that you were the one whose mind had come undone.

Go away, I said.

James did not move. His eyes still on poor Frank.

I did nothing to the dog. The dog ran off. You know I would have fetched her – in fact, I offered to fetch her back but you said not to. Surely you remember that, Eliza, that you told me not to?

The undertaker came back in, still doing up the flap of his breeches. He glanced at James as if he wondered who he was and then he said he was about to put the lid on and I should try again to fetch my mother.

She won't want to come, I said.

The undertaker coughed. The cough went on for a long time and you could hear all the various wet and dry parts of it.

Well, tell her it's her last chance to see him before I screw him down, he said, taking out a handkerchief and spitting out a quick lump of phlegm before he winked at me.

I did as he said and went and told her, but my mother would not look at me and just said I should go and see how the kiddies were doing.

I'll go, James said.

No, I said. I'll do it.

And I walked out of the house, down the steps and through the long wavy grass and down into the orchard. The morning was very still and light and hot. There was no sign of the kiddies anywhere and I couldn't hear them shouting either. For a moment I was alarmed. I hoped they hadn't gone into the lane or off into the fields, which they weren't allowed to do by themselves.

But when I got down to the bottom of the orchard, there they all were sitting in a row on the lightning tree, scowling and fighting and kicking their heels. Charlie was pinching Minnie who was half-laughing and half-crying. Honey was almost asleep, squeezed in between her and Lottie, who was sucking her thumb and in a world of her own. And Jazzy was looking properly delighted with herself and smoking a cigarette. As I watched she blew three perfect rings of smoke, a trick, I realised with a quick clench of my heart, that she could only have learned from James Dix.

As soon as Graham's got in the door, while she's simmering the stock for the risotto, Mary asks him to guess who she went to the pub with.

He looks at her.

'The pub? You went to the pub?'

She nods. Watching as he puts his bag down on the chair, looking through to find his glasses and the paper.

'Why?' he says. 'Who with?'

She turns back to the stove.

'You have to guess.'

He sits down slowly in a chair with the paper. Puts on his glasses and gazes at her over the top of them.

'Seriously, I've no idea who you went with.'

'Come on.'

'No, I give up.'

'All right. Eddie.'

'Eddie?' He holds the paper to one side and takes off his glasses. 'You had lunch with Eddie?'

She bangs the wooden spoon on the side of the pan.

'He had lunch. I didn't.'

A quick silence as he looks at her.

'You should have eaten.'

'I wasn't hungry.'

'You're never hungry.'

Mary hesitates.

'I don't get hungry till the evenings,' she says, realising only as she says it that she often, now, feels sick in the mornings.

She sees that Graham is gazing at her. Rubbing his eyes. 'How did that come about, then?'

'What?'

'Lunch with Eddie.'

'I don't know. He just knocked on the door and asked me.'

'He wasn't at work?'

'He had a day off. He's owed a lot of time.'

'Time?'

'Holiday or something. That's what he said.'

Graham looks at her.

'I wish someone owed me a lot of time.'

But later, much later, when they've eaten and cleared up and the dishwasher is thundering in the background and they are both on the sofa ready for the news, she tells him the rest. The part about the child. The boy called Oliver and the woman called Trish.

'Well, aren't you surprised?' she says, when all he does is shrug and keep his eyes on the screen.

'Surprised at what?'

'At what I just told you. The whole thing. Doesn't it surprise you?'

He yawns.

'I don't know. Not especially. Why should it?'

Mary moves closer to him. Edging across the cushions until she can put her bare legs over his trousered ones. Watching the side of his face.

'What, so you think of him as that kind of person?'

'What kind of person?'

'Someone with this whole other life going on elsewhere?'

He places a hand on her knee.

'Hardly a whole other life.'

'But a secret child?'

'Not so secret if he told you about it. And from what you're saying, it's just some poor woman he got up the duff.'

'It wasn't his fault.'

'Hmm.'

'What's that supposed to mean?'

He keeps his face steady.

'Just – I don't know – maybe he should have been more careful.'

Mary stares at him.

'You don't really think that.'

Graham says nothing, keeping his eyes on the news. She pulls her legs off him. He turns and looks at her.

'What? Now I'm supposed to agree with every little thing you say?'

She hesitates.

'I don't know why you aren't more surprised. I was so surprised.'

He looks at her.

'All right. I'm surprised. Happy now?'

She ignores him.

'It must be very odd for Deborah,' she says, even though it's the first time that Deborah's part in it has occurred to her.

The weather comes on and Graham zaps through the channels to find something else. Brushing her knee with his fingers, then moving his hand up and holding her thigh. A firm, teasing grip that might, in the old days, have signalled the beginning of sex.

'He's had a hard time, you know,' Mary says.

'Who has?'

'Eddie. He had a terrible childhood.'

'That's what he told you, is it?'

164

'What?' she says. 'Suddenly you don't believe a thing he says? I thought you liked Eddie?'

'I do like him.'

'Then why are you suddenly being so—'

Graham smiles. Looking at her.

'What am I being?'

'I don't know. So grudging about everything.'

He laughs. Mary watches him. The side of his face. The little lines around his eyes that twitch when he's tired. The upper lip with its faintly girlish pout, which, many years ago, first attracted her to him and which in some ineluctable and agonising way will always make her think of Ella.

'Come here,' she says.

'What?'

'I said come here.'

When he doesn't move, she reaches over and takes the remote from his hand, turning off the TV. Moving herself onto him, astride him. Feeling beneath her the tired trousers, the worn linen shirt, their colours and textures so familiar as to have almost become a part of him.

Blindly, eyes half-closed, he reaches up and touches her. A finger on her breast, then her waist – once half a stone too soft, now taut, defined by grief.

As she feels the first stirrings of something, he looks up at her.

'What's all this, then?'

His face is kind. Baffled. A stranger's face.

She says nothing. She bends and kisses him. He lets her do it. He doesn't say anything. Doesn't do anything. She can't decide if it matters or not. She doesn't know what it is that she wants him to do.

Upstairs, a door bangs shut. Mary stops, her hands still on him.

'What was that?'

'What was what?'

'Upstairs. You didn't hear it?'

Graham looks at her.

'What did you think you heard?'

Mary strains, still listening.

'I don't know,' she says. 'It sounded like a door. Ruby's room, or—'

'Well, it couldn't be.'

'I know.'

Graham reaches up to her, his hands searching her face, his thumb on her lip.

'Hey. Don't stop. I was enjoying that.'

'Were you?'

Mary hesitates, still listening to the house.

'Yes,' he says. 'I was.'

That night, for the first time in a very long time, she dreams of Ella. Ella undressed and ready for a bath. Water crashing from the taps in the bathroom across the landing. Ella, naked and happily clamped on her hip, the sensation of that small body against hers, its springy weight, its solid, curving warmth. The dream is long, unhurried. It seems to go on and on. More than once she lets her lips drift over that downy hair, breathing it in, staying there, leaving herself there, nowhere else she'd rather be.

In fact, the sensation of not having to hurry, of having time, is so intense that when she wakes she does not weep, but just lies there. Afraid to move or even breathe in case she dislodges the feeling that is washing over her. A feeling that she had imagined was lost to her for ever. Not loss or grief or even anger. Just, quite simply, love.

I was very angry with James and I told him so. I told him he should not have given Jazzy a cigarette.

Why not?

Because she's too young.

What's it to you, Eliza? Isn't it her business what she does?

She's a child, I said. She's ten years old. She doesn't know a single thing about anything.

He smiled.

Ah, well, but she probably knows a lot more than you think.

Don't speak about her like that.

Like what?

I don't know.

You don't know?

I just don't like the way you talk about her, that's all.

James stared at me for a moment and I stared back. I tried hard to think what it was that I didn't like. A lot of my energy was having to go into hating him and a part of me thought of how much easier it would be just to give in and beg him to slide his hand inside my dress so I could feel his fingers on the keen and shivery point of my breast the way I used to. He gave me a look then as if he could see right inside my head.

Just because you're afraid to try new things, he said.

What? What's that meant to mean?

He said nothing, just looked at me hard and then laughed again.

You're an innocent, Eliza. Even more than all those kiddies, I'm telling you. You've no idea. It's you who's the child. You're the one who knows nothing at all.

I looked at him. He was still smiling.

It's all right, he said. Don't worry about it. It's why I like you. It's why I like you best of all of them. It's why you're my girl.

I'm not your girl.

Whatever you say.

Frank was buried in the evening as the light was going and the birds were calling and the cows were coming home.

My mother didn't go and the little ones weren't allowed. It was just my father and Jazzy and me. I don't know if James would have cared to be there or not, but my father needed him to bring the cows in. He told my father that afterwards he would look in on my mother and take her a cup of tea.

I looked in the hole before they put him in. Poor Frank. I didn't like to think of him going down into that deep and murky darkness all alone. I wished the dog could have gone in with him, but my father had already put her in the woods.

Afterwards, my father would not speak. His face was white and his hands trembled and he would not say a word to anyone. We went home and he pulled up a chair in the kitchen and sat with his head in his hands. I asked him if he wanted a cup of tea and he said he didn't, he said he didn't want anything. He said I didn't need to sit with him either, but I was afraid to leave him there all alone. So I sat and watched the back of his head and I saw him wipe his face a couple of times. After that he had a smoke and then I think he went up to bed and there I was, left alone with my thoughts.

At last Jazzy came in. I saw that she'd been crying. I felt sorry for her and I put out my hand and she came over and took it, trying to plait my fingers as she liked to do, twisting them over and over each other, till I said ouch and pulled my hand away.

Jazzy looked at me. Her hair was in rats' tails and the tears had made her face dirty. She had on her oldest, most torn chemise. She was fidgeting and scratching at the tops of her legs.

I've got boobies, she said. Look.

And she put her two hands in the place where anyone could see there was only little girl's hard flatness.

Don't be silly, Jazz, I said. Of course you haven't. What are you saying that for?

But I have. Look. They're growing, aren't they, Eliza?

She bunched them up again with her hands, trying her best to make something of them. I didn't know what she was on about.

They're not growing, I said. Not yet. You're too young.

She gazed at me.

But I'm a woman, aren't I? she said.

I shook my head.

You're ten years old. You're nowhere near being a woman.

But I am. James Dix said I am.

What do you mean, James said you are? What's James been saying?

She bit her lip.

He said I wasn't to tell you.

Wasn't to tell me what?

Nothing, she said, and the look on her face was hard and tight and ugly.

At that moment there was a knock on the door, but before either of us could go to it, it opened and Phoebe Harkiss came in. She had an armful of flowers. She stood there for a moment, looking at us both.

From my ma, she said.

It's a bit late for flowers, I said.

I know. I was supposed to bring them earlier.

I did not move. I could not be bothered with Phoebe Harkiss right now.

All right, I said. You can put them in the sink.

Phoebe looked at me for a moment, then she went over and put them there, but after she'd done it she did not seem to want to go. She stood there looking at both of us with a smirk on her face.

So is it true? she said.

Is what true?

About your ma.

What about her?

She rolled her eyes and glanced at a corner of the room.

That she's up the spout again?

I lifted my head and stared at her.

She's not! Jazzy said.

Phoebe smiled, enjoying our surprise. Her face splattered with freckles and the eyes so lacking in colour they made you feel queasy.

Our ma almost died from the last one, I said. She's not having another one as long as she lives.

Phoebe cast her eyes over me.

It's not what they're saying in the village.

What are they saying in the village? Jazzy said.

Phoebe sighed. She looked over at where the flowers were and she made a worried, fussing face that anyone could see she'd just copied from women in the village.

I don't want to upset you, she said.

Either tell us at once or shut up about it, I said.

She shrugged.

Well, I suppose you ought to ask James about it.

Jazzy stared at her.

Why would we want to ask him?

Phoebe looked at her for a long moment and then, as if she couldn't contain it any longer, she laughed.

June. The weather continues hot and dry. Deciding at last to tackle the garden, they drive off together to a garden centre. About nine miles down the A12, three or four roundabouts and a turning off to the left. Very well signposted, Deborah said it was.

Mary's made a list of what they need. Compost, mulch. A long hose on a reel to fix to the tap in the yard. Some good-quality secateurs. A rake. Perhaps a plant or two.

'We could even see if there's any decent garden furniture,' Graham says as they drive around looking for a space in the busy, dusty car park.

They take a trolley, pushing it off past the wood and laminate and paint aisles, past the barbeques and parasols and lawnmowers. Then they stand together out in the dappled sunshine of the gardening section, wiping crumbs of black compost off on their jeans, trying to decide if it's crazy to plant a climber – honeysuckle or clematis – in the middle of what some are saying might turn out to be a heatwave.

'We'll just have to be very good about watering it,' Mary says. She catches him smiling at her.

'What?'

'Just – it's nice. To hear you talking like that.'

They decide on a jasmine and a clematis, as well as some small shrubs and a rose with blooms that are neither pink nor gold but somehow in between.

They spend at least ten minutes choosing a proper hose with all the different, complicated attachments. And then they look briefly at tables and chairs, but agree that none of them are very nice.

'We should ask Deborah,' Graham says.

'Why Deborah?'

'She knows all those antiques people. She'll know where we can get something old.'

Mary thinks about this.

'Old chairs are never really all that comfortable,' she says.

'All right, but a table? I don't know what you call comfortable. Maybe we should think about getting another swing seat.'

She stares at him.

'A swing seat?'

'Like the one we used to have. Didn't you used to have a thing about swing seats?'

A sudden memory of their old, green and white striped swing seat flying high. Small bare feet sticking out of it. The vivid lawn, homemade ice-lollies, the spray of the sprinkler. Laughter—

'Seeds,' she says. 'We need seeds.'

She picks out rocket, parsley, basil, coriander, three or four types of salad and pak choi.

'Pak choi? Do we grow pak choi?'

'Never. That's why I'm getting it.'

He leans over and pulls her to him, kisses her hair. She feels his arms around her.

'I don't think I'd want another swing seat,' she says.

'I know,' he says. 'I'm sorry. I wasn't thinking. I shouldn't have said it. I know that.'

They decide that he'll join the long queue to pay while she goes and gets the car. Out there in the car park, she walks fast, keeping her eyes fixed on the horizon. Wisps of clouds in a bluest of blue skies. Greyish blur of woodland sloping towards the road.

She gets into the car. Her face smacked by the sudden thick heat inside. Rolling down the windows, putting the key in, she drives it slowly round, avoiding the people pushing trolleys, waiting for a space to pull in, getting as close to the entrance as she can.

She turns off the engine then and waits, hands loose in her lap, looking out for him.

It's only as she sees him coming with the trolley, frowning a little as he struggles to get it down the ramp, that she understands what is happening to her. She grabs the box of tissues off the back seat just in time. Wipes at her face and thrusts the balled-up tissue into her bag moments before he pulls open the door.

'OK?' His hands are on the trolley as he smiles down at her, wanting the key to the boot.

'Yes,' she tells him, smiling back and realising it's not a lie.

I was lying in my bed when he came to me. Half-asleep in the early-morning shadows, my eyes barely managing to open, I saw the door move – hot fear and surprise slicing through me – but before I could even cry out, he was right there beside me, his weight pinning the sheets, his hand on my mouth.

Swear to me you won't cry out, he whispered. Swear it?

I tried to nod, but he was crushing me so hard I could not gasp or speak or breathe, let alone move my head. Slowly, he removed the hand. I licked my lips. And was about to ask him what he thought he was doing when he gave a sigh and put his head in his hands.

I'm all undone, he said.

What?

You heard me. All night, I've just lain there in the barn, weeping and sobbing like a little child. I came to tell you I can't do it any more, Eliza. I thought I could do it but I can't. I just love you far too much. I'll be whatever you want me to be. Anything you want, anything you ask, I'll do it. I fall asleep thinking of you and I wake up thinking of you. The taste of you is in my mouth, on my tongue, in my heart, I don't care what you say, everything around me – the sky, the fields, the birds, even the damnable, dratted cows, Eliza – when I look at them, all I can think about is you.

I gazed at him. I felt quite afraid. I did not think he had ever said so many words all together in all the time I had known him. I was about to try to answer him, but he threw me a look of such unbearable gentleness then, that I felt a pain somewhere deep inside me, I wasn't sure where.

I love you, he said. It's as simple as that.

I took a breath and shut my eyes. I honestly did not know if I wanted to be loved as much as all that. But something about the feeling of him right there on my bed, my limbs warm beneath the weight of him, had begun to work its spell.

I don't know what to say, I said.

His eyes were on me, drinking me up.

Don't say anything. There's nothing to say. Just please if you have any pity left in you, forgive me, Eliza.

Forgive you for what?

For everything. For what I have done, what I'm doing – for what I will do.

As he spoke, he laid a hand on my knee under the sheets and something jumped inside me. It ought to have been fear but it wasn't, it was pleasure. I was melting. My soft and liquid self returning.

What will you do? I whispered.

With so much care you would think I was made of glass, he touched his fingers to my lips. I smelled straw and dung and fresh air – the cold metal tang of farm machinery.

Hush, he said. That's enough. I've already said too much.

He stood up. Proud and tall and reckless and so out of place, standing there by the washstand in my little room. I felt myself shaking all over. And I couldn't help it – I didn't care any more if it meant he had won – I reached out my hand to him.

Stay—

He looked at me for a moment and you could see his mind working. As if he was weighing something up. He almost smiled at me and he seemed about to touch me but he checked himself.

No, he said. I mustn't. That's it, Eliza. I'm going now.

Driving home, she looks at her phone and sees four missed calls from Eddie.

'Four?' says Graham, reaching for his sunglasses. 'Four? Why on earth would Eddie call you four times?'

'I don't know,' she says. 'I've honestly no idea. He seems to have decided that we're friends or something.'

Graham laughs.

'Well, you've no one to blame but yourself for that.'

'What? Why is it my fault?'

'You've been leading him on, haven't you? All these secret pub lunches.'

'It was only one, and it wasn't secret.'

'All these confessions about his past, then.'

Mary looks at the phone in her hand.

'It's not like that.'

'I'm only joking.'

'All right.'

'What is it like, then?' he asks her after a moment or two.

'I don't know. I honestly don't know.'

Graham slows as he comes to the roundabout. Neither of them speaking. The peaty smell of warm soil and plants and garden centre in the car.

'Well, hadn't you better call him?' he says. 'Find out what he wants?'

He flicks on the indicator.

'Later,' she says. 'I'll do it later.' She turns the phone off and puts it in her bag.

She gazes out at the horizon, huge sky, sun bending through the windscreen, moving over Graham's bare arms.

'I find him quite strange to deal with actually,' she says at last.

'What – Eddie? Why? What's strange about him?'

'I don't know. All he ever seems to want to do is talk.'

'To you, you mean?'

'I suppose so. Yes.'

'Nothing wrong with talking, is there?'

Mary says nothing.

'You think he's lonely?' he asks her after a few more moments have passed.

'Lonely?' Mary feels her face heat up. 'Why would he be lonely?'

'I don't know. I don't know anything about him. But men get lonely, don't they?'

She looks at him briefly, then back out of the window.

'Do they?'

'Yes, they do.'

She thinks about this.

'So do women.'

'You're right. So do women. Everyone gets lonely sometimes.'

Mary watches as he fiddles with the radio, turning the knob till he finds music.

'I do like Deborah, though,' he says. 'Don't you?'

'Yes,' she says. 'Yes, I do.'

She doesn't call Eddie and when he doesn't try her again, she's relieved. Briefly, she rehearses some kind of a story to herself, about her phone being out of charge or on the blink or the signal coming and going, something like that. But then in the end she forgets all about it and does nothing at all.

And next day, wandering around the garden in the dewy cool of the morning – setting up the hose, trying with difficulty to tighten the fixing on the old metal tap so that water doesn't come spurting out from underneath, deciding where the clematis should go – she at first ignores the feeling. Or perhaps she doesn't even have to ignore it. She simply does not pick it up, lodged as it is deep within a web of sensations that she has, she supposes, learned to endure.

The lump of grief that never leaves her throat. The hot, shocked space behind her eyes. The tightness in her chest which the bereavement counsellor told her was anger, but which mostly feels more like astonishment or panic or even, on those rare, optimistic days, the possibility of her own eventual death.

When it happened – all through that time when they were missing and then, in the worst possible, most unimaginable way, weren't missing any more and it could not be changed, they could not ever be brought back – people told her how courageous she was. Him too, but especially her. As if a mother's courage was somehow harder won than that of a father.

But she was not courageous. They both know what happened. They know that, unlike him, she let rip and succumbed, giving in to the very worst part of herself. Even though they do not discuss it now, have never discussed it, in fact, they both know that she damaged things. Biting and clawing at fabrics, objects. Making holes. Kicking. Scratching. Damaged herself, too. Or wanted to, anyway. She banged her head against the bedroom wall till a vivid bruise bloomed there. She pulled her hair out. One time – a time she can barely allow herself to think of now – she struck a match and tried to set fire to her own clothes.

They offered her everything, everything was offered. There really was no shortage of offers of help. Talking. God. Flowers. Medication. Healing. A clairvoyant got in touch and offered to take her straight to them, straight to the precise place where they were. And that would have been very tempting, to be taken to her girls, whatever state they were in by then, to know that she had beaten the police to it and found them, that she could take them in her arms and hold them against her, no more searching for them, her babies.

Except that when, more than two weeks later, the chance to see them finally did come, she was unable to find whatever it took (she would not allow herself to believe it was courage) and she refused it, that last chance to be in the same room as what was left of her own children, and say goodbye.

They'd been warned, when they were told that both bodies would be partially covered, that they would be protected from the worst, that there was in fact not much left. Not even a hand you could properly hold, the liaison officer had said, suddenly unable to look them in the eye.

Not even a hand? For a quick moment Mary saw her girls' fingers as they used to be, warm, sticky, covered in chocolate or Marmite or poster paint. Fingers that she would grab and wipe with a warm flannel, getting the cloth down between the fingers even though they would wriggle and laugh and try to pull away. Not even a hand. They won't get me anywhere near that place, she told Graham.

They told her that whatever she decided was fine. But that she should think very carefully. It wasn't just about now. There was the future to think of, too. They found that, whatever they imagined they felt at the time, people frequently changed their minds later, wishing after all that they'd done it, that they'd taken one final chance to say goodbye.

Graham said he could not decide which was the bigger nightmare, going or not going. He said that he did not want to let his daughters down. But he admitted that he was afraid. He wept. The decision woke him up at night. It made him shake and sweat. In the end he said that he would go.

He was gone for more than four hours.

When he came back he poured himself a large Scotch – a drink that Mary had never in her whole life seen him drink – then he sat very still without speaking for a long time. After that, still without speaking, he made supper. She could not eat the supper. Neither could he. She watched him not eating it, unable to speak to him, afraid to ask him what he'd seen, afraid of what pictures he might now have in his head, loathing herself for not being able to share them with him.

And it was odd that when, however many weeks later, she saw the small, ginger-faced man sitting there in the dock, pulling down his shirt cuffs and adjusting his clothes and making himself comfortable like that, that is what she found herself thinking of. Not the terribleness of all those days of waiting. Not the loss – the small, beloved faces they would never see again, the warm hands they would never again hold. Not even the chill, raw torment of what they daily had to think, guess, imagine.

No, when she saw him in the dock that day, all she could think of was Graham's face that night. His empty face, the gulf that had widened between them – that would go on widening – and the two sad plates of food that she had scraped into the bin.

But this feeling. It stops her at last, standing there in the middle of the half-mown lawn, trowel in hand, she is unable to ignore it any longer.

She watches a Red Admiral butterfly as it alights on a half-dead rose. The dusty black torso. The dark legs. The quivering wings, opening and closing – something about the movement sickening her.

Dropping the trowel, she sits on the broken brick wall close to the old apple store, wrists on knees, waiting. What is it, this feeling, as if her insides are tipping up? Is she going to vomit again? She doesn't know. She feels oddly patient, alert, curious almost. She does not vomit. Holding herself very still, she continues to wait.

The butterfly flies off at last, jerking and lifting through the blue morning air. She can't watch it. Looking down, still waiting for the sick feeling to pass, she squeezes her eyes shut for a moment or two: a brief blackness and dizziness.

And then she looks up.

A sudden crowd of small children right there on the old fallen tree. Legs swinging, faces shadowy and smudged, big and small children, the smallest just a baby, odd, dull clothes, messy hair, pigtails and boots, all of them squeezed up together in a row, one of them she is certain, smoking a cigarette—

It's not possible. Feeling herself settle and still.

She looks again.

And the air thickens and warps and changes shape around her, birds and insects silenced as time passes – so much time passing all around her – wild and naughty rings of smoke blown into the air, laughter, small voices piping up and calling between the trees. And somehow here she is, she, Mary, at the very palest centre of it, lulled and stilled and unmistakably herself—

Mary Coles.

Her heart jumps. She feels a hand on her shoulder and turns a bit too quickly.

'Hey.' Eddie standing there and grinning at her. 'It's only me.'

Mary gasps – turning back to the children, but already the air has curved itself around them and though the sense of them remains for a few more seconds, she knows that they are somehow even now beyond her, somewhere else. Gone.

'Eddie!'

He takes his hand off her. Still smiling, but stepping back. His dimple, his glasses, sunlight on his face. She stares at him, the shock of it still pulsing in her throat.

'You OK?' he says.

She stares at him.

'Did you see them?'

'What?'

'Just now. Did you see all those children?'

'What do you mean? What children?'

'Right here – over there, just a moment ago – lots of them. Lots of little kids. On the tree.'

He blinks at her, uncomprehending, his glasses catching the light.

'On a tree?'

'Right there.' She turns back to the tree, its bark bright and blameless now in the morning sunshine. 'They were all right there, sitting there. Just a second ago. A whole lot of children, sitting right there on that tree.'

He begins to laugh. Mary allowing herself at last to take a breath. She looks at him.

'I'm not joking,' she says.

'I know you're not.'

'You really didn't see it?'

He shakes his head. 'I'm sorry.' Keeping his eyes on hers.

Mary turns back to the tree. Nothing. She looks at Eddie again.

'Did you say my name?'

'What?'

'Just now. Did you say it?'

'Your name?'

'Mary Coles. Did you say Mary Coles?'

He laughs.

'I don't think I said anything. I think I just said "Hi" or something.'

'It's only me.'

'What?'

'That's what you said. "It's only me."'

'OK.'

Mary looks around her again at the blue air, the green leaves, the queasy, dappled light. Her hands are still trembling.

'So – what? Am I seeing things? Is that what this is?' He smiles at her.

'I don't know. Are you?'

Mary stares at him, a quick, chill memory creeping over her. Thinking of the photo on the wall of his bedroom. The upside-down girl. The children. The blurred baby. And the long shadow.

He folds his arms.

'What did they look like anyway, these children?'

She gazes at him, the blood still jumping in her throat.

'I don't know,' she says. 'I'm not so sure I did see anything.'

He blinks.

'You were very sure a moment ago.'

'I know.'

'But not any more?'

'No.'

He glances at the house, then back at her.

'You got time to make me some coffee?'

The first time James Dix tried me, it didn't work. I was willing enough, but it would not go in. At first he looked annoyed, but then he stopped himself and did up his breeches again.

I don't want to hurt you, he said.

It's all right.

You wouldn't say that if I did hurt you, Princess.

I'm not a princess.

To me you are. A real, royal princess.

He lit a cigarette and smoked it. Frowning and looking at me all the time as if he had a big new problem to crack and I was it.

It was a dull, misty day – air warm, sun not broken through yet. We were behind the apple store where the ground was soft enough and the blackcurrant bushes grew up thick around us. A good and quiet place, we'd thought, for him to show me what it was that men and women do.

At last he threw down the cigarette and stood up.

Come on, he said and he took me by the hand and pulled me over to the fallen-down tree.

What are you doing?

You'll see.

Roughly, as if he was in quite a hurry now, he pushed me forwards over the tree and I felt him pulling up my skirts and tugging at my drawers.

Hey, I said.

It's all right.

I twisted round to see what he was doing and saw that he had undone the flap of his breeches again, but before I could think any more about what was going on, he was already doing it—

I felt it there for a moment, straining, stretching.

No! I cried.

He put his lips on my neck and hotness rushed up through me, up my legs and under my arms and into my throat. I felt his teeth, gently biting.

No, I said again, quieter this time.

It's all right, he whispered. There.

Oh!

You feel that?

Yes.

It doesn't hurt, does it?

A bit.

But you like it?

I don't know.

It went on and on and then it just seemed to finish. We held very still, listening to our two selves breathing, alive and wetly cupped together on that tree.

I felt the weight of him against me and his man's warmth and his cigarette breath on my neck. I watched a small black beetle hurrying over the crinkled bark, up and down, side to side, travelling to somewhere that only he knew about.

At last he sighed and put a kiss on my head. Then he stepped back and off and there was a small noise and I felt it come sliding out. Wetness going down my leg. It was pinkish. I used my petticoat to wipe it.

Is that it? I said.

What do you mean, is that it? Isn't that enough?

I saw that he was laughing at me.

We sat down. He smoked another cigarette, puffing on it faster and faster now as if he was in a right big old hurry. I pulled up grass. It was lush and damp. One handful after another, arranging the small, green pickings in the lap of my skirt.

The first time you ever did that to a girl, I said, weren't you afraid?

He laughed, then he made a face. Blowing out smoke and straight-away taking another suck.

Afraid? Why ever would I be afraid?

I don't know, I said.

Keeping his eyes on me and still smiling, he ran his fingers through his bright hair. He looked like a cockerel, I thought – yes, the cock of the yard, with his hair all standing straight up on top like that. I felt annoyed and admiring both at the same time. I looked at the pieces of grass in my lap and then back at him. He really was awfully full of himself now that he'd got me to do it with him.

What is it? he said, smiling as hard as he could. What are you thinking now?

I hesitated. For a moment I thought about telling him the truth – that I was thinking about what Phoebe Harkiss had said about my mother being up the spout and wondering what it had to do with James and if I dared ask him about it. I was also thinking about how I'd like to tell him that, even though I still liked him, he wasn't as great as he thought he was and that as a matter of fact I felt quite fed up with him, the way he was always so intent on being amused and in charge of things.

I was wondering if you'd done it with Phoebe Harkiss, too, I said, the words coming out before I could stop them.

Now he looked very angry.

For the love of God, Eliza, what's the matter with you? Why are you always so concerned with Phoebe Harkiss?

I shook out my skirt. Grass falling everywhere and over everything.

I don't know, I said.

He put out his cigarette, smoke coming out of the side of his mouth.

That girl is nothing to me. I don't know why you think she's so interesting. Really, Eliza, you've got nothing to worry about. Phoebe Harkiss is not of any interest to me at all.

I looked at him. The little bow of his lip, so awkward and pretty. Apart from the stubble on it, you might have mistaken it for a girl's.

Yes, but have you done it with her? I said.

*

He said we had to do it again.

What, on the tree? I said, thinking I wasn't sure I could be bothered to get up and go through all of that malarkey a whole other time.

He smiled and he took me in his arms. He lifted my hair. He kissed my face. Then he rolled me back so I was flat on the ground. I gasped as he pinned me.

No, he said. Right here.

And he pulled my drawers all the way off this time and parted my legs and got inside – easily because it was still slippery from before – only this time he did it slower and a bit harder, keeping his eyes on me and his mouth on mine, moving and flicking and licking and kissing me.

At first I felt nothing. I thought that my body didn't much care what was happening and it could have been anything at all going on inside me. But then something changed. The feeling of him doing it – it was like the twist of a key, building and turning. I wanted to stop, I couldn't stop, I didn't want to. I was afraid, elated. I was spilling over. I began to scream.

He clamped his hand over my mouth. I could not breathe. I pulled it off. The noise that came out of me, finally – even I had never heard it before.

We lay there. The moments tumbling past us. Every part of me red and startled and wild. My cheeks. My chest. My heart. The whole of the inside of me. I imagined blood, pouring down from deep within me, a wide river of blood pouring out of the very centre of my heart. I still could not breathe, could not speak or think – I did not know whether to be upset or not.

He looked at me. He looked me up and down – my eyes, my cheeks, my heart, my face.

Eliza, he said. Whoa. I mean it. You ain't supposed to like it that much.

She takes him up to the house and sits him down in the kitchen and makes him coffee. Not bothering with a proper pot, just getting out the instant, chucking in the granules and the milk and putting the mug down in front of him. She hands him a spoon to stir it and asks him if he wants sugar. He says no. He leans back in the chair and tilts his head and looks at her.

'You're not having any?'

She shakes her head, the smell of his steaming mug nauseating her already. Folding her arms, still standing there, already wishing he would go.

'What is it?' he says.

'What?'

'I get the feeling you're angry with me.'

She looks at him.

'I'm not angry.'

'What, then?'

'I'm not anything, Eddie. I'm just busy, that's all.'

'Oh. Sorry.'

'No need to be sorry.'

He sighs.

'Oh God, Mary. I don't know what's going on between us.'

'What do you mean? Nothing's going on.'

'We seemed to be so close. But now . . .'

Mary stares at him.

'For goodness' sake, Eddie. Nothing's going on. And nothing's changed either. Why does everything always have to be so dramatic?'

His face falls.

'You see? You are angry.'

Mary sighs. Pulls out a chair and sits.

'What are you doing anyway? You're not working today?'

He hesitates.

'I am. I'm working from home today. Well, I suppose you could call it work.' He takes off his glasses, rubs them on his T-shirt, puts them back on again. 'What?' he says, when she doesn't say anything. 'You find it odd that I work from home sometimes?' He smiles, looking down at the table, putting his hands on it. Running a finger over the notches and scratches. 'I suppose I just fancied a chat, that's all. Thought I'd come and see how you were, that kind of thing.'

'I'm fine,' Mary says, unable to stop herself glancing at the stairs. She wants to have a shower, make the bed, she ought to phone her mother.

She is about to find a way of saying these things when without warning Eddie stands up. Pushing his chair back. The noise of it scraping over the floor starts the dog barking.

'I'm sorry,' he says. 'I should probably just go.'

'What?' She bends to grab the dog's collar.

He looks at her.

'I didn't realise—'

'Didn't realise what?'

'Well, it's not a good time, is it?'

He looks at the dog, who barks again. Mary drags her across the room and pushes her into the sitting room, shutting the door. She turns and faces him, confused. He runs his hands through his hair, looking at her.

'You only needed to say, you know. That you weren't alone.'

'What?'

'I wouldn't have dreamed of bothering you if I'd known that Graham was here.'

Mary stares at him, confused.

'Graham's at work,' she says.

He blinks at her.

'Who is it, then?'

'What?'

'Who's that upstairs?'

'There's no one upstairs.'

'Then what's all the noise?'

'What noise?'

He begins to laugh.

'You're having me on, aren't you?'

After he leaves, she tips his untouched coffee into the sink. Tries not to look at the carton of already too-warm and separating milk as she puts it back in the fridge. She releases and feeds the dog, who stares at the kibble for a few baffled moments as if she's never in her life seen food before, and then, very slowly, begins to eat.

She goes upstairs. Pausing on the top step before walking across and standing for a moment on the landing. Moving backwards and forwards, she treads the boards. The floor creaking loudly under her feet. Sunshine is pouring through the big window, but the long passage that leads away from their bedroom is in shadow, the door at the end closed.

She won't have that.

She walks down the passage and flings it open. The room is exactly as she left it after she stripped Ruby's and Lisa's beds. Dust hanging in the bright, empty air. A dead fly on the window sill. A dark hoodie flung on the only chair. A faint, depressing smell of something like cheap perfume or maybe deodorant.

She looks around her. A mirror put there for Ruby, but otherwise bare walls. The old paper peeling off in places.

Silence. Too much of it.

She leaves the room and goes back down the passage onto the landing, where she crosses to the window and looks down into the lane. No one. The long, snaking ribbon of the road, hedgerows, fields. Not a soul.

What was she expecting? She doesn't know.

In the bedroom, she kicks off her shoes and lies down on the unmade bed, her head on the familiar mess of pillows, knees pulled up, a smudge of dirt from the garden reminding her briefly of something, though already the memory's ragged and half-gone, sliding from her grip as loose and smooth as a dream—

She pulls up her T-shirt and puts her hands on the warm skin of her belly, shutting her eyes, holding herself, unsure of what's been happening or how or why.

When, across the landing, a door slams loudly, she is half-expecting it. She does not flinch. She keeps her eyes closed and stays very still. She is quite proud of herself, she does not move a muscle.

James Dix and I were in love. He agreed with me that it was love. (Just like in all the songs, I said. All right, he said, pulling me to him and laughing.) But he added that he had seduced me, did I understand that? And that I was not under any circumstances to tell my father. Or my mother. Or anyone, for that matter.

Tell them what? I said as I gazed at his face, the face that seemed to grow more beautiful and enticing every time he touched me. That we love each other?

He looked at me as if he thought I might be trying to trick him.

Not that, he said. And not the other thing either.

What thing? I said, though of course I understood perfectly well what other thing he meant and just wanted the fun of making him say it.

He frowned at me.

The thing that we do, dearest. The thing that you seem to like so very much.

Dearest. I liked it when he called me that. It gave me a feeling in my heart like birds and ribbons and the petals of small pink flowers flying up in the air. All the same, I could not resist teasing him.

But why not? I asked him. Why can't it be said?

Though of course I knew the answer and in truth just the idea that we were having the conversation was making me want to pull all my clothes off and have him do it to me straightaway.

I told you, Eliza, he said, growing impatient now. Because you are hardly more than a child and it was me that seduced you and they would all say I oughtn't to have done it.

Why would they say that? I asked him.

He shrugged.

People are stupid, he said.

I laughed then. I said I did not care a frick whether he had seduced me or not, nor a fat farthing for what anyone said. I said he could seduce me a hundred times over for all I cared. For it was truly the best thing I had ever known, this seducing. It was wild. The liveliest thing. It was the bee's knees.

If I had known it would be as good as this, I said, I promise you I would have got you to do it to me a long time ago.

He looked at me for a moment and then he shook his head.

What? I said.

He smiled.

Just you. The things you say. You remind me sometimes of a girl I once knew.

What girl? I said, wondering if he meant the poor dead sweetheart in Lowestoft or the other one that also ended badly.

He shrugged and his eyes were faraway.

Just a girl. Her name was Violet. She rode ponies. She was wild and crazy just like you.

I laughed.

You think I'm wild and crazy?

But he did not smile.

Too crazy for the workhouse and too sane for the asylum, he said. That was Violet.

I stared at him, trying to imagine this new girl with the name of a flower who was a bit or maybe even a lot like me.

Was she the sad one that broke you? I said.

What? he said.

The one you wouldn't tell me about?

He drew a quick, sharp breath, as if he'd forgotten what he'd already told me.

No, he said. No, that was another one.

I thought about this.

You've known a huge, great lot of girls, I said at last.

He shrugged. He didn't say anything.

And what happened to her? I asked him at last.

He swallowed. I couldn't tell if it was with disgust or sadness.

You don't want to know that, Eliza, he said.

Our love blossomed. We had connection whenever we could. Early in the morning and late at night, usually behind the old fallen tree or the apple store. I made him show me all the different ways of putting ourselves together that might bring me to that same sweet point of shock and delight. Some of the ways were quite unexpected. He seemed intent on opening up all the most secret parts of me you'd have sworn could not be opened.

Don't be afraid, he'd say as he coaxed my body into some new and unlikely way of behaving itself. Just do as I say.

And I learned to do exactly that, because when I did, it was only a moment or two before I was gasping aloud with the pure dark pleasure of it.

Sometimes I resisted and sometimes I didn't. Sometimes I trusted him and wished I hadn't. He had his own ends in mind and he wasn't always gentle. Sometimes he teased or slapped me, left me frantic and upset and sore. But after a while I learned not to know what was coming, and even to like not knowing it. It had the effect of making the final explosion much higher and swoonier, not knowing when and at what cost it would arrive.

I had never dreamed that love could be so hot and bright and dazzling. Some days it seemed impossible to believe that the small quiet me who had once liked to sleep alone on a rough sheet and spend her nights thinking about the insects and the birds that made their nests outside her window, could now be so greedy for a man's hard purpose inside her.

You are a holy bloody terror, he muttered in my ear one morning, when he'd just brought me to a place of such deep and panicked rapture that I'd wet myself for all the world as if I was a great big helpless baby like our Honey.

Meanwhile, there was no doubt about it: my mother was up the spout. She waddled about moaning at how big and tired she was and saying how she hadn't the heart for a new one after the loss of poor Frank and how this one would certainly be the death of her.

She was always like this when she had a new one coming, so I thought nothing of it. But another part of me looked at my father's poor, tired face and the way he and my mother never said a kind word to each other, and I was uneasy. The air crackled with something and it wasn't just the death of our Frank.

Remembering what Phoebe had said, I asked James if he had ever had anything to do with my mother and when he asked me what on earth I meant, I told him.

Now he looked very angry indeed.

Oh my God! he cried.

What? I said, disappointed because he'd had his thumb lightly shoved up inside me and we were only just getting started. Where are you going?

He sprang up off the grass and straightaway began doing up his flap and brushing himself down.

To see that fucking bitch Phoebe Harkiss, of course!

Don't say that! I cried, because even though I thoroughly disliked the girl, I was shocked at his language. Please, James, don't call her that.

He looked at me for a moment. His hair flaming upwards like a cock's bright crest and his cheeks white with rage. He stared quite hard at me and then he began to smile.

Oh Princess, he said. You're right. Of course you are. What am I doing? Look at me. I'm rushing at things.

I smiled back at him. And I sat up, smoothing my skirts back down over my knees. He spat on his palms, rubbing at his hair till it was flat again.

Phoebe Harkiss is a liar, he said. She'll say anything that comes into her head.

I said nothing, but he lifted his eyes and looked at me as if he wanted to make sure that I'd heard.

I saw that there was sweat all over his face, the whole of his forehead and cheeks dripping and shining with it. I thought he looked like he was running a fever, his face drawn and his eyes glittery.

You're hot, I said.

He said nothing.

James, I said. Look at you. You're very hot indeed. I hope you're not getting sick.

He wiped at his face with his sleeve, but his eyes and his mind seemed far away.

I'm not sick, he said. I'm angry.

Well, don't be.

He looked at me.

It's not a thing a person has much choice about, Eliza.

He got out a cigarette and smoked it. I could see from the tightness in his cheeks that he was thinking hard.

When he'd stubbed it out, he still didn't say anything. He just turned me over as if I wasn't there and pulled down my drawers and carried on exactly where he'd left off, putting his thumb in at first and then getting on me from behind like you see the dogs doing it in the ditch.

As I felt him reach into me, he grabbed my hair and yanked my head back and I was about to complain but then the popping brightness of what came next seemed to blow my head off and the cry I made went on echoing in a place that felt so distant and brackish and lonely that if someone had told me that it was not even on this earth of ours, I think I would have believed them.

Mary goes to the doctor's. A tiny surgery in a long brick bungalow, right down at the end of the village, past the allotments and by the humpback bridge. Shiny brown furniture, diabetes leaflets, worn-out spider plants. A plastic box of children's toys on the floor.

The woman at the desk gives her some forms to fill in. She hesitates over the part about pregnancies and children, then writes '2' and puts down her daughters' ages as they were then. She hands the forms back, and is surprised when the woman says she can see the doctor straightaway.

The doctor seems no more than a girl, barely out of her teens. She wears a white summer dress made of cheesecloth. Sandals. A tortoiseshell comb in her long, brown hair.

'Let's just pop you on the couch,' she says.

The brown-haired girl examines her gently, prodding and pressing with cool, barely convincing hands, then gives her a tube and says that, given the symptoms, she'd like her to do a pregnancy test.

Mary hesitates, still sitting on the white paper, legs hanging stupidly from the couch.

'I couldn't possibly be pregnant.'

The doctor is writing something, her head bent, hair falling over her face.

'All the same. If you don't mind. I'd just like to rule it out.'

She sits there, frozen, her heart banging.

'What I mean is, my husband had a vasectomy years ago.'

Now the doctor looks at her.

'How many years?'

She struggles – when was Flo born? For a quick, suffocating moment, she can't even see her daughter's face, let alone locate the month or the year.

'Seven or eight years at least.'

The doctor pushes her hair behind her ears. She looks down at the form. Frowns at her computer screen, scrolling up and down. Then she wrinkles her nose, smiles.

'Do you mind? Since you're a new patient. Just so we can both be a hundred per cent sure?'

7

A heatwave. It's official now. The longest, hottest, driest spell for thirteen years, something like that. The countryside is dramatically, visibly parched. Grass withered and brown, air stretched and bending in the light, roads shimmering like water.

They eat supper in Deborah and Eddie's garden. Wooden decking, storm lanterns, citronella candles, a huge white awning. Their third or fourth supper there, it must be. Next time, Mary tells them, it really is our turn.

'Nobody's counting,' Deborah says as she passes the big bowl of salad round. 'And look, all I did was grill a bit of fish.'

Deborah is kind, Mary thinks. They're both kind. Eddie, too. He means well. She sees that now. Since that morning when he came round to see her, he hasn't bothered her again. He's stopped ringing her, and when she saw him in the Farm Shop the other day, he was exactly as he should have been. Relaxed and friendly, but not too friendly.

She worries, now, that she wasn't very polite to him that day. Perhaps all he was doing was reaching out to her. Perhaps Graham's right – that he's just lonely. People get lonely. She must remember that. Sometimes she thinks she's become so unused to normal social contact, that she's forgotten how other people behave. She doesn't know any more what's usual and what isn't.

After it happened, after it was all over and people supposedly left them in peace to pick up the pieces and try to get on with their lives again, she hid herself away. Unable to find the energy or the courage or whatever else it took to speak to anyone – not even to the people who mattered, the ones who needed to be spoken to.

She did not call her mother, for instance. And when her father went into hospital quite suddenly for an operation, all she did was send a card. It was Graham who had to ring up and find out what had happened, to hear about the complications, to put up with her mother weeping over the phone. She ignored all offers to meet with friends for drinks or lunch and when those offers finally petered out she was relieved. She knew very well that her life was shrinking around her, growing smaller and tighter, and still she did nothing to stop it. It was as if she could not remember what the point of friendships or social occasions had ever been. Without her daughters in her life, there seemed to be no point in any of it any more, not even family. The only person she could bear to be with was Graham.

She remembers how shocked she was when her sister had a miscarriage. Nineteen weeks. Her first baby. She'd never even told them she was pregnant.

'How could we?' Katie said on one of the rare occasions when they met up. 'After what you were going through? How could we possibly have told you something like that?'

For the first time since it happened, she'd felt ashamed of herself.

Katie has a healthy baby now. A boy called Sam, nine months old. But she hasn't seen him since he was born and she hardly ever speaks to her sister these days. Her mother tells her that Katie's afraid to be around her with the baby, afraid it will upset her. And though she tells her mother that's nonsense, that it's no one's fault, that one of these days she and Katie will get together, she knows it's not true. She is here and Katie is over there. And every day the gulf widens and she tries to tell herself that she minds, but the truth is she's not sure.

It's not yet dark, the air still properly hot, scented with the honeysuckle that Deborah pointed out earlier, clambering right up through the magnolia tree. Mary notices how the white cotton dress Deborah has on emphasises her slenderness, smocked at the bodice like a little girl. As soon as they finish the fish, Eddie lights a cigarette, insisting, when Deborah complains about it, that it keeps the midges away. When she starts to clear the plates, Graham leaps up.

'Ah, I see you've got him well trained,' Eddie says and Mary smiles and tells him that's a sexist thing to say.

'What? The idea that women train men to do their bidding? You don't think it's true?'

She shakes her head.

'It's the kind of thing my father would say.'

'And her father's a retired bloody army colonel,' Graham says over his shoulder as he carries the plates away.

Eddie looks interested.

'You're an army child? And you think I'm like that, old-fashioned and, what, militaristic?'

She looks at him.

'My father has the excuse of his generation. You don't.'

Eddie laughs, but she can see she's upset him. As soon as Graham is properly in the kitchen and can be heard talking to Deborah, he turns to her.

'You don't have to keep on going for me like that, you know.'

She looks at him, trying to decide if he's joking.

'Going for you?'

'I didn't mean anything by it, you know. It was just a joke.'

'I know that,' she says, watching as his face softens and his dimple appears.

'How are you, anyway? Are you OK? Why aren't you drinking?'

'I am. I'm drinking.'

'You haven't touched it. I've been watching. You're not ill, are you?'

Mary looks at her glass, just the look and smell of the wine, suddenly tart and chemical, turning her stomach.

'I'm fine,' she says. 'Really, I'm fine. How are you?'

He sighs and his face falls.

'You don't want to know.'

'What doesn't she want to know?' says Graham, picking up his napkin and sitting back down and reaching for the bottle of wine.

'Just talking amongst ourselves,' says Eddie, distributing spoons, as Deborah brings some kind of lemon dessert in tiny white dishes. 'Her being an army child. Now that I know that, well, it explains a lot.'

Graham smiles and Mary feels him glancing at her.

'What does it explain?'

She watches Eddie top up her untouched glass of wine.

'Well, let me see.' He puts down the bottle. 'You probably moved around a lot as a child, did you?'

She nods. Eddie laughs and looks at Graham.

'See? She has that aura about her. Rootless. Resilient. Able to cope. I mean it in an entirely complimentary way, of course.'

'You should meet her dad,' Graham tells him. 'Quite a piece of work, he is.'

'Do you get on with him?' Deborah asks.

Graham hesitates.

'He's all right. It wasn't always easy at the beginning, but yes, he's a good man, we rub along.' He looks quickly at Mary. 'It's been hell for them, for Pat and Ken, the past year or so. And I'm not sure we've been able to help much, have we?'

'That's not your fault,' Deborah says.

Graham looks at her.

'I know. We've done our best, they've done their best.'

For a moment no one speaks.

'And what about your parents?' Deborah says at last.

Graham looks at his plate.

'They died about three years ago. One after the other. First my dad and then my mum. Thank God.' He stares into his wine glass for a moment. 'They weren't strong in the way that Pat and Ken are. I think that this – this thing – it would have absolutely destroyed them.'

They talk briefly about Ruby, then. Graham, having drunk more wine than Mary's seen him drink in a long time, confesses that he's worried about her.

'In what way worried?' Eddie says.

Graham hesitates, then says he thinks she might have a drugs problem.

'When you say drugs?' Deborah looks at him, holding her spoon in the air. 'What kind of drugs do you mean?'

Graham hesitates.

'I don't know. I don't know what I mean, really. She drinks a lot – I mean serious amounts, way more than we did at her age. And she smokes a bit of weed.'

'Well,' Deborah says, 'they all do that, don't they?'

'But it's more than that – more than weed, I mean. I know she uses MDMA. She's been in trouble at school, stuff like that. I suppose at the end of the day, she just doesn't seem to rate sobriety very highly.'

'I'm sure she'll grow out of it,' Deborah says.

Graham sighs.

'Anyway, her mother wants her out of London for the summer, so guess who gets the lucky ticket?'

Mary shakes her head.

'We haven't discussed it properly yet.'

'And will her friend be coming too?' Eddie says.

'What, Lisa? I hope not,' Mary says, before she can stop herself.

She pushes away her dessert, half-eaten. Then checking herself, not wanting to seem rude, she pulls it gently back and digs the spoon in again, playing with it. She feels Graham looking at her.

'I know you're not very fond of Lisa,' he says, 'but at least she keeps Ruby occupied.'

Eddie sits up.

'Why aren't you fond of her? What's wrong with her?'

'Nothing's wrong with her,' Graham says.

Mary looks at him.

'You realise Ruby hates our house? You realise Veronica's going to have a hard time even getting her to leave London.'

Deborah looks at her.

'Veronica? Is that her mother?'

'Ruby will do as she's told,' Graham says.

Eddie leans across Mary to pour more wine for Graham and Deborah. Mary puts her hand over her glass. He puts the bottle down a little too heavily and places a hand on her knee.

'Now tell me something: why don't you like Lisa and why doesn't Ruby like your house?'

'It's complicated,' Mary says, pushing his hand off as gently as she can.

'Complicated? How complicated? Is she scared of it?'

'Stop it, Eddie,' Deborah says. 'You're drunk.'

Mary feels her heart contract.

'Who told you that?'

'What?'

'That she was scared.'

Eddie laughs.

'No one told me. I just made it up. I thought she might be creeped out by such an old house, that's all.'

195

Graham shakes his head.

'Ruby isn't scared of the house. It's not that. It's just that she'll latch on to any possible bloody excuse for why she needs to stay in London. Anyway, she was fine last time when she had Lisa along to keep her company, wasn't she, Mary?'

'She was,' Mary says.

'So there you go,' Eddie says. 'Young Lisa has a function after all.'

Mary looks at him.

'No one said she didn't.'

'I'm not sure you can blame London anyway,' Deborah says. 'Once kids want to have fun, they can find it pretty much anywhere, can't they?'

'Sure, but it's a little bit harder around here,' Graham says.

Deborah's eyes widen.

'I don't know about that. Just look at the bus shelter on a Saturday night. Those kids aren't sober. The only difference between here and London is they wait a whole lot longer for the bus to come along.'

Eddie laughs and so does Graham.

'Well, I think you're both great,' Deborah says. 'With Ruby, I mean. I'm sure it's not easy. Maybe you just need to keep her occupied. Send her strawberry picking or something.'

Now Graham laughs so much he almost spits his drink out.

'I'm sorry. Just the idea of my daughter, clothed head to foot in black, stumbling, half-stoned, down the strawberry rows at Wharton's farm. Well, it doesn't bear thinking about.'

Deborah makes coffee and Mary helps her. In the kitchen the lights are dim and the elderly Siamese is asleep on a blanket on the sofa.

'I'm sorry about Eddie,' Deborah says as she scrapes the plates and puts them in the dishwasher while they wait for the pot to bubble through.

'Sorry about what?' says Mary. 'What's he done?'

Deborah hesitates.

'I think he's a bit drunk. But he was in a funny mood tonight right from the start. Rebarbative. It's just the way he is. He gets like that sometimes.'

'I really didn't notice,' Mary says.

Deborah doesn't look at her. She put a soap tablet in, shuts the dishwasher. It starts to hum. Mary watches as she turns off the gas and takes the pot off the stove.

'You've been very good to him. Don't think I don't know that. He's told me, you know, about how great you've been.'

Mary stares at her.

'I really haven't done anything.'

Deborah shakes her head and her earrings move. Mary notices that she looks tired.

'All the same. He does appreciate it. We both do. He's just not very good at expressing it, you know?'

They drink coffee and the conversation drifts. They discuss the train crash in France that's all over the news. They talk about the mechanics of it – how could a huge great train like that ever gather enough speed to veer right off the track? – but not the body count, not the deaths.

They talk about a big antiques barn just off the A12 where Deborah thinks they might find a garden table. The amazing and very reasonably priced nineteenth-century French glass chandelier which she saw there a couple of years ago and didn't buy, the loss of which still haunts her now. They talk about the weather. The fact that the heatwave's supposedly set to continue right into August. And, of course, the wildfires.

'You expect them in California or Australia or wherever,' Eddie says, shaking his head and opening another bottle of wine even though everyone insists they've had enough. 'But here—'

'We thought it was an exaggeration,' Deborah says. 'All this stuff about no barbecues and being careful not to chuck cigarette ends and all that. But then we drove past this stretch of heath just beyond Leiston, didn't we, Eddie?'

He looks at his plate.

'Absolutely blackened. Burnt to a cinder, it was. You wouldn't recognise it. Nothing left at all.'

Mary gets up fast. Gasping for breath. Cold water pouring through her. The sound of chairs being pushed back as they all turn to look at her. Everything suddenly on a tilt. Deborah's little cry of shock. Eddie's astonished face. Her husband's eyes, frozen with recognition and pain.

Deborah asks if she should go after her.

'No,' she hears Graham say. 'It's all right. She just needs a moment. Please, I mean it. Just let her go.'

She holds herself very still on the edge of the little sofa in the study off the hall. Alone and in darkness, just the faint pools of light coming from the garden. Wrists on knees, her hands still shaking, managing to breathe, one breath at a time, concentrating on the in and out, calmer now.

Eddie is standing in front of her.

'I brought you a drink of water.'

When she doesn't take it, he sets it down on the small table next to her. She waits for him to go but he still stands there.

'Graham said we should leave you alone but – I couldn't. I'm so sorry, I know I should probably be able to but – I just couldn't.'

She lifts her head a little and sees the stitching on his jeans, the part of his belt where it's ragged and frayed, the end hanging off. She hears him take a breath.

'I wish I could do something. I know there's nothing I can do, but I want you to know that I wish with all my heart that there was.' He reaches out and touches her head – the sudden, startling warmth of his hand on her. 'Do you want me to leave you alone?'

'No,' she says, surprised that she doesn't.

He moves his hand over her hair. Smoothing her hair, the way she used to touch her girls.

'What are you thinking?'

She does not speak, shaking her head.

'Try and tell me. What are you feeling? Is there anything you can tell me?'

She says nothing.

'Mary?'

'Not really,' she says.

She wishes she could tell him something. But what would she tell him? Could she tell him what she did yesterday – that she walked for more than a mile, in search of a field, any field, where she could find herself sufficiently alone to shout their names. Needing so badly to have that feeling again, the simple taste of those sweet words in her mouth, even if only for a few seconds. But that just as she thought she'd found the perfect spot – a vast expanse of rough, ploughed land, deserted and unholy – the farmer appeared on his tractor. Or she assumes it was the farmer. Him waving to her. Her, silenced, waving back.

Or she could try to explain how she never stops thinking about the precious, soft hours after Ella was born. How, when the midwife saw how she did not once let her out of her arms – so close and warm against her, the fuzz of her small head tickling her nose – she nodded approval and said there was no need to check her temperature. And how this made her feel like the very best of mothers, the most valiant and effective protector of her newborn child.

Or else she could just tell him how, for some brief fraction of almost every second of every hour of this sorry, continuing life of hers, she is forced to think of them in that ditch. Is forced to think of how they spent more than two weeks rotting there in the ditch, barely covered, partially burned, hands, faces, fingers, hair, their small bodies half-submerged in the cold black water. How she thinks all the time of the night falling and the sun rising and night falling again, black and cold. And how, even once they were found, it was still necessary to leave them lying there for two more days and one more night, unlifted and unconsoled, while police and forensics completed their tests and evidence gathering.

She could tell him how, during this period, she wept and vomited and ground her teeth so badly in her sleep that she cracked a molar. How she thought about killing herself so often that one night she dreamed she'd succeeded and when she woke up and found herself still alive, she sobbed with disappointment.

She takes hold of his wrist and removes his hand from her head. Picking up the water and sipping it. Startled by its clean coldness.

'I'm all right now,' she says. 'Thank you. You go in. I'll be back in a minute.'

I can't marry you, you know, James said to me. I'm just saying, Princess. Because I don't want you to go getting any ideas in your head that aren't possible. I don't want you to end up disappointed. All right?

Yes, I said. All right.

He kept his eyes on me.

What? You really don't mind?

I looked at him. The idea of marriage had never entered my head and I told him so. He gave me a careful look, then he grinned.

Well, that's good. Good girl! Because I am hopeless fond of you – you know that?

I'm fond of you too, I said, though I was still thinking about the word hopeless – was it hopeless? In fact, I love you to pieces.

He looked uncertain.

It's for your own benefit, you see. I don't want to lead you on.

I don't care about that, I said, but I could see from his face that he wasn't listening.

I wouldn't want to leave you in the lurch and all because you got your hopes up.

I don't ever want to marry anyone, I told him truthfully. Why would I?

He gazed at me for another long moment and then he sighed.

Because it's what girls want.

Well, I don't want it, I told him truthfully. I don't want what other girls want. I just want to go on being me.

He looked at me again and then he scratched his head.

What a rare one you are. I wish all women would think the same as you.

I sat up and pulled up my drawers, putting my hand for a moment where he'd just been. I liked to feel it, the wet. It was like water but not like water, slipping over your fingers with a gritty roughness that made me think of pears when you sink your teeth in and the juice runs down your chin and you wonder if the mess is worth it and then you realise that it is.

Well, I don't know why they don't, I told him.

Don't what?

Think the same as me. I don't know why all women don't think it. It's as clear as ice to me.

He shrugged.

It's when a child comes along, that's the problem. As soon as they're up the spout, then that's it. Then they just want to sit back and start taking your money.

But you haven't any, I reminded him.

What, children?

200

I laughed.

Money!

He nodded and his eyes were hard and bright.

That's right. I haven't. Not a brass ha'penny, Princess. You know as well as I do that I've nothing. Though I can tell you that's not what the bird in Lowestoft thought.

What, you mean Violet? Or the one called Tilly? Or do you mean the dead one? I said, because I was getting more and more confused by the tangle of alive and dead women he seemed to have left behind him.

He gazed at me for a moment, his eyes like somebody dreaming.

None of those. Though it is true that Violet might have wanted marriage had she not been insane.

I said nothing, because he'd got my interest now and I wanted more. I held my breath, hoping he would go on and he did.

I was very unlucky with Violet, he said. I was not in her for more than a minute. There was no proof whatsoever that I was the father.

I stared at him.

What? I said. A child? Violet had a child?

Violet? Ah, well she would have, if she had not destroyed herself.

Now I was aghast.

You mean to say she killed herself? With a poor babby inside her?

He blinked and then he nodded. Even though his eyes were still quite serious, his face was bothering me.

Herself. The child. And the pony too.

What pony?

The one that should have been her livelihood. The little piebald that wore the feathers and the jewels and went round all the fairs. It made no sense at all. I told you. That girl was not sane.

Poor Violet, I said, though in my head I was also feeling very sorry for the poor dressed-up pony, which sounded like a grand little animal and surely ought not to have had to die as well.

He looked at me.

Not poor Violet. Not poor at all. She would have had me. She would have caught me up for life, that Violet would have. A little fish, I was, wriggling in her net.

You're not a bit like a fish, I began to say, but he wasn't listening.

Very fortunate then, that when the pony was found with its throat cut, Violet was lying right there beside it. She must have done the pony first and then herself, mustn't she? It was the only explanation.

I swallowed back a bad taste. I couldn't work out why it was, and then I could. The look on his face. It belonged to someone else, not him.

James Dix struck a match and lit a cigarette. He took a long suck and then he blew the smoke out. At last he looked at me.

I had nothing to do with it, he said. I wasn't even in the neighbourhood. That's what I told them and it was God's own truth. And don't you ever forget that, Eliza.

They walk back home together down the lane. The air still warm, the sky alive with stars. They don't speak, but after a while Graham reaches for her hand and she lets him take it. She remembers how, when she first knew him, they held hands all the time, constantly, everywhere, fingers always entwined, never letting go if they could help it, and how much she came to love the feeling of it, of being so willingly linked – and she glances down now at her hand in his larger one and can't believe these are the same two hands from that innocent time so long ago.

As if he can feel her thoughts, he gives her hand the smallest squeeze but she doesn't squeeze back.

'What?' he says. 'What are you thinking?'

She tells him she isn't thinking anything, though in fact she's wondering about whether she could tell him about her visit to the doctor's, realising to her surprise that she has no idea what she would say – would not know how to find any words that would be both truthful and satisfactory.

Reaching the house, they're surprised to find the little wooden gate open, moving gently on its hinges as if someone has just that moment left and failed to latch it behind them. He stares at it.

'That's odd. Didn't we close it?'

'I don't know.'

'I did. I know I did. I remember doing it.'

'Someone might have put something through the door,' she says.

'At half past twelve on a Friday night?' He looks at her. 'Well, if someone's broken in, we'll soon find out.'

They go in. There are no deliveries and no sign of burglars either. He takes the dog into the garden while she gets ready for bed. She undresses, washes her face and then stands at the window cleaning her teeth, her hand cupped under her chin, watching the two of them weaving their way in and out of the trees, stopping now and then before moving off again.

While the dog sniffs at something, she watches Graham stand and tilt his head back, hands in pockets, swaying slightly, gazing up at the stars. He's drunk, she thinks, and for a quick moment she doesn't even recognise him – as if he's just a fragment of some larger thing, fleeting, uncertain, distorted. She walks into the bathroom and spits in the basin.

Half an hour later, when he's come in and got into bed, she goes back to the window.

'Can you hear it?' she says.

'Hear what?'

'That.'

'What?'

'Listen. That awful sound.'

He lowers the newspaper, holding it against his chest.

'I can't hear anything.'

'You really can't? A little way off? Like someone screaming?'

He smiles. 'It'll be an owl.'

'An owl?'

'Remember when you came here that first time, in the night, on your own? You said you heard an owl?'

That night. She tries to think of it. The car. The lane. The uneasy, waiting presence of the dark house with no one inside it. She looks at him.

'It wasn't like that. It was like someone in pain. A girl screaming.'

'Then it'll be a fox. Foxes sound terrible. Unearthly. They're famous for it.'

Graham lifts his paper again. She turns back to the window. Silence. A warm, black wind stirring the trees.

'Come to bed,' he says. 'It's very late.'

She glances back at him.

'You're reading.'

'I'm waiting for you.'

She says nothing. Still peering into the garden. Far off – right down at what must be the very bottom by the fallen tree – a blob of light, moving slowly and unevenly, up and down and side to side. A firefly, she thinks.

'What have you arranged?' she asks him, still watching the light. 'With Veronica?'

He yawns.

'Arranged in what sense?'

She glances back at him.

'About us having Ruby. I'd rather know now than have to wait for you to find the right moment.'

He looks at her.

'I actually haven't arranged anything yet.'

'Right.' Mary sighs. 'Of course you haven't.'

She turns back to the darkness. The screams have stopped but the light is still there, bobbing around. She hears Graham folding the paper and chucking it on the floor.

'Look, do you really want to do this now? At this time of night? What I mean is, aren't we both a bit too tired and drunk to have this conversation?'

Mary looks at him.

'I'm not drunk.' She hesitates. 'I don't mind having her here. You know I don't. You keep on acting as if I mind it. But I don't. I realise that it's necessary.'

She sees his jaw tighten.

'Great. Nice for Ruby to know how much she's wanted.' He turns out the light and lies down.

'Don't sulk,' she says.

'I'm not. I'm very tired and I want to sleep.'

Mary watches him for a moment then she looks out of the window again. The light is gone now, but she can just about make out the dark shape of something moving down the garden. Too big to be an animal, but surely not a person?

'It changes our whole summer,' she says, frowning at the shape as it steals along the edges of the flower beds. 'I think there's someone in our garden,' she adds.

The quality of his silence makes her shiver.

'She's not even slightly a part of your family, is she?' he says at last.

Mary thinks about this. The shape is almost out of sight now, moving towards the bottom of the garden. In a moment she won't be able to see it.

'I don't have a family any more,' she says.

'Right. That's good to hear.'

'You know what I mean.'

'I do. I understand completely and it cheers me up immensely.'

He punches his pillows, turning over.

'There's something moving in the garden,' she tells him again. 'Seriously, Graham. I've been watching it for a while.'

He doesn't answer. She searches for the shape again, gazing into the black knot of the trees. Listening again for the screams that sounded human even though they couldn't be human—

'Well, whatever it was, it's gone.'

She turns back to look at him and she sees that he's asleep and has been for some time.

In the night, a storm. Not as bad as the storm that brought James Dix to us, but it blew down some big branches with all the leaves on and turned the cart in the yard over on its side and uprooted the row of currant bushes our father had only just dug in.

Our mother was upset because it also ripped out the lilies she'd planted on our Frank's grave, scattering them around the churchyard as if it intended that all the other dead should grab some for themselves. She sent Jazzy and me to gather as many of the plants as we could and put them back in.

We didn't have to take the little ones with us, because Honey was asleep and Charlie had jumped off the apple ladder and hurt his leg, even though it didn't stop him and Minnie chasing chickens around the yard. We would have preferred not to take Lottie with us either, but she yelled and cried and went around upstairs slamming doors and then banged her head so hard on the kitchen table that in the end we had to.

It was a warm, wet morning. The earth on the grave was fresh and sad and brown. There was no headstone because we were saving up, but you knew it was Frank because of how small and clean and new it was. Of the seven lilies Ma had planted – one for every year of his age – only one was left and even that one looked a sorry sight.

For a moment, we all just looked at the grave. It was hard to know what to think. It didn't seem to have anything to do with our Frank, and yet at the same time you knew it was everything.

Lottie sat down on the ground next to one of the big grey stones and she scuffed the heels of her boots around in the earth and sucked her thumb and watched in a not very helpful way as Jazzy and I gathered up some of the plants that were strewn around. We checked they still had roots and dusted the muck off and then dug new holes to plant them in.

Won't he catch cold? Lottie said.

Won't who catch cold?

Our Frank. Under the earth. It's claggy in there.

She shuddered.

Frank's in heaven, I said. He's in heaven and he's quite warm enough. You don't need to worry about him, Lottikins.

Lottie's mouth fell open.

Ain't he under the earth?

I hesitated.

Only his poor body, I said, though a part of me still felt that bodies were all that could ever matter to anyone. As I took another lily and pushed its hairy roots into the soil, I couldn't help thinking of poor Frank who must be down there just a few feet beneath my fingers. How would he look now? Would he still look like himself or would he be just a shape made of bones or would he be something worse?

Lottie was frowning.

Why is his body poor?

Because he was poorly and he died. But his dear soul survived and it's gone up to heaven to be with the angels.

She seemed satisfied with this. She put her thumb back in her mouth, but a moment later took it out again.

But I want him to come home. When's he coming home, Eliza?

Jazzy looked at me and rolled her eyes.

Never, she said as she hacked away at the black earth with her trowel. He's never coming home. Weren't you listening to a single thing Eliza said? He'll never ever come home again, Lottie, because he's dead.

Lottie stared at her.

Dead?

Yes, dead! Why do you think they buried him? What do you think everyone's been weeping about, you silly little goose?

Lottie's face went very still, but you could see her thoughts working.

But when he stops being dead, then can he come back home?

Jazzy laughed.

People don't stop being dead. Dead goes on for ever, Lottie, don't you know that? It's what's so very horrible about it. Tell her, Eliza.

It's true, I said, though even just saying it made me feel quite cold and dull inside. Frank can't ever be alive again, because you only get one chance at living and when it's over, that's it, you're dead.

Now Lottie's chin began to wobble.

Frank not dead, she said and she folded her arms and shook her head and drummed the heels of her boots on the ground.

I put my trowel down and looked at her.

Oh Lottie, I said. You know very well that he is. Don't you remember how they put him in a box and how we all cried and cried?

Lottie stared at me as if this was a new and terrible piece of information.

But what about the little dog?

What, you mean Frank's dog?

Lottie shook her head.

No, Tuffy. The Tuffy dog. Did we put him in the box with Frank?

I stared at Lottie.

I don't know what you're talking about, I said. I don't know anything about any dog called Tuffy.

Lottie's face turned dark.

Tuffy! The dog that is soft as a lamb and you put it on your face like this.

She made a rubbing motion with her fingers on her cheek. Jazzy was looking at her and shaking her head.

Shut up, Lottie. What are you on about? There was only our old dog and she wasn't like a lamb and you know very well that Pa put her in a hole in the woods.

Lottie seemed to think about this. She put her thumb back in her mouth and sucked on it for a while. At last she pulled it out and wiped it on her pinafore.

I think Tuffy was the little girls' dog anyway. But I thinked if Frank was dead then maybe he could have it too.

I felt my heart drop.

What little girls?

She blinked.

Them little girls. The ones that died.

I bit my lip.

Lottie, I said, there aren't any little girls. Whatever are you talking about?

Yes there is. The little girls of miracles that had the Tuffy dog.

Little girls of miracles! What a stupid thing to say, said Jazzy and she began to laugh loudly.

I looked at her.

She probably dreamed it, I said.

Not a dream! Lottie said. Anyway, I used to be dead too and I came back.

Jazzy had had enough. She threw down her trowel.

No, Lottie! You didn't used to be dead. And you didn't used to be a dog. You didn't used to be anything. And there aren't any little girls either. Why do you always make up so many boomers?

Not boomers, Lottie said.

Yes, they are, they're boomers. Do you know that God punishes children who make up stories about dead people? It's wicked to lie. You're a wicked child and I wish you had died instead of Frank!

I looked at Jazzy and I thought that recently she'd become almost as mean as Phoebe Harkiss. But Lottie was staring at her.

When I was dead, she whispered in her darkest voice, I just laid there on the floor with the blood coming out of me.

Lottie, I said, that's horrible. I wish you wouldn't say such things. Where do you go getting such horrid ideas from?

From the man who killed me.

What?

Lottie smiled. Her eyes were raw and furious.

He couldn't help it. He was a bad man so he just had to do it and God let him because God is bad.

Lottie! I said. Just stop it right now.

The man hit me and hit me till I was dead. Just like the little girls.

I took hold of Lottie's shoulders and looked in her eyes.

Just stop this nonsense right now or you're going straight home to Ma. For once and for all, no one killed you and you weren't ever dead.

Though you will be one day, Jazzy said. And sooner than you think, if you don't shut up with all this rubbish about miracles.

Lottie was silent for a long moment.

Not miracles, she said. Mary Coles.

I thought that was the end of it, but I was wrong.

Later, much later, after night had come down and the sky had turned from blue to black, I was sitting in the kitchen biting my thumb and thinking about poor Frank and all the awful and aggravating things he used to say and do which now that he'd gone just seemed quite ordinary and sweet.

And I was thinking, too, about whether I should go and look for James, who had gone with my father to the steeplechase at Bungay but must surely be back by now. And I was thinking about something else as well – a wavy, upset and hard-to-understand kind of thought that had not yet taken shape in my head but was already making my throat feel tight and sad – when she came and stood behind me.

At first I didn't feel her there. In fact, she kept herself so quiet and still, that when at last she reached up and tugged my sleeve, I jumped so hard that my thoughts exploded all around me, shattering into pieces.

Lottie! I cried. Whatever are you doing? Why aren't you in bed?

She was gazing up at me with hot eyes. Her cheeks were bright and her breath smelled sickly and of fever. She licked her lips.

I don't like it, she said.

What? What don't you like?

The lady.

What?

She keeps coming – Lottie looked around the room and then back at me. She held up her hands. I said to her to go away, I said: You must go away right now or I'll bite you! But every time I say it she just stays and stays—

But Lottie—

I watched as she plucked at her nightgown and stomped her bare feet and gazed all around the room again. I saw that she was on the verge of tears.

Make her go away, Eliza. Please make her—

Make who go away?

The lady!

What lady? I can't see any lady. Ouch! I said as she grabbed hold of my arms so tight with her fingers that it started to hurt. Get off, Lottie. I mean it, you're pinching me.

I prised myself away and got up.

Is it the same lady you were talking about before? I asked her as I reached for a spill to light the lamp.

Lottie was still for a moment.

It's Mary Coles.

Mary Coles? Who's Mary Coles? We don't know anyone called Mary Coles. What are you talking about, Lottie? I said as I went to the window to look out for any sign of James.

She blinked.

It's a name, isn't it?

Yes, but whose name?

It's her name and I told you, I don't like it.

Now Lottie began properly to cry.

Oh Lottie, I said. Look at you, you're just about ragged with tiredness. Why aren't you in bed and asleep?

I don't like her, she sobbed. I don't like her – I want her to go.

Her sobs were so loud that I had no choice but to go over and sit back down on the chair and pull her on my knee.

I don't know what you mean, I told her more gently now. What lady? There isn't any lady here.

She turned and nestled herself into me, hugging her small arms round my waist and pushing her face into my sleeve.

She's in here and I don't like it.

In here? You mean in this room?

Yes.

And are the little girls in here too?

Lottie let out a wail.

Not them! The little girls are dead!

I thought about this.

Look, Lottie, I said as I got her comfortable on my lap and kissed her soft hair that smelled of bed and old milk. I want you to look around the room. Let's do it now. Let's look around the room together.

And I took her chin in my hand and as calmly as I could turned her head so I could show her every inch of that empty room with its shadows and dark spaces and familiar objects that were only just visible in the light of the lamp.

You see, I said. There's no one. No lady, no little girls, no monkeys or bears or tigers either. There's no one here at all but you and me.

Yes, there is! Lottie cried – and she pointed with her finger before twisting her head back against my breast as if she could hardly bear to look.

No, there isn't.

There is! Look. Over there!

Where?

There!

Again, she jabbed her finger into the air. And so I looked. I did it. I put my eyes in the very place where she was telling me to put them.

I looked at the stone-flagged floor that I'd swept not more than an hour ago. The sheet of newspaper that Pa had pinned to the wall, that had prices for horse rakes on it. The chair he always sat in to take his boots off. The mirror. The clock. The oil lamp. The platters and the mixing bowls on the dresser. A brown jug. Some strips of sack cloth for tying birds' feet together. Ma's worn-out apron with the blue flower pattern and the blackberry stains on it. And beneath all of that, the stack of firewood, barely visible now in the dark of the fireplace which always had mice nesting in it and the rug that Ma and me had made from an old red soldier's coat she'd got from a bone man.

I looked at all of these things – things I fully expected to see, and which were indeed as precisely and definitely there as they always were – and I was about to start scolding Lottie again for telling great big booming lies, when I saw it. Something—

Human, it was. Woman. The legs long and loose in dark breeches, the face shadowy, black hair coming undone and falling over its shoulders, moving fast across the kitchen floor, slicing softly through the air towards the place where we —

Drawing breath and springing to my feet, knocking the chair out from under me and pulling Lottie into my arms, I would have cried out, but at that exact moment James came in. His hands were dirty and hung heavy by his side and his face was grey and terrible.

You have to come, he said.

What?

I froze and stared at him, his body large and sudden in the open doorway, the black dark of the night solid behind him. I glanced straight back at where the shape had been. Nothing. I looked again at James.

What? I said again.

He swallowed.

Just come.

Slowly, I let go of Lottie and let her slide to the floor. I thought she would complain but she remained silent she did not make a sound.

Why? I said. What is it? What's the matter?

His face did not change.

I need help, he said. I need help, Eliza, and I need it right now.

Mary's mobile shudders into life. The sound makes her jump.

'I'm fucking begging you,' Ruby says, 'to talk to Dad. He's somehow got it into his head that I have to spend the whole summer with you guys like I'm some kind of under-age retard or something and I thought I could get Mum on my side at least, but now he's fucking well brainwashed her into it and she won't listen to a single thing I say.'

Mary sitting on the old bench and watching the dog sniff around the bricks she's just laid over the roots of the clematis, thinks about this.

'Well, it doesn't necessarily have to be the whole summer, does it?' she says at last.

She hears Ruby take a breath.

'Doesn't it? That's not what they're saying. You ask Dad. I swear they want me on a train the very moment I break up, so they can incarcerate me in the fucking countryside.'

Mary brushes a ladybird off her arm.

'I'm sure it won't be for the whole holidays.'

'Won't it? Try telling them that and see what they say. Seriously, Mary, will you talk to him? I mean it, I think I might be able to bear a long weekend or something but any more than that is going to be fucking torture.'

'Torture?' Mary says, still watching the ladybird's dark blur of wings. She hears Ruby gasp.

'Yes, torture. Don't you get it? That's exactly what they want. It's supposed to be awful. It's some kind of a punishment for whatever it is that I'm supposed to have done. Mum wants me away from all my friends and all my social life that I've taken so long to build up and basically away from any possibility of the tiniest shred of fucking pleasure I have left in my life.'

Mary hesitates.

'And you don't think it might be good to get out of London for a while?'

Ruby lets out a wail.

'Oh my God. Please don't tell me you're in on it too? You were my last hope. I thought you at least still had a mind of your own?'

Mary thinks about this. She thinks about her mind and she wonders, for the first time in what she imagines is probably quite a while, whether it really is her own. At the same time, she reaches out with a hand and tries to wave at the dog, who is now starting to scratch at the earth under the bricks.

'Hold on a moment,' she tells Ruby, 'I just have to shout at the dog. The thing is,' Mary says as she wrestles the dog away from the roots and forces her to sit at her feet, 'your dad is really quite worried about you. And so am I. I'm worried about you. And I know for a fact that your mum is worried—'

She hears Ruby gasp.

'Worried? What in fuck's name is wrong with you all? It's ridiculous. I've done absolutely nothing for ages except try to please you all, but at the end of the day, it just doesn't work, does it? All I am is a bloody scapegoat. Lisa thinks that too. She thinks it's really unfair. The trouble with you guys is you're so fucked up by what happened and you're just looking for someone to take it out on.'

Mary is silent. Letting go of the dog and smoothing a hand over the leg of her jeans.

'That's what Lisa thinks, is it? And what else does Lisa think?'

Ruby sniffs.

'All right and I'll tell you another thing, but you won't like it. I haven't even told Mum this, but your house is scary. I don't like sleeping there. It seriously creeps me out. I'm not being funny and

I swear I'm not making it up. And it's not just me either. Lisa felt it too.'

Mary says nothing. She stays calm. The air is warm and bright and sharp around her. It smells of apples, leaves, soil, baby's fingers, the fuzzy brown hair of small girls. She doesn't feel at all upset. She doesn't feel bad or afraid or worried. In fact, she realises she hasn't felt so perfectly and conveniently comfortable in a very long time. A sinking euphoria, that's what this is, blurring all her edges, a bit like the medication they gave her straight after it had happened.

'Mary?' Ruby says.

'What?'

'You still there?'

Mary swallows.

'I know,' she says.

'What?'

She hesitates. Feeling Ruby on the other end of the line, waiting.

'I know there's something in the house,' she says at last.

Several hours later, she runs into Eddie in the Farm Shop. Both of them buying milk. He's carrying Deborah's big straw basket with the flowers on it. 'Mary Coles!' he says. 'Now isn't that funny – I was just on my way to see you.'

Her spirits drop. She knows she won't shake him off now. He waits while she pays. Outside in the sunshine, he stops and looks at her more closely. 'Mary? What's the matter? Are you all right?'

Mary tries to smile.

'I'm fine. Why? Don't I look fine?'

He hesitates.

'You look very pale.'

'I'm always pale.'

'No, really. I don't think I've ever seen you so pale. You look like a ghost of yourself.'

'Well, I'm fine, really.'

He smiles.

'All right. If you say so.' Keeping his eyes on her face, he puts his hand into the basket and brings out something wrapped in newspaper. 'Here.'

'What?'

'I wanted you to have it.'

'Oh, but Eddie!' Mary unwraps it, pulling off the paper, the glass suddenly cool beneath her fingertips. 'You can't possibly give me this.'

He grins.

'It seemed to chime with you – that time I first showed it to you, remember? I could tell it meant something. You showed an interest. You even saw things in it that I'd never noticed.'

The shadow. Mary tries not to look for it now. It might not be anything – might not ever have been there, she thinks.

'But that doesn't mean I should have it,' she tells Eddie.

'Yes, it does. Really. Please don't make me explain it. I just wanted to give it to you. I feel that you're its rightful owner.'

Mary looks again at the picture – the country lane, familiar and barely changed except for the presence of those long-ago faces – all those small children lined up against the hedge, the stout little girl staring straight ahead, the other child hanging upside down, skinny dark legs in dark stockings, hair sweeping the dust. She sees with relief that it all looks quite different in the bright sunlight – bleached out and in some way benign. She turns back to Eddie.

'But what about Deborah? You had it on your bedroom wall.'

He makes a face.

'She won't even notice it's gone. She never liked it – she's not keen on old stuff. And anyway I told you, there are two more of the things at home waiting to be framed.' He lifts his eyes to meet hers, his face suddenly shy. 'Your hair really suits you like that, by the way. I've never seen you with it up.'

'Oh.' Mary, hating herself for flushing, reaches up and touches the clip she'd forgotten all about. 'I had a shower and forgot to take it out.'

'Well, it's good. Makes you look a bit French.'

'French?' Mary laughs and his face falls.

'Anyway. You should wear it up more often.'

Mary doesn't know what to say. She looks at Eddie, suddenly worried that she hasn't thanked him properly.

'How are you, anyway?' she says. 'How's your boy?'

'My boy?'

'Is he OK? When does he break up? Will you get to see him soon?'

Eddie looks at her for a long moment.

'It's nice of you to ask,' he says. 'No one ever asks me that. I'm trying to arrange a visit at the moment, in fact, but it's difficult. Deborah gets quite upset if I even mention him.'

Mary looks at him.

'Does she? Why?'

'It's complicated. It's not her fault. Just maybe best if you don't go mentioning him to her, OK?'

'OK,' Mary says.

Clutching the basket to him, Eddie looks at the ground.

'It's just, some of the stuff I told you – it's best if it stays between us.'

'All right,' she says, unsure what she's just agreed to.

She extricates herself and walks back home down the lane carrying the picture and the milk. Away from Eddie, she feels oddly light, unencumbered – noticing all over again how bright the air is, dancing with insects and bits of something seed-like that seems to come floating down from the trees.

When she gets to the house, she sees that the gate is swinging open again. She closes it and goes inside and moves briskly across the kitchen, fast and purposeful, ignoring the feeling that there are other people in there – hands and skirts and faces, the plump wrist of a child, a blur of voice and limb and the quick childish gasp of breath.

She unclips her hair as she goes, shaking it out over her shoulders and, putting the milk on the table and, drawing back the heavy bolts on the back door, she lets the dog out into the garden. And she stands there for a few moments, holding the picture and still hardly daring to look for the long shadow of the man who waits just around the corner for she doesn't know what.

James dragged me down the garden with him but before we even got near, I could hear it – a thick, throaty sound that wasn't crying and wasn't screaming, but something else much worse. And as we went round the old fallen tree and he began to pull me behind the apple store, I knew that whatever was there, I could not look at it.

At first there seemed to be nothing and for a quick second my spirits calmed. Then as my eyes got used to the dark and the faint moonlight, I saw that she was further back, in the dry, grassy shadow cast by the old wall, the same hidden place where him and me so often had our fun with each other.

You could see that she'd dragged herself quite a way across the grass, because even the tallest stems were flattened and broken and slicked with a trail that shone blackish in the moonlight. She must have got herself as far as the wall before reaching out with her hand and scraping her nails against the cold brick and giving up.

Her pinafore was dirty and torn and her skirts all hitched up and you could see the backs of her legs, which were smeared and bloody. One of her boots had come off and was by the wall, the other still on, but unlaced. She was lying with her head on one outstretched arm almost as if she was sleeping, but the other was twisted harshly round and pointing the wrong way entirely and the hand was bloody and partly severed and one of the fingers was hanging right off.

There was blood all over her neck and face and in her hair – it came from her mouth and nostrils and even her eyes – and I saw with a shock that she was burned and blackened under the arms and around the chest, as if her clothes had been set on fire and then put out. But that wasn't the worst thing. The worst thing was that she was looking right at me and her mouth was still moving.

I couldn't help it, I turned away. I thought I would begin to be sick. I was gagging and heaving. I wanted to run, but he grabbed me by the shoulder.

You've got to help me, he said.

What? I cried.

We have to finish her off.

I covered my face with my hands. I was shaking so hard I could not breathe. When I took my hands away, there was wet there. I did not know if it was sweat or tears.

Oh God, I whispered. Oh God, oh God, James. What have you done?

I swear she's not meant to still be alive, he said. Honest to God, Eliza, after what I did to her, I don't know how she can be.

With his eyes still on me, he picked up a spade.

'Have you moved any of my tools?' Graham asks her. 'From behind the apple store?'

She looks at him, standing there on the step in his old gardening clothes. 'No,' she says. 'What tools?'

He scratches his head.

'There was the rake and the hoe and a couple of spades. And a mallet, I think. I don't know. I can't remember what I left there.'

'And they're gone?'

'All gone. Really annoying. It was the brand-new hoe, the one we got the other day. But my fault I suppose for leaving them there. And for not getting around to doing that fence.'

Mary stares at him.

'You think that someone came in from the fields?'

He shrugs.

'Must have done. How else? Don't fret. It doesn't matter. Nothing we can do about it now.'

He looks at the table. Eddie's picture propped against the fruit bowl. 'What's that?'

Mary explains and shows him that it's just around the corner. 'If you went around there,' she says, pointing into the photograph, 'you'd come to this house.'

This house. She looks at it again. For a moment she doesn't know what it is that's changed. Then she does. In the picture the lane now seems entirely light and bright, all shadows gone.

Graham frowns at her over the top of his glasses.

'But why would he give it to you?'

'What – Eddie?' Mary feels the colour go to her cheeks. 'I don't know. I asked him that myself and I didn't get much of an answer. You know what he's like. He didn't say anything really.'

After the girls were taken, after weeks had passed and they realised they were probably gone for ever but still didn't know why or in what circumstances, Mary slept.

She did not expect to be able to sleep – did not think she would ever in her whole life sleep again – but she did. She slept. Curled in a coma of her own making, rigid, defended, on her side of the bed, the safe side. It was a sleep without dreams or hope, without any sense of refreshment or of life waiting for her. Even now, if she lets herself think about it, she can precisely recall the taste of that sleep: its black deadness, its grip and flavour. Back then, of course, she would rather have died than slept. Death is what she would have chosen. But she could not leave Graham to cope on his own, so she made do instead with that hard, black, dirty sleep.

While she was sleeping, they came to get things. Anything would do, they said. Hairbrush, baby teeth, bed sheets. For the DNA. And it was very good that she was sleeping, because just the thought of these things would have been enough to break her down all over again. She was very glad Graham did not give them the baby teeth – tiny, jagged, bone-coloured fragments she kept in a dark velvet compartment of her mother's old jewel box. Instead, he gave them Ella's *Mr Men* toothbrush and one of Flo's unwashed raggies.

But Mary did not know any of this till later. She slept through all of it. Waking only to eat and drink and go to the toilet and listen to phone messages, before groping her way back down into the numbing stupefaction of that sleep.

And when at last she had to be woken, it was only because the officer came. Even now she does not know why it was a police officer and not one of the family liaison officers who they'd come to like, trust and dread all at the same time. But it wasn't one of them. It was someone they'd not seen before.

Her name was Claire. She had short blonde hair and small gold studs in her ears and there was a knitted thing in the shape of a teddy bear on the keys that hung with the handcuffs at her waist. Claire said no to a cup of tea. She stood there in their kitchen and the look on her face was enough.

'We have a significant update for you,' she said. 'Where do you want to be told and who do you want present?'

She wakes in the night and she's cold, so cold. She gets out of bed and goes over to the drawer and, shaking all over, she pulls out a jumper, leggings, socks, anything she can find. She puts them all on. Then she picks up a hot-water bottle and, still trembling with cold, she creeps downstairs to the kitchen, puts the kettle on.

A spider is crouched on the counter. Huge, dark, motionless, waiting for something or someone. She brushes it off and it glides across the floor, through the muck and dirt. Dirt? As the kettle chugs to a boil, she bends to look more closely. She's never seen the floor so filthy, so covered in dust and muck. And whose are the black boots? The apron with blue flowers flung over the chair. Why is there a sheet of newspaper pinned to the wall? Where have all the feathers come from?

Straightening up, confused, and lifting her eyes, she sees that the half loaf of bread left out on the counter is furred with mould, a forest of blue-green hair. Worse than that, her fingers, held out in front of her, are suddenly dark and soft at the tips, her flesh blackening, dying. She gasps—

Sitting up in bed. Graham has the light on and is staring at his phone.

'It's Ruby.'

'What?'

'Veronica says she's taken something.' He jumps out of bed. 'She's in King's. I've got to go. I'm going.'

Still struggling to wake, Mary starts to get up, but he stops her.

'There's no point you coming. I mean it. Go back to sleep.'

Mary stares at him.

'What's she taken?'

'I don't know. Some pills.'

'What, on purpose?'

'I don't know.'

'I should come.'

He touches her head.

'There's no point. Nothing you can do. Stay with the dog. I'll call you as soon as I get there.'

The spade he had was dark and sticky with something. It was the one he had used to do her. She was watching us and moaning now. Her face was terrible. And her leg without the boot was twitching as though it was not attached to her but had a life of its own.

James was frowning, his face like a child's face, the lower lip pushed out.

It was her screaming, he said. I told her to stop but she would not. She went on and on, squealing like a ferret in a trap, I could not shut her up. You know what she's like.

I stared at him. I wanted to say that I wasn't sure that I knew what Phoebe Harkiss was like. I took a step away from him, felt the rough wood of the apple store at my back. I watched as he lifted the spade.

No, I cried out as softly as I could, for fear someone should hear me. No, no! Stop it, James!

He paused, his eyes sliding over to me.

She's a nasty piece of work, Eliza, he said, still gripping the spade in his two hands. She would not stop. Don't you see? It was going to rouse the whole neighbourhood. Also – he let the spade fall again and shut his eyes for a second – I'll admit I was very angry with her. For the things she'd told you. For the damage she'd done already and the further damage I can promise you she intended to do.

I held my breath. I could not think. Thoughts were skittering around in every direction. Our whole lives and all of the good things we'd had and said and done, pouring down into a place of darkness, an abyss.

I don't understand, I told him.

Yes, you do.

I don't.

He raised a finger.

Don't say that, Eliza. You do understand. You know very well that you wanted this.

Wanted it! I cried at him in horror. I don't know what you're talking about – who on earth could ever want this?

He looked at me and shook his head.

Easy to say that now, Eliza. But I've lost count of the number of times you've brought up the subject of Phoebe Harkiss with me and not in a good way.

I stared at him, my heart thudding so hard a taste of sick came up in my throat. When I tried to speak, it came out in a whisper.

You think I wanted you to hurt her? Is that what you're saying, James? That you thought I wanted you to hurt Phoebe Harkiss?

He sighed and let his hands drop down by his sides.

I don't know what you want, Eliza. Honest to God, I never do. But what I know for sure is that now we're in this together and you need to help me deal with it.

I took a step back away from him.

Why?

What do you mean, why?

Why would I help you with this?

Why? Because we love each other of course and because you're my girl and like I said before, we're in this together.

I was about to tell him that this was untrue, that seeing Phoebe Harkiss on the ground like this had banished all thoughts and feelings of love from my mind and that I wasn't at all sure any more that I wanted to be his girl. But then as he grasped the spade in both his hands, I saw something in his eyes that I had not seen before.

He came very close to me. His face in my face. I saw that he was sweating so much that it was running from his hair and down his temples and dripping into his shirt. His clothes were wet. The snake on his neck glistened wet. When he spoke, the slow and deliberate softness of it turned my insides cold.

All right, he said. All right, you win. You just walk away. Walk away now, Eliza, and leave me to it. Go on. Just do it.

I said nothing. I stayed very still. He bent his head closer to mine.

Do it, he said.

I waited a moment. My chest was tight. I could not speak. He licked his lips.

Why aren't you walking?

I said nothing.

I'm waiting.

Another quick silence.

I'm waiting, Eliza. Why aren't you walking? You're free to go – look at me, am I stopping you?

I snatched a breath, my blood jumping. He watched me for a moment and then he laughed.

Or do you want to stay and help me? Is that it? Would you like that? Would it give you pleasure to help me? I mean it, Eliza. I want an answer. Are we in this together or are we not?

I bowed my head. Out of the corner of my eye, I caught a small, dreadful movement from the ground where Phoebe was. I realised I was shaking all over.

Well, Eliza? he said. Give me a sign that you understand me. A nod will do. Give me a nod, Eliza. Because I swear that I won't proceed any further without a sign from you.

I could hardly breathe. My fingers were icy but my body felt as if it was on fire. I thought I was going to faint, but at last I must have nodded, because he stepped away, satisfied.

I let my eyes go back to Phoebe. One terrible thought chasing another in my head now.

222

Why is she burned? I whispered.

James stood the spade down in the earth and leaned on it a moment. He lifted one hand and rubbed at his hair.

Well, I thought if I could only get her in the apple store, I could set it off. Chuck something in that would make it burn. An accident. That's what they'd think.

Oh God, I said.

But she wouldn't burn. Like a witch, she resisted the flame and it just smoked and sputtered away like some old biddy's pipe.

He laughed. And as he laughed, Phoebe moaned. I saw that more blood was coming out of her eyes. I felt some more sick come up in my mouth but swallowed it back.

James stepped forwards and lifted the spade. I couldn't help it, I cried out for him to stop.

But he paid no attention. He whacked her so hard that all you could hear was a dull crunching sound. She gave a small whine, almost a shout—

He looked at me.

There, he said. You watched me do it, Eliza. We're finishing her off. We're in this together now.

And I turned away as he lifted the spade once more with two hands and brought it down straight like a blade.

Mary stands in the kitchen, one hand on the old pine table, holding herself still and watching the space between the chair and the dresser. Air, white-painted wall, skirting board. She can't take her eyes off it, that space. The dog gets up out of her basket and walks towards the same place and, head on one side, stares and begins to growl.

Mary can't help it, she takes a step backwards, away. She looks at the dog.

'What?' she whispers. 'What is it?'

The dog, listening, tilts her head the other way and looks at her.

'What is it?' Mary says again. 'Is something there?'

The dog gazes at her and looks again at the space. Then at last, as if something has changed, she relaxes and goes over to her water bowl and starts drinking. The sound of her lapping filling the room.

Mary glances around her. There's a bottle of PLJ lime juice on the counter. Without warning, the yellow plastic lid pops off and hits the floor, rolling across the stone flags. Mary jumps so hard she almost cries out. Immediately the dog runs over to the door and whines.

The phone rings. Graham. He tells her that Ruby's all right. She's fine.

'They didn't even have to pump her stomach,' he says. 'They tried to make her vomit but it didn't work. They gave her charcoal. They want to monitor her for a bit longer, but they're sure she's going to be fine. Medically, anyway.'

Mary listens, still staring at the PLJ bottle. She asks him what Ruby took. He gives a short laugh, but she thinks she hears a catch in his voice.

'Would you believe, she took about two weeks' worth of her mother's anti-depressants. Sertraline, I think it's called.'

Mary thinks about this. Veronica on anti-depressants? He'd never mentioned that. She bends to pick the yellow lid up off the floor.

'My God,' she says.

'I know.'

'But why on earth – do you know why?'

She hears him sigh.

'Well, that's the million-dollar question, isn't it? We'll give her a couple of days, wait till she's feeling a bit better. But then she's certainly got some explaining to do.'

'But what?' Mary gazes at the small piece of plastic in her hand. 'You're saying you think she meant to hurt herself?'

Graham hesitates.

'God knows what she meant. A cry for attention, Veronica says. But I would say that girl has plenty of attention, wouldn't you? I mean, honestly, so much of the bloody time.'

Mary tries to think about this – about whether Ruby has their attention or not. She puts the lid back on the bottle.

'How's Veronica?' she says.

She hears Graham take a breath.

'Upset. Furious. Relieved. Shaken. She's all right,' he adds and Mary thinks she hears gratitude in his voice, that she bothered to ask.

He tells her that he's going to stay over in London till tomorrow at least. That Ruby is seeing a psych person. That he's going to make sure Veronica eats something. That he'll call Mary later to give her an update.

'I just feel she needs me at the moment,' he tells her, and Mary isn't sure whether he means Ruby or Veronica. She tells him that's fine. Of course it's fine. She understands.

'I love you,' he says before he says goodbye.

'Me too,' she says. 'I love you too.'

She turns the phone to silent and lays it carefully on the table and sits down. And suddenly there it is – a smell she remembers from childhood. Hot, feverish skin and hair, poorly breath, the bright metallic tang of long-ago sickness.

She looks around her.

Everything is in its proper place. Chairs, bench, cooker, sink. The big casserole dish washed and turned over to drain. The flowers she picked that morning and put in an old jam jar. The picture Eddie gave her propped on the dresser next to a pile of bills. She can't see anything wrong anywhere.

Then her eyes go to the calendar on the wall by the fridge. A present from her mother. Bright yellow spring flowers, celandines or something, a Swiss mountain in summer. All the squares blank and white, their empty life. As she watches, the page moves, unmistakable, blowing upwards, as if a breeze had lifted it.

Gasping, she tries to stand, scraping her chair on the old stone floor. The noise does it, it does the trick. At last she feels the presence drift, wobble, diminish.

Gone.

She notices her phone on the table, blinking. She picks it up, her hand trembling. Five missed calls. In the few moments since she said goodbye to Graham.

'Eddie,' she says, 'what is it?'

The last blow had gone into Phoebe's chest. You heard a crack and a snap like the wishbone on a chicken. There was so much blood it seemed as if her heart was spilling out. I tried not to look, but I couldn't help it, I did look. The sight of her lying there with her bodice quite bloodied and open and every private part of her on display made the ground beneath me feel light and soft and tipsy.

James, I said. Oh my God, James. What have we done?

He did not seem to hear me. He threw down the spade and fished around in his pockets and lit a cigarette.

Thank Christ for that, he said as he chucked the matches on the ground. Now, do we burn her or bury her?

I watched as he sucked on the smoke, taking several long drags and blowing out furiously before throwing it down and crushing it hard with his foot.

Come on, he said. I need ideas, Eliza.

I stared at him. The way he'd flung down that spade, you'd have reckoned all he'd just done was finish spreading a patch of manure or something similar. You could imagine it was a perfectly harmless and ordinary day and he was going home to his tea in a minute which was waiting on the table. As if he knew what I was thinking, he scratched his head and yawned and then he smiled at me.

I'm awful hungry, you know, Eliza. I'd kill for a bang sandwich. Or a sausage. I'd love a sausage.

I stayed silent. I had no answer to that.

Oh, he said. And did your pa tell you by the by that we cleaned up at the races?

He's standing there just as he said he would be, on the edge of the corn field. His car askew on the verge as if he pulled in abruptly, the door flung open against the hedge.

Mary sees that he's wearing jeans. A crumpled shirt, untucked. His hair bent and untidy, as if he just got out of bed. A sheen of sweat on his face.

For a moment he just looks at her.

'Mary. You came.'

The sun is hot on Mary's head. The dry, baked smell of the corn. An aeroplane moving overhead. The emptiness all around them. She feels suddenly trapped, lured.

'Are you all right?' she says. 'What is it? What's happened? Should I call Deborah?'

The smile disappears.

'Please don't. That would actually be the worst thing you could do.' He hesitates. 'And anyway she's not here. She's in London today.'

'In London?' Mary's heart speeds up.

'With her mother. They had stuff to do.'

She takes a step back, away from him, looking at him.

'What's the matter, Eddie? What's going on? Why did you call me?'

He smiles at her.

'Can we just go for a walk?' he says.

The moon had slid behind a cloud and the sky was black and starless, the whole world dark. I felt as if the life I knew before had ended, that I had walked straight out of that one and into another that was as sudden and frightening as the devil's own hell.

James sat down on the ground not far from where her body was and he patted the grass next to him.

Come here, he said. Come on. Come to me, Princess.

I looked at him but I didn't go. I stayed where I was. The piece of ground he sat on had blood on it. I could not have gone and sat in those sticky black shadows for all the tea in China. I was about to say so, but then something caught my eye.

I gasped.

James! Look!

Even though Phoebe's chest had blood still coming out of it and her freckled face was shocked and still, her eyes wide, the leg with the boot on was moving.

James was fishing around in his pockets for another cigarette.

Don't worry about it, he said, turning his head and watching for a moment, before going back to what he was doing. It's what they do, when they're dead. She's gone but the leg don't realise it yet.

I stared at the leg, twitching and twitching, and I thought of Phoebe who I'd always hated but who was gone – not just for a while, which I wouldn't have minded – but for ever and ever. She could never come back. I couldn't help it. I began to cry.

James found the cigarette and lifted his head and looked at me.

For Christ's sake, Eliza, he said as he put it in his mouth and struck a match. I tell you it's nothing to worry about. I swear I've seen the exact same thing happen once or twice before and you can take it from me that on all those occasions the folks were goners.

I stared at him.

All what occasions?

He waved the match to put it out. Shaking his head, looking at me through narrow eyes, breathing out smoke.

It was only a couple of times.

What was only a couple of times?

Forget it. I didn't mean it like that.

What, James? What have you done?

He looked at me, then down again at the cigarette in his hand.

When you have lived as I have lived, Eliza—

I could not listen. I turned my head and looked away and then I went and sat away from him, as far away as I could possibly get, my back against the apple store. I tried to swallow my tears, for I knew there was no use to them. A strange kind of calm was coming over me. Everything bad that could ever happen had happened now. We were firmly in hell and it was almost a relief to know there was no possible way out. I sat back and looked at him.

How many people have you killed? I said.

She takes him to her bench. Out on the grass path, recently mown and now with a scattering of molehills, by the tall reed beds towards the golf course. She can see that he's still shaky, not himself at all. She still doesn't know why he called her. He says he can't explain it right away, that he just needs to calm down.

'Talk to me,' he says.

'What about?'

'Anything. Tell me what you've been doing today. Tell me anything. I just need to hear you talking.'

Mary hesitates, then she tells him about Ruby. She can see that he's genuinely shocked.

'I'm so sorry,' he says. 'I can't believe it. She seems like such a sensible, level kind of girl. I'd never have dreamed she'd do something like that.'

'Neither did we,' she says. 'We thought she was fine. It seemed to come right out of the blue.'

He looks at her.

'Poor Graham.'

'I know.'

'And poor you. Both of you. And when's he back?'

She tells him she doesn't know. Tomorrow, probably. It depends on what happens. He and Veronica are taking it one day at a time.

Eddie looks at her.

'He gets on OK with her, does he? This ex of his?'

Mary tells him the truth. That Graham and Veronica are not the best of friends, but that it's amicable. That he always tries to do the right thing by her, to behave well, because of Ruby.

Eddie looks interested.

'I realise I never even asked you what the situation was.'

'The situation?'

'Did he leave her for you? Sorry,' he adds, watching her face. 'Is that a bit personal?'

'Yes, it is and no, he didn't. She left him. For someone else. But it didn't work out. With the person she left him for, I mean.'

'So she made a mistake and now she wants him back?'

Mary stares at him, shocked.

'No. Of course not.'

'What I meant is – I suppose I just thought he must have left her for you. That's just the feeling I'd got.'

'Well, he didn't.'

'All right.'

For a while they sit and don't speak. Eddie smoking a cigarette in quick, nervous puffs.

'What a lovely spot,' he says and she tells him that she comes here every day.

Surprise on his face.

'Every day?'

'Almost every day. Whenever I can. I suppose it's the only time I'm ever properly alone.'

She watches as he puts out the cigarette and places the stub next to him on a slat of the bench.

'And you brought me here,' he says, looking pleased.

She shrugs, says nothing. Wonders if she's already regretting it. Aware, suddenly, of the smell of him. Sweat and soap. Other people's soap.

'What a day,' he says. 'Look at that. What a sky.'

She tilts her head to look at the clear wide blueness of it, not a single cloud, the hot sun bearing down on them. He turns away from her suddenly, shielding his eyes against the light.

'That bird. Can you see it? See how it just keeps on falling and falling out of the sky?'

'A kestrel probably,' she says, wondering why the sudden sight of the back of his head makes her feel sorry for him.

'Is it a kestrel?'

'I don't know. Graham would know.'

'He knows about birds?'

'A bit.'

'He knows about most things, doesn't he?'

'Some things, yes.'

'Is there anything he doesn't know about?'

She does not answer him. They both watch the bird for a moment, climbing and falling and climbing again.

'Does he know about you?' he says.

'What do you mean, does he know about me?'

'Does he know what goes on inside your head? What you think about. What you want.'

Mary says nothing for a moment, then she shrugs.

'You're assuming that I know those things,' she says.

Eddie hesitates. Leaning forwards, his wrists on his knees. She hears him sigh.

'I had this dream. A couple of nights ago. The weirdest dream. One of those dreams that are so clear they almost don't feel like a dream. And in the dream – believe me, Mary, I know how this sounds – you told me you were going to have a baby.'

Mary feels her heart tilt. She turns and stares at him.

'A baby?'

He shakes his head.

'I know, I know. Dreams don't really mean anything. It's probably just because of what we talked about at the pub – and me telling you about my son and all that.' He takes a breath. 'And I promise I would never have told you, except – well, it wouldn't let go of me. I couldn't shake it off. And it felt like I wouldn't be able to stop thinking about it until I'd told you.' He turns to look at her. 'And then I was at work and – I don't know how to describe it – I just sort of panicked.'

'Panicked?'

She stares at him. He looks away.

'It was like I had no choice: I just had to see you. To tell you. About the dream. Seriously, Mary, I felt almost sick with panic. It's never happened to me before. I got in the car and drove here as fast as I could. The only reason I stopped the car by that field is my heart was pounding so hard I honestly thought I was going to crash.'

Mary looks at the ground. Swallowing. Looking at her hands in the lap of her jeans. Her eyes suddenly filling with tears.

'See?' he says. 'I told you it was crazy.'

She swallows again.

'It's not crazy.'

'It is. It is crazy.'

She clasps her hands together, suddenly afraid.

'I'm pregnant,' she says. 'I think I am. I think I'm going to have a baby.'

James, I said, we have to do something. Before they go looking for her – before they find us here.

James nodded, but he seemed in no hurry. He lit another smoke. Held it over to me but I shook my head.

I mean right now this minute, I added. Before someone comes.

He nodded again.

The field, he said. We'll put her in the field. The clods are still quite claggy from the storm. It'll be easy enough to dig there.

I stared at him.

Are you mad? And in a month or two when they dig up the potatoes, what then?

He nodded. The moon came out again, turning his face grey, then bluish, then silver. I thought that he looked like a bad fairy king.

You're right. Good girl. Well done for using your head. What, then? What'll we do? We could take her to the river at Bly, I suppose. Put her in a sack and make sure it sinks? But I'm not sure how we'd get her there.

Easy, I said, because I was very angry with him now. We toss her in my father's cart and trundle her along the road for everyone to see.

For a moment he looked at me as if this might really be a plan, but when he saw that I was ribbing him, he smiled.

He stares at her. Catches his breath.

'But I thought – after what you told me – it wasn't possible?'

'It's not. You're right. It's not.' She blinks. 'It's not possible.'

She waits, pressing her lips together, holding herself very still. She feels him looking at her.

'So – then how?'

'I don't know.'

'But are you sure?'

'I don't know. Yes. I suppose so. I mean, they did a test.'

'The doctor did?'

'Yes.'

She thinks of it for a moment. That beige room with its mottled walls. The doctor's face. Her thudding heart. Confusion. The memory of it making her heart race again.

A breeze stirs the reeds. They both watch as the bird drops through the air before gathering itself just in time and heading back up into the sky. She feels him looking at her.

'What does Graham say?'

'I haven't told him yet.'

'You haven't?'

'No. Not yet.'

'But you will.'

'I don't know.'

'What do you mean, you don't know? You have to tell him.'

Mary looks at her knees.

'It only just happened. I don't even know why I'm telling you. I haven't decided what to do yet.'

'Do?'

'I don't think I can have it. I can't, Eddie – if it turns out to be true, that is.'

He glances at her.

'True? But what are you saying?'

'Well, it can't be true, can it? How can it be?'

'You think they've got it wrong?'

'Well, they must have, yes.'

'But you say they did a test?'

She looks at him, her eyes filling up again.

'Please don't make me think about it,' she says.

Far off, the sound of a dog barking. Someone calling to it. Whistling. She feels him watching her again and she looks at him, noticing that dimple in his unshaven cheek.

'Well, miracles happen,' he says at last.

'Miracles.' She hears herself laugh.

He shakes his head.

'That's what it was. In the dream. Someone kept on saying it. A miracle, they said, it's a miracle.'

She lifts her head, looks at him. 'I can't have a baby, Eddie. I just can't.'

'What do you mean, you can't?'

Mary says nothing. She glances down and for a moment she sees his arms, his hands resting on his knees. The chunky metal wristwatch that looks like it means business. The light hairs on his forearms. The deep blue veins on the backs of his hands. His fingers, knuckles, nails.

'I just can't,' she says again.

'Look,' he tells her after a few more moments have passed, 'I wasn't joking when I said it was a miracle. If anyone deserves a miracle, it's you. So maybe you should just think of it as a gift?'

'A gift?'

'My mother had a child that drowned. A boy.'

She stares at him.

'What? You mean your brother?'

He hesitates.

'My half-brother, yes. He drowned at Christmas. Can you imagine? Christmas Day – Christmas morning – in the pond.'

Mary feels her blood jump. He takes a breath.

'But she went and got pregnant again the very next year and this time she had twins. What a blessing it was. A miracle, you see.'

She looks at him.

'I thought your mother died when you were ten?'

He blinks at her. Feeling around in his pocket for his cigarettes.

'Ah, but you see, all of this was long before I was born.'

'And the twins?'

'What?'

'They're still alive?'

He sighs. Pulls out a cigarette, looks at it.

'I've told you about my family. It's a messy business. God knows where the twins are now.'

'But are they boys or girls?'

'Girls. Women, I suppose. I don't know how old they'd be now.'

233

'You don't even know? You've never tried to find them?'

He rests his arms on his knees for a moment, lighter in one hand, cigarette in the other. Staring into the long grass.

'I haven't,' he says. 'You're right. I feel ashamed now that I haven't bothered. I ought to have a go at finding them, I suppose.'

You did something terrible, I told him.

He shrugged.

I wasn't intending to harm her. But what could I do? She asked for it. Come on, Eliza, we've been over this. It's not my fault.

Not your fault? Whose fault was it, then?

You know what a spiteful little bitch she was.

No one asks to be killed, I said.

I don't know what else I was supposed to do.

I stared at him in horror, then I couldn't help it – I started to laugh. But almost as soon as I'd started, the taste of the laugh in my mouth turned bad and I stopped.

You are unbelievable, I said.

He looked at me carefully for a moment then he stuck out his lip in a sulky way.

A spiteful little blabbermouth, she was. You've no idea. I swear, I had no choice. I simply couldn't trust her any more. She said she'd go straight to her Ma and tell her everything she knew about me.

Now I stared at him.

Everything? What do you mean? What was it that she knew?

He shook his head then and blew out a long breath of smoke and looked down at his boots. I saw that they were unlaced just like Phoebe's boot was unlaced and there was mud all over them. His breeches too. He shook his head.

Nothing at all, he said. I mean it, Eliza. She had nothing on me. At the end of the day, it was all just guesses.

But what? What are you talking about? I don't understand. What thing did she guess?

He shrugged. His eyes were calm.

I don't know. Whatever it was that I'd been doing, I suppose.

A chill ran through me.

What had you been doing?

He raised his eyes and gave me a sticky look.

Nothing. I wasn't doing nothing.

I held my breath. Tears were coming up in my face but I swallowed them back down. Talking to James Dix in this mood was like swimming in a swamp – the more you kicked, the more you got sucked down.

I wish you'd never come here, I said. I wish I didn't know you. I would give the whole world not to know you. I wish that storm tree had flattened you and left you properly dead.

For the first time, he looked quite shocked.

You don't mean that, Princess.

I do, I said. I do mean it. I mean it with all my heart. I can't love a murderer, James, I just can't.

He said nothing. Far off somewhere in the woods, an owl was calling. A terribly sad and lonely sound. I glanced over at Phoebe. No part of her was moving now. Her skin shone white in the moonlight. I used my apron to wipe the tears off my face. For a long while both of us were silent. I thought about everything James and me had done together – all the laughing and touching and dear little promises and happiness – and I waited for him to say something, but he didn't say anything. He did not speak.

But I won't have you go to jail or be hanged, I said at last. I won't do it. I can't.

His face lit up.

That's right, Princess. I knew it!

What? I said, the speed of the change in him almost making me regret what I had said. What did you know?

That I could rely on you. I knew it. Oh Eliza, you do love me, don't you?

I wasn't all that sure I did love him any more. I pressed my lips together. It was like I wanted to press all the kisses out of them, the memories of all that warmth and kissing.

It's not about love, I said.

What then?

I shook my head. The truth was I didn't know what it was about. Perhaps all I wanted was for nothing to change – for everything to stay sweet and steady and the same, for the summer to go on exactly as it was. But I also felt impatient for something: what? I could hardly be bothered to explain it to myself, let alone try and make him see it.

But I looked at him sitting there and, remembering the peppery smell of the back of his neck and the way his eyes could melt me and all the times we'd had connection, the things we'd done, the backs of my knees went hot.

I've a better idea, I said. Of what to do with her.

'Don't go home,' he says as they make their slow, sunlit way back along the rough-mown path by the golf course to his car. 'Do you have to go? If Graham's not even there? Come back to ours for a bit.'

She hesitates. Looking at him.

'Is Deborah there?'

'I told you. She's in London today. Seeing her mother. I'm getting her from the station later.'

Mary says nothing. A quick picture of Deborah on a train, her pale hair falling over her shoulder as she pushes down the window to open the door.

'What?' he says.

'Nothing.'

'You looked worried.'

'I'm fine.'

She does not look at him and then she does. He reaches out and touches her hand, just for a moment, the lightest touch.

'Go on,' he says. 'I'm asking you. I'm begging you. I really want you to come.'

At the house, Mary's startled to see Deborah's bag on the chair in the sunny, coir-matted hall. A cardigan flung over it.

She stops in front of it for a moment. Then follows Eddie into the kitchen. Watching as he goes over and fills the kettle, plonks it down and switches it on, turning back to her.

'She has another bag, you know.'

'What?'

'The bag. Out there. It's not the one she took with her. To London.'

'Oh.'

He comes over to her then – crosses the room and stands in front of her. She has no idea what he's going to do, and then she does. He puts his two hands on her shoulders. The unexpectedness of it – almost painful. She feels a flush spreading up from her chest to her neck, her cheeks.

'What are you doing?' she says.

He keeps his eyes on hers for a moment, then takes his hands away. 'I don't know. I haven't the faintest idea.'

He walks away, crossing the vast, blond space of the kitchen – its airy cleanness odd and alarming to her now, even though she's eaten several suppers in here, even, one weekend, let herself in to feed their cat – and goes over to the polished counter of the island.

'An island!' Deborah said as she showed them around the house that first time. 'I don't know what it is about islands, but I've always wanted one, haven't I, Eddie?'

Now he takes mugs off hooks. Puts them down on Deborah's island. Opens a drawer for a spoon. Goes to a cupboard by the sink, takes out a big, unopened box of tea bags, rips the cellophane off. Glancing across at her.

'Sit down,' he says.

Mary does nothing. She doesn't sit. He glances at her.

'She's not here. I told you.'

'What?'

'Deb. She had lunch with her mum and then they were looking at wallpapers or something. For the long-awaited, bloody extension. She's going to text me when she's on the train.'

Mary says nothing. At last she pulls out a kitchen chair and sits down. Looking at the sagging sofa by the Aga, where the elderly Siamese lies curled and motionless on a blanket that is thick with hair.

She feels Eddie watching her.

'Do you need to call Graham?' he says. 'To see how she's doing?'

She shakes her head.

'I know he'll call when he has news.'

For a moment neither of them says anything. Eddie looks at her.

'This must feel so hard for you both. After everything that's happened – your daughters – after what you've already had to go through.'

The kettle comes to the boil. He pours water into the cups. Mary watches him in silence. He lifts his head and looks at her.

'What?' he says.

'What?'

'You. What are you thinking? You're thinking something. I can see it all over your face.'

She smiles. Shakes her head.

'I don't know. It's just that – well, you're the only person I've ever met who dares to do that.'

'Do what?'

'Refer to it. To the girls. And to what happened.'

He makes a face.

'Deb always says I don't think. That I just go blundering in.'

Mary looks at him.

'I wouldn't call it blundering.'

'You wouldn't?'

She takes a breath.

'When we were at the pub that time, and you asked me about the girls – you suddenly out of the blue asked me their ages and what they were called – well, this may sound strange, but I can't tell you how much I liked it.'

He looks at her. Lifting the tea bags from the cups.

'Really? You didn't mind it?'

'It was lovely. Lovely of you. Yes, really. A lovely thing to do.'

He sighs.

'It wasn't out of the blue actually. And it wasn't me blundering, not that time. I'd been thinking about it for a long time. Wondering whether I should. Trying to pluck up courage, I suppose.'

Mary stares at him.

'You had?'

'I wasn't sure, you see, whether it was the right thing. I very badly didn't want to upset you. Make you think about them, I mean.'

She looks at him.

'You didn't upset me. Not at all. And anyway, I want to think about them.'

'You do?'

Mary nods, suddenly both elated and embarrassed. He gazes at her.

'Of course. Of course you do.'

She sits up in her chair.

'No one ever asks me about them any more. Literally never. Not even family, no one. People go out of their way not to mention them.

No one ever says their names. Even Graham. Especially Graham. He just can't do it – he can't say their names.'

'He can't?'

'Not yet. It's not his fault. He just can't. I don't blame him for that. But what it means, you see, is that no one ever mentions them at all. Whole days – weeks – go by and I don't ever hear them mentioned—'

Her eyes fill with tears and she turns her head away quickly. A long silence. She turns back. Watching as he pours milk into the cups.

'I'm sure it's just that they're afraid to,' he says at last. 'The people, I mean. They probably think you'll find it upsetting.'

Mary watches as he puts the milk bottle back in the fridge. She shakes her head.

'Well, I wouldn't. I wouldn't find it upsetting. What's upsetting is to have to live my whole life never talking about them as if they were—'

He turns from the fridge to look at her.

'Dead?'

She nods, feeling herself flush. A kind of shame creeping over her. But confidence, too. A little bit of confidence. Allowing herself to glance at him.

'That's right. As if they were dead. Sometimes I still can't believe it. That they really are definitely dead. Not temporarily dead or just dead for the time being in some awful, painful way, but completely dead and gone – lost to me, completely lost, for ever and ever.'

Eddie is silent for a moment.

'It's impossible. To think about.'

She holds herself very still, her cheeks still burning.

'It is, yes.'

'If you believe it is for ever.'

She looks at him.

'What does that mean?'

He hesitates.

'Well, I suppose some people would say it's just this life—'

Mary shakes her head.

'I don't believe that.'

'You don't?'

'No. No, I don't. Why, do you?'

He keeps his eyes on her.

'Not really, no.'

They're both quiet again. Very gently, he places the tea in front of her.

'But they're not dead to you, are they? That's what you're saying, isn't it? That they aren't.'

Mary stares at him. She shakes her head. Tries to speak but finds she can't. He leans back against the kitchen counter, folds his arms, looking at her.

'You carry them around with you, don't you? All the time. Anyone can see it. They're in your eyes, in your gestures, the way you move your hands, your head. It's impossible to be around you without feeling and seeing them.'

She nods, tears now coming to her eyes.

'That's it. That's it exactly. How do you know that? How can you say it? Do you think it's mad? Doesn't it sound very strange?'

He shakes his head.

'Not at all. Not to me anyway. Though I think it's true that a lot of people might not get it.'

Mary looks at him. She smiles at him and he smiles back and then for a moment they both laugh. She gazes at his face, unable suddenly to take it properly in, to get enough of it.

'Some days it feels like they exist more strongly than ever,' she tells him. 'Since we came to this place. I don't know what it is about it, the cottage, I felt it from the very first time. They never came here, never lived in this place, yet somehow there's a connection – a continuing. I feel them all the time. Everywhere. In the garden especially—'

'The garden? Why the garden?'

'I don't know. I can't explain it. I only have to walk out into the garden to feel them, to feel that they're right there with me. I didn't feel it when we first got the house – it was something that grew slowly, creeping up on me. Now it's unmistakable. They're in the garden. I spend time with them every day. You think that's mad?'

He smiles at her. Picks up his tea.

'What do you want me to say?'

She feels herself start to laugh.

'That it's not mad. That I'm not going out of my mind. That you think it's OK.'

He smiles.

'I think it's OK.'

Mary takes a breath, holding her hand out in front of her. Realising she's trembling.

'Some days the feeling's so strong I almost don't know what to do with it.'

Eddie looks at her.

'Do you need to do anything with it?'

'I don't know.' She gazes at him now, a kind of euphoria building inside her. 'Really, Eddie – I don't know.'

He is leaning back against the counter now, looking at her.

'What were they like?' he asks her at last.

She looks at him, her heart lifting.

'The girls? What, I haven't told you?'

He smiles.

'You've never told me anything. But I suppose I've never asked.'

'You told me all about your boy without me asking.'

He smiles again.

'That's right. You're right. I did. Well, then. Tell me. It's your turn. I'd just like to be able to imagine them, that's all. Your girls.'

Mary smiles and then she laughs.

'It's difficult. I don't really know how to describe them.'

'Try.'

She shuts her eyes, opens them again.

'I don't want to make you think they were perfect or anything like that. They were just normal children, I suppose. Quite a handful, quite annoying sometimes, same as any kids that age. Monsters. That's what we called them, the little monsters. They could be pretty impossible, both of them. Ella was probably the worst.'

'Ella was the big one?'

Mary nods. 'Twenty-one months between them. She was just so bright, Ella was. Right from the start. She could read at three years old – I'm not exaggerating – not just the odd word, but proper books, a whole book. She'd make up stories as soon as she could speak and I had to write them down for her—' Eddie laughs and

Mary smiles. 'She was so bossy! Then later she wrote them down herself, of course.'

'You think she'd have been a writer?'

She shrugs. 'I don't know. It's easy to get carried away. I mean, lots of kids make up stories, don't they? Maybe, though. But it wasn't just that. She could do maths, too. Anything, really, she was so quick, she could pick anything up. She had such an imagination. I think it might have got her into trouble one day.'

'Why do you say that?'

Mary hesitates. 'We worried about her sometimes. She couldn't always tell the difference between what was real and what wasn't—'

'She told lies?'

'Not exactly. Not lies. You wouldn't call them lies. She'd say things and you knew she really did believe them. But she seemed to live in a slightly different world from everyone else.'

'She sounds a lot like you.'

Mary smiles. 'Me?'

'You don't think you're like that?'

'I haven't thought about it. But she wasn't that much like me. I can't do maths at all, for instance. She had my impatience, though. And my hair—'

'She had your hair?'

Mary laughs. 'Exactly the same! Very long and dark and out of control. Always tangled. But she wouldn't let me cut it.'

He looks at her.

'I'd love to see a photo of her.'

Mary takes a breath, shakes her head.

'I haven't been able to look at pictures yet. Graham can. It's funny, isn't it? He can't speak about the girls, but he can look at them.'

'And you're the other way round.'

'Yes.'

'I wonder why that is.'

'I don't know. I don't know why I can't. I don't mind talking about them, not at all. But I just can't seem to look at pictures yet. I think I worry that once I started—'

'What? Once you'd started what?'

She looks at the table. 'I'd never be able to stop.'

She's silent for a moment. Eddie picks up his tea.

'And the little one? What was she like?'

'Flo?' Mary laughs. 'About as different from Ella as it was possible to be. The most laidback child ever. Lazy, though. My God. She let Ella do just about everything for her. All our fault, I know that. We spoiled her, I think, it was hard not to, because she was such an easy baby, especially after Ella.' Mary lifts her tea, looks at it, puts it down again. 'The big thing you need to know about Flo – the thing you couldn't have helped knowing if you'd met her – is she was absolutely mad about Peppa Pig—'

'Peppa what?'

Mary laughs. 'Peppa Pig! It's a character, on TV. You won't know it. Your boy's probably too old. I'm sorry, but Flo was obsessed. She never stopped talking about Peppa Pig this, Peppa Pig that. Her lunchbox, her trainers. She had this dressing gown that she never took off, she even wore it to school once. She wanted to go to Peppa Pig World – can you believe it, there's a Peppa Pig World? We were going to take her for her birthday.' Mary feels Eddie looking at her. 'Oh God. I'm sorry. I'm going on too much now.'

He shakes his head. 'Please keep going. I like hearing it.'

'It wasn't just Peppa. Flo loved all those things. She was never one for dolls, but animals, soft toys. She had this dog, a little blue dog called Tuffy. I think he was originally Ella's but somehow she got hold of him. He went everywhere with her. After they – when they were missing – I kept him with me. Partly I knew Flo would have worried about him, but also, well, he had her smell on him. I even took him to bed at night.' She looks at Eddie. 'It's ridiculous, I know—'

'It's not. It's not ridiculous at all.'

She hesitates. 'We put him in her coffin. Tuffy. It's what she would have – well, it was just the right thing. It felt like the right thing. I can't tell you how hard it was, though, letting him go.'

She looks at her tea again. Then lifts her eyes, trying to smile.

'I haven't talked about all of this stuff in such a very long time. Peppa Pig. My God, I used to have to listen to that word about eighty-five times a day. And Tuffy, too. Just saying it all aloud, sitting here in your kitchen like this—'

She notices that Eddie is very still, very quiet.

'What?' he says. 'What about it?'

'I don't know. It's . . .' Mary thinks about it, hugging herself, her teeth chattering, suddenly very cold.

'Does it hurt?'

'I don't know. Should it hurt? Do you think it should hurt? Is it weird, do you think, that I'm sitting here, wanting to tell you all about Peppa Pig and Tuffy?'

She shakes her head, starts to laugh. Eddie smiles, looking at her.

'You love it, don't you? You just do. You love it.'

'What?'

'Talking about them. You love talking about them. Just now, listening to you. You came completely back to life. I've never seen you like that before. All lit up. You changed, you really did. For a few moments you were someone else.'

Still hugging herself, Mary looks at him.

'They were everything to me, my girls. My whole life. Everything. I suppose they made me who I was. When they died, my heart stopped. I ceased to exist. My heart just stopped when they died.'

Eddie is quiet. His eyes on her.

'And what happened?'

'What?'

'On that day.'

'You mean how did I lose them?' Mary takes a breath, looks at the floor. At last she lifts her head, meeting his gaze. 'I took them swimming,' she says.

That day. It took just a few minutes for her to bring the car round from the car park to the front of the leisure centre. Expecting to see them waiting where she had left them, at the foot of that sloping, concrete walkway – wet hair and sandals and rolled-up towels. At first, not finding them there, she did not panic. She realised, angrily, that against all her instructions they must have gone back up to the snack machine. Flo, it would be Flo, moaning for chocolate.

Risking a ticket by leaving the car on the yellow line with the indicators flashing, she ran up the slope to reception. They were not by the snack machine. And then, finding nothing, no one, in fact no children anywhere at all, not even in the small hallway that led down to the changing rooms, then she did at last panic. Running up and down the walkway and around the glass reception area screaming, calling, crying out to anyone she could find, demanding to know if the people waiting in the queue had seen two little girls in identical purple fleeces – one with long, dark curly hair, the other shorter, fairer, in fact quite blonde.

People started to help her. One of the tracksuited girls came out from behind the desk. Checking the changing rooms, the foyer, the poolside, then three or four of them going back out onto the walkway, rushing up and down that windblown slope, calling their names.

Might they have gone to the car park? Was that possible? they asked her. Could they have been looking for her there? Her heart banging hard enough by now to make her want to retch, afraid to leave any part of that place uncovered yet knowing that every single time she moved, she was going against her own perpetual instruction to them: if you are ever lost, if you ever can't find me, don't move. Stay put. Stay in the exact place where we said we would meet.

And then, after minutes or maybe longer, when the duty manager was called and then the manager and then, finally – after what seemed like a very long time but was probably still less than half an hour – the police, even then she refused to sit still or stop looking for them or to believe that anything could have happened in the brief amount of time it took for her to run to the car park and get the car and bring it round.

'You left the two of them alone?'

'It was less than two minutes. I've done it before. They're sensible girls.'

'It's a busy road.'

'They were holding hands. They know not to go anywhere near the road.'

'The older one would stay with the younger one? You're sure of that? She wouldn't leave her?'

'Never.'

'You're certain they wouldn't go wandering off?'

'Absolutely certain, yes.'

Two little girls, aged seven and five. Sisters, yes. One dark, one fair. Identical purple fleeces. Navy sandals. Rolled-up swimming towels.

'And the towels – what colour are the towels?'

The towels. She froze, failing at this last hurdle, unable now to see the towels – even though she'd been rubbing at her daughters' sopping hair with them at some point in the last hour, which now felt a hundred years ago.

'Blue,' she said, and then, beginning to cry, 'or maybe green. I don't know. We have both colours. I don't know which ones they were.'

A moment as the policeman took this in.

'You say at first you thought they might have gone to the vending machine?'

Flo had been difficult all afternoon. Ever since Becky the babysitter left. Tired and scratchy. Moaning that the armbands pinched. Refusing to get in the pool and then refusing to get out. Naughty about getting dressed. Lashing out at Ella for no reason at all. And then insisting that she wanted something from the machine in the foyer.

'You can have a drink at home.'

'I want a Kit-Kat.'

'Forget it. You've had a big plate of chips and that's enough.'

'But I'm still hungry!'

'You'll have to wait.'

'But I brought my money!' Flo's mouth, wobbling now, her whole face on the edge of tears. Unzipping the pocket of her fleece, showing the few dull coins nestling there among the screwed-up foil and fluff and crumbs.

She ignored her. When Flo was building to a tantrum, it was sometimes the only way. Keep on going. Distract her. Keep up the momentum. Don't lose pace, don't get caught—

'I'm going to get the car now.' Pulling keys out of her bag. 'You going to come or wait for me here with Ella?'

'I want Kit-Kat!'

'I said are you coming or waiting?'

Flo began to cry.

'Right,' she said. And she turned and left them and went to get the car.

Mary lifts her head and looks at him.

'This really has been the strangest afternoon.'

'Strange in a good or a bad way?'

'I don't know. I really don't know. It's like you said – I don't feel like myself at all.'

'Who do you feel like?'

246

'I don't know. I've no idea. Someone very odd. My old self perhaps.'

'I like your old self.'

'Do you?'

'Yes. She's lovely. She's so bright and awake and alive. Look, you haven't drunk your tea.'

'I know.' She looks at him. 'I'm sorry. I actually don't think I can.'

Eddie sighs. Shakes his head.

'Mary,' he says.

'What?'

'I don't know. Just that. Just Mary.'

Neither of them speaks for a few moments. Mary thinks, vaguely to herself, that she should go. But the thought feels like no more than a bunch of words, not especially important or true, and she lets it float for a moment and then wobble, bend and burst—

'What are you thinking about?' he says.

She smiles. 'I was thinking about those bubbles. You know, that you get in a little pot with a wand and you wave it around or you blow them.'

He laughs. 'My God, that takes me back. I remember those. Do they still make those?'

'The girls loved them, especially Flo. She tried doing it with washing-up liquid once, but it didn't work as well.'

He nods. 'It can't just be ordinary old soap, can it? They must put something else in.'

'Maybe.'

'Either that or it's just very cheap soap. And that's what makes the bubbles.'

'You think so?' Mary says.

He looks at her.

'I can't tell you how badly I want to kiss you,' he says.

They sit together on the vast L-shaped sofa. Deborah's sofa, with its acres of linen cushions, its neutral-coloured throws. They haven't kissed, but he's insisted on opening a bottle of wine. She doesn't know what he wants. She doesn't really care. At least three feet of sofa separate them.

'Come here,' he says, patting the clean linen cushion next to him. 'Come on, come and sit closer to me.'

Mary shakes her head. Trying not to think about what it might feel like to be closer to him. Her head on his shoulder. His hand inside her shirt.

She blinks.

'I have this stash of pills,' she tells him. 'Stuff they gave me when it happened, to keep me calm, to calm me down. I've saved them up. I've got loads of them.'

She sees that his face changes.

'What are you saying?'

'I don't know.'

'You're saying you've thought about killing yourself?'

She glances down at her knees in their blue jeans, her feet on Deborah's startling cream rug.

'I probably wouldn't do it.'

'But you think about it.'

'Yes. Of course, I do. Yes.'

He says nothing. At last he picks up the bottle and comes and sits beside her. Puts a hand on her knee.

'You shouldn't do that,' she says and for a sudden strange moment they both look at his hand. He doesn't take it away. 'And I don't know why I just told you that. About the pills.'

'You can tell me anything. You know you can.'

She looks at him.

'I'm dead inside, Eddie. My heart, it's empty. It's what I tried to tell you, before. I have nothing to give anyone.'

She sees him smiling. He takes his hand off her knee.

'Ah. Your great big empty heart. I have to say, I've never met a less empty person in my whole life.'

She picks up her wine, looks at it, puts it back down.

'Will you forget what I told you? Everything I've said today. Please forget it.'

He sighs.

'It will go no further. But can I just say I'd like you to throw those pills away?'

Mary looks at him. She picks up her glass, drinks from it.

'I like Deborah,' she says.

'I know. I know you do. She likes you too.'

She sighs. Looks again at her feet on the rug.

'He almost left me, you know, Graham did.'

Now Eddie stares at her. 'Graham?'

'You're surprised?'

'Yes. Yes, I am. Very surprised. Why on earth would he do that?'

'The same reason anyone would. He fell in love.'

'Love?'

'Well, supposedly, it was love. He had someone else anyway.'

He sits back on the sofa.

'You're telling me Graham had an affair?'

She bites her lip.

'I don't know if he'd call it that. This woman he met through work. A designer. Not even that young or anything. Older than me. A nice person, apparently. I'm sure she was. I never met her. But I knew people who knew her.'

Eddie is still staring at her.

'This was recently?'

'Yes. No. Well, two or three years ago is when it began. It only stopped when – well, it stopped after the girls—'

She hears him take a breath.

'I'm not sure he even slept with her. I don't know. But what does it matter? It was real.'

'Real?'

'He said he loved her. He did love her. What can I say? If you think you feel love for someone, then you do. You love them. He loved her.'

Eddie is staring at her. 'And he knows? He knew. That you knew?'

She takes a breath. 'He came and told me. He was very confused. Confused and upset. And guilty. He didn't like lying. In fact, he hated it. He's honest in that way.'

'Honest? You call it honest?'

Mary shakes her head, hesitating a moment.

'Before it – before what happened – he was going to leave me. Or I was going to leave him. Whichever. We were talking about it seriously, about separating. It seemed like the only right thing – but we hadn't told the girls. That was the part I didn't think I was going to be able to bear. What to say to them. I mean, of course, Flo wouldn't really have understood, but Ella—'

Eddie puts out a hand, taking hers. She glances at him, allowing herself a breath.

'But then, well, I suppose what happened – it meant we never had to tell them. And then, somehow, time passed and—'

'And what?'

'Well, look at us.'

He looks at her.

'You stayed together? Some people would be driven apart.'

'I know.'

'But not you.'

'No. I'm sure it's all down to him. Anybody else – well, I can't imagine – but he is a good man. We need each other.'

'And love?'

'What?'

Mary looks at him.

'Do you love each other?'

She shakes her head.

'I don't think about love.'

'I don't believe you.'

'All right. We love each other. I love him, anyway.'

'And does he love you?'

'I don't know.'

'You don't know?'

She hesitates.

'I don't think it's about love. I'm not sure that love is always enough. I think that you perhaps also need imagination.'

'Imagination?'

'If you're both grieving, you do.'

Eddie is silent.

'I don't know what you mean,' he says.

She looks at him.

'You don't?' She shuts her eyes. 'He loves me. I think he does. But sometimes I come into a room when he's not expecting me and he thinks I can't see him and I find him sitting there and he just looks so – completely alone. He looks—' She takes a breath. 'He looks like someone serving a life sentence.'

Eddie says nothing. Both of them silent for a long moment. The little clock on the mantelpiece whirring the half-hour. He pours her more wine.

'Don't,' she says. 'I mustn't. I really should go.'

She feels him looking at her.

'I love you,' he says.

She lifts her head.

'What?'

'I love you, Mary. I wasn't going to say it. In fact, I promised myself that whatever happened today, I wouldn't say it. But there you are. I broke my promise. I'm sorry. I just love you.'

She feels herself tense.

'You can't.'

'But I do.'

'No – you mustn't say it.'

'Why mustn't I?' His voice – his face – suddenly elated. 'I'm an adult. I'm not stupid. I know what love is. I knew it the first time I saw you. Ever since that time you both came to dinner.'

She looks at him.

'One meeting? It's not possible.'

He smiles.

'What, you don't believe in love at first sight?'

'No, I don't. Of course I don't.'

He shrugs.

'Well, whether you believe it or not, it won't change what I feel. I love you. Like you just said, if someone feels it – and I feel it. That's it. It's a fact. It's the truth.'

The truth? Mary looks at the fireplace, the huge stone fireplace. The rug. The firewood neatly piled, not a piece out of place. The interiors magazines. The collection of carved figures, angry faces, weapons raised.

'I should go,' she says.

He reaches for her hand. Holds it in his.

'Do you remember that time? When we met? The first time you came here for dinner? You were very flustered.'

'Flustered?'

He laughs.

'You weren't in the greatest of moods. You surely remember that? You didn't want to be here at all, did you?'

'I don't remember,' she says, though she does.

'You looked gorgeous. You had on these red trousers. Silk, I think.'

'Velvet.'

'What?'

'They were velvet.'

'Well, they suited you. You looked amazing. You should wear them again.'

'I gave them to the charity shop,' she says, remembering with a sliver of relish the pretty things she chucked in a carrier bag and dumped there the next day.

'You didn't.'

'I did.'

He strokes her hand, holding it in both of his.

'Well, that was a mistake. A big mistake. I'll have to buy you some more.'

'Don't be silly.'

'It's not silly.'

'I don't want you to buy me anything.'

'I will. I want to—'

'Eddie,' she says. 'I mean it. I have to go.'

He puts a hand on her shoulder.

'Not yet.'

'I must. I have to.'

'Please. I'm saying please. Mary, just look at me. I don't want you to.'

She turns to look at him. Thinking that he looks so young, suddenly, like a boy, that he could be about sixteen.

'We can't do this,' she says.

'I love you.'

'Please don't keep saying that.'

'Why?'

'It's not true and don't you see, it spoils our friendship? You've been so kind to me today, this afternoon. I've loved talking to you. I've loved everything about it. But I don't want to do this. What you're asking of me, Eddie, it's not fair – there's nowhere possible for this to go—'

'You could love me back.'

'I can't.'

'Don't? Or can't?'

She looks away. Bright early-evening sunshine slanting over the garden.

'Both. It's both.'

He shakes his head. She feels him smiling at her.

'All this time. I've been falling in love with you. You must know that, Mary. At least don't say it's a surprise.'

She looks at him.

'It is a surprise. I had no idea. I like you a lot. Of course I do. You're a good man.'

'I don't want to be a good man. I have no ambition whatsoever to be a good man.'

'You're my friend. I want to be your friend. I don't want to hurt you.'

'That old chestnut.'

'I mean it, Eddie.'

He blinks. 'Well, you will. You will hurt me. If you don't at least respect me enough to believe in what I'm telling you. You will hurt me very much.'

She looks at him for a moment, unsure what to do or say. Then she hears it. Her phone. She gets up quickly and goes back into the kitchen, takes it from her bag, looks at it. She puts it back in the bag and picks up her cardigan, starting to pull it on.

'Graham's on his way home,' she says, walking back into the room. 'He's bringing Ruby back with him.'

'He's not staying in London?'

'He's changed his mind. He says Veronica needs a break.'

Eddie looks at her and something in his face seems to change.

'I'm sorry. I'm forgetting all about what's going on. You have to go. Of course you do.'

He walks over to her and very gently, he starts to do up the buttons of her cardigan. She can't help it, she laughs.

'I don't need it done up.'

'You might get cold.'

'I'm not cold. It's still so warm out there.'

'All the same. Want to send you home in one piece.'

She bends her head to watch as he carries on doing it, his fingers stumbling as he struggles to push the buttons into the holes.

She lets him do a couple of them up and then she can't help it – something about the careful closeness of his fingers, all that newness and possibility and warmth – she reaches out and pulls his head to hers.

The sun is low in the sky by the time she gets back home, the light pink. Darkness still hours away.

Wandering down the garden with the dog to get the washing in off the line and then perhaps uncoil the hose and water the plants, Mary realises that she is drunk. Not much. Just enough to make her limbs feel light, her edges blurred. The second thing she realises is that she can smell smoke. A hot sharp odour hanging on the evening air. The dry dirtiness of old-fashioned cigarette tobacco, reminding her of old men, maybe an old army friend of her father's.

She stops for a moment, trying to decide where it's coming from. The air still warm, clouded with tiny evening insects. Unmistakable now, the smell – is someone standing smoking behind the old apple store? Her heart begins to race. Is there someone in the garden again?

She looks at the dog. Watches her sniff the air as she squats on her usual bit of lawn. There's no growling, nothing. No sign that anything is wrong.

Calling to the dog to follow her, she walks a little further. Reaching the washing line and – on a whim, a hunch – not touching it but instead ducking her head and moving on past it.

'Come on,' she calls to the dog who doesn't follow but stays where she is, standing next to the rosemary bush.

Not put off, she keeps on going. As fast as she can now, stepping around the old fallen tree, where the long grass prickles at her knees, and finding herself looking into the mass of dark, scrubby bushes beyond the apple store, where the ancient and gnarly hedge with its broken fence gives onto the field.

The hacked and beaten body of a young girl is lying there.

8

On the edge of Yarrow's field, where the turnips were pulled in winter for cattle feed, was a ditch used for drainage. For the longest part it was a normal kind of shallow ditch and in hot weather it mostly dried up. But if you went to the place where it snaked around and met the woods, it got so deep for a stretch that even in the height of summer it was filled with thick black mucky water.

It was in this stretch that we put Phoebe Harkiss.

Later, when I tried to think about how we did it – when I tried to imagine how James must have wrapped her in a piece of sacking and put her over his shoulder and how we must surely have gone there together in the silty darkness of that terrible night, loading the sack with some stones from the field and putting her in the cold stinking water and watching till you could no longer glimpse any part of her above its black surface – I found myself struggling. I could not see it.

And I'd wake in the night, my heart nearly bursting out of my chest with panic and fear. Not because Phoebe was dead. Not even because I knew for a fact that it was James Dix who had killed her. But because I could not for the life of me remember anything about what we'd done with her.

When I told James this, he said it was just as well.

Don't you see? he said. It's God's way of protecting you.

I stared at him and told him I could not see what God had to do with it. But he just smiled.

I tell you it's normal. I've done it my whole life. I make myself forget things all the time.

You do?

He shrugged.

What you don't think about, you don't know. It makes you inno-cent, Eliza. It takes the thought right out of your head. It means you won't turn into a blabbermouth like that evil little witch.

I tried to think about this.

But I do know it, I said at last. I do know for sure that we both put her in the ditch. I don't think I'll ever be able to forget such a terrible thing. I just can't quite remember the feeling of doing it, that's all.

He looked at me then and his eyes flashed cold.

Well, you should try and forget it, Eliza.

I shook my head.

I can't.

I'm telling you to try—

I can't, James. I can't ever forget it.

He leaned forwards, putting his face closer to mine. I wondered if he was going to kiss me, but instead he showed me his teeth.

Listen to me. You need to forget what you know – forget it all – if you don't want to end up like her, that is.

Something tight and cold sank through me. I stared at him.

What do you mean, end up like her?

He shrugged and drew away.

That's what killed her, isn't it? Her big blabbermouth. Why don't you ever listen to a single word I say, Eliza? She had such a mouth on her, that one did. We didn't put her anywhere. We didn't do anything. We've not had anything to do with Phoebe Harkiss. I've barely ever spoken to her in my life and that's a fact.

But—

I was about to disagree with all of this when he grabbed me. He grabbed hold of my neck, gripping it so tight that I gasped.

That's all you need to know, Eliza, if you value this little beating heart of yours and you want to stay alive.

Graham gives her a glass of water from the tap. She sips it, glad for once of its sharp, chlorinated taste. But when she sees that he is trying to make her a sandwich – slicing the bread and hacking at the Cheddar with a butter knife – she tells him she can't eat anything.

'You've got to. It's what you need. It will calm you down. Low blood sugar. Look at you, you can't stop shaking.'

'How can I eat anything when I've just been sick?'

Now he looks at her, shaking his head.

'Alcohol in the afternoon.'

She shakes her head.

'It was nothing. I told you. One glass of wine.'

Graham stops for a moment, the knife in his hand. He looks at Ruby, still sitting on the bench where she put herself when they came in, the dog sniffing at her feet, bags piled on the floor in front of her.

'Why don't you take your stuff upstairs and sort yourself out?' he says to her.

Ruby stares at him, but doesn't move. She keeps on sitting there. Giving the dog's ears a stroke before pulling her sleeves down over her wrists.

'I want to know what she saw.'

'What?'

'Out there. What did she see?'

Graham puts down the knife. Looks at Mary. She lifts her eyes and looks at Ruby, unsure what exactly she's looking for. Same old dark clothes, pale frowny face. Her black hair skewered up on her head with some kind of a clip.

'Are you OK?' she asks her. 'How are you feeling?'

Ruby shrugs.

'What did you see? He says you saw something. I want to know what it was.'

'I'd rather not talk about it.'

'Why not?'

Mary looks at the floor.

'I don't know if I saw anything.'

'But you thought you did?'

'I don't know.'

Graham comes over, puts his hand on her shoulder.

'Look, my love, whatever you think it was—' Mary waits, her whole body stilled by his touch. She does not move. Holding her breath. 'It wasn't there. You know that.'

She lets out her breath.

'All right,' she says.

And she believes him, because how can she not? She knows that when he got home and couldn't find her anywhere in the house and came down the garden calling her and then found her, white-faced and shaking and sobbing on the ground by the fallen tree, he listened to what she had to say – listened hard, his two hands holding on to her. Then, once he'd taken it in, he let go of her and went straight round the back of the shed and looked. Not knowing what he would find, ready to deal with it, whatever it was.

She waited, still weeping and trembling, for his cry of shock.

But he came back immediately, his face tight, concerned, purposeful. He knelt down and put his arms around her, his head close to hers, his lips against her face.

He told her there was nothing there. Absolutely nothing. Just bushes, he said. The same old bushes. And a few too many nettles and brambles and an old dog rose that had seen better days.

He took her, then – still trembling with shock – down through the garden and into the house. Where she didn't even say hello to Ruby but went straight through the hall to the toilet and, still seeing the thick, brownish blood that had been coming from the girl's eyes and nose and mouth, she vomited.

That's when she told Graham about the drink with Eddie.

'You two,' he said. 'You can't stay away from each other, can you?'

She could not tell if he was joking or not.

Now, though, he squeezes her shoulder.

'All right,' he says. 'We're going to go back down there and I'm going to show you.'

She stares at him.

'What, now?'

'Yes, now. You too, Ruby, if you're so keen to see. The dog as well. We'll all go down there. Family expedition.'

Ruby shakes her head. For a moment, Mary thinks she sees fear in her eyes.

'I don't want to. I'm not going down there. I hate that place.'

Graham looks at her.

'What do you mean? What place?'

'The horrible fucking shed thing. That whole bit at the bottom of the garden, I hate it. It's creepy and dark. It creeps me out. And people can get in. You said yourself that someone got in there and took your stuff.'

Mary watches as Ruby gets up and goes over to the fridge. Opening it and standing staring at its contents as if they might at any moment multiply or change.

'I don't want to go down there either,' she tells Graham.

He looks at her.

'For goodness' sake, Mary, don't be ridiculous. We're going down there so you can see for yourself that there's nothing there. Otherwise you'll never be able to get it out of your head. You know you won't.'

Ruby turns to look at her again.

'Get what out of your head?'

Mary says nothing. Watching Ruby's face, solemn and childlike, still lit by the eerie light of the fridge, she feels herself shiver.

'All right,' she says to Graham. 'All right. Come on, let's do it.'

So, while Ruby picks up her bags and goes upstairs, they make their way together down the garden, past the washing line – clothes still hanging there, pale and still and warm in the blue dusk. Skirting around the old fallen tree, towards the shed.

'We ought to pull this thing down,' Graham says. 'It's not doing anything, is it? Look at it.'

'What?' she says. 'Pull down the apple store?'

He looks at her.

'An afternoon's work. That's all it would be. Get some light in. Ruby's right about it being creepy – it's because it's so bloody dark. It needs to come down. You'd notice the difference. It would mean you could see right across the fields.'

Mary says nothing. Looking at the broken roof, the greenish moss on its rotten walls. Some dry, grassy stuff poking out from under the eaves, a couple of grey feathers, the nest of some bird perhaps—

She stops, unable to make herself go any further. But he takes her hand and pulls her, straight into the shadows behind it. She stares into the greenish dark of the bushes. She sees nettles. The dense prickly mass that is the rose. She doesn't see anything else.

Graham lets go of her hand and he stands there, hands on hips, looking around him.

'I should really get my hedge trimmer and tackle this whole area,' he says.

Mary doesn't say anything. Listening to the hum of some insect. A bird cawing loudly in the field beyond. Nothing else.

Moments pass. She tries to summon the cigarette smoke again, to remember its particular, dry, old-fashioned odour. But it doesn't come. All she smells is evening. A darkening sky. Bright leaves. The earth cooling.

Graham takes her hand. Squeezes it.

'OK?'

She nods. Glances up at the house. Sees that Ruby's window is open. She knows that Ruby never opens windows unless she plans to smoke. She thinks about saying that, but stops herself just in time.

'How is she?' she asks him then. 'Do you think she's OK?'

He hesitates.

'I don't know. I've no idea really. In the car just now, I tried to talk to her. But she wasn't interested. Wouldn't say a word. You don't mind me bringing her back here, do you?'

Mary looks at him.

'How can you even ask me that?'

He sighs.

'Veronica was in such a state. It's all been such a shock, all of this. I don't think she can cope on her own at the moment.'

Mary looks at him.

'You never told me she was on anti-depressants.'

'Didn't I? Well, she's had her issues, Veronica has. I don't know if the drugs are helping much really.'

'All the same. You never told me.'

He looks at her.

'You feel that's important?'

'I don't know. Is it?'

He takes a breath. Looks away down the lawn.

'So I've just said we'll have her here for now. Nothing fixed. We're just going to take it a day at a time.'

Mary looks at him.

'I'm surprised you managed to get her to come.'

He hesitates.

'She wasn't keen. But I've got to take her back to the hospital next week anyway. I suppose I've played it down, the length of time. I've

260

told her we'll see what happens after next week. They want her to see a psychiatrist.'

'What, she hasn't already?'

'Just the one in A & E. They want her to have some formal help. That's the other bit I haven't told you.' He looks at his hands for a moment. 'It turns out she's been cutting herself.'

Mary stares at him.

'My God.'

'I know. A bit of a shock.'

'But what do you mean? Cutting herself where?'

'Her arms. Her thighs. I haven't seen it. She wouldn't let me anywhere near her. But Veronica has. All those great big sweaters she always wears, even in summer? Well, now we know.'

Mary is silent. She thinks of the streaks of blood she saw on Ruby's sheets. Her sleeves always pulled down over her hands.

'And Veronica knew all of this?'

'Not for long. She hadn't known for long.'

'But she knew and she didn't tell you?'

Graham looks at the ground, rubs at the back of his head.

'Poor Veronica. I don't think she knew what to do. She really has been at her wits' end.' Before Mary can say anything, he holds out his hand to her, taking hold of her fingers, reaching for her. 'Please, sweetheart. Don't go blaming Veronica for everything. All of this, it's been very difficult for her too, you know.'

She says nothing. He holds on to her hand for a moment longer.

'What about you, anyway?'

'Me?'

'Are you all right?'

'I'm fine.'

He lets go of her hand.

'Are you?'

'Yes. Why wouldn't I be?'

Graham looks at her in the careful, attentive way she's come to dread.

'I still think you should talk to someone,' he says. 'You spend far too much time alone in this house.'

She throws him a cool look.

'I like being alone in this house. And anyway I do talk to people. I talk to Eddie.'

'To Eddie?'

'This afternoon. I told you. We talked for ages.'

'Right.'

'We went for a walk and we talked and then we went back to his and we drank wine and we talked some more and do you know, it was great. It cheered me up, actually; it really did.' She looks at him. 'Don't you want to know what we talked about?'

'What did you talk about?'

'The girls.'

Graham stares at her. She watches his face go still.

'The girls?'

'That's right. I told him all about them.'

She watches his face, stricken. A chip of ice in her throat. He shakes his head.

'Why did you tell him about the girls?'

'Because he asked me. He asked me everything about them, actually, and I told him. I told him lots of silly things, things I haven't even dared think about in all this time. I told him about Tuffy – remember Tuffy? – Tuffy and Peppa Pig, all those words I hadn't said aloud in ages. It felt good. We talked and laughed about them.'

'You laughed?'

'Yes, we did. I told you, it felt good. It made me feel better. It was very nice, to be asked about them and to be allowed to talk in a normal way. It made me realise how very much I've missed having someone to talk to about them.'

Mary finishes, unable any longer to stand the pain on his face. Real pain. He is looking at her and then he isn't looking at her. He drops his head. For a moment neither of them speaks.

'I'm sorry,' she says at last.

She looks up at the sky, darkest blue, almost black now. The end of day, beginning of night. She thinks that maybe she can see a star. Graham sits down on the bench, brushing leaves off. Gazing into the long grass.

'Are you OK?' she asks him.

He shrugs. 'Not really.'

'I'm sorry.'

'It's all right. You don't have to be.'

Mary sits beside him on the bench. Glancing at him. She thinks of reaching out and placing a hand on his leg, his knee, a comforting hand, but finds she can't quite bring herself to do it.

'It was horrible, you know,' he says at last. 'Seeing her lying there, in A & E. Her mouth all black from the stuff they gave her. All those wires on her. It was even worse than I thought it would be. When I first saw her, I thought—'

Mary turns to him.

'What?' she says softly. 'What did you think?'

He hesitates.

'I suppose I thought that she was dead.'

It was young Miss Narket that came and told us about Phoebe. She was a busybody and always liked to be first with local news. Her hair was dirty and her cap falling off and her face was wild from lack of sleep, but she wasn't going to be stopped from getting her story out. I held my breath and listened while she gave it to my mother.

Only I was expecting her to come and help me with the hymn books, wasn't I? And then, when there was no sound nor sign of her, I thought it tremendously unusual and I got quite worried and sent Addie Sands to go and see what was happening and that's when she found her.

Found who? my mother said.

Her mama! Poor Mrs Harkiss! And in such a state, screaming and crying and on her knees praying and demanding God's help in finding the girl. On top of being a widow, she lost a daughter to diphtheria last year and I'm not sure if you've heard but the son has gone lame and can't help at the Smithy any more. I tell you, that woman has had nothing but bad luck since a year last November and I honestly do not think she can take any more strain and worry and now this.

My mother, standing there by the gate, her hands covered in flour and her belly poking out as big as anything, regarded Miss Narket with careful eyes.

I expect it's nothing, she said. I expect it's a prank. My own kiddies disappear from time to time – Charlie is a terror for doing it – and I don't give it a second thought; in fact, I'm glad of the peace and quiet, if you really want the truth. She's probably gone off and hid somewhere and is waiting at this very moment to be found.

Miss Narket looked at my mother and then she looked at me.

That girl's not got a tricky bone in her body. She wouldn't hide.

All kiddies like to hide, my mother said. You don't have to be tricky to want to hide sometimes.

Miss Narket shook her head.

Not that one. She has a nice, plain imagination, that one does. I don't know about your children, but young Phoebe Harkiss don't have any of those kinds of mischievous ideas in her head.

I thought about Phoebe Harkiss's nice, plain imagination and wondered what Miss Narket would say if she knew that her beloved little helper had gone around telling half the village that the Narkets bathed in the same water as their pigs and that they all, as a consequence, had nasty, weeping sores in unmentionable places.

As if she knew what I was thinking, Miss Narket looked at me and scowled.

And another thing. We had a church trip planned for Saturday to go and ride the donkeys at Yarmouth. I know that she was very much looking forward to it and would not have missed it for anything.

I tried to picture Phoebe Harkiss on a donkey. Her freckled hands grasping the tuft of the animal's neck, her gingery body wobbling as she clung on. Part of me wanted to give her a small shove and watch her topple off.

I wondered, then, what she would do in Yarmouth. I wondered whether she'd want to have a go at the machine that you hit with a hammer and the thing slid up. The High Striker, James had said it was called. I was wondering about all of this and wishing, slightly, that I could go along to Yarmouth with them all, when I remembered that Phoebe Harkiss was dead and lying in the black water at the bottom of Yarrow's ditch and wouldn't be going anywhere near any donkeys or fun fairs ever again.

Thinking that last thought made me flush bright pink to the roots of my hair. I remembered James's dark threats. The way it had felt when he grabbed my neck. I looked away quickly, worrying that either my mother or Miss Narket would notice.

Well, Saturday's still some way off, my mother pointed out. I dare say she'll be back by then.

She's such a friendly girl, I said, still feeling badly hot in the face. I do hope nothing bad has happened to her.

Miss Narket gave me a sharp look. She folded her arms and turned back to my mother.

Three murders there's been in this county since March, did you know that? And all of them young girls and all of them the bodies hacked at and partly burned and then left barely covered at the edge of a field somewhere.

My stomach dropped and I felt the blood go to my cheeks. But my mother's face didn't change.

I knew it was in the Gazette, she said. But thanks very much for giving me the unpleasant details.

When their girls were at last allowed to leave the ditch where they had lain for so long, their bodies were put into bags and driven to the hospital in a private ambulance. Mary and Graham were asked if they wanted to be there while this happened and they thought about it and said they didn't. But then in the morning they changed their minds. As if he had known this would happen, Dave, the youngest of the family liaison officers, was at their door almost as soon as they'd put down the phone.

'Don't even think about it,' he said when they tried to apologise.

It had rained that night, but it was a bright day. Puddles shining on the black roads, the hedgerows pale with the beginnings of blossom. He drove them there in silence, the two of them sitting in the back, their fingers laced together like teenagers.

Mary had thought, or hoped, that it would all be over very quickly. But getting them from the ditch to the ambulance took much longer than she'd expected. She saw that it made Dave tense, the waiting. When he caught her watching him, he leaned over and touched her arm.

'A lot of formalities, I'm afraid.'

By the time the ambulance was ready to leave, the afternoon had fallen away and the light was starting to go, the air cold and damp, a raw mist rolling in across the fields. And once they'd turned off the power and lost the strong lights, and there was only what came from the vehicles, it was a shock, feeling for the first time that thick darkening air all around them. She saw that they were in the middle of nowhere, in a world that would go on for ever and ever in this way: wide open to the elements and empty and relentless and black.

They were asked if they wanted to go in the ambulance with the girls and Mary started to say yes – the swift, unhesitating response of a parent who wouldn't dream of not accompanying their child to hospital or anywhere else for that matter. But before she could continue, Graham stopped her. Taking hold of her arm and speaking in a low voice to the driver. Telling him that no, it might be better if they followed.

And so she did as she was told. She let them drive her away. And as they drove – all four vehicles moving with such terrible, hushed slowness over that huge and darkening earth – she did not dare allow herself to look back even for a moment at that place that had for a while contained their girls.

She wishes now that she'd fought harder to be with them on that last journey. Wishes that she hadn't allowed herself to be led and persuaded and put in a separate car like that. It was no one's fault. She blames herself. What could she have been thinking? Did she really imagine it was an opportunity that would come again?

She used to be the kind of mother who knew how to focus, who could cope with anything – able to find any amount of nerve and courage when it came to her girls. When the school secretary phoned to say that Flo had fallen off a climbing frame at break and needed to go to hospital, she not only got herself there in ten minutes flat, but kept her distracted in the ambulance with stories about Spongebob Square Pants and Peppa Pig – continuing the stories later as she held her on her lap while the shattered arm was cleaned and dressed and put in plaster.

In fact, so entirely alert was she to this task, so numb to every other idea or sensation, that she didn't realise until much later that at some point during all of this she'd somehow cut her own hand and it had bled all over the pale cotton of her shirt.

'Mummy, don't cry,' Flo whispered to her as the nurse passed her bunches of rough, blue paper towels to clean it.

'Mummy isn't crying,' said the nurse. 'Are you, Mummy? Look at how very good and brave your mummy is.'

Mary waits until Graham has left for work. Then she goes into the room they call the snug – the only room where she can be sure not to be overheard by Ruby – and she closes the door as softly as she can and then she rings him. He picks up at once.

'I don't know how to say this,' she says, standing in the cool, fusty room next to the old armchair flanked by the stacked-up cardboard boxes that she can barely look at. 'But the way I behaved. I don't know where it came from. Please can you forget it. Forget it ever happened. Forgive me, I mean. I'm really very sorry.'

There's a pause. She waits, trying not to look around the room, trying not to see him too clearly in her head either.

'What do you mean?' he says.

'The things I did. Yesterday. Things I said. I shouldn't have. I didn't mean to do what I did.'

'You didn't mean to kiss me?'

'No, I didn't.'

'You didn't?'

'You know I didn't. I'm sorry. Please let's just forget it, Eddie.'

He says nothing. There's a long silence. At last she hears him exhale, a long, slow breath. Smoking, she thinks.

'Look, Mary,' he says at last, 'it's cool, all right? You can relax. But you're asking too much of me. I told you honestly how I feel about you – and you responded honestly. When people say and do things, it's usually because they mean them. You can't just undo it all. You can't just undo life when you feel like it, take it all back.'

Mary feels herself freeze.

'I'm not trying to undo anything. I'm trying to apologise and ask that you—'

'I love you,' he says. 'Everything I said. I meant every word. My heart is in your hands. I mean it. I wouldn't mess with you, Mary.'

Mary shuts her eyes. When she opens them, she sees all over again where she is. In that room, surrounded by their things.

'Please,' she says, sitting down on the chair next to the low coffee table where she sees with relief that Graham has put all the photos back in their green floppy wallets. 'Please, Eddie, I'm asking you not to say that.'

'But what if it's true?'

She takes a breath, puts her hand to her face.

'It's not true. It can't be true.'

She hears him pause.

'I can't stop thinking about you, Mary. I woke up this morning and all I could see was your face. Your eyes. Your beautiful hair. I fall asleep thinking of you and I wake up thinking of you. The taste of you is in my mouth, on my tongue, in my heart. You've no idea how much time each day I spend thinking about you.'

Mary says nothing. Her heart thudding as with one hand she opens a flap of the wallet, slides out the top photograph.

'Mary?' he says.

In her hand, Ella and Flo are standing by a low brick wall. Where were they? The wall is familiar. Is it the little children's zoo in the park? Ella is wearing a bomber jacket, blue and red from Gap, Mary remembers the one. Staring straight ahead and smiling. Her hair tied back. Her arms lifted, spread against the wall. Flo is gazing off to the left, holding Tuffy by his ear.

'Mary? Are you still there?'

'I'm here.'

'You went very quiet. Are you OK?'

Mary stares at the photograph. She does not cry. She does nothing. Says nothing. She does not breathe.

She goes up to Ruby's room, taking the stairs softly, lightly, two at a time, finding her hunched in bed, blind pulled down, duvet round her knees, earphones in her ears. The door's open just enough that she can put her head in, but as soon as she does it, Ruby scowls.

'Can I talk to you?' she says.

Ruby's face doesn't change. She takes out one earphone, holding it an inch from her ear.

'What about?'

Mary pushes the door a crack and takes a small step into the room. Mess immediately exploding all around her. Smell of warm clothes and deodorant. Dirty cups and plates. Towels on the floor. She tries not to look.

'What are you doing?'

'Listening to music.'

'What sort of music?'

'Just music.'

Mary hesitates.

'I wanted to see if you were OK.'

268

'I'm OK.'

Ruby waits for her to go. She doesn't go.

'You're all right? You don't mind staying here? With us, I mean?'

Ruby shrugs.

'I don't have any choice, do I?'

Mary takes a step closer to the bed.

'Can I sit down?'

She doesn't wait for an answer, but puts herself on its edge. As the mattress moves under her weight, the duvet is pulled off Ruby's knees. Ruby yanks it back, but before she does so, Mary sees a bright plastic lighter, a packet of something she doesn't recognise.

'I want to talk to you,' she says. 'Can you take those out for a minute?'

Very slowly, Ruby removes the other earphone. Keeping them both in her hand. She looks at Mary, holding her gaze in a direct, faintly insolent way that Mary knows is supposed to make her uncomfortable.

Mary sighs. Choosing her words carefully.

'Look, Rubes, I know you're angry. I know that, OK? I'd just like to be able to understand why, that's all.'

'Why?'

'Why what?'

Ruby looks down at the bed. The earphones in her hand.

'Why do you need to understand? What's the point?'

Mary takes a breath, touches her hand.

'You poor thing. You've had such a tough time recently, haven't you?'

Ruby says nothing. Shrugs. But as she presses her lips together, Mary thinks she sees her chin wobble. She puts a hand back on the duvet, close to where Ruby's leg is. Immediately the leg moves away.

'We've all been very worried about you,' Mary says. She watches Ruby's face. 'Do you realise that? I hope you do realise that.'

'Whatever,' Ruby says.

'You don't care that everyone's been worrying about you?'

Ruby shrugs. Looking away. Mary sees her chin wobble again.

'Are you anxious about anything?' she asks her. 'Is there something we don't know about?'

Ruby looks at her.

'What do you know about?'

Mary hesitates. 'All right, is there anything you'd like to talk about?'

Ruby blinks.

'Why would I talk to you?'

'Because I care about you.'

'Why do you care?'

Mary looks at her hand on the bed.

'Why do I care? Oh God, Ruby. Where do I start? So many reasons. Come on, you know very well how much I care about you.'

Ruby mutters something Mary doesn't catch. She lifts her head.

'What?'

'I said you're not my mum.'

Mary takes a breath.

'I know I'm not your mum. I'm not trying to be your mum. Why would I try to be your mum? You've got a great mum who loves you very much. But that doesn't mean I can't care as well, does it?'

Ruby says nothing.

Mary looks around the room. The mirror. The chest of drawers with clothes spilling out. The window with its tattered old blind, Ruby's incense burners and joss sticks lined up along the sill. The faded, peeling wallpaper. The blackened, soot-charred remains of what was once a small fireplace.

'We should paint this room for you,' she says. 'We really should. We could make it a lot nicer, you know.' She looks at Ruby. 'Get you some better curtains as well. Would you like us to do that?'

'Do what you like.'

'You don't care what it looks like?'

'Not really.'

'You don't think it's worth making it nice? If you're going to be spending a bit of time here.'

'I'm not going to spend any time here,' Ruby says.

Mary is silent a moment. Something occurs to her.

'You're not still scared, are you? Of the house, I mean.'

Now Ruby lifts her head, suddenly alert.

'You fucking well know I am.'

Mary stiffens. She tries to breathe, smoothing her hand over the duvet.

'Really? What are you scared of?'

Ruby narrows her eyes.

'How can you act all surprised like that? You were the one who told me there was something, remember? You said it. You said you knew.'

Mary takes a breath.

'You're right. I did say that.'

'Well, then.'

'Look, when I said that, I think I was just talking about a feeling. A vague feeling I sometimes get. I just wanted to tell you I understood and that I felt it too. I didn't mean it was anything to be frightened of.'

Ruby looks at her.

'So what do you feel?'

'What, in this house?'

Ruby nods, waiting. Mary hesitates, looking around the room.

'I don't know. You get a sense of other people, don't you? It happens in lots of houses. Old houses. Sometimes you almost think you can hear them.'

'Hear what?'

'I don't know. The things that used to go on. The people.'

'What people?'

Mary tries to smile.

'I don't know. No one in particular. Just – I suppose whoever it was who was here before.'

Ruby is watching her.

'You've seen him. Don't lie. I know you have.'

'What? Seen who?'

'The ginger guy. I know you've seen him.'

Mary hesitates.

'What, the young man with the red hair? Yes, I've seen him. I know who you mean. I think he must live in the village.'

Ruby looks at her.

'But why is he always here?'

'Here?'

'Everywhere. All over the fucking place. In the garden.'

Mary's heart sinks.

'You've seen him in the garden?'

'Yeah, down the bottom of the garden doing stuff – I don't know, digging around. And by the old shed thing. He's the one who took Dad's tools, isn't he?'

'Is he?'

'Well, come on, it must be him, mustn't it?'

Mary tenses, her body suddenly light and still.

'Ruby. You've never told us any of this.'

'I'm telling you now. Come on. You've seen him too. He's always here, outside in the lane, looking at this house.'

'Is he?'

'For fuck's sake. You know he is. And the kids, too.'

'The kids?'

Ruby hesitates.

'All those children. The little kids.'

'You've seen them too?'

'Not really.'

'You haven't seen them?'

Ruby blinks.

'I know they're there. I've heard them. So have you.' Mary feels Ruby watching her. Her eyes on her face. She hugs herself, suddenly bone cold, trying to stop her teeth knocking together. She makes herself meet Ruby's gaze.

'And you're saying this scares you?'

'I don't know why it doesn't scare you. You know that time Lisa and me came back that time to watch a film, after we'd been to that dinner down the road with you?' Mary nods. 'Well, Lisa went to the toilet and I was putting the DVD in and I looked up and he was there at the window.'

'What? Who was?'

'Him. That man. Ginger guy. He was staring in through the window, his face pressed right up. It was fucking terrifying. I thought he was going to try and come in. He kept his whole face pressed right up against the glass for about ten seconds.'

Mary stares at her.

'Seriously?'

Ruby rolls her eyes.

'I'm not making it up.'

'And then what?'

'What do you mean?'

'What happened? What did you do?'

'I didn't do anything, did I? I was too fucking scared even to move. I shouted for Lisa to come, but when she came she couldn't see him.'

'What do you mean she couldn't see him?'

'I don't know. She just couldn't. And I couldn't either then, so I suppose he must have gone.'

Mary thinks about this.

'But for goodness' sake – a man at the window, Rubes. You should have called us. Why didn't you phone your dad immediately?'

Ruby smiles.

'What would you have done?'

'I don't know. We'd have done something. Your dad would have. He'd have called the police.'

'The police?' Ruby starts to laugh.

'What's funny about that?'

Ruby shakes her head.

'It's not like that. What the fuck would the police do? He's not a burglar or anything.'

Mary takes a breath.

'What is he then?'

'I don't know.' Ruby looks at her again. 'I don't know what he is. I thought you might know.'

'Me? Why on earth would I know?'

She feels Ruby staring at her, inspecting her face.

'Well, come on, it's something to do with you, isn't it?'

Mary shakes her head, trying to smile.

'I don't know what you mean.'

Ruby keeps on looking at her.

'That's right. Of course you don't.'

Mary stares at her.

'What do you mean? What are you saying? Please stop this, Ruby, don't talk like that, I don't like it.'

'Why don't you like it?'

'Because it's horrible. You're giving me the creeps.'

Ruby looks down for a moment at the earphones in her hand.

'I told you the first time I came here, didn't I, that I didn't like the house? Lisa feels it too. I told you. But there's no point telling you anything, you and Dad, because you never listen. And anyway even if you did listen, you're no use. You're the very last person who'd be able to help.'

Mary stares at her.

'What do you mean? Why am I the last person?'

Ruby lifts her head and looks at her.

'Well, it's why you're not scared of it, isn't it?'

'What?'

'The thing in the house. Ginger guy. And the kids. Everything. You say you don't know about it, but whatever it is, even Lisa agrees, it's definitely coming from you.'

I had thought that once Phoebe was safely laid in the ditch, that would be the end of it. I told myself I hated and despised James – that even though he had made me feel more alive than anyone else I had ever known or perhaps would ever know – still enough was enough. I wasn't going to wait around like some simple little fool for him to grab and threaten and hurt me whenever he felt like it.

But another part of me felt very sorry for him. I saw that, despite all his fine, bold talk, he was angry and anxious. Anyone could see he wasn't sleeping at night and there was a rash of small scabs across his forehead where he wouldn't leave off scratching. One night I was sure I heard him being sick in the barn. He was bothered and listless and his face looked worn out with tiredness.

And my heart missed him. And so did the rest of me. At night, I'd lie in my bed and pull up my chemise and whisper to myself about all the things we'd done and a little flame of madness would light up inside me, only to go out again as soon as I remembered I was all untouched and alone. But one morning, sitting on the yard wall in the hard sunlight and watching as Lottie and the twins pulled the moss from between the cracks, I suddenly felt that nothing in the world was worth anything if I could not feel him against me again. I jumped down so fast I heard a ripping noise.

Lottie looked up.

Your dress!

What?

You've torn it. Look, Eliza.

I pulled it down.

It's all right, I said.

Ma will be cross.

No, she won't.

Where are you going?

Nowhere.

Yes, you are.

None of your business, I said.

Go away, he said when, having searched every other place, I found him at last, hunched in a dark and dusty corner of the tool loft above the cowshed. I mean it, Eliza, just go.

I stood there on the ladder, half up and half down, looking into the shadows of his poor, wild face.

What do you want? he said when I still didn't move. Can't you just leave me alone?

What did I want? What I had wanted was to ask him to touch me, hold me, come up close to me and lift up my skirts and say sweet things and beg to do what we always did – for hadn't we after all done it enough times in the private, gritty dark of that place while the cows chewed and shifted around beneath us?

But I saw now that he did not want it. I saw that his face that had once contained nothing but desire for me was blank and empty. I had thought that I'd be the one who'd stop loving him first – I did not think I could love a murderer. But it turned out I was wrong. He had nothing left for me: there was no trace of our love left anywhere on him – not in his eyes or his mouth nor any part of him. I knew it was already hopeless but I said it anyway:

I came to be with you, I said.

I propped my elbows on the rough wooden boards of the loft and stared at his boots which, though I did not like to think about it, still had the black, caked mud of Yarrow's ditch on them.

James did not look at me. Instead, he walked over to the bench. I watched as he picked up a small sharp knife that was used for slitting the young pigs. He held it, frowning, testing the blade against his fingers.

Well, don't, he said.

What?

You can't be with me, Eliza. I'm afraid you can't. Not any more. I'm sorry but it's for your own good.

My own good?

Yes, your own good! Is that so difficult to grasp? It's over, Eliza. It has to be. We're finished with each other now.

Finished?

I can't have you anywhere near me, he said.

My mouth dropped open. I felt my insides dissolve and fall away.

But I love you! I cried.

He said nothing. He shrugged. Keeping his hands on the knife, twisting it around and around. Now and then you saw sunlight squeeze itself from between the broken tiles of the roof and move along its ragged edge.

I swallowed. My mouth was dry.

I thought I was your princess, I said, and when he did not answer: What is it, James? What is it that's different? I don't understand. Don't you love me any more?

His face did not change.

Something terrible has happened, he said at last.

I felt my heart swerve. I took a breath.

I know, I whispered. I know that—

He turned and inspected me with cold eyes. There was so little love in them that it seemed to stop my breath.

No, he said. Not that. I don't mean that.

I stared at him.

What then?

He looked at me for another long moment, but his face stayed empty and he did not speak.

Hot. It is still so hot. The longest, hottest, driest spell in more than thirty years, the man on the radio says.

Mary goes again to the doctor's. This time the woman on reception remembers her, smiling at her kindly and telling her how well she's looking. This time, too, she doesn't wait long. An elderly lady offers her a torn and crumpled copy of The People's Friend. She thanks her and looks at it briefly. Who is the people's friend, anyway? she wonders. Who are these people? Has anyone ever really been their friend?

She puts the magazine down and watches a dribbling toddler in a bib who is clutching on to a low table and pushing beads up and down a bright, curving wire while its mother holds a beaker containing a purple drink.

She sees that the child – who every now and then takes both hands off the table and, patting the air, screams with delight – has never had a haircut. Long, fine curls clustering behind each ear. It won't be long now, she thinks. The tall chair, the scissors, the grave and unfamiliar little face that for a quick moment will make the mother want to cry.

When Mary is called in, it's brief and efficient. The doctor smiles a little too hard and talks to her in a friendly, careful way. She scrolls up and down her screen, asking her some slightly difficult questions, which she tries her best to answer truthfully. The doctor knows all about her now. It was inevitable, she thinks, with people talking and also with the internet. Even Eddie and Deborah admitted they'd Googled them that time. It could not really have been prevented. What was she imagining? That they would come here and start a new life and no one would ever know anything?

She leaves the doctor's with a prescription. Tomorrow she will drive into the next village to get it made up and then she will put it where she keeps the rest, in the old jewellery box at the back of the wardrobe.

As she leaves, she sees that the toddler has stopped playing and launched itself into a full-scale tantrum – the mother shaking a large rattle in its face to calm it down.

It won't work, she thinks, with a sneaking jolt of satisfaction. If it were me, I'd scoop him up and whisper naughty things in his ear. Wicked and exciting things. The story of the Bad Cat. All the mischievous and crazy things he'd done. He'd forget all about the tantrum. It always worked with Ella.

'What bad cat?' she'd say, quietening immediately. 'What's he done? Can I see him? Is he here right now?'

For such a long time she could not put her hands in their school coat pockets – Ella's duffle, Flo's anorak.

When she finally did, she found a dull, brown stone from the garden. A boiled sweet, sticky in its waxen wrapper. A shrivelled conker. A crumpled Pokémon card. In Ella's coat, a half-eaten bag of smoky-bacon crisps (she has no idea how she got the money for that). In Flo's, a handful of dust that might once have been autumn leaves. A ball of foil from a chocolate bar. A blue button covered in denim. And fluff. So much fluff.

She thought she would cry when she found all these things, but she didn't. She put every item, including the sweet and the half-eaten crisps, in a box and she sealed it with brown tape and put it away. After that, she washed the anorak and took the duffel coat to the dry-cleaner's.

She has no idea why she did any of this.

Walking back through the village, the phone lights up the moment she looks at it.

'Mary, please listen for a moment. You can't cut me out like this – it's just not fair. I just need to talk to you.'

She takes a breath.

'All right,' she says.

'What?'

'I'm listening. Talk.'

'I mean face to face. I can't do this on the phone.'

'I can't see you, Eddie.'

'Why not?'

'You know why not.'

She hears him sigh.

'I'm sorry,' he says. 'I'm so very sorry. You've got to believe me, Mary. I'm feeling terrible – really, I can't believe I've been this stupid. The very last thing in the world I wanted to do was ruin our friendship.'

A short silence. She listens to it. Feeling herself soften.

'You haven't ruined it,' she says.

'I have. I did. I know I did. It's all my fault. I said too much. I shouldn't have told you what I felt. I just went rushing in like a lunatic. It's my fault. It's what I do. With women, I mean. It's what I always seem to do.'

'With women? With what women?'

He laughs.

'What I mean is, I'd do absolutely anything to go back to how things were.'

278

Mary takes a breath. Thinking of all the time they've spent with Deborah and Eddie. The suppers, the chat. What Graham likes to call village life.

'We can do that.'

'Can we?'

'I think so. I don't see why not.'

She hears him hesitate.

'It's what I'd like.'

'Would you?'

'Honestly, Mary, you've no idea. I'd like it so much.'

Mary swallows. Almost at the cottage now, she stops and gazes up at the windows, bright with late-evening sunshine.

'You've been good friends,' she says. 'You and Deborah. And you too. I appreciate what a good friend you've been.'

She hears him hesitate.

'Well, it's mutual.' He takes a breath. 'I think you're lovely.'

She can't help it, she shivers.

'Please don't start that.'

'All right. All right, I'm sorry.'

'You don't need to apologise.'

'All right, I'm not sorry. But thank you. Thank you so much. And I didn't mean it about the women.'

'Didn't you?'

'You can't tell when I'm joking?'

'I don't know.'

'Well, it was a joke, OK?'

'OK.'

'Tell me you believe me, that it was a joke?'

'I believe you.'

A pause.

'And you? You're all right?'

'I'm all right.'

He laughs. 'And Graham? Is he OK? And the girls? How's it going with the girls?'

Mary hesitates.

'Girls? You mean Ruby? It's only Ruby.'

She hears him pause.

'What, Lisa's not there?'

279

'Lisa? No. Why would Lisa be here?'

'But I thought – isn't she supposed to be coming to stay?'

'Is she?'

'Oh well, maybe not.'

'Well, is she?'

'Look, perhaps I got that wrong. Just forget I said that, OK?'

Mary turns around again, away from the house. She walks several paces down the lane then stops and stands there, gazing into the hedge.

'What do you mean?' she says as softly as she can. 'Why would you think that Lisa was coming to stay? What on earth made you think that she was here?'

She feels him hesitate.

'Please forget it. I blundered, OK? I got it wrong. I told you, it's my great big mouth.'

Mary thinks about this.

'Have you been talking to the girls?'

A brief silence.

'Only messaging.'

'Messaging?'

'Yeah, well, we message now and then. You know. Facebook.'

'What? You're saying you're in touch with Ruby and Lisa on Facebook?'

'For God's sake, Mary, it's nothing. Once or twice. We kept in touch a bit, that's all. About music and stuff. Since that time I showed them my vinyls, remember?'

Mary still stands in the lane, feeling herself begin to tremble.

'You never told me that.'

He laughs.

'I suppose it never came up.'

'But – I had no idea.'

'Of course not. Why would you? And anyway, why would I tell you? What, you think I should make some kind of formal announcement? Would you really have been interested? Is it so very important?'

Mary says nothing. Very carefully, she ends the call. She glances up at the house again, looking up at the bedroom windows, the sun so bright on them now they seem to be on fire.

*

Lottie came and found me. She had Honey with her. Both of them standing there with their brown Sunday dresses half-undone and no aprons or shoes on. Lottie had Honey tied to her wrist with a piece of string. Our mother sometimes did that, if she couldn't watch the babies herself and wanted to be sure they wouldn't wander off.

I'm afraid we came to tell you something a bit bad, Lottie said and she snatched a look at Honey, whose face was greasy with something like butter.

Bad? I said, taking the corner of my apron and wiping Honey's face.

Lottie grinned and looked at Honey again.

You won't like it. Not at all. She folded her arms and turned her head from side to side. No, no, no, you ain't gonna like it at all.

I looked at her. I was getting tired of her tricks. I knew she wanted the attention and I didn't feel like giving it to her. I sighed.

All right, I told her. Spit it out.

Lottie looked at Honey again. Honey laughed. You could see from her gummy smiling face that she didn't understand a thing about what was going on.

Lottie took a breath and frowned.

Well, this girl, see? I don't know who she is, all I know is that she's dead like our Frank. But she's not in heaven. She's lying all alone in a place where she's covered with black water and she wants me to tell you she's very unhappy indeed and she don't like it.

I stared at Lottie. For a few dark, woolly moments I did not understand a word of what she was talking about – and then suddenly I did. The blood came to my face. I shook my head and took a step away from her.

There's no girl, I said.

Lottie's eyes widened and she looked very interested.

Why?

What do you mean, why?

Why isn't there?

Because, Lottie, I'm telling you there isn't.

Lottie thought about this. She looked at Honey.

Then why did she say that, Eliza? She came and she said it. Tell Eliza! That's what she said. She said that you would know who I meant.

I took a breath and I crouched down right in front of Lottie so I could look in her face. Honey thought it was a game and laughed, reaching out a hand to pat my cheek. I pushed it away and she did it again, harder.

Stop it, I said.

Pat-a-cake! She began to laugh.

Not now, I said. I turned back to Lottie. Look, Lottie, I said. I don't understand a word you're saying but I'm telling you you're to shut up right now.

Lottie gazed at me.

She said if you don't understand, then maybe I should go and ask James.

I froze.

No, I told her quickly. Don't ask James. Promise me, Lottie, you won't say any of this to James.

Lottie pressed her finger against her lip and put her head on one side.

Why not, Eliza? Why won't I?

Never mind why. Just promise me.

Lottie stared at me. Her cheeks turning pink. She glanced around her as if she was getting ready to run.

I want to. I want to tell James.

You mustn't.

But I want to!

I took a breath.

James would be very angry, I said. He really would, Lottie. He wouldn't like it.

Lottie stared at me.

Angry with me?

Yes. With you.

She looked excited.

Why would he be angry with me?

I suddenly felt faint, so I sat myself down on the ground. I was having to think so fast that I felt quite dizzy.

Lottie, I said, would you like a kitten just like Jazzy has got? A little furry kitten all of your own?

Now Lottie gasped. She pressed her hands together and nodded.

Well, I said and I took her small, dirty hand in mine, the one that hadn't got the string tied to it. It won't be right now this very moment. You'll have to be very patient. But as soon as the next litter of kittens is born in the village, I shall go and get you one.

Lottie stared at me. Her mind working so hard that her whole face went still.

When will it be?

Very soon.

But when?

You'll have to wait for them to be born, won't you? But I happen to know there's a cat in the village with a great big fat belly. The fattest. It won't be long now.

Lottie gasped.

Won't it?

It won't.

Lottie thought about this.

I don't want a black one, she said. Or a white one.

What kind do you want?

One with stripes. Like Miss Sands' tiger!

Addie Sands doesn't have a tiger.

In the Big Book of Animals, she does.

All right, I said. You mean a tabby? You want a little tabby kitten like Lupin?

Tabby! Honey shrieked.

Lottie looked at her.

Shut up, Honey, she said.

All right, I said. All right, I'll get you a dear little tabby. Would you like that?

Suddenly Lottie's face fell.

Ma won't let me.

If you don't say a word about any of this to anyone, and especially if you don't go and talk to James, then I'll speak to our mother and explain to her why you should have one. You know that she'll listen to me. If I tell her you've been a very good girl. Would you like that?

Lottie nodded. Her top-knot was bouncing now. Honey was gazing at me.

Me too, she said.

No, said Lottie. Not you, Honey. It's me who talked to the dead girl, so it's me that gets the kitten, not you.

Honey's face crumpled and she began to cry. Lottie turned back to me.

Why did the girl say that James was wicked, Eliza?

My heart missed a beat.

What? I said.

Did he hit the girl very hard? Did he hurt her? Is that it?

For a moment I could not speak. The shock spread through my bones and all my thoughts seemed to come at me at once. Lottie kept her eyes on my face.

Why are you crying?

I'm not.

Yes you are.

Lottie, for goodness' sake, I'm not crying!

You are crying, don't lie. Every day you cry and cry and me and Honey don't like it, we don't like it at all, do we, Honey?

'Is it true?' Mary asks Graham, walking into the kitchen and slamming the cupboard door so hard that the dog jumps out of the way. 'Is Lisa coming to stay?'

He looks up from washing the salad.

'Ah. Lisa. I was going to talk to you about that.'

'Just tell me if it's true or not?'

'It's not like that. Who told you, anyway?'

'Never mind who told me. I just want to know if she's coming.'

Graham reaches for a tea towel and dries his hands.

'I was going to talk to you about it tonight. Just that, as we have to go to London tomorrow anyway, Ruby asked if—'

Mary pulls out a chair and sits down. Straightaway the dog comes over and pushes her nose into her hands. She shoves her away.

'She hates this house, Lisa does. Do you know that? Just like Ruby does. They both hate it. They think there's something wrong with it. Do you realise that?'

Graham gazes at her. 'What? Something wrong with what?'

She shakes her head. 'You've no idea, have you?'

'No idea about what?'

Mary puts her head in her hands. She feels tears coming. Pinches them away.

'Just that they don't like it here, that's all. Both of them, they hate this house.'

'What don't they like?'

Mary shrugs. 'They're scared. They think the house is frightening. Creepy. You remember what Ruby said when she first came here? She said it to me all over again the other day. And Lisa feels exactly the same way, apparently. You ask Ruby if you think I'm making it up.'

Graham comes and stands in front of her.

'I don't think you're making anything up. But I do think you're a bit tough on Lisa. She always seems very happy to be here. And I also think you're perhaps overreacting.'

Mary says nothing. She feels the kitchen doorway darken. Looking up, she sees her.

'It's true, Ruby, isn't it?' she says. 'That you find this house scary? Please just tell your dad what you told me.'

Ruby pulls her sleeves down over her hands. She doesn't look at Mary.

'It's all right,' she says in a quiet voice.

'What's all right?' Graham says.

'The house. It's OK.'

Mary looks at her.

'That's not what you told me.'

Ruby hesitates.

'Well, all right, there is something a bit—'

'A bit what?' Graham says.

Ruby takes a breath.

'It's not that I think there are ghosts or anything.'

Graham laughs.

'Oh, great. Well, I'm glad we've cleared that up, then.'

Ruby glances at Mary.

'It's only the man, really.'

'Man?'

Mary looks at Graham.

'She means the man with the red hair. The young guy. The one I saw in the garden. She's seen him too.'

Graham chucks the tea towel on the table. He looks at Ruby.

'In our garden? You didn't tell me that.'

Ruby looks at the floor and shrugs.

'I didn't want to worry you.'

Mary says nothing, looks away.

'Ah, well, you know what?' Graham says to Ruby. 'I honestly don't think that chap is anything to worry about. Though I can't say I'm keen on people coming in our garden. We need to fix that.'

Now Mary stares at him.

'You've seen him too?'

'Once or twice, yes. Not in the garden. I'm sure he was up by the woods one time with his girlfriend when I was walking the dog. He waved to me. He seemed quite friendly. The girlfriend seemed nice too. Quite a young girl with very long hair. And I've seen him in the fields. I think he must work for one of the farmers or something.'

Mary looks at Ruby.

'Well, there you go, a farm labourer. So you and Lisa can calm down now, can't you?'

Graham smiles. 'Farm labourer. Now there's an old-fashioned word.'

She looks at him. 'What would you call it?'

'I don't know. Just labourer sounds a bit Victorian, that's all.'

'Anyway, you don't need to worry,' Ruby tells them. 'Lisa's not coming any more. She can't.'

Graham opens the fridge, takes out a beer.

'Really? Well, that's a shame, darling. Why not?'

Ruby shrugs. 'She's got stuff on in London. I don't know. Parties and there's this guy she met or something.'

Mary feels herself relax.

'A new boyfriend? That's nice.'

Ruby looks at her.

'Why? Why is it nice?'

'Come on, Rubes,' Graham says. 'She's only trying to make conversation.'

Ruby looks away. 'Whatever.'

In the morning, Graham takes Ruby to London for her appointment. Mary waits for them to go, trying to hide her impatience as he unlocks the car for Ruby, then comes back to pick up his wallet and keys, returning once more for his glasses and a kiss – quick, dry, apologetic almost – and then yet another time—

'My phone.' He makes a face.

He is about to leave, but stops in the doorway.

'We're having lunch with Veronica, by the way. Is that OK?'

She stands there in her bare feet on the cool stone flags looking at him.

'What do you mean? Of course it's OK.'

He keeps his eyes on her.

'I don't know. I just thought I should mention it, that's all.'

'Why?'

'No reason. More that not mentioning it didn't feel quite right.'

She looks at him. She sees that he's missed a bit, shaving. A small forest of coarse dark hairs on his jaw.

'It's fine,' she says. 'Why wouldn't it be? Have fun.'

He looks at her. 'You know it's not for pleasure.'

'OK.'

She waits again for him to go, but he doesn't.

'It's partly so we can work on Ruby together. Before the appointment.'

'Work on her?'

He sighs. 'In getting her to commit to this therapy, or whatever it is they want her to do. She's got to feel we're united. Supporting her through this together.'

For a quick moment, Mary sees Graham and Veronica sitting together in a candlelit restaurant somewhere. White tablecloths and shining glasses. The united parents of Ruby.

'Of course,' she says.

'Of course what?'

'I mean, it's important that you both support her.'

Graham looks at her.

'Thanks.'

'Thanks for what?'

'Nothing. Just thanks.'

A small something inside her – a tight, hot burning thing she hadn't been aware of before – flickers and seems to go out. She ignores the feeling, waiting for him to go. But still he hesitates.

'You're OK?'

'I just said I am.'

'No, not with that. I mean are you OK generally?'

She nods. 'Of course I am.'

'There's no of course about it.' He keeps on looking at her. 'You promise you'd tell me if you weren't?'

Mary nods, knowing very well that she is long beyond promises. Graham waits for another moment, still searching her face as if there was something else he wanted to say. At last, telling her he'll see her later, he goes.

When she's sure she's heard the car drive off, she takes her tea and walks down the garden, the grass cool and damp under her bare feet, the dog trotting along behind her. She sits on the old bench. Shutting her eyes. Feeling the sun on her face, her neck, and in the roots of her hair. The bird racket above her is huge, vast and loud. But then at last it stops and there it is, the thing she's been waiting for. Silence.

She opens her eyes.

A small girl is making her way down the garden. Four years old, she'd guess – four at the most, maybe less. She wears a rough brown printed dress, light hair twisted up on top of her head. The dress is quite undone at the back, almost to the waist, unbuttoned or maybe buttonless. Some kind of greyish underclothes visible beneath it. Something about her familiar.

She is walking slowly through the long grass and carrying something wrapped up in a piece of cloth, holding it out in front of her as carefully as if it were made of glass.

Attached to her by the wrist on some kind of a lead – a piece of string, is it? – another child, this one younger, with the wispy curls and round face of a baby. Her pale skirts are bunched up and tucked into odd, big pants and she stumbles along beside the older girl, trying to keep up, catching at the air now and then with her free hand to keep her balance.

There is a thickness to the air, a stillness. Apart from the children, everything else has stopped – no sound, no living thing anywhere, no feeling of aliveness, of anything alive.

Mary feels her blood rushing in her ears. Her mouth dry, she swallows and, very slowly, puts down her tea. Wiping her hands on her clothes, she stands, gazing after them as they continue on across the lawn, watching as they squeeze themselves through the very deepest and darkest part of the hedge.

She thinks it's over. But the thick silence continues and then she sees her. The older girl – a long-haired teenager, this one – wading through the long grass, her head bent, her step measured and sullen, her face hidden by the grubby cotton flaps of a bonnet—

And then they're gone, and everything resumes. The air bright and light and thin again. Birdsong. Plants and leaves vivid and trembling in the sunlight.

Mary looks at the dog. Sniffing, unconcerned, at a patch of dandelions. She tries to breathe.

After a moment or two, her phone trembles in her pocket. She ignores it. When it trembles a second time, and then a third, she turns it off.

James was right. I didn't know anything. All I knew was that it was all Phoebe's fault. What had happened had come down between us like a hard wall of iron. He had no itch for me any more and no lightness of heart to put it into action either.

I tried not to miss him, but I did miss him. The smell of all his hot, hairy places. The sound of his voice, calling me. His hands on my clothes. The feel of his fingers finding their way through my hair. Even the look on his face after he'd spilled himself into me – a look so tight and harsh and mysterious that when I asked him what he was thinking and he said 'nothing', I believed him absolutely.

Was it really true that I would never gaze on that face again, never see that look? The nevers were all Phoebe's fault. The things that would never happen, the pleasures I would never feel again. They kept me awake at night, the nevers did. They made me sick. If this was what love was, if this was how it felt to lose it, then I'd rather not have had it in the first place.

But something else was also making me sick. I wasn't a fool. I knew what was happening. My spit tasted like a mouthful of nails and my bodice would barely lace up. I remembered how, when she was expecting Jazzy – or was it Frank? – Ma had liked to lick the handle of the small, beat-up tin they used to fetch the milk in. I had laughed at the idea of it, amazed and disgusted. But now I astonished myself by wanting to run my tongue along its cool, blunt curve and taste its iron tang.

I tried everything. I danced up and down in the yard till bright spangles of hotness came floating down in front of my eyes. I threw myself off the highest rung of the ladder in the barn and let myself roll around in the rat mess and the dust. I made myself swallow comfrey juice and then vomited until water poured out of my eyes and small red pinpricks appeared on my face. I did everything painful that I could think of that might put a swift and violent stop to what was happening inside me.

And all of it was pointless.

You're looking very bonny, Eliza, Miss Narket said.

Meanwhile the constabulary had come to the village to search for Phoebe. They sucked up the light, crawling along the edges of the lanes and fields, poking and nosing around like a line of flapping black crows. Only unlike the crows, you knew that no amount of hand clapping would be enough to scare them off.

Mary hears someone calling her name. She turns and sees Deborah in a bright skirt and sandals, picking her way down the weed-covered steps into the garden. Straightaway, the dog runs towards her, barking. Mary calls her off.

'Do you mind?' Deborah laughs and puts a hand down to stop the dog jumping up. 'I rapped on the window and couldn't get any answer so I guessed you must be out here. I was just on my way to the shops and Eddie said you weren't very well, so I thought I'd come and see if you needed anything.'

Mary stares at her for a moment.

'I'm fine. I'm perfectly well.'

Stroking the dog's head with one hand, Deborah glances up, shielding her eyes in the sunshine.

'But Eddie said he'd seen you and you were looking very pale or something and he was worried about you.'

For a moment, Mary struggles with this.

'I don't know what he meant. I'm fine.'

Deborah laughs.

'Ah well, that's good. Glad to know all's well. I know he's very fond of you.' She looks at Mary for a moment. 'He says you've been a very good friend to him recently. And I think he's needed it. I wanted you to know that we both appreciate it.'

Mary feels the blood go to her face.

'I haven't done anything.'

Deborah smiles. 'Well, that's not what he says.'

Mary shakes her head, tries to smile.

'I don't know what he's talking about.'

A brief, awkward silence. She looks up, lets her eyes go to the house. There's a face at Ruby's window. Suddenly unmistakable – a quick, pale movement. Swish of hair. Her heart contracts.

'All the same,' Deborah is saying, 'after what you guys have been through. I think you're so brave. And kind as well. More than kind. Seriously, he's very fond of you. Never stops talking about you, you know.' She hesitates, glancing around her. 'Goodness, isn't it lovely out here? I always forget how huge your garden is. And I love the way you've left it to go so wild.'

Mary tells her it's more through lack of energy than intention.

'Well, I like it,' Deborah says. 'It's very special. It's got an atmosphere.'

That's right, Mary thinks, that's right, it has. She glances back up at the window again. Nothing. She asks Deborah if she'd like some coffee and is relieved when she says she doesn't.

'Can't stop. It's book group tonight and I've got a million and one things to do before tomorrow when Eddie gets back.'

'He's gone away?'

Deborah blinks.

'London. Just for the night. He's got various friends there. He wasn't going to go till next week but one of the people he was seeing, their plans changed or something.'

I told James I needed to talk to him. At first he looked very cold and doubtful, but eventually he agreed to meet me behind the apple store. I told him frankly then what was happening to me, that I was in no doubt, that it was perfectly obvious, that I knew all the signs.

At first he seemed quite unconcerned. He looked at me and he laughed. He said I had a good imagination and that was a fact.

I do not see how you can be in the family way, Eliza, he said. What I mean is, I promise you it is very unlikely.

I asked him what he meant by that and he told me that he had always been very careful. I thought about this.

What does careful mean?

His face went tight.

If you knew how people came to be in the family way, you wouldn't have to ask. You would just get it, Eliza.

I told him that I did know all of that very well and remembering all the things we'd done, I didn't think he'd been careful enough. Very slowly, as if he needed time to think, he rubbed at his face. Then he shook his head.

You're a young girl, he said. You're very innocent.

When I protested that he of all people knew very well that I was not innocent, he looked at me thoughtfully.

If you really believe you are burdened in this way, he said at last, then all I can say is it is not by me.

Now I grew properly furious.

What are you saying, James? That I went around giving myself to other men?

He blinked.

I did not say that.

What, then? You're saying that you had nothing to do with it? That you did not have connection with me whenever you felt like it?

He shrugged.

You're very young, he said again. And very pretty. Any man would notice you, Eliza. And I like you – very much – you know that I always have. But I do believe this is all a very fanciful story you've allowed to take root in your head.

I stared at him. I could not believe what I was hearing.

In my head? I said. In my head?

He sighed. I watched as he leaned against the apple store and folded his arms.

You remember that I told you once about the woman in Lowestoft? The one who died?

I felt my heart jump.

Yes, I said. What was it that she died of?

I knew he would not tell me and I was right.

Never mind about that. It was a long time ago and it was all quite unfortunate. But you remember that there was also another one?

Violet, I said. The one who was too crazy for the workhouse and too sane for the asylum. She died too, didn't she? Along with her poor pony.

He looked at me as if he was startled that I should remember.

What happened to Violet? I asked him. And what's she got to do with it?

He stared into space as if he hadn't heard me.

I told you before. Violet destroyed herself and the pony too.

But why?

He tilted his head and frowned.

Well, I don't know what it is with some women. But they get to know me and then, well, it all somehow seems to speed up.

It? I said. I don't know what you're talking about. What is it exactly that speeds up?

James jutted out his bottom lip. I saw that he was trying to seem unperturbed, but was not managing it. In fact, talking like this seemed to be exciting him. His eyes were a little too alive and bright. It seemed he could not dim them however hard he tried.

Well, let's just say they seem to get ideas.

Ideas?

I watched him carefully, but the whole time he spoke, my blood was chilling. I was struggling to stay level and calm.

He bit his lip.

They get it in their heads that I've promised them things, don't they? And then when they don't get whatever it is they think they want – well, they seem quite prepared to fabricate.

Fabricate?

Just like you, Violet said I'd had relations with her. Many many times she said we'd done it.

And you hadn't?

He scratched his head till the hair stood up on end in a bright red coxcomb. He blinked twice as if he'd just woken up and seen what was around him.

I had never been near her. Not one time. It was all some fancy story that she'd dreamed up. She was a lively girl a little like yourself,

Eliza. A lively girl with a lively imagination to match. I'm not saying you're like this. But some women would do anything to catch a man.

Now I began to understand the meaning of his words. And as I did so, something in me started to fall. It was my heart, dropping like a stone.

And what about Phoebe Harkiss? I said.

I saw him tense.

Phoebe Harkiss?

Was she also a lively girl?

He looked at me and he did not answer.

Well? I said.

When he spoke, his voice was slow and cold.

You ought to be very careful, Eliza, he said.

Careful about what?

The things you talk about. You don't want to end up in the asylum, do you?

My mouth fell open.

What? I said.

He kept his eyes on me.

It's just that some of the things you say, they make no sense at all.

When they first knew for certain what had happened to their girls – when the police officer called Claire with the short blonde hair and the gold studs and the knitted thing that hung with the keys at her waist, when she came and took them into the other room and sat them down and told them what she had to tell – Mary found herself down on the floor.

She did not collapse, or faint or fall. Instead, she simply laid herself down on the old beige carpet with its drift of grey dirt and fluff. She put herself down there and she stayed very still.

And Claire and another officer – were there two or even three of them in there? it seems absurd that even now, after not that many months, she cannot recall – knelt down on the floor beside her and took cushions from the sofa and put them under her head and her knees. And she knows that she let them do it and that she lay there. Helpless and unwitting as a person after an accident. Not yet daring to let herself think about what they'd just said.

She knows too – and this still appalls her – that a strange kind of comfort seemed to spread over her. Euphoria even. She felt like laughing, though she did not laugh. Or did she? She knows that someone touched her hands. And found them very cold. Her hands and feet, so cold. To her they might as well have been dead. Sloughed off, discarded, no longer a part of her.

Shock, someone said. She's in shock. Can you hear me, Mary? Just try to breathe.

And so she did as she was told. She lay there, doing her best to take slow gasps of that quiet and terrible air. She kept on doing it. One breath after another. She was surprised at how easy a thing it seemed. Almost a pleasure, she felt it was, even though she knew that each breath she took was carrying her that little bit further from her girls.

9

On Saturday morning, as she sits on the bench drinking tea and throwing a tennis ball for the dog while trying at the same time to read the papers, Mary sees Graham in his paint-spattered DIY clothes, carrying a bag of tools down to the bottom of the garden.

'Decided I couldn't put it off any longer,' he says.

'What?'

'That shed. I thought I should just get on with it.'

She stares at him, suddenly afraid.

'The apple store?'

'If it ever really was used for storing apples, yes.'

'You were the one who told me that.'

'Was I?'

'You said it when we first came here.'

Graham thinks about this.

'Well, I don't know where I got that from.'

'You said it was on the deeds.'

He frowns.

'All right, well, I don't care what it is. It's had it. It's going.'

Mary hesitates. A cloud moves and the sun is suddenly in her eyes. The dog runs up with the ball. She reaches out a hand to take it, but the dog holds on, so she lets go.

'What, but you mean you're going to pull it down just like that?'

He looks at his trousers. Takes hold of the old tie that he uses for a belt and pulls it tighter.

'It's half-rotten anyway. It won't take much. And it's not like we'll ever use it for anything, is it?'

Mary glances off down the lawn. The apple store is hidden by a thick screen of trees, thicker now they're all in leaf. She can't even see the dark edge of it. Inexplicably, her heart speeds up.

'It's just it's been there a very long time, that's all.'

'An old shed?'

'Yes.'

'And that's a reason to keep it?'

'No. No, I suppose not.'

He picks up the tools again.

'You'll see, it'll make a big difference to that bit of the garden. Open it up. Get some light in there.'

'Light?'

'Well, it's a dark corner, isn't it? Dark and gloomy. It's not just you who gets the heebie-jeebies when you go down there.'

The heebie-jeebies. She's not sure any more. If Mary tries now to think of what she saw – the young girl, her body, her bloodied face – she can only hold it in her mind for the smallest second before it slips straight out again.

She looks at him. The dog nudges at her hand. Drops the ball at her feet. She bends forward to pick it up.

'Is that why you're doing it?'

'What?'

'Because I got scared that time?'

'Not really. Not just that, no.' He stops, looking at her. 'What is it? I don't get it. You really don't want me to?'

Mary shakes her head. She realises her hands are trembling.

'I don't mind. I don't mind what you do.' She throws the ball and the dog runs off. 'Do you want some help?'

'From you? No thanks. I offered to pay that layabout of a daughter to give me a hand, and she seemed quite keen yesterday, but now – surprise, surprise – she won't even get out of bed. But don't worry. Help is on its way. In fact, here he is. Help has just arrived.'

He lifts a hand and waves and she turns and sees Eddie letting himself in through the side gate.

I knew that it was over between James and me. My heart felt dead, squashed, all life and happiness gone out of it. I knew that he would never love me or touch me or look on me kindly again. It was as if our love had never happened, but also as if it was the only thing that had ever happened. I hated him for loving me and I hated him for stopping. I could not think straight any more. I cried myself to sleep at night and cried myself awake as well. At last Jazzy came and told me to please be quiet.

The little ones won't sleep with all the noise you're making.

I stared at her. What noise? I hadn't known I'd been making any noise.

You do it every night, she said. All this crying. It's too much. It makes everyone miserable. Go to sleep and in the morning you'll surely feel better.

I didn't tell her that I wished there was no morning. That I wished I would not wake up, wished that God would just be merciful and take me in my sleep. But there was no such thing as mercy: the days stretched out ahead of me, days and days and hours and nights and I did not know how I would get through them. And meanwhile in my body, everything was changing.

Now when I crept into Ma's room and lifted my skirts and looked at the shape of myself in the glass, I saw the beginnings of something that wasn't like me at all.

My mouth still tasted different – blacker and sparklier – and sometimes my toes pinched in my boots. I felt dizzy and saw pink lights flying off in all directions if I stood up too sudden or quick. I could not stand the warm udder smell of the milk in the pail. Or the fatty after-whiff when the candle blew out. But I liked the clean sharpness of vinegar and sometimes woke in the mornings wishing I could glug it down.

Meanwhile Lammas Day had been and gone and the weather stayed fine. The wheat was thick and gold and higher than our Jazzy's head. The men were all out from first crack, hoeing the turnips and lifting the barley and corn while we gavelled and raked to make it ready for the bind-pullers. And a man had come from London with a camera. He walked around the fields staring at people and had a boy with him that carried the black cloth on legs and the machinery for doing the pictures. The reason he had come had nothing to do with Phoebe. He wanted to make pictures of the harvest, he said. To show rich people in London what real sweat and toil looked like.

He'll be lucky to get a picture of that, Pa said. But if he wants to see a whole lot of good-for-nothings lying around in the dinner hour and swilling beer, then he can be my guest.

Still, I knew my father liked it that people in London might see the farm. He let the man photograph a row of black sows and some chicks that had hatched in Frank's old bicycle basket, as well as a cow at her fullest and heaviest just before the milking.

Pa was worried about the harvest. They were short on labour this year in the village and Ma was much too far gone now to help with the gavelling, so he said I had to do it.

I shut my eyes. I did not see how I would get myself to that baking-hot field, let alone lift a fork.

Jazzy will give you a hand, he said.

But who will do the elevenses and fourses? I said, thinking of all the men that would need their dinner bringing.

It will have to be the twins, he said.

The twins aren't reliable. They'll get up to some mischief. And anyway Charlie can't carry things because of his leg.

My father thought about this.

Lottie's big enough. She can do it.

What, all on her own?

Minnie can help her. And Honey, for that matter. Honey can help.

Honey's a baby, I said. Honey's no help.

All right then, she can tag along.

What? With Lottie and Minnie?

I don't see why not.

I sighed. My father never did understand the first thing about babies.

Lottie's four years old, I said. She's cleverer than Minnie but she can't look after Honey. She'll get caught up in something and forget what she's doing.

Pa looked at me.

Then we'll tie them together, the way your ma does.

I still don't think she'll manage it, I said.

Pa said nothing. I knew we were both thinking the same thing. That we had never felt the loss of our Frank more keenly than now. Our Frank who even from the age of three or four was sturdy and sensible and who would work till his small fingers were rasped and specked with blood and who wasn't afraid to lead the big horse along as the men tossed the sheaves in, even though he barely came up to that great beast's nostrils and had once almost got trampled to death when a young rabbit went scampering under its feet.

Pa told me to wrap up some bread and cheese in a cloth.

What for? I said.

For Lottie. So she can try taking it through the orchard and down to the field where the men are. Maybe it's simpler to leave Minnie with Charlie, but Honey can go with her and you can watch them to see that they do it all right.

I thought about this.

She doesn't even know who the men are, I reminded him.

She knows James. Tell her to take it to him.

I knew he was right. Lottie did know James. All the babies did. I think they could have found their way to James Dix even if he was stuck somewhere in a hayfield halfway to China.

Graham says it shouldn't take them more than an hour or two, both of them working together like that. But the walls are thicker than he'd thought and by midday he and Eddie are still trying to finish breaking up the first wall. An hour later they've managed to prise its shattered remnants away from the rest of the structure, but the second wall won't move. Three-quarters of the thing still standing there, its dusty, rotting insides half exposed, its bulk still blocking out the light.

Mary watches from the landing window, pacing up and down for a moment or two, the boards creaking under her feet. Then she goes into the bathroom and locks the door and sits for a moment on the hard, cold edge of the bath, looking at the dusty cracks between the floorboards and wondering if she's going to vomit. No, she thinks, she won't vomit. Why would she vomit? She hasn't done that in a while.

She hears Ruby get up out of bed and walk down the passage to the toilet. She's in there a long time. At last she hears it flush. Heavy footsteps coming back, stopping outside the bathroom. The latch on the door lifting. The door rattling.

'Mary?'

'What?'

Mary lifts her head, looks at the door.

'I need to wash.'

She takes a breath.

'Can you just give me a moment?'

Ruby says nothing. She does not speak or move. Mary knows that she is standing there, just on the other side, her eyes fixed on the door.

She waits a moment, then she gets up and opens the door. Ruby in pyjamas and T-shirt, her eyes still dark with yesterday's slept-in make-up.

'That's not what I call giving someone a moment,' Mary says.

Ruby doesn't react, but her face is interested.

'What were you doing?'

'None of your business.' Mary looks at her. 'If you get dressed quickly, you could go and give your dad a hand.'

Ruby stares at her.

'With what?'

'Apparently you said you'd help him pull down the shed.'

Ruby shakes her head.

'I didn't say definitely. I said it depended on how I'm feeling. And I'm feeling like shit.'

Mary thinks about this.

'Why?' she says.

'Why what?'

'Why are you feeling like shit? What's the matter?'

Ruby shrugs.

'Nothing's the matter. I often feel like shit.'

Mary looks at her. 'Do you?'

'Yes.'

Lottie and Honey went out of the kitchen door and down through the orchard, squeezing themselves through the gap in the hedge and out to the place where the men lay with their caps over their faces on the flattened grass under the harvest tree. I followed behind, just far enough away that they could feel they were doing it by themselves.

I don't know if James was surprised or not, but as soon as he clocked them, he held out his arms. He scooped shrieking Honey into the air, at the same time pulling Lottie into his lap and kissing her so hard that she squealed.

I watched them all from the shade of the hedge, pulling my bonnet over my cheeks, my limbs like lead, my mouth dry.

What are those? Lottie said, pointing to all the young rabbits that lay dead under the tree.

James laughed and I saw his hand go under her petticoat.

Well, they're the young'uns that got caught, aren't they?

Lottie caught her breath and I saw her shiver as he blew some quick breaths on her neck.

Who caught them?

I saw him plant a kiss on her head, the tops of her ears. She shrieked and pulled away, laughing.

No one did. They should have got out of the way, that's all.

I want one, Honey said and she settled her body against him and twisted her head around to look at him as she slid her thumb out of her mouth and then back in again.

I watched as he ruffled her hair.

One what? he said.

She means one of the babies, Lottie told him.

What? he said. She wants a rabbit?

A wabbit, Honey said.

James laughed.

Then you shall have one. We'll skin one and make you a little fur coat all of your own, shall we?

And me! Lottie cried. I want one too! Eliza said she'd get me a kitten if I didn't tell you anything, but I'd very much rather have a rabbit!

James looked at her.

Tell me anything about what?

I saw Lottie freeze.

Nothing, she said.

Tell me what? said James.

Lottie gave a little gulp.

I'm not to tell you, am I?

James lifted his head and saw me watching. He held my gaze for a long moment but there was no love there, only a kind of uncouth brazenness that made my throat tighten. Then he patted Honey's head and, as if he'd never known me or had a single thought about me in my whole life, he let his eyes drift away.

*

302

At one thirty, she takes them beer and sandwiches, setting the tray down on the parched and scrubby grass before standing back to look.

'Part of the problem is that it's surprisingly well dug-in,' Graham explains, leaning against his spade and rubbing at his face with his sleeve. 'Someone actually went to the trouble of digging proper foundations, just for a garden shed, would you believe?'

'It's more than a shed,' Eddie says as he lights a cigarette. 'It's an outbuilding. They were farmers, weren't they? And anyway, they did things properly then.'

As he draws on the cigarette, he lifts his eyes and looks over at Mary. She meets his gaze then looks away.

'But it's also his fault,' Graham says, smiling and indicating Eddie. 'Because we've got to keep the bloody shelves intact. Means we can't just hack away at it, which would be so much quicker.'

Eddie grins, blowing out smoke.

'A whole set of hundred-year-old apple racks. How could I not want them?'

'What are you going to do with them?' Mary asks him.

He smiles at her. 'I thought you weren't speaking to me any more.'

Graham looks up. 'Why wouldn't she be speaking to you?'

Eddie grins. 'Mary's sulking. About something I said.'

Mary feels her cheeks growing hot.

'Don't be silly,' she says.

'Anyway,' Eddie puts out the cigarette, 'I don't know what I'll use them for. Does it matter? I just have to have them. Don't worry, I'll find a use.'

Graham laughs. 'Firewood. That's what I'd use them for.'

'It's more than a hundred years old anyway,' Mary says, 'the shed. It's closer to a hundred and fifty.'

'Mary reminded me we've got the deeds somewhere,' Graham tells him.

Eddie flicks open a can of beer.

'If it was up to me I wouldn't even be pulling this thing down. I don't know why you're doing it. I think it's beautiful. Don't you agree, Mary? Isn't it beautiful?'

Mary says nothing.

'If it was in good nick, I wouldn't,' Graham says. 'But look at it, it's completely rotten. Five years and I reckon it would have collapsed anyway.'

Mary can't help it – she lets her eyes go to the shed. The wood spliced and exposed where the first wall has come away. The black earth floor, light falling on it for the first time.

'Give me a shout when you want tea,' she says and she walks as fast as she can back towards the house, leaving them both standing there.

But just an hour later, Graham comes and finds her. His clothes are dark with dirt, his face white and shaken.

'I'm sorry. I didn't want to tell you, but you'd better come. We found something. Something horrible. Oh God, Mary. I don't know what to do.'

It wasn't just the man from London with the camera poking and prying around the village. The constables were going round all the families and houses asking questions. They said it didn't mean anything, but they had to do it to get a picture of what might have happened to a young girl who had gone missing seemingly without a word or a by-your-leave. A young girl with her whole life ahead of her and nothing whatsoever to be ashamed of.

I didn't like her at all, Jazzy stupidly told the constable. I'm glad she's gone and good riddance. She gave me a kitten that she already knew was poorly.

I scowled at her to shut her up – the fear starting up inside me so fast I could barely breathe – but of course the constable was very interested and wanted to know as much as she could tell him. I watched as his hairy hands wrote 'kitten' in thick lead pencil on a piece of paper that was mostly empty but had a lot of lines on.

Jazzy looked down at Lupin, who was curled so upside down in her lap that all you could see was the creamy white triangle of her chin.

Not this one, by the way, she said. It wasn't this one. This one's the dearest little cat in the world. It was another one.

At that moment, Lottie, who'd been sitting in the corner, put down her slate and came over. She stared at the constable for a moment, then asked him if she could rap her knuckles on his big tall hat.

It's a door, she said. And if I knock on it, you'll have to let me in.

He looked surprised but he laughed and bent his big head down. She rapped on the hat.

304

There you go, she said. Can I come in?

The constable laughed and winked at me.

What a card your little sister is.

Yes, I said. A card.

After that, because she knew he'd taken a shine to her, Lottie went and fetched her slate. She thrust the drawing in his face.

What is it? Is it a cat, a candle, a leaf or a pair of shoes?

Lottie, I said. Not now. Can't you see this isn't the moment?

But Lottie didn't care if it was the moment or not and anyway the constable was finding her very amusing.

Don't worry, he told me. My daughter's got kiddies of the same age. Five, is she?

Four! Lottie shouted, a little too loudly. I'm four years old.

We're the ones that are five, whispered Minnie, but no one heard her except Charlie.

The constable gazed at Lottie.

Well, my word, and what a great big girl you are for four. Now let me see – he put his head on one side and smoothed his fingers over his moustache – I'd say it's a pair of shoes.

Lottie laughed quite rudely and told him he was wrong.

A candle, then?

She shook her head. He bent forwards to see it better.

It's not a cat, is it?

Lottie came closer and rested the palm of her hand on the constable's big black leg. It was the same thing I'd seen her do with James. It gave me a cold, tight feeling in my throat.

It's not any of them, she said in a voice so quiet it was almost a whisper. Do you give up? Shall I tell you? It's Mary Coles.

The constable looked at her.

Mary Coles? Is that a little friend of yours, then?

Lottie shook her head.

Not little. She's big. Mary Coles is big. A big pretty lady with black hair and a very sad face. She's the lady whose little girls were taken away by the—

Lottie, I said. That's quite enough.

Lottie threw me a mischievous look, then glanced back at the constable. A sharp black dread shot through me. She had the look on her face that meant she was starting to enjoy herself.

The little girls are dead, she said.

The constable stiffened.

Dead? What little girls?

Lottie blinked at him and held up both hands and sighed.

The little girls of Mary Coles. And one day we'll be dead too. Just like the girl in the black water. The man will come and I'll be dead and Honey will be dead and—

Lottie! I said. Stop it right now. For goodness' sake, whatever has come over you?

Lottie gazed at me and her chin began to wobble. She clutched at herself.

My tummy hurts, Eliza. I've got a tummy ache.

Come here, I said and I pulled her to me and took her on my lap. She began to suck her thumb. I smoothed her hair. The constable looked at us both.

Do you know what she's talking about? Who is this man? Have you seen him here in the village?

I tried to laugh.

It's nothing, I told him. It's just a silly game she plays. The Mary person is a made-up person. She tells a lot of boomers, Lottie does. I don't know where she gets the ideas about the dead children from. You make it all up in your head, don't you, Lottie?

And I kissed her head, but Lottie looked up sharply.

Not boomers! she said and she began to cry.

The constable put down his pencil and took off his helmet and put it in his lap. He scratched his head. He was looking hard at Lottie. My blood was jumping and I felt shaken right down to my boots, but I smiled as brightly as I could at him.

Lottie's very excited because she's getting a new kitten soon, I said. Aren't you, Lottie? A little tabby kitten all of her own. Remember how I promised you, Lottie?

Straightaway Jazzy looked at me.

She's not getting a kitten.

Yes, she is.

It's not fair. I'm the only one with a kitten.

We want a kitten! shouted Charlie and Minnie together.

Lottie looked at them and began to cry.

Don't want a kitten! I don't want one, Eliza.

306

She turned her face to my chest and kept on crying. The constable looked very bewildered. Jazzy turned to him.

I'm the one who likes kittens, she said. It's me. I told you: I had a kitten but it died. Phoebe knew it would die, because it was very poorly. James said she was a very bad girl to let me take it when she knew it was so sick. He said he would punish her for it.

No, he didn't, I said. Of course he didn't. Shut up, Jazz. You're making it up.

But the constable looked interested.

And who is James? Is James your brother?

Oh no, Jazzy said. James is just a man.

I felt Lottie stiffen.

He's the man who's going to kill us, she said. We don't really know him, but Eliza does.

For a moment everyone stared at her. I flushed hot to the roots of my hair.

What do you mean? I said. I don't know him any better than you do. We all know him and like him very much and you know very well that James wouldn't hurt a fly.

Lottie thought about this.

He wouldn't hurt a fly perhaps. Not a teeny tiny little fly. But I do think he would hurt a child.

I looked at the constable – I was getting desperate now.

James helps my father out on the farm, I said. He's perfectly all right, but he didn't know Phoebe Harkiss. When the first cat died, James helped Jazzy pick out another one. That's all it is.

I watched as the constable drew a line under something I could not read. He put his helmet back on and put his writing things away in his coat.

All the same, I'd like to talk to him.

I shut my eyes. I had a vision of the sky falling down on me like a great big black pack of cards.

Why? I said.

Just to find out what he knows.

Someone – Mary can't any longer remember which one it was of all the many trauma and bereavement counsellors they saw – told her that grief is not really grief, but love. It is love, they said. Or a corollary of love. Another branch. Or simply normal love expressed, through force of circumstances, in a different way.

Strange, then – because these bones have nothing whatsoever to do with them, could never in any way be linked to anyone she has ever loved – that grief, simple, pure and heart-shaking grief, is what she feels as they wait for the police to arrive.

She sits in the kitchen, dry-eyed, calm, decisive even – it was she, after all, who called them, who went and Googled what you had to do and then reported it. But inside, somewhere in the very rawest part of her, her heart feels like it's dying all over again.

Eddie – who squeezed her shoulder and patted Graham's arm before he left – told them not to go jumping to conclusions.

'People find bones all the time,' he said. 'They've obviously been there for years. It's a shock, but you mustn't think about it too hard. It may not be anything.'

But less than ten minutes later, the phone rang.

'I can't believe it,' Deborah said. 'This is awful. What a terrible shock. And after all that you've both been through as well.'

She reminded Deborah of what both Eddie and Graham had said. That what they'd found could easily be the bones of an animal. A large dog. A sheep. A small horse. A beloved pet that someone had decided to bury long ago under the floor of the apple store.

She heard Deborah thinking about this.

'All the same. Until you know for sure, you'll be in shock. You won't know what's hit you. Don't underestimate it. The impact, I mean.'

Deborah asked if there was anything she and Eddie could do. Did they need supper? A drink? Just someone to come over and be with them until the police came?

Mary told Deborah that they were OK. That they wouldn't worry till they had to. That they were keeping an open mind.

Yet even as she said it, she saw them all over again. The bleached nubs of what looked like vertebrae lying there in the dark, disturbed earth. The gleam of what might have been part of a ribcage. An unmistakable jaw bone with some teeth attached. A dirty, webbed fragment of what might once have been a skull.

Later on the day of the constable's visit, James came and found me.

I was pegging out washing, the sun hot on my back. I had not been alone with him in a long time and at first I couldn't help it, even though my mind knew it was hopeless, my body felt a quick, hot rush of hope. In the old days, he would have looked around to see that no one was near, then he would have grabbed me hard and held me tight, whispering to me about the things he intended to do to me later.

But of course he didn't do that. Instead, he just stood there considering me with so much coldness on his face that my knees felt weak. I told myself it was better that I didn't notice. I picked up a sheet from the basket.

Did he come and find you? I said.

Did who come and find me?

The constable. Did he ask you some questions? What did you tell him? Did he ask you if you knew her? What did you say?

James kept on looking at me as if I was some stranger he'd just met in the street. Worse than a stranger, since he might have been polite to a stranger, yet now his eyes were terrible, quite hard and dead. When he still didn't speak, I put the wet sheet back in the basket and turned to face him.

Speak to me, I whispered. James, it's me, remember? Please, I beg you, talk to me.

He took a step back away from me. At last he shook his head.

I haven't the faintest what you're on about, he said. Knew who? Why would he ask me if I knew someone?

I stared at him.

Why Phoebe Harkiss, of course.

Straightaway, almost before I could finish getting the name out, he stepped forwards and gripped me by the wrist, his fingers so tight on me that it burned.

Don't! he said.

What?

Don't ever say that name to me again, he said. I mean it, Eliza. Never again as long as I live do I want to hear that name on your lips.

I stared at him, my heart up in my chest.

All right, I whispered.

I mean it, you know.

309

I know. I know you do.

He looked at me for a moment, then he let go.

Anyway, he said, I didn't come here to talk about that. I came to tell you that you need to take a dose.

What? I said. A dose? A dose of what?

He frowned at me.

Salts, I think. Salts or senna. There's some I've met in the city who use gin, but I reckon you're too young for that and I doubt anyone here'd give it to you.

I stared at him. Felt my blood beginning to rise up into my head.

What do you mean? I said. Take a dose for what?

What do you mean, for what? The thing you told me about, of course. So you will get your – you know—

I told him I did not know what he meant. He stared at me.

Your courses. The thing that should happen if you— What, you're saying you don't know what that is? You've never had that?

Had what?

Eliza, for goodness' sake, the thing that happens to all women!

I bit my lip and looked at the ground.

I don't know if I am a woman yet, I told him, because it was the truth and also because I did not know what he was talking about.

He folded his arms and looked at me. I knew that look. It meant that something had taken him by surprise and now he was turning things over and over in his mind.

All right, he said. Well, in that case you've been very unlucky. And I am even more sure that I had nothing to do with it. But you still need to get yourself a dose of something.

I stared at him. The way he said it – get yourself a dose of something – made me feel like the loneliest person on earth. It was a struggle to keep the tears from coming.

I don't know how to get whatever it is, I said. But I suppose I can ask my mother.

No, he said quickly. Not your mother. How about one of the Narkets?

Miss Narket's white accusing face came into my head.

I'm not going to Miss Narket about this, I said.

Well, you can't go to your mother either.

Why not? Why can't I?

I watched as a shadow went across his face. I waited.

Why not? I said again.

He took a breath.

If you tell your mother about this, I will never speak to you again as long as you live.

If I had wondered why he did not want me to ask my mother, it wasn't long before that question was answered. That night her time was up and she began to scream.

My mother generally slid babies out between one household job and the next and, more often than not, got up and cooked the dinner afterwards. But not this time.

We'd never known the pain go on so long or heard her scream so hard and loud with nothing to show for it. In the end our father could not stand it any longer and he sent me to fetch the doctor. By the time I got back with him it was beginning to be light. Ma's face was yellow and the room smelled nastily ripe, like blood. The baby was stuck, half in and half out. Jazzy was sitting at the bottom of the stairs with the twins and all three of them were crying. My father had his face in his hands.

The doctor rolled up his sleeves and pushed his hands in and twisted. Out the child slipped. I stared at the long, blue body. It's eyes were black and open wide but it wasn't moving.

I gasped.

Is it dead?

The doctor smiled and thumped it hard. A loud cry came from somewhere. I realised it was the child. My father looked up.

Another bonny boy, the doctor said – and because my mother could not take him, he handed him to me.

My father was weeping.

Will she be all right? he said, not looking at the child in my lap but at my mother who was drenched and feasy and did not quite seem to be in the room with us.

The doctor said that he thought Ma would live, but that this had better be the last time.

The last time of what? said Jazzy.

Never mind what, my father said.

The last baby, idiot, I told her.

And I looked at him, my new brother. I held him in my arms as the sun came up. He had a slick of dark black hair that made me think of Frank, and his hands were like brown, wrinkled walnuts just out of the shell.

But it was only as Jazzy handed me the cloth to dry the cheese and wet off him, that I rubbed at his hair and realised that it wasn't black at all. It was the brightest, most flaming red.

The girls' room. At first they did not touch it. It was impossible. They could not face it. They left it exactly as it was. Duvets, crumpled and slept in. Old vests and socks. Ella's meerkat poster, its corner curling off the wall where she had picked at the Blu-tack. A fairy skirt. Lego bricks. Farm animals. The doll with its face scribbled on by Flo. A one-legged Action Man that she liked to take in the bath. Ella's bead-making set. Crayons tipped on the floor—

For a long time – apart from one shameful vodka-drinking night when she crept into the bottom bunk only to wake, hours later, dribbling and sobbing, among the warm, Flo-smelling nest of soft toys – she did not let herself go in there. Neither, as far as she knew, did he.

Instead, she began to focus on the guest room, the room they never used. She had never before paid much attention to this room, but now she saw all of its possibilities. Sunny and spacious, clean. Best of all, no one ever slept there. It was empty.

She changed the bed. Washing and even ironing the linen. Making it up with piles of pillows and layers of neatly folded blankets and quilts.

'What are you doing?' He stopped in the doorway, staring at her as she attended to it. She lifted her head, flushed, caught out. 'Who on earth are you expecting?' he said.

She looked down at the quilt. It was the one she had made herself from patchwork odds and ends when she was a teenager. Laura Ashley remnants. She hadn't got around to finishing it until almost fifteen years later, needing something to occupy her restless, excited fingers as she waited for Ella to be born.

Each hexagonal patch was different. A sprigged floral here, a stripe or a check or a polka dot there. She put a finger on it. Looked at him.

'I'm not expecting anyone,' she said.

When they moved, someone else came round to pack up the girls' room. A friend, or she thinks it was a friend, it seems awful now that she cannot remember. Someone they used to know, anyway – one of the many who faded so neatly and completely from their lives afterwards.

Some of the stuff went straight into boxes, some in the bin, some of it to charity. Mary knows exactly which shop it went to, and for a while she had to take a long and stupidly inconvenient detour through the town, simply so that she could be certain of avoiding its window.

I went to see Miss Narket. I told her I was sick and needed a dose of something. She made a point of not looking at me, but her face went stiff and she sat up straight. You could see it was the best thing that had happened to her since Phoebe Harkiss didn't turn up to help with the hymn books that day.

At last she stood up and came over. I knew she wanted a closer look at me. I had to let her, but I did not like it. Although she was called young Miss Narket, she was not young. Her skin was smooth but it had hairs on it and just like all people that are close to God, her breath smelled bad.

What is it? she said. Is it your stomach?

I nodded and touched the part of me where the trouble was. The part that had recently begun to flutter as if a butterfly was stuck in it.

Have you been bilious?

Somewhat.

And the other? Can you do it?

The other? I didn't know what she meant so I told her I wasn't sure.

She tutted.

When you go to the privy, young lady, how is it? Do you manage it or don't you?

I told her that I managed it.

She sat back down in the big brown chair and picked up her sewing. Her nails were thick, like claws. I did not know how she got the needle in and out. I saw that there was a fat black Bible on the table next to her with a lump of cheese on top. The cheese had a bite taken out of it and yellow crumbs had fallen on the Bible's cover. She saw me looking at it.

I don't know what you've come to me for, she said at last.

I felt my cheeks grow hot. I could not tell her that James suggested it.

I don't have anyone else to ask, I said.

What about your ma?

I can't ask her. She's just had a baby.

Miss Narket's face twitched. She lifted her eyes from the sewing.

And I hear the child's a carrot-top, is that correct?

I nodded. She kept her nasty, glinting eyes on me even as she pulled the needle through the cloth.

So what do you make of that, then?

What?

The red hair. What do you make of it?

It's from my father's side, I told her. My father's Uncle Perry. He had two girls, twins, both of them more than six foot tall and both with the brightest red hair down to their waists.

This was what I'd heard my father telling people and I didn't see what was wrong with it as an explanation.

Miss Narket looked at me in silence for a moment and then she laughed. I realised for the first time how much I hated her. Understanding it gave me a funny feeling. Like having to run up a hill when you knew you'd much rather go down it instead.

I turned to go.

Where are you off to now? she said.

I told her I had some errands to run.

She didn't ask me what the errands were. She carried on sewing.

You should go and ask Addie Sands, she said. About your little problem. You tell her what's really wrong with you and I expect she'll sort you out.

When the police – an unnecessarily large group of three men, two dogs, two cars and all their noise and talk and radios – have at last gone, and when they've explained everything to Ruby and sent her off to walk the dog, Graham says he's going to shower.

But a few minutes later, he comes and stands in front of her.

'All right. I'm sick of this. I need to know what's going on.'

'What?' Mary glances up, confused, her head still full of it all: police, garden, shed. She looks at him – towel around his neck, hair still dripping from the shower.

'You two. What exactly is going on between you?'

'What?' she says it again, feeling the blood leave her face. 'What do you mean? Going on in what way?'

He breathes out, blotting at his face with the towel. Looking out of the window then back at her. Pain, or fury, or perhaps something else, in his eyes.

'You know who I'm talking about though, don't you?'

She looks at him. For a moment she doesn't know what to say. She says nothing. At last she takes a breath.

'I assume you mean Eddie? And when you say going on, can you please be more specific?'

'Specific?'

'Do you mean, am I having an affair with him?'

She watches as he closes his eyes.

'What?' she says. 'You don't mean that?'

He looks at her.

'I don't know what I mean.'

'Well, then.'

He shakes his head.

'There's something – an atmosphere – between you two.'

She thinks about this.

'An atmosphere?'

'An excitement, then. Something significant. Call it whatever you like. I'm not an idiot. You can pick it up a mile off.'

Mary says nothing. She feels him watching her.

'You're saying you don't know what I'm talking about?'

'I don't know.'

'The way he looks at you. Or doesn't look at you. All that stuff about you sulking. And anyway you were in the strangest mood this morning.'

She stares at him.

'Why does that have to be to do with Eddie?'

Graham looks at her for a long time.

'He seems to know things.'

'What things?'

315

'I don't know. It's the way he talks. He mentioned a friend who'd gone and had the snip. A vasectomy. Why would he go out of his way to mention that? The way he said it, well, it was just so obvious he knew about me. Does he know? Did you tell him about me?'

Mary shivers. Suddenly knowing that she can't lie.

'I'm sorry. It just came up. I didn't mean to tell him and I probably shouldn't have. But we talked about a lot of other things too. He's just a friend. A good friend. There's nothing to feel guilty about. He's been very kind to me.'

'Kind? Is that what you call it?'

Mary looks at him.

'Why? What do you call it?'

Graham says nothing. He holds the towel against his face. For a moment they are both silent.

'So what else does he know?' he asks her at last. 'This very good friend of yours. Did you tell him that we never manage to have sex any more? Is that why he looks at you like that, thinking he's maybe in with a chance? In fact, perhaps he is – in with a chance, I mean – because did you tell him that you can't really stand to have me anywhere near you these days?'

Mary looks down at her hands on her knees.

'You know that's not true.'

Graham sits down. Pulling the towel from around his neck and staring at it for a moment. His shoulders sagging.

'Isn't it?'

She tries to look at him.

'You know it isn't. I've tried. I try. I keep on trying. All the time, I try.'

He looks away.

'Oh, well done. Aren't you wonderful? Heroic. It's always some great big, valiant effort for you, isn't it?'

Mary swallows back something that might be anger, might be tears.

'That's not fair.'

'Isn't it?'

'You know it's not.'

He looks at her for a moment.

'I just can't believe you'd do it.'

'Do what?'

'Tell him that. Why would you? And talking to him about the girls as well. What kind of a relationship can you have that you would tell him all these intimate and private things?'

The girls.

Mary is silent. Remembering her hands reaching for Eddie, pulling his face to hers. The quick shock of him against her. After she'd kissed him, after she'd felt his face, his mouth, the heat of him close against her, they didn't do anything else. They could have done, but they didn't.

The girls.

'Why did you do it?' she says to Graham, suddenly furious.

'What? Do what?'

'Decide we shouldn't have any more children.'

He looks startled.

'What do you mean, why did I? I didn't decide it. We both decided it.'

'Did we?'

'You don't remember? The conversations?'

'Not really.'

'We talked at length about it.'

'Flo was still tiny.'

He presses his lips together.

'She was almost a year old.'

'She was nine months.'

He shakes his head.

'Now I've no idea what you're saying.'

She looks out of the window. At the bluest of blue skies.

'I don't really know what you think about any more,' she says to him. 'Honestly. I don't know what's in your head.'

'What do you mean? There's nothing in my head.'

'Exactly.'

Graham makes a noise of impatience.

'I'll tell you what I think. I think that it's not any of that man's business to know those things. I was shocked, if you really want to know.'

'Shocked?'

'Yes, shocked. Very shocked. I'm still shocked. Shocked and – I don't know, I suppose I felt betrayed.'

Mary lifts her head and looks at him.

'Well, now at least you know how that feels.'

He stares at her.

'What?'

'To be betrayed.'

'How dare you?'

She lifts her head, suddenly calm.

'How do I dare? How do I fucking dare?'

She thinks of the day when he came and told her – after the school run, after she'd had to make a second trip with Ella's forgotten lunchbox – how he was waiting there in the hall as she put her key in the door. Tears standing in his eyes. His lip trembling. So much pain on his face.

I can't lie to you, he told her. I just can't do it. I respect you far too much to lie to you.

Respect. What bollocks, she thought.

Mary stands up. Picks up the forms they've been left with – a sheaf of printed papers, standard procedure for reporting the discovery of human remains, the police said. Yes, they said, almost certainly human, but that's all we can tell you at this stage. Forensics will come and take them away, assess them for us.

She sweeps the papers up off the old pine table – their presence there suddenly making her feel uneasy, almost ill – and she folds them carefully and puts them on a high shelf of the dresser. She turns back to look at Graham.

'I just want to tell you that I'm not sorry,' she says. 'Not for a single word I just said. I don't take anything back. I mean every word of it and I don't care what you think. I think I'd dare do anything now. Isn't that frightening? It frightens me. But what the fuck else is there left to lose?'

She watches him, sitting there as if he isn't with her – as if he's in another place entirely. He does not speak. Or if he does, she doesn't hear him. And for a moment she's not sure either whether she spoke those last words aloud or just thought them.

At last, without looking at her, he gets up and he leaves the room. She does not go after him. A minute later, she hears him in the snug and seconds after that, she hears a Springsteen track turned up very loud.

The shock of the music – she didn't know he'd got around to wiring up the speakers – stops her for a moment. It's the first time in so long – and certainly the first time in this house – that she's heard music. As she listens, everything else drains away and all she feels is the loud, lifting brightness of that old forgotten pleasure.

Addie Sands was the Sunday school teacher. She was kind. She used to give us bread dipped in salty water. She loved all children, and when I was still small, she'd sometimes keep me on after the class to give my ma a break and carry me around the village in her arms.

You were a lovely babe, she told me once. I always liked to talk to you because you were so bright and beady and you listened to every word I said.

The little ones still went to her for Bible class. Lottie and Honey liked going very much because they loved to collect the colourful ribbons that she gave out for good deeds and good thoughts. But Jazzy thought she was too old now and was always on at our mother to let her stop.

I went to see Addie, but she was out. I peeked through her window, which was always clean and homely, and I saw a copper kettle and some plants and a hag-stone hanging above the whitened hearth and a cup and saucer on the table as if someone had just that moment been sitting there. But when I knocked on the door no one came.

I waited a while in case she'd just gone around the back. But still no one came, so I gave up and went back down her crumbly path with its double rows of orange snapdragons and pinks and phlox and stocks and all sorts of other cosy cottage flowers whose names I could not remember.

I felt quite downhearted and lonely then. I thought it would have been quite a comfort to sit at that table with Addie and watch her lift that cup off the saucer and put it to her lips. I hadn't known how much I'd wanted to talk to her, and I didn't think I'd have had much of a problem getting up the courage to tell her my troubles.

I knew that if James found me, he would demand to know if I'd got the medicine – and walking back down the lane I went over in my head what exactly I would say. In fact, I prepared my story so thoroughly that I almost began to believe it myself. Yes, I'd had a dose. Salts – or was it senna? – something like that anyway. Miss

Narket had, unsurprisingly, been a dead loss, but Addie had been very kind and she had helped me. Everything that he had been so keen that I should do, I had done. All I had to do was wait now. There was nothing else to it. Everything was going to be all right.

They come the next morning and take away the bones and half of the soil from beneath them too.

Mary and Graham stay in the house. They agree that they'd rather not have to see them – the two men and a youngish girl in their white clothes and masks. The dark van. The aura of studied respect that surrounds the whole operation. The memories it kicks up. They are very relieved indeed that there does not have to be a tent.

She sits with him in the kitchen, neither of them speaking.

'What is it?' she says.

'What do you mean, what is it?'

'Why are you so angry?'

He doesn't look at her. He seems to think for a moment.

'I'm not angry. I'm just tired.'

She leans back in her chair.

'We're both tired.'

'That's right. We are. We're both tired.'

At last he gets up and walks over to the sink, flings the rest of his coffee down it. Picks up his wallet and his keys. Calls to the dog. She watches him.

'Where are you going?'

He glances out at the garden.

'I don't know. I just know I can't stay here while they're doing this. Do you mind?'

'Do I mind what?'

'I'm going to walk the dog. I won't be long.'

'It's all right. Be as long as you like.'

He hesitates a moment in the doorway, looking at her hard as if he's searching for something. She waits for him to speak, but he doesn't. He doesn't say anything. At last, he turns and leaves.

When the men have finished and one of them, the older one who earlier introduced himself as Nick, is putting his head around the door to say goodbye, Mary asks him if it's all right for them to take the police tape away now – the blue and white tape that she can still see fluttering down there beyond the washing line at the end of the garden.

Nick says of course. He's sorry. It no longer needs to be there at all. They'll go back and remove it straightaway.

And that should be it, he says, glancing at Ruby, who for once is up and dressed and watching the men from her perch on a stool by the window. They'll leave them in peace. He gives Mary a small printed card. The office will be in touch if anyone finds anything.

'Anything?'

'Anything that might affect your property. Anything requiring further investigation or whatever.' He smiles at her and glances again at Ruby and unzips the front of his suit, revealing the bright green and yellow of a Norwich City T-shirt. 'But you shouldn't worry,' he says. 'It's not likely that they'll want to take it any further. Those bones, they're pretty old. Well over a century is what we're guessing.'

'And they're definitely human?'

'Oh yes. We're pretty sure of that, yes.'

Later, when Graham is back and they've still barely spoken to each other, eating a subdued lunch of cling-filmed leftovers straight from the fridge, Ruby comes and finds them and asks if Lisa can come and stay just for one night. If they say yes, then she can get on the one-forty train and be at the station just after four.

'She's got no money or anything,' Ruby says. 'But she reckons she can blag it.'

'Why hasn't she any money?' Graham says. 'And is it really worth her coming here for just one night?'

'It's worth it to her,' Ruby says.

'What do you mean, it's worth it to her?'

She makes a noise of impatience.

'She's got to go somewhere. She doesn't care where she goes. She just needs to get away. And I suppose I thought that maybe for once we could behave like normal human beings and help her just this one fucking time.'

Graham starts to speak, but Mary interrupts him.

'Away from what?' she asks Ruby.

'What?'

'What is it that she's got to get away from?'

Ruby scowls.

'My God, I can't believe it, do you really always need to know everything?'

Graham glances at Mary.

'I think we do, yes,' he says.

'All right, she's had this great big fight with her parents, OK? Her dad hit her or something. Satisfied now?'

Mary stares at Ruby.

'He hit her?'

Ruby folds her arms.

'Yes, he hit her.'

'That's terrible. Why on earth would he do that?'

'I can't go into it. It's not important. Look, she's calling me back in a minute. I just need to know right now if it's a yes or a no.'

Graham says, 'OK, tell Lisa she can come.' But Mary tells him she's not sure.

'You don't think you should just have a quick word with her parents first? At least speak to her mum to check it's OK?'

Ruby lets out a wail.

'You can't speak to them. Don't you see, if you speak to them it'll fuck it up completely!'

'But do they know she's coming here?' Mary says.

'Of course they don't!'

Mary turns to Graham.

'I'm not sure I'm happy about this. I just don't feel we really understand what the situation is.'

'I just told you the situation!' Ruby says.

'Yes,' Mary says. 'But if she was my daughter, I wouldn't want other parents taking her in even for a night without them first telling me they were doing it.'

'She's not your daughter,' Ruby says. 'Why can't you stop acting like everyone's your daughter? You don't have any daughters left, haven't you fucking well taken that in yet?'

A quick, shocked silence. Mary feels something drop away from her. She sits down, suddenly exhausted.

Graham folds his arms, his eyes on Ruby. When he speaks, his voice is quiet, stunned.

'I'd like you to apologise to Mary right now.'

Ruby says nothing. No one speaks. After a few moments, she turns and leaves the room. They watch each other's faces and listen as she goes upstairs and along the passage. When she reaches her room, she slams the door hard.

Graham never once said he blamed her for leaving the girls there at the leisure centre. Not for a single moment. Even though the police questioned her hard about it, still it was not something they ever referred to between themselves.

Partly, they both knew very well that he would have done the same thing. If anything he was more relaxed than she was, letting them wait in the unlocked car while he popped into a shop, for instance. Or insisting it was fine to drop them down the road from school some mornings and watch them walk up to the gate.

When they finally did have a conversation about it – a very long time after they knew what had happened – she realised, with a lick of shame, that it was she who blamed him.

'Why can't you be angry with me?' she said. 'Why can't you just be honest and hate me for it?'

'Hate you?'

'You know what I'm talking about.'

He looked at her.

'I don't. I don't know. I actually haven't a clue. Why on earth would I ever want to hate you?'

Mary looked at him, then. Taking in the maddening kindness of his face. His patient willingness to think well of her.

'I left them standing there. At least four minutes, maybe more.'

The timing was something they'd gone over and over. Was it three minutes, or four? Could it have been five? Six, she'd told the police at last in tears, I can't honestly be sure it wasn't six.

'I'd have done the same,' he said. 'You know I would. Many people would have.'

'No,' she said. 'It's not true. You've no idea, Graham. Many people wouldn't have.'

He blinked at her.

'It was no time at all,' he said.

'I left them there.'

He shook his head.

'What are you trying to say?'

'The fact will always be there, that I left them. I left them and I walked away and while I was gone, he took them.'

He took them. There, she'd said it. Three words that she could hardly bear to utter. Words that took her straight to a place of stinging black terror.

Quickly, as it always did, it played over again in her head. The moment in court. The careful adjusting of the shirtsleeves. Making himself comfortable. We will never be comfortable again, she'd thought. Even if we both live to be a hundred, proper, ordinary human comfort is something we will never know again.

She saw that Graham did not know how to answer her. Good, she thought, I've finally shut him up. She waited.

He came up and put his arm around her.

'Why be so hard on yourself?' he said at last. 'After all this time. I don't honestly see what it's going to achieve.'

This was so far off the mark that she couldn't help it – she laughed.

Two or maybe three days after they'd lost them, when they were still stuck in that hellish place of un-life, waiting for news, any news, one of the family liaison officers had happened to ask Graham where he thought they were.

'What, the girls?'

'Yes. The girls.'

Even at the time it had seemed an odd question. The only question, perhaps, but unaskable all the same.

She'd watched with a cold kind of interest as Graham touched his face, running his fingers over his sleepless, three-day beard.

He shut his eyes and he sighed.

'They're dead, Mike,' he'd said at last. 'I think they are probably both dead.'

She had never in her life hated anyone more than she hated him at that moment.

Mary assumes that Lisa will not be coming. But when she returns from walking the dog, she sees Graham standing in the lane with Ruby. Holding his car keys. He lifts a hand to stop her speaking.

'Ruby and I have had a long talk,' he says. 'It's all sorted. I'll fill you in later.'

She stares at him.

'What, you mean she's coming? You can't be serious? You're saying you've given in? You've said that Lisa can come?'

Graham looks at Ruby.

'They're going to keep right out of our way. And you needn't worry about supper, by the way. I'm sending them down the road for fish and chips.'

This time, possibly for the first time, she's the one who calls him. He picks up so fast that for a second or two it throws her.

'Look,' she says, 'I wanted to say I'm sorry. About the other day.'

'The other day?'

'You were right. I was sulking. And I shouldn't have been. It was silly. I overreacted. About the girls. I'm sorry.'

She hears him suck in his breath.

'You hung up on me.'

'I know,' she says. 'I shouldn't have done that. I'm sorry.'

'And I called you, you know. After we found the – after the awful thing with the apple store. I was quite worried about you. Yesterday and the day before. I called you several times.'

'I know.'

'I only wanted to see how you were. You could at least have answered your phone.'

'I'm sorry,' she says again.

'Why didn't you?'

'Answer my phone?' She hesitates, searching for something truthful. 'I don't know. I just didn't feel I could speak to you.'

'But why not?'

'I don't know. I think – maybe I was afraid to.'

She hears him laugh.

'Afraid? You're afraid of me?'

Mary takes a breath.

'Not of you. Of what might happen. Of what we might say to each other.'

She hears him hesitate.

'You mean of what I might say or what you might say?'

'I don't know. Both.'

'You're afraid of us?'

'Maybe.'

'And now?'

'What?'

'What about now? Aren't you afraid of what might happen now?'

Mary thinks about this. She looks out of the window – looks right down the garden, at the place where the police tape was, the place where until this morning the bones were. A hundred years or more.

'Mary?' he says. 'Are you still there?'

She says that she is, but at the same time she wonders if she really is. A hundred years, she thinks. And there's her whole long empty life, hours and hours of it and years and years of it, stretching out ahead of her.

Eddie is silent for a moment.

'Why did you call me?' he says at last.

'I told you. I wanted to apologise.'

'Only for that?'

'I think so.'

'There's something else, though, isn't there?'

'I don't know,' she says.

'You do know.'

'All right,' she says. 'I'm going for a walk. To my bench.'

'Right now?'

'Yes. Right now.'

He hesitates.

'And you want me to come?'

'Only if you want to.'

'If I want to? You know I want to.'

'Well, then.'

She hears his surprise.

'You want to see me now? You really do? After all of this?'

'Yes,' she says. 'I think so. Yes, I do.'

Walking up the lane, I was intending to go into the house and up to my room but as I went past the kitchen door I heard such a commotion, what with the baby crying and Jazzy talking and everyone generally yapping at each other that I knew I could not face it. So I took myself round the back and down through the orchard instead.

I did not know where I was going; in fact, I had no plan at all. But it did not surprise me when I found myself in our old familiar place behind the apple store. And there I lay down on that piece of ground that used to be so full of excitement and sweetness and I couldn't help it, I put my two hands on my chest, my knees, my thighs, trying to remember how it felt to be touched by him. And before I knew it I had slid my underclothes down and, licking my fingers, I put my hands where I knew that he would have put them and tried to do the exact same thing that he would have done to me.

Oh, it had been such a very long time. Hundreds and hundreds of years, it seemed. I wanted him so very badly.

I tried it fast and frantic and I tried it slow. I tried not to think about what I was doing and then I did, I let myself think of it. In the end, I couldn't help it, as my cheeks grew hot, I let my mind go wandering away from my own body and off, over every particular part of him – all the parts I'd been trying for so long to stop myself thinking about.

I thought about his face. His eyes. Those hands. His chest, his shoulders and his wrists. The strength of him and the vigour and the push. The body that was always hard and ready for me. The sweet, sky-high feeling of him reaching out for me—

But it was no use. None of it worked. My body was just my plain old girl's body, the one I had before I knew him – the one that did not feel or know anything much and certainly did not care what happened to it.

So I stopped my work. I let my stupid fingers drop to the ground. And then, as if it wanted to make its point, the fluttering started up in me again. Not a butterfly at all this time, but a tiny, trapped bird attempting to stretch its wings.

I knew it was all over then. I kept myself exactly where I was and I pressed my face against that warm dry earth. There was no reason any more not to weep, so I let the tears come.

I cried until there were no more tears left in my face or my body or anywhere else in my whole sorry existence. And after that, I did nothing. I carried on lying there on the ground, my clothes still torn half off me, and I heard the rough, unlikely sound of my own heart beneath my bodice and I couldn't help listening for the other smaller one that must be beating in there too and something about the act of listening for it seemed to still and soothe me, and calm me down.

Minutes passed. I don't know what it was that made me lift my head and open my eyes, but something did. And that's when I saw it. Not the grass or the patch of hot blue sky that soared above or even the black shadows of the hedge or the greenish mildewed wood that was the apple store, but something much worse.

A few months after it was all over, a teacher from the school called at the house, bringing with her some of their exercise books and artwork. Barely into her twenties – round, pale face, heavy bosom and big, blue-framed glasses. Miss Savage. It had always seemed the wrong name for a primary school teacher.

'I didn't know what to do,' she said, obviously distressed as she handed over a couple of Tesco carrier bags filled with sugar paper and painted cardboard, glitter already spilling out of them onto her hands. 'It didn't seem right to bring it, but it didn't seem right not to either.'

Mary was very proud of herself. She was calm, welcoming. They sat at the kitchen table. She made Miss Savage a cup of tea, even offering her a piece of cake, which she refused, batting it away with glitter-covered hands. Mary kept on noticing how young she was. How she put her big, young, unmarried fingers around the mug and clung to it with something like gratitude.

'You needn't look at them now,' Miss Savage kept on saying. 'I just couldn't bring myself to throw them away, that's all.'

But Mary did. She did need to look at them and right now was the only possible moment. She pulled something green out of the bag, something stiff and curling from its heavy dollops of paint and glue. Egg cartons stuck on, poster paint yellow. Green paper leaves. Some wool for grass. Dancing daffodils. She recognised Ella's writing, orange felt-tip, turned to brown on the green of the paper.

Her hands trembling. Moving her eyes away. Wanting to put it straight back in the bag but also to crush it in her arms. Greedy to be alone with it. Suddenly resenting the teacher's presence, yet disliking herself for resenting it. Understanding the risk she had taken.

'It's very kind of you,' she said. 'You are very kind. You did the right thing. We would always have wanted to have them.'

She looked up and saw that the teacher was pulling tissues out of her pocket. Taking her glasses off. Crying.

'It was terrible,' she said. 'Taking the labels off their pegs. It took us a while to get round to it. I don't know why I'm telling you that. I'm so sorry. But it just was. It was the worst thing I've ever had to do in my life.'

Later, when the teacher had gone, Mary stared at herself in the mirror. She stared at herself till the shapes were blurred and all the lines had changed and it looked like something not quite human was standing there.

What kind of a life could she live now? What was left for her? What kind of a person could she possibly be?

Her skin crawled. She itched all over.

She tried changing her clothes, but the new ones were just as bad, so she changed back again. She put on a jumper, but it hid nothing. She put on earrings, tore them off. It was her face, that was it. She thought of the honest kindness of the young woman's face – upset, plain, open. It made her want to weep.

She tied her hair back and began to scrub herself clean. All her make-up off, everything. But she found she could not bear herself like that either. In fact, if anything, that was worse. Because, when she looked at herself in the mirror, stripped and cleaned of everything that she had once used to disguise herself, she no longer saw herself at all, but them, just them, her two girls staring back at her.

I sat up. The thing in front of me was the thing that we had put in the ditch at Yarrow's field. It was covered in blood and muck and worms and was lying there in the weeds and grass and staring back at me with dead, accusing eyes.

No. It was not possible. I shut my eyes. I opened them again. It was still there. One of the hands had opened and come away from the body. It was outstretched, the bone coming through the skin, its sharp white fingers reaching for me.

I gasped, pulling myself away across the grass as fast as I could. But as I moved, it seemed to follow, the whole body moving now in small jerks and starts. I knew it would not be long before I felt the bone-cold hardness of those fingers on me.

I began to scream and I did not stop until my father came running from the house to find me.

Get it away from me! I cried.

My father's face was stiff and white and appalled. He stood there watching as I sobbed and beat my two fists on the ground.

Get what? he said. What, Eliza? Whatever do you mean? Get what?

I looked back at where it had been. There was nothing. Just a patch of scrub and dandelions, a bee hovering in the mild air above them.

My father took a step closer. He was staring at me.

Eliza, he said. Whatever has happened to you?

I felt him looking at my bare legs, my bare thighs and whatever else he could or could not see. I tried to pull my skirts down, but I was crying so much I could not speak or move my hands. I knew I could not explain why I was lying there sobbing and crying with my clothes half off, so I did not try.

I said nothing. I gave a little moan. He continued to stare at me. I could see his thoughts forming and still I could not speak.

Who did this to you? he said. I need to know. Tell me now, Eliza, who did this terrible thing to you.

I said nothing. I did nothing. I did not need to. I realised then that it was very simple. All I had to do was let him look.

He is already sitting on the bench when Mary gets there. He pats the space next to him and she sits down. Feeling him looking at her.

'I like your dress.'

She glances down at what she's wearing. An old denim dungaree-skirt thing with pockets, grass-stained around the bottom.

'It's just my gardening dress.'

He smiles.

'It's nice. I like all your dresses.'

'I don't really wear dresses.'

'No, I know you don't. You wear jeans, don't you? I like all your jeans too.'

Mary can't help it – she laughs. And before she can do anything he has pulled her to him, putting his arms around her. She doesn't try to stop him. She waits. Held against him like that. She does nothing.

'I can feel your heart,' he says after a few seconds have passed.

'Can you?'

'In my chest. It's pounding in my chest.'

'In your chest?'

'Yes. Straight through from your chest into mine. Can you feel it?'

'No.'

'Listen.'

'To what?'

'To that. Listen. Come on, surely you can feel that?'

She laughs again, trying to pull away.

'No,' he says. 'No, I'm sorry, I'm not letting you go. You can struggle all you like but you're staying right here.'

Mary waits, obedient.

'My arm,' she says at last. 'Ow. You're crushing my arm.'

'Sorry.'

He releases her, but only a little. She feels his lips against her cheek. His breath in her ear.

'Go on,' he says. 'Say it.'

'Say what?'

'I shouldn't be doing this, Eddie. I ought to go. We really shouldn't be doing this, Eddie.'

Mary tries to laugh but doesn't manage it. She pulls away slightly. Realising that she is trembling.

'I don't really care what we do.'

'You don't?'

She shakes her head and he pulls her to him again. She feels him kiss the side of her head.

'That's a dangerous thing to say.'

'I know.'

He waits a moment. So does she. She can hardly breathe. She does not want to breathe. Heat and light causing the air all around them to shimmer and bend.

'Do you know what this field is called?' he says at last.

'What do you mean, what it's called?'

'Fields have names. Or they did in the old days. I found a map at the library. There's one called Glebe field. And there's Hulver. And Nut Tree. This one is Yarrow's field.'

'Yarrow? Why Yarrow?'

'Who knows? Perhaps the name of some long-ago farmer. I know there aren't any Yarrows round here any more because I checked.'

'You checked?'

'Just in the library.'

'What were you doing at the library?'

'I like to look things up. I always have. The records. Archives. It's amazing what you can find out.'

She smiles at this. His liking for facts.

'Like my picture,' she says.

'What?'

'The old photo. The one you gave me.'

He hesitates.

'That's right. I'd forgotten about that. What have you done with it?'

'Nothing. Just kept it. It's on the shelf in the kitchen.'

'You still like it?'

'I love it.' She doesn't tell him that some days she is afraid to look at it, that some days it can seem to buckle and twist under her gaze until she is certain she can see something in it that cannot possibly be there. How can one picture contain such a presence, so many shadows? She's losing her mind, she sometimes thinks when she looks at that picture, going mad.

'Does Graham know about it?'

Mary turns her head.

'What? That you gave it to me? Yes.'

'He doesn't mind?'

'No, of course he doesn't.'

Eddie pulls her closer.

'You're right. Those little girls in the picture – maybe it was their father who owned this field. Maybe he was Yarrow. Mr Yarrow. I know that you like to think of it as your field,' he adds.

'It isn't?'

'No. I'm very sorry to break it to you, but it belongs to Yarrow.'

She laughs.

'Yarrow,' she says.

'What?'

'Nothing. Just I like the sound of it, that's all.'

Moments pass. At last, he lets go of her. Picking up her hand instead and holding it in his. Mary sighs.

'It was a person, you know. The bones. The bones that you and Graham found, under the shed.'

He hesitates.

'I know. Deb told me.'

'She knows?'

'I think Graham told her. Before they came to take them away.'

Them. Mary turns and she looks at him. Tears standing in her eyes. He puts both arms around her.

'Oh don't,' he says. 'I mean it, darling. Please don't cry.'

They sit there for a very long time. His arm around her. Her head against his chest.

'I didn't think you'd let me do this,' he says. 'I didn't think you'd ever let me do it.'

She shuts her eyes for a moment, opens them again.

'Do what?'

'Have you this close. Hold you like this. Is it OK?'

She smiles. We're just friends, she thinks.

'Are we?' he says. She glances at him. She must have said it aloud. 'Funny sort of friendship.'

'I don't care,' she says.

He's silent a moment.

'We're friends,' he says. 'We're definitely friends. But if it was up to me, we wouldn't waste time sitting here like this.'

She looks at him.

'Why? What would we do?'

'You really want to know?'

'I don't know.'

He sits up straighter, points.

'You see that little dip, just before you get back on the path that leads up to the golf course?' Mary nods. 'Well, we'd go and lie down there in the long grass. And I'd take all of your clothes off one by one – pull off your lovely, funny garden dress as well as everything else – and then I'd make very passionate love to you. Twice.'

'Twice?' Mary starts to laugh. 'I'm too old for twice.'

'All right. Once then. If that's how you want it. It would take a while anyway, getting you to relax.'

'Would it?'

'You know it would. You know what you're like. You'd have all your reasons. You'd say you didn't like it there and that you couldn't get comfortable and that you kept on feeling things—'

'Things?'

'I don't know. Creatures. Wildlife. Mice. Snakes. You'd probably tell me you were afraid of snakes.'

'I'm not afraid of snakes,' Mary says, remembering the python she picked up to show Ella at the children's zoo. Its surprisingly hot, dry weight in her hands.

'All right, but you'd say you were. And I'd have to reassure you. And then you'd confess to me that it wasn't snakes you were afraid of at all, but something else.'

'What?' she says, interested now. 'What would it be that I was afraid of?' She looks at the side of Eddie's face. 'Tell me,' she says.

He turns to look at her.

'I don't know. I don't really know what you're afraid of. I'm making it all up. I suppose the truth is I've only ever kissed you once and I just wish I could do it again, that's all.'

Mary thinks about this.

'Thank you,' she says.

'It's my pleasure.'

'I appreciate that you're so honest.'

He nods. 'I am. Searingly honest. Well?' he says.

'Well, what?'

'How about it?'

She laughs and so does he. She looks at him.

'I'm sorry, but I don't think we can.'

'Why not?'

'Because I think that's what I'm afraid of.'

'What do you mean? What are you afraid of?'

She hesitates.

'I suppose I'm afraid that I might start to like you too much.'

'What? You don't like me now?'

'Yes, I do like you. You know I do. But I might start to like you a lot more.'

'What, and that wouldn't be a good thing?'

'No, it wouldn't. You know it wouldn't.'

'Even though I'd be such a fantastic lover?'

Mary laughs.

'It wouldn't be a good thing. And I wouldn't really care if you were a fantastic lover or not. I suppose I'd just be worried – that you'd be too nice to me.'

He looks surprised. 'Too nice?'

She closes her eyes, sun warming her face.

'You'd hold me. You'd say nice things. I know you would. I worry that you'd do it in a way I wasn't used to and it would upset me because I'd realise no one had ever done it to me like that before—'

She breaks off, thinking about what she's just said. For a moment she's quiet. Feeling him looking at her, his fingers reaching for hers.

'Are you all right?' he says.

Mary looks at him. Looks at her hand in his. Tears standing in her eyes.

'And then at the end, you'd ask me if I was all right and just the simple fact of you asking me that would make me want to cry.'

He squeezes her hand and for a while neither of them speaks. She sits there with her hand in his and then at last, very gently, she takes it away, replacing it on her lap. She lets out a sigh. Thinks she feels her blood slowing down, her bones relaxing.

'And then afterwards,' he says, 'when we were lying together in the long grass and I'd banished all your fears of snakes, I'd ask you if you were still afraid.'

'Afraid?'

'Of what might happen? Are you still afraid, Mary? I'd say. Or has it happened now, the thing that you were afraid of?'

Mary puts her hands to her eyes.

'It would have happened,' she says. 'It would definitely have happened. And I'd tell you that. I'd say yes, it's happened. And what then?'

Eddie thinks about this.

'Well, we'd probably just lie there together in the long grass and the sky would be huge and blue just like it is right now, today—'

'It's always blue,' Mary says, tilting her head back to look at it. 'All this summer, isn't that just what it's been? Blue and blue and nothing but blue.'

'And I'd take hold of your hand – like this – and we'd weave our fingers together and block out the sun for a moment.'

'Why would we do that?' Mary gazes at their two hands knitted together.

'Just for a game. Just to see if we could. Maybe we'd have a look for the kestrel, too. But we wouldn't see it.'

'Why wouldn't we?'

'Because it wouldn't be here.'

Mary looks around her.

'I don't think it's here now either. If it really was a kestrel. The one that we saw that time.'

'We don't know for sure.'

'That's right, we don't.'

Eddie takes Mary's face in his hands and he kisses her and for a moment she lets him. He holds her face for a longer moment, looking at her.

'This is agony,' he says, releasing her again.

'I'm sorry.'

'You don't love me, do you?' he says.

She says nothing. He looks at her.

'Where are you with Graham?' he says at last. 'How are things between you? Are you OK? Have you told him yet – about the baby?'

Mary hesitates and she feels him watching her face. She does nothing. 'What?' he says.

She looks down at her hands in her lap. Her heart churning. She licks her lips.

'It's complicated,' she says.

She feels him still looking at her. She almost can't bear it. At last he sighs. He puts a hand on hers.

'There never was a baby, was there?' he says.

Mary glances away at the fields, the blue sky, her heart still racing, all of the blood coming to her face.

'I don't know what's been happening to me,' she says. 'This whole summer. Something's been going on. I haven't been myself.'

He's silent a moment.

'Well, of course you haven't.'

'No, it's not that. It's like I've had to switch whole parts of myself off. Whole parts of who I am shut down.'

He takes a breath.

'That's just called grief.'

Mary shakes her head. 'No. No, it's more than that.'

She thinks for a moment about whether it's worth trying to say it aloud to him, whether it's something she can even dare to articulate to herself. And before she can stop it happening, her mind starts to take her in there, around the house – rooms, walls, landing, windows, fireplace, table – racing out fast into the garden, in darkness now – face at the window, night coming down, soil in her mouth, a tree falling, doors slamming—

'What? Mary, what is it?'

She puts her hands up to her face.

'I think it has to do with the house,' she says at last.

'The house?' Now he looks surprised.

She hesitates.

'I suppose I've been deciding what to do. How to live. Whether to live. Whether it's going to be worth it.'

'What's that got to do with the house?'

'I don't know.' She shakes her head. 'I don't know.'

She hears him sigh.

'I'm not going to ask you what you decided. About living, I mean.'

'No, that's right, please don't.'

'You don't want to answer that question?'

'No, I don't.'

Eddie says nothing. He looks off across the fields for a moment, then before she can see what he is looking for, he turns and looks straight back into her eyes.

'Run away with me.'

Mary laughs.

'I'm serious. Let's go. Today. Now. I have money. Just pop home and get your passport. We need never come back.'

She laughs again.

'I'm deadly serious.'

'I know you are,' she says.

It turned out that my father didn't need many reasons to go looking for James. It turned out that he had actually been holding it all in for some time. My father was a peaceful man generally and not a

337

hard person at all, but once his blood was up, you did not want to let yourself too near him.

I asked him very quietly if any of this had to do with my mother and the new baby?

His face went dark. It was a look I hadn't seen in a while but I knew it very well from the old days of Isaac Roper.

What do you mean? he said. In what way could it have anything to do with them?

I shrugged.

I don't know what you're talking about, he said.

All right, I said.

All right? What exactly are you trying to say to me, Eliza?

Nothing, I said.

He told me, then, that in the village, people had been saying things for some time. More than a month ago, a man had come up from Ipswich with a handcart selling cloth from the draper's there to measure people up for Sunday suits. And among the titbits of news he brought with him was that, back in the spring, a man had been going around breaking into various houses in the town and taking valuables. And someone had seen him leaving through a pantry or back kitchen window and had reported that he had red hair. He'd had a case of jewellery and a couple of silver salvers and a brand-new silver snuff box that belonged to the draper's own late uncle, who used to be the rector there.

I suppose I didn't want to believe it at first, my father said. He seemed honest and willing enough. And he worked hard and seemed so good with the little ones and all of that. But it turns out he's no more than a common thief.

He hasn't stolen anything from us, I pointed out, though even as I said the words, something cold went through me.

My father gave me a sharp look.

I don't know why you're suddenly standing up for him.

I didn't know either, so I stayed quiet. Isaac Roper had been right all along, I thought. A murderer, a swindler or a housebreaker – James was all of those things. Call the constable, Isaac had said – and he'd been right. It was all almost exactly as he had said. My father folded his arms. I saw that he looked very uneasy.

The things he did to you, Eliza. I don't want to discuss it, but there will be consequences. That man will be punished. He will have to pay.

That man. I nodded. As well as the coldness, a big, hard shiver was starting to spread through me. It started in my head and trickled its way down through the centre of my body to the tips of my feet, my fingers, the very edges of my toes.

Maybe I was thinking about Phoebe Harkiss. Or maybe I was thinking about the other murdered girls that Miss Narket had mentioned to my mother a while ago and which I'd had to make a big effort not to think about. I could not tell which it was, but it was as if my mind had suddenly cleared and I could see much more than I wanted to. I could see it all. The bad things that were behind us. And the vast terribleness of what lay ahead.

I'm afraid there's more, my father said.

He told me then that Miss Narket had recently gone to visit her married niece in Lowestoft and it turned out that the niece had a friend who did charitable work at a home for distressed gentlewomen down by the docks and all the talk around there was of a good-looking red-haired man who'd gone around the whole of the previous year seducing any woman he could.

It was said that he'd been most lavish and convincing with his affections. He'd married at least two of them, one of them a young girl barely out of childhood, and promised marriage to several others. He'd left a girl of only sixteen in the lurch with one small kid and another on the way, and some people said he'd also gone around with her sister who was not yet twelve.

He seemed to be a collector of stolen goods and of women's hearts. A liar, too. And a conniver. He could slip and wheedle his way in and out of any situation or responsibility, petty as a child and always quick to blame others for his own failings and wrong-doings.

I am afraid he is a con man, Eliza, my father said. A chancer. A person who does not seem to care a fig for the trail of chaos and harm he leaves in his wake.

I shut my eyes. It was the only way to stop the tears coming.

Then he must surely be very unhappy, I said with a sob.

My father looked at me as if I was mad. He said he didn't care a jot if a criminal such as him was unhappy. In fact, he hoped very much that God would see to it that he was.

Why didn't the police catch him, then, I said, if he was so very busy doing bad things?

My father said it wasn't that simple. He said that he'd had such a wide variety of different names, this man, that the police seemed to stand no chance whatsoever of keeping up with him. John Allen. Horace Doddington. George Gandy. Ted Mullins had been the last one. At least two women had been promised marriage by Ted Mullins, my father said.

I asked him what the rector had been called.

What rector?

The dead one whose snuff box got taken.

He said he didn't know it, but I was not at all surprised when a few days later he asked around and discovered that the rector's name was the Reverend James Dix.

Meanwhile three men from the village and my father had looked all over for the man who called himself James, but he was nowhere to be seen. He had vanished.

I didn't know whether to be glad or not. I didn't want to think about where he might be, though I suppose a part of me didn't want anything to have happened to him.

But I also didn't want to think about what might happen if he turned up. So I didn't do anything. I tried not to think about it. I stayed in my room and prayed that the fluttering in my belly would stop.

People had wanted to lay flowers at the leisure centre but the council declared it unsafe, so they laid them at the school instead. Piles and piles of bouquets, wrapped in cellophane and tied with string to the black-painted railings or spilling over onto the pavement.

There were toys, too. Many people made a point of bringing two of everything. Two pink roses. Two dogs. Two teddy bears. A pair of dolls. Someone wrote both of their names in shells, though later these got kicked and became unreadable.

There were cards and messages. 'Rest in peace, little princesses, you're safe from harm now.' 'We didn't know you, but we know you're together in heaven.' There were football scarves, even though neither of them were interested in football. A Barbie balloon, even though they both hated Barbie. Someone put a frozen pizza there.

One or two people tried to light candles but were stopped – it was a school, after all. And when stuff overflowed onto the zigzag yellow line, the police were forced to remove it. In the end, so many bright-coloured bits of tissue and plastic and feathers came off and got sodden in the rain and blew into the gutter, that the street sweeper made a point of coming by twice every day to clear them up. It was said that he went out of his way to do this because he remembered the little girls – the smaller one used to wave to him sometimes – and he didn't want the display taken down any sooner than it had to be.

They never went near the school or saw any of this for themselves, but they knew about it because it was in the papers, all of it, and of course on TV.

Back home, Mary finds no one in the house. Feeling hot and tired, she decides to take a shower. Going upstairs and pulling off her clothes and dropping them on the floor and standing under the water before it has even run properly warm.

Stepping out, dripping onto the mat and reaching for the towel off the hook on the door, she glances out of the window and immediately she sees her. A young girl, the same one, she's certain, that she saw in the garden – long-haired, in a strange and floppy cotton hat, drab brown clothes, walking down the lane in the still bright, late-afternoon sunshine. She walks slowly, dragging her feet, her face gazing down at the ground. When she reaches their house, Mary watches, expecting her to continue on past, but no—

She holds her breath. She cannot move – standing there still wet, the towel wrapped around her, tense, afraid even, watching as the girl seems to move towards the house and then out of sight. She can't see the gate from where she stands but she's certain she hears the sound of the latch lifting. She waits in a kind of terror for what must surely happen next. The sound of feet on the step. The quick rap on the door.

But no, there she is again, stepping back through the gate and moving off, the long ribbons of her hat falling down her shoulders as she continues slowly on down the lane. Mary keeps watching her until the tall yew hedge is in the way and the girl is entirely swallowed up into its vast, dark shadow.

For a moment she stands there, relief thudding through her. Then, slowly, she begins to dry herself again. Aware, at last, of a familiar dull ache starting in her belly, something tells her to look down at the towel. What she sees there does not surprise her. Thank God, she thinks. Thank God. At last.

She dresses and goes downstairs. The kitchen clock says almost seven. There's no sign of Graham and the girls and she wonders briefly if they're in the garden, before seeing the note-pad propped on the kitchen counter. 'At pub. Join us?'

She stands at the sink and runs the tap to fill a glass with cold water. She is still standing there and drinking it, suddenly more thirsty than she's been in a very long time, when the man from the coroner's office calls.

He apologises for ringing so late and asks her how she is. He tells her he'll cut straight to the chase. They'll be getting a formal letter in the post in the next couple of days. But he thought that she and her husband would be relieved to know that the remains are far too old – a hundred and fifty years at least – for them to need to take the case any further.

Slowly, Mary puts down the glass of water.

'The case?'

'Well, we can't say exactly how she died. There are things that point towards a blow to the head. Possibly some damage to the thoracic spine, the ribcage. It wasn't natural causes, let's put it that way.'

She pulls out a chair, sits down.

'A she? You can tell it's a she?'

'Oh yes. That part's easy. Definitely female. And quite young. Between fourteen and sixteen years old, they reckon. And evidence of a foetus, too. So a young, pregnant female.'

'What?'

Catching her breath. Watching the bright surface of the glass of water as it wobbles in front of her.

'Which may or may not have something to do with why she died. Though we'll never know for sure, of course.'

Very carefully, as if it were the most fragile thing in the whole world, Mary picks up the glass and sips from it.

'But – so, I don't understand. What happens now?'

'What happens?'

'You mean there's nothing you can do?'

'Do?'

342

'To find out what happened to her.'

There's a pause. Mary senses him looking at his watch. Wanting to wind it up now.

'After all this time? Well, it's not like there's a missing persons case to follow up. And any perpetrator's going to be long dead. And as I said, these remains are at least a hundred and fifty years old.' He coughs. 'Not quite antiquities yet, but – you've heard the expression a cold case? Well, this isn't even a cold case. This one's packed in ice and buried at the bottom of the bloody Arctic Circle, if you'll excuse my French.'

James Dix came to me in a dream but it wasn't a dream: there was nothing soft or unlikely about it, it was big and bold as real life. In the dream, I tried everything in my powers to make him want me again but he didn't – he said he couldn't and he wouldn't ever again – so instead I told him what I'd seen behind the apple store. That got his attention straightaway.

It's not possible, he said. You know it's not. You know very well where she is.

Where?

Why, in Yarrow's ditch, of course. Where we both put her. Wherever else could she be?

You don't think she could have moved?

Please God, Eliza! You put her there yourself. It was even your own idea. Don't you remember that we tipped her into the thick black water and watched her sink and then, when we were quite satisfied that she was gone, we came back to the house and washed ourselves at the pump and played a game of hearts and ate like horses and had a good old laugh about it all?

I gazed at him in horror. I did not remember the part about washing or eating or playing cards and I certainly did not remember having a good old laugh. That day had lodged in my mind as a cold and dark and terrible day, the very worst day of my whole life and especially since it was also the beginning of everything being over between him and me.

But I saw her, I said.

He smiled.

You've been dreaming.

But—

I tell you, the dead are the dead and they can't move. They stay right where they are. That's the beauty of the dead. You know just exactly where you are with them.

I tried to think about this.

But I tell you, James, she was there. I saw her. There was no doubt at all about it. She was so very real—

It was a dream, Eliza.

Covered in muck and worms and – oh! – reaching out for me, she was – her horrible fingers – I saw the bones . . .

James continued to smile.

A dream, he said again.

I looked at him, the eerie contentment on his face, the chill, frank beauty of him, and I took a breath.

And now? I said.

What about now?

What if I'm dreaming now? Talking to you like this. What if all of this is a dream? What if I'm simply dreaming you saying all of these things to me?

He frowned at me then, rubbing at his hair just as he always did in real life. He yawned.

I don't know, Eliza. How can I know if your whole life isn't one long dream and one day you'll finally wake up from it and—

And what?

He looked at me with a sudden tenderness.

And be released, he said.

And he bent his head to kiss me, and I was so startled by the sly spark of his lips on mine – a thing I had ached to feel for so very long – that I awoke.

At half past eight, Graham and the girls still aren't home, so Mary walks the five minutes down the lane to the pub.

The verges have all been mown and the grass lies in piles where it was chopped, a couple of blackbirds wrestling a worm from underneath. The sun has gone and the sky is mauve, the air still warm but moist with the promise of dew. Two kids with scooters are playing in the road, chatting and laughing and swearing. Mary hears a woman calling to them from somewhere behind the cottages.

She goes around the back of the pub, through the car park, her feet loud on the gravel. Graham and the girls are sitting out on the darkening lawn in the exact same place where she and Eddie sat that day, which already feels like a very long time ago. For a moment she's stopped in her tracks by the sight of them. A relaxed and smiling man and two teenage girls. A family. Then Graham sees her standing there and waves. She goes over.

'We'd have waited,' he says. 'But we didn't know where the hell you were.'

Mary looks at Lisa. She sees that her lips are drawn on in a dark pencil and she has a dirty leather jacket around her shoulders. Pale hair sticking up around her small head. As she leans forwards to wipe her finger around the salty inside of a ripped crisp packet, Mary glimpses black underwear, the freckled top of a breast.

'I went for a walk,' she says in the brightest voice she can manage. 'It was such a lovely afternoon. Hello, Lisa. How're you doing?'

Lisa nods but doesn't speak. Graham asks Mary what she wants to drink. She says she won't have anything.

'Aren't you eating?' she says.

Graham throws her a helpless look.

'These two refuse to have anything except crisps. They keep insisting they're not hungry.'

'Lisa ate on the train,' Ruby says.

Mary looks at Lisa.

'I thought you didn't have any money?'

Ruby picks up her glass.

'She managed to find some.'

'Did you?' Mary asks Lisa.

At last Lisa raises her eyes. Mary sees that the make-up is less dense than usual, a little less convincing. Without it she looks younger, smaller.

'I found a fiver,' she says.

For a moment Mary wonders if she's been crying.

'Do your parents know where you are?' she asks her.

Graham puts a hand on her wrist.

'Darling,' he says, 'it's all right. We've talked about it. I'll fill you in later. It's all a bit complicated.'

Lisa looks at her.

'It's all right,' she says.

Mary stares at her.

'All right for who?'

Ruby makes an angry noise.

'Can you just leave off interrogating her? She's had a fucking awful time today if you really want to know.'

But Lisa looks at Mary.

'I meant, it's all right that you're worried. I don't blame you for worrying. But I left my mum a note. You don't need to worry about anything. I've sorted it. She knows all about what's happening.'

'So what is happening?' Mary asks Graham when they've sent the girls off home and he's persuaded her to change her mind about a drink and ordered a last-minute plate of lasagna for himself.

He makes a face.

'As far as I can gather – and all right I admit I didn't want to press too hard – it's the age-old story. Unsuitable boyfriend. Someone they don't approve of anyway. I got the feeling he might be older. And there was a fight. But I'm not sure it's true that her father hit her. Her stepfather, it turns out. But I'm sure there's a whole lot more to it than that.'

Mary looks at him.

'Meaning what, exactly?'

'Oh, I don't know. It's just – those girls. It's part of why Veronica and I felt Ruby shouldn't be in London.' He hesitates. Picking up the beer mat and putting it down again. 'Actually I don't have any evidence that Lisa's using anything. But Ruby, she's just got so reckless.'

'Reckless?'

'Well, casual. About herself. Her body. About taking things.'

'You mean drugs?'

'Or pills, medicine – anything she can get her hands on really. You'd think after what she did to herself – ending up in hospital – well—'

'You think she ought to know better?'

'You'd think she'd at least be scared.'

'You want her to be scared?'

Graham blinks.

'I want her to stop taking stupid risks, yes.'

Mary thinks about this.

'And you think she's safe here?'

'How do I know?' He sighs. 'And then of course there's the cutting.'

Mary is about to say something when he puts his head in his hands. He stays like that for a very long time.

'I'm sorry,' she says at last.

'It's not your fault.'

'No, I mean I'm just sorry.'

'Sorry for me?'

'You know what I mean.'

Without looking at her, Graham reaches out and puts a hand on her knee. She looks at the hand for a moment, before putting her own hand on his.

'Anyway, I'm sure she'll grow out of it,' she adds.

'Grow out of it? Grow out of being unhappy, you mean? Will she?'

'Most kids do, don't they?'

He takes a breath.

'I'm just not sure I can cope with all of this right now. I mean it literally. I'm not sure I have the strength. I'm genuinely not sure.'

Mary squeezes his hand.

'You're just tired.'

'I am. That's right, I am. Very tired.' He lifts his head. 'Anyway the point is, Lisa's here now. And she promises me that her mother knows where she is.'

Mary shakes her head.

'And you believe her?'

'What can I do? If she's lying to me, seriously, then what can I do?' He looks at her and sighs. 'Look, I know you don't like her – and God knows, I'm not necessarily sticking up for her over all of this – but all I can say is, she's been a good friend to Ruby.'

'Has she?'

'She was there at the hospital, you know, when they took Ruby in. And I actually get the feeling that she's a bit more responsible than Ruby when it comes to all this so-called partying.'

'Do you? What on earth gives you that idea?'

'I don't know. Just a feeling I get. She's more together than Ruby. Ruby's so all over the place, but Lisa seems more mature, don't you think? More of a young woman. I get the sense that she knows what she wants, knows what she's doing.'

Mary thinks about this. Graham takes her hand, holds it in both of his.

'Anyway she's not our responsibility, is she? And she's going back tomorrow afternoon. Just try and bear with it if you can till then.' He looks at her. 'And don't think for one moment that Ruby's getting away with what she said to you, by the way. I haven't even begun to deal with that.'

Mary shuts her eyes.

'Don't worry about it. It really doesn't matter.'

'Of course it matters.'

'She's just angry, isn't she? She's very angry.'

'What the hell's she got to be angry about?'

Mary hesitates.

'Lots of things. She's got lots of things to be angry about.'

A girl brings the lasagna. So hot that steam fills the air, illuminating for a moment the cluster of midges hanging above them. The sky is black now, the air cooling. Scent drifting over from the lilies in the flowerbeds.

Mary tells him about the call from the coroner's office. The pregnant teenage girl, the violent death. Graham listens with a serious and attentive face while he pokes at the lasagna with a fork.

'Did it upset you?' he says at last. 'Hearing all of that?'

Mary looks at him. 'Does it upset you?'

He picks up his drink. She watches him thinking about it.

'I don't know. Poor girl. But it's a long time ago, I suppose.'

'What difference does that make?'

He looks at her. 'Well, time. All that time. It pushes things further away, doesn't it?'

'Does it?' Mary says.

'You don't think so?'

She takes a breath.

'I think that only someone with not very much imagination could think that.'

He scoops a forkful of lasagna.

'All right. I don't have very much imagination, then.'

'I didn't mean it like that.'

'I suppose I just meant there's a kind of distance, isn't there? More than a hundred – hundred and fifty – years. Surely you agree about that?'

Mary thinks about this. Trying to decide what distance means and whether there is any or not.

'Do you think Lisa's pregnant?' she says.

Now he stares at her. Putting down his drink.

'What on earth makes you say that?'

'I don't know. I don't know what made me say it.'

He pushes his fork around the plate, scoops up a fold of pasta and offers it to her. She shakes her head.

'I don't think so,' he says. 'All right, I suppose there's always a possibility, but – well, I don't think she's pregnant, no.'

Mary is silent for a long moment.

'I thought I was pregnant,' she tells him then. 'Until tonight.'

'What?'

'And then, just now, a little while ago – just before I came here, in fact – I got my period.'

Now he puts down the fork and stares at her. Something on his face that she cannot read.

'What? Pregnant? Sorry, what are you saying?'

She blinks.

'Just that. That for a while, I think I honestly began to believe I was.'

She watches his face as he struggles to take it in – shock and bewilderment – and for a moment, in some vague way, she feels ashamed.

'But how could it even be possible?' he says at last.

She shakes her head.

'It's not.'

'So – then, but how could you think it?'

'I can't explain it,' she says, telling the truth now.

'You can't?'

She licks her lips, gazing at him, almost afraid. At last she shakes her head.

'I can't even explain it to myself,' she says.

He is still looking at her.

'But you're not. You're not pregnant?'

349

'No.'

'Then – I still don't understand. What on earth made you think that you were?'

She hesitates.

'All those things. Exactly the things I felt both times with the girls. Tiredness. And sickness – most mornings – I had them all.'

'You had symptoms of pregnancy?' She nods. 'You never told me. That's what the sickness was? You felt all these things and you never said anything to me?'

She shuts her eyes.

'I didn't know what to think. And it wasn't just that, anyway. There were other things too.'

'What do you mean? What other things?'

'Remember how I was with Ella? Always so jumpy and tired and hearing strange noises, everything so loud and odd, everything I ate tasting all wrong.'

'But then why didn't you go to the doctor's?'

'I did. I did go to the doctor.'

He lets out a breath. Hands dropping to his lap.

'You went to the doctor and you never told me?'

'You were busy with Ruby.'

'That's not fair.'

'I'm sorry. I don't know if it's fair or not. It's how it felt to me at the time.'

Graham passes a hand over his face.

'What did the doctor say?'

Mary hesitates. Remembering that when the young woman with the long brown hair and the cheesecloth dress checked the pregnancy test, when she smiled at her and said, 'Well, that's all OK, then. We'll just have to work on the basis that you've had a bit of a virus or a vomiting bug or something,' she did not seem able to hear her. That instead, something massive and unexpected went sweeping through her. A kind of devastation. For a moment the room was entirely, violently dark.

'That's it? You're sure? I'm not pregnant?'

The doctor blinked at her.

'I didn't get the feeling you were expecting to be? After what you said about your husband and—'

She went on to say something chatty and conciliatory – about statistics, about vasectomies and their occasional yet rare failure rate, something like that.

But Mary was no longer listening. No longer even there. The most terrible chill pouring through her.

And maybe it began because she hadn't been honest about what had happened to her own children, her own real children. Writing them down on that form as if they still existed. A lie, of course, and yet a lie that had, briefly and quite unexpectedly, given her an immense and secret pleasure.

Or maybe it wasn't that at all. Maybe it was something less easy to define, something to do with what Graham had just said. Distance. And probability. After all, if you can lose two little girls outside a leisure centre on a sunny afternoon, if you can wake up one morning a mother and the next morning not a mother, if you can lose the one thing you were living for in a space of one quick, blameless and unremarkable afternoon—

'The doctor told me I wasn't. But I suppose I wasn't able to take it in. Literally unable. I didn't believe her.'

'You didn't believe what she told you?'

'I was just so very sure. I knew that I was.'

'But you weren't.'

'No. No, I wasn't.'

Graham pushes away the plate of food.

'I can't believe it. All of this has been happening to you and you've told me nothing. Nothing.'

'I'm telling you now.'

'Wonderful. I appreciate it. Thank you.'

'Please don't be angry.'

'I'm not angry. I'm—'

'What? What are you?'

'I don't know. Something else. You telling me all of this now. It makes me feel – lonely.'

Mary glances away at the darkening sky. The beginnings of a moon.

'I couldn't have had it anyway. Even if I had been pregnant. I couldn't have had it. You know that.'

He turns to her.

'What do you mean? Why couldn't you have had it?'

She shuts her eyes.

'Come on, Graham. Look at us.'

He takes a breath. He puts his hands to his face.

'You wouldn't have had it? You're saying you wouldn't have wanted to have our child?'

She looks at him. Tears standing in her eyes. Shaking her head.

'Would it have been our child?' he says then.

She keeps her eyes on him, trembling now.

'Who on earth else's would it be?'

I cried hard when I woke from my dream about James Dix because I knew then that my dreaming life was the one I wanted, not my waking one, which had always been small and empty and drab.

And, lying there awake and alone in the bleached light of that early morning, I dared at last to remember what he'd said to me that day in the tool loft above the cowshed – the day he had told me that he was finished with me for ever, that he could not have me anywhere near him, that it was for my own good, and all because something terrible had happened.

At first I hadn't understood. I had thought that he meant the thing that had happened with Phoebe Harkiss. I could not think of anything more terrible than what he had done to her and the way I had helped him hide it. But then he told me. He told me what the terrible thing was. Still holding the knife in one hand, he reached out with the other and he drew me close and he kept me there while he let me know exactly what it was.

It's you, he said. You're what's happened to me, Eliza. You've got inside me, under my skin, right here into the very centre of my heart.

I searched his face, my eyes wide now, my heart lit up again and beginning to dare to hope.

Oh James, I said.

No, he said. No, Eliza. You don't understand.

I gazed at him.

But I love you too. You know I do. My heart is the same. My heart is full with it, you cannot possibly ever know how much.

He put down the knife and he took hold of me with both hands. My wrists. Gripping them so hard they began to burn.

Yes, he said. But you don't get it, do you? It's a bad thing. It's terrible—

352

Terrible?

Look at how I am, Eliza. Look at what you did. Is this how a man should be? I am not good. I am all on edge. Look at me.

On edge? I said, hardly daring to breathe now. But James, my dear, if you truly love me—

His face was cold now.

Love? What is love? Please pay attention, Eliza. Please try and listen to what I say. You are nothing but a child. You haven't even the slightest understanding, have you, of what you've done?

I stared at him.

What? What have I done? All I ever did was love you, James.

Stop it, he said. Stop talking about love. Don't you see, I don't want your love? Your love isn't good. It's bad. It makes me do bad things—

He let go of me very harshly and he picked up the knife again. I watched him hold it and turn it, handling it as if it were a thing of great interest to him.

Bad things? I said.

Why do you think I killed her? Your love, Eliza. It has a kind of poison in it. It's not right.

Poison? My heart was thudding now. I had no idea what he was saying. If anyone had poisoned anyone, then it was him – he'd poisoned me. His love was the one that contained the poison.

I thought of the small alive thing that was growing so fast inside of me that it felt frightening. Each day, more and more now, all sensations, all feelings, were turned inside out, the edges of me made of nothing – thinner than paper and more stinging than salt. I blinked away some tears.

Not right? I said, for I was becoming very confused. This is just me, James. The ordinary, young Eliza that you know and like. It's only me, for pity's sake. What is it you are so afraid of? What isn't right?

He shook his head and he put down the knife again, turning his whole body away from it as if he was somehow afraid of it. I saw sweat on his face. It was the same look I'd seen on him so many times before. I watched as he wiped himself with his sleeve.

I'm not well, Eliza. I can't see straight any more. I'm not at all well, and it's all your fault.

I stared at him.

My fault?

If I can't have you, then – well, I have no idea what I might do.

I took a breath, trying to keep myself steady, all my thoughts spinning and colliding. I did not understand a thing he was saying.

But you can have me, I said, keeping my voice as calm and quiet and careful as I could. Don't you believe me? Here I am, James, I am yours.

I said it and I meant it, but even as I spoke the words, my heart was plummeting because I knew that wasn't it.

No, he said. Don't you see, that can't happen? It's you. It's all your fault. I wish I'd never met you. I wish I'd never lain down under that tree and I wish I'd never listened to you and watched your pretty face and kissed you and—

What? I was wild now, shaking all over, I was beginning to think he was quite mad. What are you saying? I don't understand you, James. I've done nothing. What in God's name have I done?

I held my hands out to him but, as if he was afraid of what he might do, he was already backing away from me.

Don't come near me, he said. Don't come anywhere near me. I'm telling you, Eliza, this is over now. I've had a lucky run of it but my luck has run out. It is over now.

And he backed away and went towards the other tools. The sharp tools that were there to be used on the crops and on the animals – the blades and the castrating knives, the sickles, the weed-hooks, the spikes.

I stood and watched him and I felt hopelessness wash over me. I was drowning in it. I knew there was nothing I could do. I was gasping for air.

What are you doing? I said.

You know what I'm doing.

But I don't know anything.

That's right. You don't know anything. Let's keep it that way.

I took a step away.

I've done nothing but love you, I said again, my voice hardly more than a whisper now.

He looked at me as if he'd never seen me before, but also as if he could never see me well enough.

That's it, Eliza. That's exactly it. Listen to yourself. That's what you've done.

Is there nothing I can do to stop you? I cried.

354

But it was pointless to ask. I already knew the answer. The answer had been there all along.

Things that Mary did not see coming: the day when, taking the girls to nursery, going around to get Flo out of the car, she stepped into the road holding Ella's hand just seconds after a heavy lorry had thundered by. Standing there in its ripe, diesel backdraught, a cold and sickening realisation passing through her.

Or, the time with Flo as a baby, in their old kitchen with the flagged-stone floor. Handing her to a friend because the soup was about to boil over. Realising in less than two seconds that the friend – a young man not used to babies – hadn't quite got her. Even though he reacted just in time, pulling her awkwardly into his lap and balancing her there.

Mary doesn't remember what she said, what she did. All she remembers is the fragile eggshell curve of that moment: Flo's small head, its skin so thin that a pale blue vein shone through her temple – and all that cold stone beneath her.

Did she snatch her baby back? She doesn't think so. She thinks she was polite, that she just got on with stirring the soup, her hand trembling. And the young man – it was clear that he had no idea what had just happened. 'Hasn't she got the most amazing eyes?' he said.

Twelve or thirteen days into the trial, he – the defendant – finally broke down. He admitted taking the girls to the ditch. He even admitted pouring petrol on their bodies, to attempt to set light to them. But it was because he had panicked, he said. It had all been a terrible accident. He had never meant to kill them.

He said that he wished that he could turn the clock back. He really was very sorry now. It was pure chance, he said, that he happened to be passing the leisure centre on that day – 'I was on my way to see my mother. She's in a care home near there.' It had happened in a moment, their deaths, an instant. He did not remember anything – did not know how it had happened. All he knows is he had not intended it. Afterwards he had been in a state of shock, of disbelief.

'What did you do?' his QC asked him. 'After you had killed them and left them there half-burned in that ditch. What did you do?'

A pause. The court was very still. Mary found herself looking up, away, at the high, colourless walls of the court room. A long way above them, light – sunshine – poured in through a window.

'I went home and I think I had a shower then I played on the PlayStation and I made myself a sandwich,' he said.

'A sandwich?'

'That's right.' He allowed himself a quick, careful glance at his questioner. 'I was hungry. I always eat like a horse when I'm stressed.'

A pause. The QC's face did not change.

'And is it true that you also put some sheets in the washing machine? That you washed some sheets?'

'I don't know,' the man said.

'Think about it. Did you wash some sheets?'

'I might have,' said the man – and yet again he wept.

In the morning, Ruby comes down earlier than usual, while Mary is still clearing away the breakfast things. She has on a plaid shirt that Mary's never seen before. Tracksuit bottoms. Dirty, thick socks slopping off her feet.

She opens the fridge and takes out a Diet Coke. Goes into the sitting room, shutting the door. After a moment or two, Mary hears the crackle of the TV coming to life. Loud voices. Music. The volume being ratcheted up.

She goes in and starts to open the curtains.

'Hey!' Ruby says.

'What?'

'I wanted those closed.'

Mary hesitates, trying to decide whether she has the energy for a row. She twitches them back halfway across.

'We need a little bit of light in here,' she says.

'Why?'

'Because it's depressing otherwise.'

'But I can't see the TV.'

'You can. You can see it well enough.'

'I can't. I'm not joking,' Ruby adds in a milder voice. 'It's my eyes. I really can't.'

Mary turns and looks at her.

'What's wrong with your eyes?'

Ruby blinks.

'I don't know. Just they always hurt in the mornings, that's all. I think I might have some kind of infection or something. I looked in the mirror just now and they were bright red.'

Mary looks at her.

'Have you been smoking?'

'Fuck's sake. Why would I be smoking?'

'Have you been smoking weed?'

Ruby shifts on the sofa.

'I don't really do that any more, if you really want to know.'

'Why not?'

'What?'

'Why wouldn't you do it?'

Ruby gazes at the TV.

'What is this? Some kind of Spanish fucking Inquisition?'

Mary looks at her.

'Where's Lisa, anyway?' she says, only just realising.

Ruby tilts the Coke can to her mouth.

'Oh, she went.'

'What? Went where?'

'Dunno. Back to London, I suppose.'

Mary stares at her.

'Lisa's gone? But when? How did she get to the station?'

Ruby looks at her.

'How do I know? Maybe she got a ride or something.'

Mary comes and sits down on the sofa. She picks up the remote and pauses the TV.

'Ruby. Look at me.' Slowly, Ruby turns her head. 'I need to know right now where Lisa is and if she's safe.'

'Why?'

'You bloody well know why.'

Ruby sighs.

'She's fine. Don't worry. It's nothing bad. I think she'd just had enough, that's all. She suddenly wanted to get back.'

'Suddenly? So – what? She just got up and walked off out of the house without telling anyone. What time did she go?'

'How do I know? I was asleep.'

'Then how did you know she was going?'

'She told me she might. Last night. She said I could have her things. She gave me this.' Ruby plucks at the collar of the shirt.

Mary lets out a breath.

'But why?'

'Why what?'

'Why on earth would she give you her things?'

'What do you mean, why would she?'

'Well, why didn't she want them?'

Ruby looks at the paused TV and yawns.

'For God's sake. How am I meant to know?'

'You didn't ask her?'

'Not really.'

Mary hesitates.

'Seriously, Ruby, why didn't she tell us she wanted to go? Dad would have given her a lift to the station. Should I call him? Do you think we should go looking for her?'

Ruby sighs.

'For fuck's sake. Just calm it, will you? Stop overreacting to everything. She'll be fine. She's not a child.'

'She's sixteen years old.'

'That's not a child.'

Mary looks at Ruby.

'Can you phone her please? I want to know exactly where she is.'

'I can't do that.'

'Why not?'

'Because she left her phone.'

'She what? No one leaves their phone.'

'She did. She said I could have it. She said she didn't need it any more. That phone is a piece of shit anyway. Someone's getting her a proper one.'

At first, when Mary hears the sharp knock on the door, she jumps. Her first thought – entirely, almost frighteningly irrational – is that it's the odd girl in the brown clothes and the floppy hat, come back down the lane and standing there wanting to come in. But when she goes over and pulls it open, she sees that Deborah is standing there.

'I'm sorry. I'm so sorry. I didn't know who else to go to.'

Mary sees that her shirt is only half done-up, the strap of a pink bra showing. Her eyes are red from crying. Her hair twisted into a clip, but falling out of it, down her back. Mary brings her in and pulls out a chair and offers her tea. But she says she doesn't want anything and, after standing for a moment clasping her hands and staring around the room, begins to cry again.

'It's Eddie,' she says. 'He's gone.'

'Gone? What do you mean, he's gone? Gone where?'

'I don't know. I've absolutely no idea. I was actually hoping you might know something.'

'Me?'

Mary feels her blood jump. Deborah looks at her.

'All I know is this time it's for real. He's not messing around. This time he means it, I know he does. Oh Mary, I don't think he's coming back.'

'This time?' Mary stares at her.

Deborah shuts her eyes.

'Let's just say it's not the first time.'

'Then he'll be back.' Mary struggles to take this in. 'Surely? That's reassuring, isn't it? If he's done it before? It means he'll be back.'

Deborah shakes her head.

'It's different this time. He's not answering his phone – but he sent me this text. It was horrible. It just felt like—'

She begins to sob. Mary puts a hand on her arm, her shoulder.

'Felt like what?'

'It felt so final – I don't know – like he was saying goodbye.' She looks at Mary. 'Oh God. I don't know what's wrong with me. I feel like I might faint.'

Mary goes to the tap and runs it for a few seconds. Brings Deborah a glass of water. Watches while she drinks it.

'You're saying you think he's left you? Properly left you? But why on earth would he do that?'

Deborah looks straight through her.

'That's right. That's it. Yes, that is what I think. He's left me. Oh God.' She begins to sob again.

'Breathe,' Mary tells her. 'Deborah, I mean it. You need to calm down. Just sit for a moment and try to take some breaths. There.'

Deborah breathes, but her chin wobbles. Mary touches her arm. 'You've tried calling him?'

'Lots of times. It just goes straight to voicemail.'

Deborah looks at her. Tearing a piece of kitchen towel from the roll that Mary hands her. Blowing her nose.

'He said to forgive him. In the text. That's all. Forgive me, he said. Nothing else. Just that. But forgive him for what? What does he mean? What am I supposed to forgive him for this time? Honestly, Mary, I didn't know what to do – who to go to. Then I realised: I had to talk to you.'

'Me?'

'Well, obviously. Because you and he are so close. It's all right – he's told me all about it. These past few weeks. I know all about how amazing you've been.'

Mary looks at her, her insides growing hot.

'I don't know what he's told you, but I really haven't done anything. I don't know what he's talking about. Amazing about what?'

Deborah stares at her.

'But I thought – he's spoken to you, hasn't he? All those long talks you've had. He said he'd told you everything.'

'Everything?'

'About his problems?'

Mary catches her breath.

'What problems?'

Now Deborah's mouth drops open.

'You mean he hasn't told you? About his illness?'

'What?'

Deborah tears off another sheet of kitchen roll. Holding it in her hands and seeming to want to steady herself, then looking out of the window.

'These last few months have been very hard. The whole summer, really. Ever since he was signed off work—'

'What? He hasn't been working?'

Deborah makes a face.

'Oh God, no. Not in months.'

Mary thinks about this.

'I thought he had a lot of days off? Holiday? I thought he was owed—'

'Holiday?' Deborah laughs. 'Really? Is that what he told you? He was signed off work ages ago.' She blows her nose again, then she gives Mary a long look. 'So he's been lying to you too?'

Mary stares at Deborah, feeling the room tilt. Grabbing on to the table, lowering herself into a chair.

'I don't know,' she says.

Deborah sighs.

'The first time I met him, he told me a load of lies. He said he'd never been married, can you believe it? That he'd been alone all his life. That I was the first woman he'd ever loved and wanted to commit to.'

Mary stares at her.

'And it wasn't true?'

Deborah shakes her head.

'He'd been married three times before. Three times! Married and divorced. Three ex-wives. Can you believe it? He's a serial marrier, if that's the right term. But they call it something else now, don't they? Love addict or something?'

Mary says nothing.

'Funny thing is, he's actually not that keen on sex. Love's what he likes, the thing he does really well. Being in love. Falling for people. Head over heels. The whole, romantic rigmarole of it. He's a fantasist, you see. But he's so convincing. I think he even convinces himself. He just lets himself fall in love.'

'He does?'

'Oh, yes. Over and over and over.'

Mary looks down at her wrists in her lap. Suddenly cold, the world tightening around her. She looks at Deborah.

'But you?'

'Me?'

'Well, but you fell in love with him?'

Deborah sighs.

'I did. Oh God, yes. I was crazy about him. He knew exactly what he was doing, of course – he gave me so much attention, you see. Knew exactly how to reel me in, get me to respond to him. And yes, I thought he was wonderful – so sensitive and caring, asking me all these questions and – well, he just seemed really interested, in a way that no one had been interested in me before. Stuff about losing my mother, all of that. He was so kind. He listened. He made me feel so – understood. And by the time I found out about all the lies, well, it was too late, I suppose.'

'Too late?'

Deborah makes a face.

'Well, I wasn't going to abandon him, was I? And I suppose by then I really did love him – I do love him. And we had all these honest, searching talks. And he agreed to have some help. And I think he did mean it, at the time, anyway. And for a while it actually was fine, or I thought it was. A new beginning and all that. I suppose I thought I'd cured him.'

She laughs and then she looks at Mary. 'I know he really likes you. He never stops talking about you. I could see it was doing him good, the friendship with you, and I encouraged him to see you. Funnily enough, I thought he was being completely honest with you. It didn't ever occur to me that he would lie to you. What a stupid bloody idiot I am.'

'You're not an idiot.'

'All the same. It should have occurred to me, shouldn't it? That's the problem with me. Again and again, I put it all behind me and I trust him and—'

Mary watches as Deborah puts her head in her hands.

'But has he ever seen a doctor?' she says.

Deborah lifts her head, shuts her eyes.

'Oh God. So many doctors. They did put him on something for a while that seemed to be helping. Or at least, I thought so. At first, it felt like he'd turned a bit of a corner. But, you know, he's not a child. I can't watch over him all the time.' She lifts her head. 'Anyway, the point is, I don't think he's been taking it at all.

'And then recently he's been a lot worse – more unstable. Sleeping all day. Missing doctor's appointments. But he said you were helping him – because of everything you've been through, you and Graham, that you'd changed things for him. And I knew there wasn't anything funny going on between you, obviously. Not that I wouldn't put it past him, and not that you're not a very attractive woman, but I suppose – well, I suppose I just trusted you.' She blows her nose again, looks at her. 'Oh, Mary. I'm so sorry. I feel terrible. I honestly thought you knew all of this?'

Mary is trembling. She tries to say something but finds that she can't speak. Deborah goes on: 'And then it all got a lot more serious when we found we couldn't have children. That he couldn't, I mean. I honestly think he was doing all right until then. But that just seemed to tip him over the edge. It's so important to him, having kids – kids of his own. I'd have been very happy to look into adoption but he wouldn't even consider it. In fact, he's been more and more obsessed with the whole thing – being a parent, a father – and he just went to pieces, couldn't cope with it at all—'

Mary is staring at Deborah. She feels her stomach tighten.

'But what about his son?'

'What?'

'He told me he had a son. A boy. In London.'

Deborah looks at her.

'Oh, what? You mean Ollie?'

'That's right.'

Deborah sighs.

'Ollie does exist. But he's not his son. Of course he isn't. He's the son of someone we – well, an acquaintance. Someone I used to share a flat with.' She sighs again. 'Oh dear. I'm afraid he's done this before. Used Ollie in this way, I mean.'

'Used?' Mary feels her hands go to her face. 'Used in what way?'

Deborah thinks for a moment.

'Lied about him. Made stuff up. Talked about him as if he really is his son. Oh, don't worry, I know, he can be very convincing. Like I said, I do sometimes think he manages to believe it himself. But it's not true, none of it is. He's never had a son. Far from it. In fact, it was very embarrassing because it got so confusing for poor Ollie that his mother had to ask me to stop him contacting them.'

IO

That last day. A Sunday. I remember every part of it. The parts that I knew about and the parts that I didn't. The worst parts of all were the ones in shadow. The ones that I could hardly bear to think about – would never even dare to guess at.

I woke that morning to a cool sky. A hush. Everything stilled and slowed. Even the cows – their low, steady moan as they waited to be milked – muted and unlikely and far away.

I stood at the open window, trying to work out what it was that was different. The air, it no longer smelled of summer – was that it? I waited. All around me, something was happening. For a few uncanny moments it seemed as if everything was unfixed, hesitating, ready to be taken backwards, started over again and undone.

Then the feeling stopped. Time ceased to drift and became more certain. Everything resumed. Trees, walls, gates, suddenly clear and bright and solid. And once the day had got itself going, it moved along with a cold and horrible speed.

My father was whistling to himself, spreading pork fat on two pieces of bread. One was for himself to eat, the other for my mother, who had taken to her bed since the new baby came. I asked him if they'd found James yet and he said no, they hadn't found him, but they most certainly would.

How do you know he hasn't gone back to Lowestoft? I said. How do you know he hasn't gone away to Yarmouth or Cromer?

Or China? said Jazzy, who was blacking the little ones' boots ready for Sunday school and kept on having to shout at Honey to get out of the way.

Our father looked very serious. He put the knife back down on the plate. It rocked there for a moment, catching the bright yellow sunshine.

He's been seen in Yarrow's field, he said. They think he may be hiding out in the woods.

Hiding? I said.

My father looked at me.

All I'm telling you, Eliza, is he's still here. He's getting ready for us. That man hasn't gone anywhere yet.

That day – a school inset day. 'Insect days', the girls liked to call them. Mary always forgot to put them in her diary and often had to find childcare at the very last minute. Though sometimes Graham took time off and other times, as on that last terrible day, she managed to split the time with a babysitter and work from home in the afternoon.

The day began badly. Upstairs after breakfast, stumbling accidentally into a conversation about when and how they should separate and if they should have some more counselling before they even thought about it, she and Graham had fought. Graham wanted more counselling, she did not. Graham accused her of giving up on the marriage and she accused him of lying about still seeing his lover.

'If I was still seeing her, then why would I want to bloody well bother with counselling?' he said.

'The counselling's a smoke-screen,' she told him. 'You just want to be able to think well of yourself. You want it to look like you're doing the right thing.'

Both of them had raised their voices and Graham had kicked out in passing at the chest of drawers, causing two bottles, one of Calpol and one of perfume, to fall to the floor. The bottle of Calpol had no lid on and had spilled all over the floor. Ella had come in at that moment and what she had seen had made her cry.

And Mary had been furious with Graham, really bitterly furious, because he was the one who'd been reckless, the one who hadn't cared enough – who'd first raised his voice at her in anger even though she'd begged him not to. And now she did not know what and how much Ella had heard.

'Sometimes Mummy and Daddy get cross with each other,' she whispered as she mopped the sticky pink mess off the floorboards with a towel, then pulled her daughter onto her lap and held her there. 'Just like you and Flo get cross with each other.'

Ella thought about this.

'Flo hits me sometimes and I hate her.'

'Well, Daddy and I don't hit each other—'

'But you want to.'

Mary smiled, kissed her head.

'No, honey. People who love each other don't want to hit.'

'And you and Daddy love each other?'

Mary looked down at her daughter's soft, dark hair.

'Of course we do. You know we do. But most of all we love the two of you, our precious girls.'

Ella was quiet for a moment. She took hold of Mary's wrist and played with her gold bangle as she often did, twisting it around and around.

'But Flo does it.'

'What? What does Flo do?'

'She hits me and she bites me and sometime she kicks me too.'

Ella was tugging at the bangle, trying to get it off. Mary kept her hand there, letting her.

'Flo's a baby who doesn't know any better,' she said. 'And anyway it's not just Flo. You know it's not. You're as bad as each other. I've seen you hit her too, you know.'

'I'm not a baby,' Ella said.

She slid the bangle off Mary's hand at last and held it.

'No, you're not. You're a big girl, who does know better and who knows she shouldn't hit people.'

'Should Daddy know better?'

'Daddy doesn't hit people, but he should know better than to shout, yes.'

'And kick things.'

'And kick things, yes. He didn't mean to do that. He just got cross and lost his temper.'

Ella sighed. 'Grown-ups lose their temper.'

'They do. Yes.'

'And did you lose your temper?'

'I did. I'm sorry. Mummy should know better as well. I'll try not to do it again.'

Sitting there in her lap, Ella was silent a moment. She leaned back against Mary, then twisted her head around to look at her.

'I don't want you and Daddy ever to hurt each other.'

'Of course you don't. We never will. That's a promise. Are you feeling better now?'

Still holding the bangle, Ella blinked. 'Are you better?'

Mary smiled. 'I'm better. Are you?'

'I'm better.'

'Good. We're all better then. Can I have my bangle back now?'

Ella looked at the bangle.

'Is Daddy better?'

Mary looked up to see Graham standing in the doorway. His face was pale. She thought that he looked exhausted, wrung out, drained, not like anyone she knew.

He looked at his daughter and he smiled but he didn't say anything. Then he turned and went back downstairs. It was the last time he ever saw her. Mary held out her hand for Ella so that she could push the bangle back on. It took her a moment or two to do it, but she got it on.

Mary did not take the bangle off again for a long time.

While they were waiting for the sitter to come, both girls wanted to watch TV. Mary said no, but they kept on pestering her, so finally she gave in.

'Just ten minutes and no more,' she said.

'Just until Becky gets here?' said Ella.

Mary smiled.

'Nice try. Ten minutes and then we turn it off, whether she's here or not.'

She took the opportunity, while they were sitting still, to check their hair for nits. The school had sent home a note asking for them to be checked regularly. She aimed to do it at bath time but almost always forgot and then once she'd had a glass of wine, she was too tired to do anything.

But there'd been several outbreaks lately, so she'd stuck a note on the fridge. Nits! it said. And under that: small soda waters, muesli, mayonnaise, handwash. And under that, Graham had written: AND MORE NITS! And under that Ella had written, in pink felt-tip: AND GUMMI BEARS! – and Mary had added 'please'.

She went to get the comb and some kitchen towels. Flo was in a bad mood. She wriggled and huffed and twitched and complained.

But Ella sat very still, tilting her head this way and that, breathing heavily, her eyes fixed on the TV. Mary told her that she was a good girl.

'I've got a lot of hair, haven't I?' Ella said.

'You certainly have,' Mary agreed. 'It takes some going through. But at least you know how to sit nice and still. Unlike another person I could name.'

A giggle from Flo.

'I don't mind being checked,' Ella said, her eyes on the TV. 'I'd rather be checked than get nits.'

'I like it when I get nits!' Flo said. 'I do. I like wolves and I like monsters and I really, really, really like nits.'

Mary looked at Flo.

'What have wolves and monsters got to do with it?'

'All the bad things, I like them all,' Flo said and she reached over and tried to hit Ella on the head with Tuffy.

'Shush!' Ella said. 'Get off. I mean it, Flo. I'm trying to watch TV.'

'You're a bad thing,' Flo said. 'Well, you are, aren't you?'

'Shut up,' Ella said.

'You shut up yourself!' said Flo.

'All right,' Mary put down the comb and swigged the last bitter dregs of her coffee. 'That's enough, both of you. And that'll do for now. I think you're both OK.'

'Flo,' Ella said, her eyes still on the TV, 'have you farted?'

Flo said nothing. She lay on her front with her woollen legs sticking up at the back of the sofa and her arms dangling down on the rug. Walking Tuffy along and then pushing him under the sofa.

'Ugh!' Ella said. 'You have. Mummy, she has!'

Flo said nothing. Laughing to herself and kicking her feet.

'You're making it worse!' Ella said. 'You're spreading it around!'

'I'm swimming,' Flo said. 'I'm a wolf who's swimming. He's swimming and swimming and swimming. He can do the crawl.'

There were angels in the programme on TV.

'Not religious angels,' Ella explained to Mary. 'Not church ones or anything. It's a different kind of angel.'

'Wolf angels!' said Flo. 'Nit angels!'

'Don't be stupid,' Ella said.

'Fart angels!' Flo shrieked, and then Ella grabbed her and they both laughed and rolled around on the floor till Flo got kicked in the eye and cried so much that the TV had to be turned off.

'Thanks for ruining everything,' Ella said.

'I don't know where Tuffy is!' Flo sobbed.

'He's here,' Mary said. 'Look, under the sofa, where for some strange reason you decided to put him.'

She picked up the dog and gave it to her.

'But can we go swimming?' Flo said, gasping out the tears as she sucked her thumb and rubbed Tuffy against her cheek. 'Can we?'

Mary looked at her.

'What, you mean today? You want to go swimming today?'

She pulled Flo onto her lap. Her warm girl's body. The tops of her ears. Her unbrushed hair. She kissed the fusty crown of her head, breathing her in.

'Yes, today!' Flo said.

'Yes!' Ella said. 'Can we?'

Mary's heart sank. She didn't feel much like taking them. But Flo had only just stopped being scared of the water and was starting at last to enjoy it. And Ella was practising for her first badge.

'I don't know,' she said. 'It depends how Mummy's day goes. We'll see, OK?'

'We'll see means no,' Ella said.

'It means it depends.'

She kissed the top of Flo's head once more and pushed her off her lap. Looking at her watch. Becky was late. She ought to go get her stuff together. Trying to think where she'd parked the car last night.

'You could bring your work?' Ella said. 'Flo can stay in the baby pool then you won't even have to come in with us.'

'Not the baby pool!' Flo said.

'If you go in the baby pool I'll give you a horsey ride,' Ella said and Flo made a little noise of pleasure.

Mary thought about this. A quick, tempting vision of sitting on the chairs by the baby pool with her laptop and a coffee, instead of standing shivering with all that chlorine lapping around her thighs.

'Maybe,' she said. 'Maybe.'

But in her heart she'd already decided she'd do it, she'd take them. She wouldn't say it now, but she'd surprise them later when she got back home. It would be worth it for the look on their faces.

And that was it, the decision made: her girls, already falling away from her, their lives already as good as over, the course of that day already set.

I don't know if my father went to search the woods by Yarrow's field that morning, or if the man who called himself James Dix had ever been there at all or had all along been somewhere else altogether.

In my heart, I thought it very unlikely that he would bother to hide himself in those woods. Why would he need to? He'd always had the knack of keeping himself very quiet and low if the mood took him, hadn't he? I didn't see why this would change just because a bunch of men were searching for him. I doubted, also, that he would ever be keen to hang around near Yarrow's ditch, for obvious reasons.

The police were no longer thick in the village. A man, a labourer from Wroxham, had already been caught for the murders of the three young girls. And in fact it was beginning to be said that Phoebe Harkiss had never been quite as innocent as was previously thought and might have run off with a sailor to Gorleston or something similar – but that didn't mean he should be stupid enough to lay a trail for them.

Why would the man who called himself James Dix want to hang around the farm like a lame rabbit simply waiting for the men to come and find him? Why wouldn't he just get going, put some distance between himself and all of us? Take himself off to Yarmouth or Cromer or somewhere else, like I said?

What was keeping him? Why would he bother to wait around for even a few more hours longer than he needed to? What on earth could there be left for him to do here on the farm?

After Jazzy had collected the eggs and swept the kitchen floor and cleaned the tallow off the candlesticks, she got the little ones ready for Sunday school.

Lottie said she wouldn't go.

You have to, Jazz said.

Don't have to.

Lottie, come on, you do.

Lottie rubbed at her eyes.

Don't want to. Not going. Not today.

Why not?

I don't know.

You do know. What is it? Tell me, Lottie!

Lottie lifted her eyes and looked at Jazz.

It's because I'm frightened, that's what it is.

Jazzy laughed.

Frightened? Whatever is there to be frightened of?

Lottie looked down at the ground. She seemed to be searching for something. At last she put her finger in her mouth.

Wolves. I'm afraid of wolves.

Don't be silly. There aren't any wolves.

Lottie coughed.

I'm afraid of Miss Sands.

Jazzy laughed.

No, you're not. No one's afraid of Miss Sands. She's the kindest teacher in the whole world.

Lottie made an angry face. She blew out some air.

Well, I'm afraid of Jesus, then.

You're not afraid of Jesus.

I am. He's a bad man.

Now Jazzy looked at me.

You shouldn't say a thing like that, Lottie. Not about our Lord. That's a wicked thing to say, isn't it, Eliza?

I went over to Lottie, bent down to her.

Why would you be afraid of Jesus, Lottikins? You know very well that Jesus loves all the little children.

Lottie bit her lip and looked at me.

Well, I don't want it.

What don't you want?

Don't want him to love me, not at all.

She hugged her arms to her chest as if she was cold. I put my hand to her head. I thought that she looked quite pale.

What's the matter? I said. Are you sick? Is something hurting?

She shut her eyes and then she opened them again.

Him. It's him. He's gonna hurt me.

371

She means Jesus, Jazzy said.

No! Lottie shouted. Not Jesus.

I took hold of Lottie's hand. It felt quite hot and alive. I didn't think she was sick.

Lottie, listen to me. No one's going to hurt you, I said.

She fixed her eyes on me, then, and there was something about the look that turned my blood cold. Her eyes suddenly dark – too dark. No longer the eyes of a little girl, but full of dread and complication – a much older person's eyes.

She folded her arms.

If I fall out of the highest window in this house, Eliza, she said, will I be dead?

I gasped.

What? I said.

If I land on my head, will I? Because I really want to. I want to fall out of the window and be dead.

I stared at her. And I was about to tell her to stop all this talk of being hurt and being dead – and that she would certainly not die, not until she was a very old and fragile lady of at least a hundred and ten. But then our father came in and told the kiddies they had to hurry up and get to school and not keep Addie Sands waiting.

Now Lottie started to fret and wail. She stamped her foot.

Not going! Don't want to go! Don't want to!

Our father folded his arms.

Do you want a spanking?

Yes, Lottie said.

I tried to think.

I'll cut you a switch, I told her. From the elder. As a special treat. Would you like that? A magic switch that you can use to keep yourself safe.

Lottie hesitated.

I'd like it, she said. But I'm not going to school.

Our father looked at her.

You will if she cuts you a switch, he said. Otherwise you'll get a good hiding from me and I can tell you right now that you won't be happy about it.

Lottie said nothing. I went to the table and picked up the knife.

*

The tree in the lane was small, but it was black with berries. Some people in the village believed it was uncanny – that a spray or a switch from its boughs could guard you like the most ferocious dog.

I didn't know what I believed, but as I chose a long, slim branch and moved in with my blade, I sensed a flick of movement from beyond the hedge and had a quick, chill certainty that someone was watching me. For a moment, I froze.

He's there, I thought. He's back.

I waited but I saw nothing and at last the feeling eased, the air around me loosening and growing loud and bright. Clatter of birdsong. Sun on my face. I breathed again.

Turning, I saw that the man from London was there, setting up his apparatus. He had a shiny leather bag on a strap. Some wooden legs. The camera looked like something you would use to blow on the fire with. The boy who was meant to be helping wasn't doing much – just whistling away to himself and picking berries in the hedgerow.

The man looked at me with his head on one side. He had a bushy moustache but not much hair on his head and there were dark shadows under his eyes.

Want to have your picture taken? he said.

I shook my head. He looked surprised.

You don't?

No thanks, I said.

He touched his moustache, which was yellow at the edges.

Well then, can you fetch your brothers and sisters? I want a picture with some kiddies up against this hedge. They let me do it the other day, he added.

Did they? I said.

He smiled.

Larking around in the wheelbarrow, they were. I got some good ones, didn't I, Tommy? He looked at the boy, who nodded, his mouth full of berries. Tell them it's the man with the camera, he said.

I hesitated.

They've got to go to Sunday school.

The man smiled. I saw that his teeth were yellow too.

Tell them I'll give them a ha'penny. A ha'penny each.

They don't want money, I said.

He kept on smiling.

Well, I won't keep them and that's a promise. They know the score. Just a minute or two of standing still for me, that's all it is.

He clearly expected me to do it, because he put the leather bag down in the grass and folded his arms and stood there in the lane waiting. I thought it wouldn't do any harm to entice them all – and especially Lottie – out into the sunshine. So I went back in and asked who'd like to have their picture taken.

Me! said Jazz.

And me! said Charlie and Minnie together – and Minnie picked up her skipping rope and rushed around getting her boots on, while Honey made a small undecided noise and sat down on the floor and drummed her feet.

Well, you'll have to get a move on, won't you? our father said.

I handed Lottie the switch I'd cut.

Here you are, I said. Here it is. Your sword.

She looked at me as if I was trying to hand her a snake.

Take it, I said. I told you, it will keep you safe.

She said nothing, but she reached out her hand and she took it. She hit the table with it briefly, once, as if testing its powers. And I waited, thinking she would start to make another big old fuss about going outside, but she didn't. Her eyes were dark but her face was very calm. She seemed to have changed her mind about everything. Maybe the switch had done it. She turned and went out into the sunny lane with the others.

I watched as they all stood in front of the yew hedge by the gate, the twins holding hands next to Jazzy, Lottie and Honey standing on the other side. They waited while the man fussed around with his camera, twiddling the knobs and moving the cloth and the boy turned cartwheels in the dust to amuse them.

At last he was ready.

Where's that baby off to? he said, as Honey started to wander off out of the picture towards me.

I caught her up in my arms and carried her back and set her down next to Charlie, who tried to catch hold of her but she wouldn't let him. She stretched out her hands and started to turn around and around on the spot, laughing and making herself dizzy.

The man didn't seem to mind. He asked me again if I wouldn't like to be in the picture after all? I said no.

Suit yourself, he said. Now then: everyone keep very still – and look at the camera!

Honey didn't keep still. But the twins did: they stared at him, their faces frozen, Minnie clutching her rope in one hand and Charlie's hand in the other. Lottie kept still too, but she didn't look at the camera. She didn't do anything. She seemed to be somewhere else entirely – gazing down with a quiet and solemn face at the branch of elder in her hand.

All right, said the man. Here we go—

He put his head under the cloth and, just as he did so, Jazz swung her legs over the top of the gate and turned herself upside down. Her hair hanging in the dust. Minnie gave a little squeal and Honey hiccupped.

The man laughed and punched something under the cloth.

Eureka! he said. There it is.

Is it over? Minnie cried.

It's over, I said.

The man pulled his head out.

That was a saucy trick, young lady, he said to Jazz as she jumped off the gate and pulled down her dress and shook the dust out of her hair. But you could see that he didn't mind that much; in fact, he seemed quite excited about it.

I handed Honey's bonnet to Jazz.

Now hurry off to school, I told them. All of you, I mean it – run along as quick as you can. Addie's waiting.

And I watched them go, all five of them, trailing off down the lane in the bright and dusty air. Minnie jumping and hopping with the skipping rope, Charlie kicking along beside her, waiting for his turn. Honey – tired and fretful – at last starting to cry and having to be picked up by Jazz, who managed to go along with her wedged on her hip the way our mother did. And last of all, Lottie, with that face full of shadows, carrying the switch in both hands and swishing and smacking it against the hedge with all the strength that she could muster.

Just above my head, I heard a warbler, its bright liquid sound pouring down from somewhere in the elder.

And I called out to Lottie and I waved, but she did not look at me. She did not once look up. She did nothing. She did not wave.

*

A man's body is found on the railway line between Melton and Woodbridge, and for a brief and terrible half-hour while the police struggle to identify him, Deborah prepares herself for the worst.

But that's before she gets the email. A lengthy and rapturous and barely punctuated email from Eddie, sent from an undisclosed location, describing exactly how hard and unexpectedly he fell for Lisa, how deeply sorry he is to have let Deborah down like this, to have caused her all of this pain, how very much he did not want to hurt her, how he would have done almost anything to spare her this.

He was the last person in the world, he says, who would have expected to fall in love with a sixteen-year-old. But he did and it is what it is and he is madly, crazily in love and the fact is he's happier than he's ever been in his whole life. And no, he can't explain it or justify it, but neither does he think he could have done anything to stop it happening.

The heart wants what it wants, he tells Deborah in the email. And he hopes she won't mind him telling her all of this, but he respects her far too much just to leave without saying anything. He feels that the very least he owes her is some kind of an explanation. He thanks her for all the happiness she has given him and he will never forget her and he wishes her well and he hopes she will find it in her heart one day to forgive him.

Graham has to sit down when he hears the news.

'Lisa! But he didn't even know Lisa! They'd met – what? – once? Maybe twice?'

Ruby tells them that Eddie and Lisa have been messaging each other for a while.

'Messaging? What, you mean on the internet? You email someone for a few weeks and it's the basis on which to elope?'

'They haven't eloped,' Ruby says.

'What, then? What do you call this?'

Ruby makes a face. 'I guess they just wanted to spend some time together, didn't they?'

'What, a sixteen-year-old schoolgirl and a forty-something married man?'

'Lisa's leaving school. And she says he's thirty-eight.'

'All right,' Graham says. 'But more than twice her age. And she's a complete idiot if she wants to leave school at sixteen.'

Ruby says nothing. Mary looks at her.

'Did you know about this? Did you know that they were planning it?'

Ruby frowns.

'I don't think they were planning it. Lisa just got very pissed off with her parents the other day and they just suddenly felt like they'd do it, that's all.'

Graham almost laughs.

'Great. Let's all do anything we suddenly feel like doing, shall we?'

But Mary looks at Ruby, her stomach beginning to churn.

'They felt like it? You mean, they just decided it on the spur of the moment, or what?'

'I don't know. I don't know when they decided it. Why? Does it matter? Why is it important?'

'It's not important,' Mary says, though to her it suddenly is, very important. 'I just wondered how long they'd been planning it, that's all.'

'They met up a couple of times in London,' Ruby says. 'And she did try to tell her mum and dad about it but they wouldn't even listen and then they banned her from seeing him and that's when they decided to do it.'

'My God.' Graham shakes his head. 'I actually thought Eddie was a decent kind of person. I honestly thought he was better than that.'

'So she used us?' Mary says, feeling her cheeks growing hot. 'That's why she wanted to come here? To see him?'

Ruby puts a hand out to stroke the dog.

'I don't know. Maybe. What else was she meant to do?'

'Wonderful,' Graham says. 'What a very mature way to get back at your parents. So this was what it was all about, then? The fight?'

Ruby shrugs.

'They were idiots, weren't they? Her parents are just so fucking uptight. I told you, they wouldn't even let her see him. That's all she was asking, just to be allowed to meet up for a drink or something. It's their own fault. If they'd just let her see him, then none of this would have happened.'

That night they go over and stay with Deborah until her sister and brother-in-law arrive. She insists that it's not necessary but they tell her that it is.

'You've had a big shock,' Mary tells her. 'You need company. I don't want to leave you all alone.'

'Turns out I've been alone for a very long time,' Deborah says.

The sister brings a bottle of whisky, half a cooked chicken and some sleeping pills. The brother-in-law is holding his car keys and keeps on looking at his watch.

'I'm picking his mum up from the station in a minute,' he says.

'His mum?' Mary catches her breath.

Deborah looks at her.

'She's devastated. She can't believe it. She's always been completely supportive of me and we get on like a house on fire. I told her she doesn't have to take sides, but she insisted on coming. She's furious with him, poor Jane.'

Mary stares at her.

'But I thought his mother was—'

Deborah looks at her.

'What, oh, he gave you all that stuff about his mother dying when he was ten, did he?' She shakes her head. 'That's us, I'm afraid.' She looks at her sister. 'We lost our mum when we were – well, I was ten and you were older, weren't you?'

The sister nods.

'Car crash,' she says.

Deborah folds her arms and looks at Mary.

'His mum, Jane, lives in Berkshire. She's a district nurse. A lovely woman, who thinks the world of him. We see her all the time.'

For a few moments they all stand together in the middle of Eddie and Deborah's huge, clean kitchen. The knives in their block. The mugs on their mug tree. The bowl of fruit on the island.

Mary feels Graham's fingers searching for hers.

'We should make a move,' he says.

She goes over and puts an arm around Deborah, kisses the side of her head.

'You know where we are if you need us,' she says.

Back home, they open a bottle of wine – 'I can't take any more fucking tea,' Graham says – and sit together on the old bench in the thick, starry darkness of the middle of the garden. The dog wanders in and out of the shrubs and bushes, sniffing.

'What's she looking for?' Graham says. 'What is it that she's after in there?'

'Toads,' Mary says. 'I think she can smell toads.'

'You think there are toads in there?'

'She brought one out the other day. I had to make her drop it. Though I think she was more frightened of it than I was.'

Mary calls to the dog, who comes over briefly, tail wagging, then goes straight back to the bushes. Graham looks at her.

'What did you call her just then?'

Mary hesitates.

'What? The dog?'

'Tuffy? Did you call her Tuffy?'

Mary smiles.

'Do you mind? You don't think it's too weird? It just seems like quite a good name for her, that's all.'

Graham is gazing at her. He looks back towards the bushes.

'You've been calling her that?'

'Well, only sometimes. When we're out here in the garden on our own. I suppose I'm trying it out. We really can't keep on just calling her "the dog", can we? What?' She looks at him. 'Is it a bad idea? You don't like it?'

She watches his face. He's smiling.

'I think it's a very good idea. As long as Flo wouldn't mind.'

Flo. She hasn't heard him say it in so long. A shiver of warmth through her arms and down into her fingertips. Flo. She swallows.

'I don't think she'd mind. I think she'd like it. In fact, I think she'd love it. It would make her laugh, wouldn't it?'

For a moment, she almost hears it: the naughty, out-of-control giggle that was the sound of Flo laughing.

'Where did that name come from anyway?' Graham says now. 'Tuffy. She made it up, didn't she?'

'One of her silly words,' Mary says.

Graham takes a breath.

'All those silly words of hers.' He's silent for a moment. 'Well, I like it,' he says. 'That's it, then. From now on, it's official. She's Tuffy. Tuffy!' he calls and the dog looks up for a moment, then returns to the bushes.

'See,' Mary says. 'She already knows it.'

Graham laughs and turns back to her.

'It doesn't guarantee obedience, of course. And we'll have to check it with Rubes.'

'Of course. Of course we will.'

He's silent a moment.

'You know what I heard the other day? I heard her talking to Lisa about Ella.'

Ella. Mary turns to him, startled all over again.

'I shouldn't have been listening really. It was wrong of me. I suppose I was eavesdropping. I was just trying to find out what they were up to, that's all. And what I heard was—'

He stops for a moment.

'What?' Mary says.

'She was telling Lisa about when Ella was a baby. How she used to carry her around for us. Walking up and down the hallway with her in her arms to get her to sleep. Hours and hours, she'd do it. Do you remember that?'

Mary looks at him. A sudden memory of Ella's mousy head on Ruby's shoulder. The white baby blanket. The ferocious eight-year-old with the long dark plait.

'Yes. I remember.'

'She was telling her all of this in such a proud voice, with such, I don't know, such sweetness. I just – I didn't know what to think. For a moment, I almost thought I was imagining it. She's so hard these days, so tough. I didn't think she had any memory of stuff like that. It didn't really sound like her.'

Mary thinks about this.

'Of course she remembers. And anyway that's just the part she shows us.'

'What?'

'The tough side.'

Graham says nothing. For a moment they're both silent. Mary sees him turning and glancing back at the house, at Ruby's lit-up window.

'Do you think she's OK?' she says.

He shakes his head. 'How can you tell? I've absolutely no fucking idea. What's she thinking? What's she doing? I'm beginning to think I'm never going to be able to talk to that girl.'

Mary looks at him.

'You can. You can talk to her. You don't realise. It's fine. It will be fine. You're very good with her.'

'No, I'm not.'

'You are. You are, you know. You forget how good you are.'

Mary thinks of Ruby as she was back then, before Ella was even born, six years old, the day she met her. Cartwheeling over the lawn as Graham watched, unable to take his eyes off her. An odd lump in her throat as she stood there watching the two of them, trying to take in the hugeness of what her life was about to turn into.

'Anyway, it will all change,' she says then. 'You'll see. Any moment now, she'll change all over again.'

He picks up his wine glass.

'Why do you say that?'

'Because she always does. Ruby changes all the time. Haven't you noticed? That's what teenagers do. Like you just said. So many different Rubies, and just when you think you've got used to one of them, up comes another.'

She feels him thinking about this.

'That's nice. That's a lovely thing to say,' he says at last. 'I like it. It feels hopeful. Fluid, anyway. Flexible. And true. I suppose things always do. Change I mean.'

Mary takes a breath.

'Sometimes they change for the worse.'

'That's right. Sometimes they do.'

From where they sit, she can just about make out the outline of the old fallen tree. For a moment, as she watches, it isn't there at all. Just an open, empty space. She gasps.

'What?' he says. 'What's the matter?'

'Nothing. Just for a moment I thought – the tree. It wasn't there.'

'It's very dark.'

'No. I don't mean that. I mean it suddenly just wasn't there at all.'

He yawns.

'That tree's been there a very long time. It's not going anywhere.'

'I can see it,' Mary says. 'I can see it now.'

Still unnerved, she watches the tree as its outline comes back into focus.

Graham sighs.

'This garden,' he says. 'I hope we can still – I wish I'd never done it now, of course. Pulled that thing down. It could have just stayed there, couldn't it? You were right. If only I'd left it. We'd never have known.'

'Wouldn't we?' says Mary. She hesitates, feeling him looking at her. At last he reaches for her hand.

'Of course,' he says. 'You knew all along, didn't you?'

'I don't know,' Mary says.

'Yes, you do. You did.'

Neither of them speak for a moment.

'Anyway, I guess it will fade, with time,' he says. 'I suppose one day we just won't think about it any more.'

Mary looks at her hand in his.

'Don't say that.'

'You don't want it to fade?'

'No.'

He smiles.

'All right,' he says. 'I won't say it.'

She lets go of his hand. Glances back at the tree. Not allowing her eyes to go beyond it, though – to the place where the apple store stood, open now to the fields, the stars. She shivers and takes a breath, tilting her head back, looking up at the vast blackness of the sky, pricked with stars.

'But it feels like home,' she says.

'What?'

'This place. It does to me. I love it.'

'You do?' He leans forwards. 'I never thought I'd be able to feel it about a place where we don't have them. Where they've never lived.'

'But you do feel it.'

It's not a question. She doesn't expect an answer. There is no answer. No answer, probably, that she could bear to hear.

She breathes in then, a deep breath. After a few minutes, he puts his arm around her. She's glad of it. She leans her head against him.

She thinks again about Eddie, his constant talk of love. Love is nothing, she thinks. It's nothing. Just the very smallest sliver of a so much larger and more complicated thing.

He asks her what she is thinking.

'I'm thinking about magpies,' she says.

'Magpies?'

'Well, a magpie actually. Just one. I thought I saw one, just now as we walked back. In the lane.'

He turns to look at her.

'Do you even get magpies at night?'

'I don't know. You're the bird person. You didn't see it?'

'No, I didn't. I thought one magpie was bad.'

'Bad?'

'Bad luck.'

'You don't believe that,' she says.

He laughs.

'You really think it was a magpie?'

'I don't know. I saw a black-and-white bird in a country lane in the middle of the night, that's all.'

'That's all? That's not enough for you?'

She laughs and he hugs her to him.

'That's nice,' he says.

'What's nice?'

'I've forgotten what your laugh sounds like. I like your laugh.' She laughs again, puts her lips on the bristle of his cheek. Warm, familiar, slightly stale and tired. 'I'm sorry, by the way,' he says. 'Sorry about the way I behaved. Over you and Eddie.'

'What?' She feels herself stiffen.

'I think I was just jealous of your friendship. All that talking. All that intimacy. I didn't want you to be telling him things that you wouldn't tell me.'

Mary takes a breath.

'I didn't. Tell him things, you know. I didn't tell him very much anyway.'

'It doesn't matter if you did.'

'I'm saying I didn't.' She doesn't add that she did a lot of other things, things that she now feels so ashamed of she can hardly bear to think of them. She feels Graham hesitate.

'All right. Don't worry. I believe you.'

'And he didn't tell me much either. Nothing that was true, anyway.'

Silence as they both think about this.

'Poor Deborah,' he says.

'Yes. Poor Deborah.'

He pours her more wine.

'And you,' he says, still holding her. 'What about you?'

'Me?'

'Are you all right?'

She swallows. 'Interesting question.'

'You're not all right?'

'I've no idea. Are you all right?'

'It's been a very difficult day.'

'Yes. Yes, it has.'

'Tomorrow will be better.'

'Will it?'

He squeezes her to him.

'Well. We can hope.'

They sit very still. Far off, there's a noise, sudden and low and thrilling.

'The owl,' she says.

'Yes,' he says. And then, 'It's Flo's birthday tomorrow, isn't it?'

Flo. She does not miss a beat.

'Today, you mean.'

'What?'

'It's today. It's already today.'

Listening to his breath in the darkness as he realises. The damp, dewy darkness. Everything is changing – yes, she thinks, she can feel it. Something is over. It doesn't even feel like summer any more.

She shivers. Waiting.

'Of course,' he says. 'You're quite right, of course you are. Today.'

The girls adored to hear the stories of their births. They knew every single detail off by heart. Each time it all had to be told in the exact same order – the timings thrillingly precise, the narrative almost biblical in its momentum.

They knew that Ella was born in winter and took eight hours to make her way into the world.

'Eight whole hours!' Ella counted under her breath. 'But that's more time even than we're at school.'

'That's right,' Graham said. 'And it was the middle of the night. Your poor mummy. The middle of the night in a freezing January. You certainly picked your time, Ella.'

'I was the easiest!' Flo said. 'I taked no time at all. I came out at lunch.'

They all laughed.

'That's right,' Mary said. 'Four hours. And you did – you arrived on the dot of one. Just in time for lunch.'

'Typical Flo,' said Graham, ruffling at her hair. 'Her mind always on her tummy.'

'And did she eat lunch?' Ella said, looking at her sister with a flash of envy in her eyes.

'Lunch? Babies don't really eat lunch.'

'No, I know that! But did she have some milk?'

'I'm sure she did,' Graham said. 'Babies always seem to be born hungry.'

And Mary looked at him and she smiled, remembering something that he had almost certainly forgotten. That while she fed Flo, while she watched the small miracle of that newborn face and felt the first prickle and tug of the milk coming down, he unwrapped a sandwich, Cheddar and tomato on rye, that they'd bought that morning in the hospital canteen – only five or six hours earlier, but already a whole other universe ago – and as Flo sucked, he fed it to her, bite by perfect bite.

At last Graham looks at his watch.

'One thirty? I don't believe it. Where have the last few hours gone?'

'Go on,' she says. 'You go in.'

'You're not coming?'

'I just want to sit out here a little bit longer.'

'On your own?'

'It's fine. Look, it's still warm. It's lovely.'

He looks up at the night sky.

'I'm sorry. I think I'm just too knackered.'

She smiles at him. 'I know you are. Go on. You go. Take the dog in with you.'

He looks at her.

'You want the wine?'

'Take it in. I've had quite enough.'

He bends, a hand on her shoulder. Kissing her head.

'Don't be long, will you? I mean it. Don't get cold.'

'I won't.'

He hesitates.

'I love you.'

'I love you too.'

She watches as he picks up his glass and hers, the bottle too, and makes his slow way towards the house, the dog trotting after him.

He's not old, she thinks, but right now he could be. Suddenly old and tired and a little bit frail.

Almost afraid for him, she watches, holding her breath, willing him to get there, to make it. For a second or two as he nears the house, the night swallows him and he is gone. Then he turns on the kitchen light and it is all the other way round. He is illuminated. She and the garden plunged into darkness.

Some time before the police officer whose name was Claire came and told them – several hours in fact before she was woken again from that terrible, drowning sleep and they were sat down together in that room and given the update that they'd been dreading – Mary knew. She knew with a dreadful, piercing certainty that it had happened: her daughters were no longer alive.

The way she knew was this.

Early afternoon. Outside it might have been raining. She got up and went to the bathroom, sat numbly on the toilet, trying not to think of anything, not to think, not to hope, it was a habit now. All she needed was to relieve herself – a basic thing, an animal thing. And when she was done and she went back into the room, blank and silent, her eyes still barely open, ready to put herself back into the dark safety of the bed, there they both were—

She cried out.

She saw them for a good few seconds. Both of them standing there in their unzipped fleeces, warm and present and rosy and certain. And she thinks they were smiling, that they seemed quite happy (though later, when she tried to think about it, tried desperately to conjure their faces, she could no longer be so sure).

What she did know was that despite them being right there in the room, they were also somehow beyond, apart, out of her reach. She could not have gone to them, could not have gone any closer, could not have touched them. And before she could do anything – before she could even call out for Graham – they were gone.

And a cold dread began to take root inside her. A choking sensation. A feeling of such blunt and grim hopelessness that she did not think she would survive it.

Graham held her. She knows that she made no sense at all when she tried to tell him. His fingers were rough, unfamiliar. His clothes smelled of ash, of fire.

'It's all right,' he said. 'It's all right.'

He put her in the bed and she went back to sleep. She slept. She dreamed of nothing. The afternoon rolled on. But she knew exactly what would happen next and it did.

Someone came and woke her. A police officer, the woman called Claire, was downstairs.

'We have a significant update for you,' she said.

Mary saw that Claire's face was steady but her hands were trembling. Graham was fetched and the next thing that happened was that someone drew the curtains in the sitting room.

My father and the other two men, they didn't find James. Or at least I don't think they did. I don't know where he was, but I would guess it wasn't in the wood.

Maybe he did come to the house. Maybe he walked right up to the gate and in through the door and into the kitchen. Or maybe he went to the orchard, to the apple store. Maybe he sat for a while on the old fallen tree – the thing, after all, that had brought him right here into the centre of our family – swinging his legs, having a smoke. I'm not sure what he would have been thinking. I suppose that he would have been looking for me, waiting for me.

My father wasn't a harsh man. I don't think he liked to fight. He hadn't the chops for it. But he was brave enough when he had to be, and he was fair. And though he was quite a bit older than James and a bit more brittle and sad and a whole lot less strong, still he could have been brutal if he felt that it was called for. If he felt that his family might be harmed. If he had managed to find him.

I don't know what would have happened then. I don't know who would have hurt who or taught who a lesson. My father had two men with him, but I also know that James would have fought quite viciously, wild and cornered and bloody, with nothing to lose. Still, I don't see that anything good is to be had from thinking about it or trying to guess. It makes no difference to what will happen next.

What will happen is, James will go to the cowshed. He will climb up that sturdy wooden ladder and haul himself into the loft where the tools are kept. He will stand for a moment, his hands hanging loose and ready by his side, looking along the rows of all those familiar and useful instruments, some of them honed to sharpness, some of them not.

He will look at the dibbers and the scuppatts and the flails and the drain spades. The scythes and the rakes and the swabs. He will look at the small blades with teeth on them that are kept for slitting the pigs. He will look at the weed-hooks – the sharp curved sickles fitted to a long wooden handle, which my father taught our Frank and me to use to chop weeds off right at the base where they grow in the ground.

He will look at all of these tools. He won't be in much of a hurry. He will think about it all quite properly. It will take him a while to decide.

Will his heart be banging? Will he feel crazy? Or angry? Righteous? Or ashamed? Will he tell himself that it was love that did this to him, love that brought him here – that a girl has put a hex on him, has put him on edge, stuck him in a tight corner, fixed his mind and scrabbled his thoughts and thrown him on a path that must surely lead to hell?

Or will he tell himself that God will surely forgive him for what he is about to do? That it's all part of His plan for those innocent little children that dare to laugh and play without thought or care or fear on this dark, dark earth?

It is too late for me to answer any of these questions.

All I know is that he will stand there for quite a few minutes staring at the different sharpened implements hanging ready on their different nails. Then he will reach out his hand and take down two of the whetted pig knives and put them in his jacket. And last of all he will select the biggest and the sharpest of the weed-hooks.

Then, whistling to himself, he will set off down the lane to the school. And less than ten minutes after that, Addie Sands will start to scream.

*

At first, standing there in the kitchen doorway, Mary's confused. Knowing very well that Graham left the kitchen light on, waiting for her to come in and lock up and come to bed. And knowing that if it weren't for the fact that the room is lit – actually quite brightly lit by the overhead light – she might be forced to doubt what she is seeing.

On the kitchen table, their metal coffee pot from this morning. A trivet. The old chipped white jug with the wooden spoons and ladles in it. A plate with a knife and some browning peel, the core of a pear. A folded section of the newspaper. And next to that, a small pink rose bud, broken off from a larger stem and saved, standing in a jam jar.

And right next to all of these things, her head resting on her arms, long, fair, almost colourless hair spilling across the old pine table, a young girl.

Mary catches her breath.

Looking around the kitchen: everything else exactly as it should be. The steady hum of the fridge. Their wine glasses and the rest of the bottle where Graham left them by the sink. A couple of pans on the wooden draining board. The dishcloth draped over the tap.

She looks at the dog, curled in her bed and asleep, not even barking. Why isn't she barking? The air smells all wrong – of blown-out candle.

Mary looks again at the girl. Her heart begins to race.

It wasn't Addie's fault. She didn't know what to do except come and find us. What else could she have done? They needed help. It was already too late for most of them, yet even so she swore she would have done anything rather than leave them.

She could hardly speak as she staggered up the lane. Her tongue stopped, all thought gone. Blood on her skirts, her wrists, her neck. Her mouth wide open. Hair falling down.

They'd been clearing up. Folding up the mats, stacking the slates, putting the chalks in the pot, tidying up the baskets of ribbons that Lottie and Honey were so keen on.

Lottie had been quiet all morning, Addie said. But she had ribbed her and jollied her along and finally she had begun to brighten a little. She and another girl, I think it was Effie Saunders, had been asking about her canary, which was singing in a corner of the room. Addie let them each give it a pinch of seed and they laughed and clapped their hands, even Lottie did, as he cocked his yellow head and, watching them with his beady eye, pecked it up.

She said that when James Dix walked into the room he looked so purposeful and was smiling so hard that the little ones thought he must have come to bring them home.

She said that Jazzy whooped at him and Honey jumped up and laughed and held out her arms. It was only Lottie who turned and screamed. And when Addie saw what it was that he had in his hands and, frozen tight to the spot, said – What is it, what is it? – and when he didn't reply but just stared wildly at them all, then she hushed the children and told them to keep themselves very still.

The first swipe he took wasn't even one of our kiddies. It was Mrs Brand's son, Thomas, who was only three and had a poorly eye. They didn't know if he was killed or not, but Addie said that he lay there without moving, with his feet sticking up in the air and the blood pouring out of him.

It was at that moment that Addie began to scream, praying to God to please have mercy and help them.

Honey was next. Addie said she ran straight to him. I don't know what she was thinking – whether she thought that it was all a game and Thomas was just playing dead, or what. She was only a baby, after all. She didn't know about people and badness and what someone having a knife might mean.

Addie told us it was quick, that she would never have realised. That he brought one of the small pig blades down on her head, her small soft neck, and that was it, she was gone.

She said that Minnie and Charlie were fierce. Charlie kicked and Minnie tried to bite him. They did not let go of each other. Charlie stayed alive for a while afterwards, holding on to Minnie and telling her it would be all right.

Lottie and Jazzy were clinging together, screaming and wailing and sobbing.

What a bad man, Lottie shouted. I never loved you at all, I always knowed you were bad. What a bad, bad man!

I don't know what happened after that. All we knew was that when he'd finished doing them all – the two little Saunders kids and Joshua Bennet and young Sarah Dean who was the only one of her mother's five children to survive diphtheria – he took one look around the place and, still smiling to himself, he turned and left.

Jazzy fought bravely, Addie told us. So did Lottie. They fought like a pair of little tigers, she said.

And I thought that Lottie would have liked that, to be called a tiger – especially since she had always been keen as mustard on the pictures of the ferocious tigers in the Big Book of Animals.

What is certain is that almost all of them died – the whole class of kiddies – all of them except for little Caroline Lunden, who had her face sliced so bad she lost her sight. We know that he made no attempt on Addie herself. And that Lottie and Jazzy were the last and that they would not be separated, they held on to each other right to the very end.

That's when he used the weed-hook, Addie said. To get them apart.

She stared at my face.

God forgive me, she said. I should not have told you that.

She isn't sleeping, the girl. Even without being able to see her face, Mary is certain of it. She's awake.

One small fist resting on the table next to the coffee pot, fingers clenched, the rough knuckles tanned, the other hand cupped on her belly. Long hair, almost down to her waist – fair, a little bleached by the sun perhaps, unbrushed, frizzy on top. The clean curve of her cheek, just visible. The tattered frill of her sleeve. Small dark flowers on her dull brown cotton dress. A thicker patch where it may have been darned. A barely discernible odour in the room. Perspiration? The faint, greasy musk of unwashed teenaged skin or hair. Girl, grass, earth, hay. A whole summer of days spent in the orchards and fields and lanes.

A faint, shaking movement from her shoulders now. Small intake of breath. The hand on the table unclenching for a moment. Is she weeping?

Mary has not moved. Standing there by the door, her breath held.

She knows what any normal person would do. Any normal person would challenge her. Ask her who she is and how she got in and demand to know exactly what she's doing in their kitchen at gone two in the morning. They'd want to know how old she is and where she lives and is there someone they ought to phone?

Are you all right? they'd say. You can't just sit here. What is it? What's going on? Are you in trouble?

A normal person would certainly wake Graham.

Mary will do none of these things. What she will do is, as calmly as possible, given how fiercely she is shaking inside, she will pull out a chair and – oh, so slowly and softly, moving a pile of Graham's clean socks and pants out of her way – she will sit down at that old pine table with its roughness and knots and whorls and she will wait.

When Mary was a child she was afraid of everything. Wolves, monsters, bees, wasps, fires, drowning or being sick, doors opening, doors closing, people coming round, the toaster popping up.

Her mother took her to see a psychiatrist.

'I found her at our bedroom window,' she told him. 'She asked if she'd die if she fell out. I told her that she most certainly would and she seemed pleased.' Her mother broke down. 'She said she didn't want to be alive any more, that if she died, she'd be safe. She's four years old, for goodness' sake. Safe from what?'

Mary's mother told the psychiatrist that she didn't know where she'd gone wrong. That she'd always done her best with Mary, but the list of fears seemed endless, in fact it was growing. Their lives were becoming unlivable. She was frightened of her own daughter, frightened for her. She could not deal with this any more.

Mary doesn't remember all of this being said. She doesn't remember her mother being upset and she especially doesn't remember wanting to throw herself out of a window – she only has her mother's word for that.

What she does remember is that no one talked – either on that afternoon or on any future afternoon – about what frightened her. The things she seemed to know, the thoughts that would ambush her seemingly out of nowhere – the risks and possibilities and certainties that lay just around a corner that only she seemed able to see.

She does not remember seeing the hanged man in her room, the vision that so unnerved her mother. And she only has a vague memory of lying in bed with her toy panda and speaking what her parents liked to call gobbledygook. But she remembers the perpetual sense of dread: the pans of milk that were always about to boil over, the phones and doorbells that were about to ring – as well as the people who were constantly on the verge of hurting themselves: tripping up, scalding, burning, bursting into tears.

When the father of a girl at school – someone she hardly knew – died in a car crash, she was sick for a week because she'd seen it coming. And when the little boy next door got meningitis and she saw him crawling happily along the floor in her room and rushed to tell her mother, she was called a liar and told that he'd died in hospital an hour earlier.

Too much to bear, all these thoughts. Sometimes she thought she would suffocate under the weight of them.

She also remembers that brown office and the large desk and the fact that when she reached out and tried to pick something up off it, the psychiatrist smacked her hand.

'I think this child just needs a bit of discipline,' he told her mother.

'That didn't hurt,' Mary said.

I went up there with my father. Standing and watching as they brought them out, one after another. Winding sheets and sacking could not hide the pitiful shapes of them, nor the dark, spreading stains. I saw things: the gaping toe of a small black boot. A dirty knee. A loop of hair. A finger. There was screaming from the mothers, a low, groaning silence from the men.

My own ma could not speak or think. She pulled and tore at her clothes. She scratched at her flesh. She started to burn things. I think she wanted to set the house on fire. My father took her somewhere, I don't know where he took her. I don't want to know.

And then, at the end of this long, dark, terrible day, with the whole of the village still out looking for him, he finds me here. Sitting in the thick grey gloom at the table in the kitchen, all of my weeping done now (or is it just begun?), barely a sob or a breath left in my body. I sit here with the candle out, I don't know if I blew it out or someone else. I don't know who did it. I don't know anything. I sit here in darkness.

I smell him first – that, before anything else: a terrible stench. Muck, sweat, blood. He stinks of the darkness and of the woods. He smells of death. His limbs hanging loose, his eyes as mild as if he's just come to help with the milking, something in his hands that twists and gleams.

You did this to me, Eliza, he says. See what you made me do? All those little kiddies. You think I wanted that?

I think that I don't know what he wanted.

Answer me, Eliza, he says.

I don't know what answer to give. He licks his lips.

A dull ache inside me. Is it fear? I feel my hands go to my belly: the shape of my baby floating there, small as a fingernail, alive and waiting. He holds out a hand. I can't look at him. I can't breathe. Yes, fear. Panic rising in my throat.

Come on, Eliza—

I feel my insides drop.

Please, I whisper. Please—

He doesn't smile.

What, Eliza? Please what?

I shut my eyes.

Please, James, just leave me here.

He takes a breath.

You know I can't do that, he says.

Later, that first night back from the hospital, Mary woke from the deep hush of sleep, the still nameless baby breathing beside her, to hear Ella calling from her room across the landing.

Graham, not quite awake, muttered something.

'It's OK,' she said. 'I'm going.'

Ella was standing up in her cot. Her baby-gro a size too big, the feet of it falling off her, hair standing up in a fuzz.

'Baby,' she said. 'Baby.'

Mary bent and kissed her, touched her hair. Yawning. The moonlit room was cold and pale.

'Baby's asleep,' she said.

And she tried to settle her back down, but she wouldn't be settled. Squirming, chuntering, beginning at last to cry.

'Baby!' she sobbed.

At last it dawned.

'You want to see her? You want to see the baby?'

Ella, thumb in her mouth, nodded.

She padded back across the landing and picked up Flo wrapped in her shawl and carried her in and held her out. Ella blinked. Keeping her thumb in her mouth and reaching out with the other hand and touching her sister – patting the small, asleep bundle of her – satisfied.

'Baby.'

'That's right. Baby's still here. Look, she's perfectly safe. You can see her in the morning.'

With the new baby held in the crook of her arm, she settled Ella back down, pulling the blanket over, stroking her warm head, her back.

'Go back to sleep,' she whispered, even though she could tell from her breathing that she already had.

The new baby was now awake, gazing at her with faraway, liquid eyes. Back in bed, she latched her on and fed her.

Who are you? Mary wondered. Who on earth are you? Where have you come from? Why are you here? What are we doing here together?

Somewhere between the first and the last suck, they both fell asleep.

Mary sits at the kitchen table, the lights out now – did she do that? She has no memory of turning them off – back door flung right open, wrenched so hard she thinks it must almost have come off its hinges.

There's a smell of burning – soot, and something greasy. The blown-out candle – candle fat? Out there, coming in through the open kitchen door, damp night air, dew, honeysuckle and something else, a noticeable stench: stagnant pond or animal dung.

Her two hands are on the table. Rigid and flat and pressed down so hard that she feels her wedding band digging right in. In her ears, the sound of her own heart.

Her cardigan is on the floor. She picks it up, trembling, tries to get it on. Her fingers so stiff she can barely move them. Cold – that's it – she's so very cold.

And the house: still now. Yes. Very still – for once. At last.

She has no idea what just happened.

By the time she goes up to bed – climbing the stairs as slow and careful as an old person – there's a faint redness in the sky. The grey already lifting. Birds beginning. Another day not far off.

She pulls off her clothes and sinks into bed beside him, her husband. Side of his face, the freckled curve of his shoulder, his quiet breath. The jeans flung on the chair. The glass of water and his watch by the bedside.

For a moment she looks at him with relief – as if she just came out of a bad dream: razzed and on edge, unable quite to believe it.

You knew all along, he said, that there was something.

Did she? Does she?

I don't know anything, she thinks as she lays her cheek down on the pillow and tries to close her eyes. I never knew a thing, not a single thing.

When, a few minutes or an hour or a hundred years ago, the girl turned her head and seemed for a second or two to see her, a spark of something seemed to pass between them, but whether it was sorrow or fear or something more like recognition, Mary isn't sure. And does it matter? All she knows is that everything seemed to stop – and she felt a silence in the room so pure and pristine and static that she could not have explained it to anyone, let alone herself.

I know nothing, she thinks.

A long time ago – or not that long at all, depending on how you want to think about it – the girls started coming into their bed in the mornings. Earlier and earlier, they came in, sometimes before it was even light. One time it wasn't much after five.

Graham wasn't happy about it. 'They need to learn to stay in their own beds. We shouldn't be encouraging it.'

'I don't encourage it,' Mary said. 'And they'll grow out of it soon enough.'

But it wasn't true. She knows that now. She did encourage it. She did. She relished those early mornings.

The creak of the door, followed by the small footsteps padding across the landing. The half-asleep lifting of the covers, a brief tussle as they each established themselves against her: knees, elbows, always too many of them. And the bed-smell of them. Wet saliva. Warm hair. Thumb-sucking. And then both of them quickly asleep – all of them, actually, Mary too, the sweetest, lightest, most taken-for-granted kind of sleep.

The girls didn't grow out of it. They never got a chance to grow out of it.

For a long time, she couldn't think of this memory, could not let herself go anywhere near it.

And now?

When they died, my heart stopped, she told Eddie. My heart just stopped when they died.

In the bed, beginning now to sob, Mary moves herself closer to Graham. She can't help it. She thinks that her heart will burst – that she won't survive this. But then she thinks a lot of things. She thinks he's asleep. He's not asleep.

He reaches for her.

'How long has it actually been?' Eddie asked her when she sat with him that afternoon on the huge linen sofa in the room with the fireplace and the African figures and the piles of magazines.

She did not hesitate.

'Seventeen months,' she said. 'It's been seventeen months.'

He caught his breath.

'That's nothing. That's no time at all.'

'I know.'

'That's like it happened yesterday.'

She bit her lip.

'I know.'

He touched her face, then. Kissed the tips of her fingers. And she remembers with a snag of shame that she let him do it.

And he played with her wrist. Her metal wrist watch. Turning it around and around. The way Ella used to play with her bangle. Gently, she pulled her hand away.

He was looking at her.

'It will get better, you know.'

'Or maybe it won't,' she said. Trying to keep her voice from being harsh. Understanding that he only meant to be kind, that

397

people – most people, everyone in fact – their impulse was only, always, to be kind.

'And if it doesn't?'

'What?' she said, her mind wandering to the stash of pills that she had collected so carefully over the months and which still lay at the back of the wardrobe, safely wrapped in a cotton handkerchief at the bottom of the same jewellery box that contained her girls' milk teeth.

'Well, do you think you can live with that?'

She sat there in silence. It was the big question, the one that meant nothing and also everything – the question that she knew she would be trying to answer every single day for the rest of her life.

'It's not seventeen months,' she told him at last. 'It's not even yesterday. It's now. It's happening now. It's always just about to happen. Don't you see? That's what I live with. It will never be over, never.'

She saw that he was struggling with this.

'And you're saying that's what you want – that you'd rather live like that?'

'Like what?'

'Not being able to put it behind you, in the past.' He stared at her, beginning at last to realise. 'You don't even want it to be over, do you? You have no inclination whatsoever to move on.'

'Move on?'

She looked at him and she couldn't help it. She began to laugh.

They conceived each of their children easily, happily, with no thought whatsoever about the possibility of failure, trouble or danger. They wanted babies – they made babies. It really was that simple. God, fate, the world, the universe, their strong and willing bodies. The love they shared and in which they trusted. Everything, it seemed, was on their side.

She liked to say that she knew the exact moment.

'It was as if each of them had their own particular flavour and it made itself felt immediately, literally that second,' she liked to say. And even though he laughed, she knew that he believed her absolutely. That was the thing about Graham. He always got it, he always understood.

But on that dark winter's morning when they brought Ella home from the hospital and, wrapped in her white blanket in her straw Moses basket, they laid her in the middle of their vast double bed, she found herself suddenly unable to bear the sight of that tiny asleep face and those tight-curled hands and she wept.

He discovered her there, in the armchair. The front of her night-dress wet with tears.

'It's because she's so small,' she said. 'And the bed's so big.'

He knelt down, put an arm around her, kissed her shoulder, her wet and salty cheek, her neck.

'What? You'd have liked her to come out bigger?'

Still crying, she buried her face in his jumper that smelled of the hospital and she laughed.

'I don't want her ever to go out in the world,' she said, taking the box of tissues that he passed her.

'Fine,' he said. 'That's easily fixed. We'll keep her at home. We'll have special locks fitted.'

She laughed again, blew her nose.

'I love you,' she said.

Behind the apple store, no moon. Blackness of weeds. Prickling tangle of the hedge. The outline of the old tree. My breath, hurting in my chest because of what he's done to me. A sudden loosening. Blood running down my arm, my legs.

He is standing above me now, looking down. So high, I think, so tall and high, his pale face bobbing up there in the darkly waving tops of the trees.

I try to look at him. His face going in and out, blurry and sharp, sometimes there, sometimes not.

Blood. My hair is sticky with it. The bodice of my dress, soaked. But it doesn't matter because here we all are, riding in the cart, all of us – my father and mother and all the kiddies. Jazzy and Lottie and Charlie and Minnie and Honey and dear Frank coming with us, too. Even the dog, her black ears streaming in the wind. I ask my father where we're going and he says the sea.

The sea, Eliza, we're going to the sea—

The sea. I try again to take a breath, but something is stopping it. Blood again. His face, coming closer now.

What is it, Eliza?

I blink. Something bubbling in my throat, a terrible taste, like old tin cans.

I thought it would hurt a lot more than this, I say.

He smiles.

I wouldn't ever hurt you, Eliza. Not if I could help it. You know I wouldn't.

I feel my eyes closing.

We're going to the sea, I tell him.

It's called the High Striker, Eliza.

No, I say. It's not right, it's not right—

It is, that's what it's called.

The last thing I feel is not pain at all but the bright smashed feeling as the cart rolls around the corner and the lane drops down and suddenly there it is—

I turn on my side and see the dark, mouldy wood of the apple store.

Don't leave me, I say. Please, James. Don't leave me here.

When I open my eyes again, I see that he has a spade in his hands.

Don't worry, he says. I won't.

That holiday on Elba, the holiday when they bought the dish. Two or was it three years ago? Sitting in the little osteria as the sky grew velvety, they all watched as a goatherd brought his whole flock hurrying past. Hundreds of goats of every possible size and shape and colour, bells clanging, bleating loudly, hooves scraping through the dust.

The girls were dazzled. They shrieked and laughed and clapped their hands. Even Mary was amazed at how the animals just kept on coming and coming, seemingly endlessly rushing past them out of the black darkness until the sound of the bells receded into the distance and—

Silence. Ella looked at her.

'Is it finished?'

And Mary was about to tell her that it was, but no, a whole minute later, here was the very last one, the smallest goat of all, a little grey one, skidding around the corner as fast as he could, bleating loudly and struggling to catch up.

Flo screamed with delight, but Ella, watching it disappear around the corner, was upset. What if this one didn't manage to catch up with the others? What if he was lost? How did they know for certain that the man would wait? Would he have counted them? How would he know there was one more left to come?

Mary leaned over to cut up Ella's spaghetti.

'Ah, but didn't you know, the goat who's allowed to go last is always the bravest and the cleverest.'

Ella stared at her.

'He is?'

Mary smiled and looked at Graham.

'It's the rule in the goat world, isn't it, Daddy?'

Graham put on a serious face.

'It is. It definitely is. Only the very bravest goat is allowed to go last.'

Ella listened, fork in hand, napkin tied around her neck, tears still standing in her eyes.

'What a brave goat!' she said.

Mary smiled.

'That's right,' she felt Graham squeeze her knee under the table. 'He's a very special goat. That little goat is definitely the very bravest of them all.'

Seventeen months. That's all it's been. But one day in a future which she can scarcely imagine but which she knows lies only just around the corner, it will have been seventeen years.

Seventeen years.

But she won't think of that now.

There was another holiday. Easter, was it? She rented a house by the sea, just her and the girls without Graham, and the three of them woke early, to the most perfect morning. Let's walk to the harbour for breakfast, she said.

She remembers every detail. Bright sun, blue sky, the air, sharp and chilly. Sea smooth, brown as a pebble, barely a ripple on it. Not yet eight in the morning and not a soul about, not even a dog walker, the beach eerie and wide, emptier than she'd ever seen it.

At first the girls walked along with her. Ella chattering about this and that. Flo singing and laughing, every third or fourth step a little skip and a hop.

But soon they both got lively and, electrified by all that space and light, they started to run ahead and, because it was so safe and because she knew they could not come to any harm, she let them.

She remembers it all perfectly, the bright elasticity of that moment. The sand beneath her feet. Glittering sea. Early morning sun in her eyes. The two small girls in jeans and T-shirts, tearing ahead of her over that wide, unearthly landscape.

She thinks that what happened next is they got to the harbour, but the place where she thought they could get breakfast was shut and the sun went behind a cloud and the day turned that little bit greyer and colder and by the time she'd got them back to the house and bought cereal and milk from the Co-op, Flo was scratchy and all Ella wanted to do was watch TV.

But in fact, she tells herself, that's not what happened. It's not what happens. Not what will happen now. What will happen is, she will keep on following them over that stretch of bright, early-morning sand, the two people she loves most in this world, small dots of darkness getting smaller and smaller and further and further away.

And she ought to worry, but she isn't worried. She could call them back, but she won't do that. She won't do any of these things. What she will do is she will just keep on walking – nothing but that. It's far simpler than she ever realised, the simplest thing in the world, just to walk, just to keep on going, to follow them forever, her girls, her daughters, her eyes on them both, keeping them safe as they race together over this wide, exhilarating earth.

Acknowledgements

A heartfelt thank you to Alex Bowler and Dan Franklin at Jonathan Cape, Claire Wachtel at HarperCollins US, and Iris Tupholme at HarperCollins Canada for their many meticulous readings and invaluable insights. They turned out to be right about just about everything, and anyone who thinks that novels are not edited these days should see an early draft of this one.

Big thanks, too, to the brilliant (and brilliantly unstoppable) Karolina Sutton and everyone at Curtis Brown: your passion and excitement is a real inspiration.

Finally, thank you doesn't begin to describe what I owe my former agent, Gill Coleridge of Rogers, Coleridge & White. When I was nine years old, I used to dream of being an author. She made it happen. After twenty years together, this novel is dedicated to her, in friendship, gratitude and with so much love.

penguin.co.uk/vintage